THE
FATAL
CURE

JEREMY THOMAS FULLER

BOOKS BY JEREMY THOMAS FULLER

THE METALWOOD SAGA

Season One

The Metal Wood

The Stone Flame

The Death Edge

The Fatal Cure

The Prime Trees

Season Two

The Absent Memory

The Crystal Curse

The Silent Binds

The Twin Fury

The Splinter Soul

STANDALONE

Attention Deficit

THE FATAL CURE

THE METALWOOD SAGA
BOOK 4

JEREMY THOMAS FULLER

**STARMIST★
ENTERTAINMENT**

STARMIST ENTERTAINMENT

166 Geary Str STE 1500 #1259
San Francisco, CA 94108
United States

jeremythomasfuller.com
instagram.com/jeremythomasfuller
facebook.com/jeremythomasfuller
bsky.app/profile/jeremythomasfuller.com

Cover designed by Maria Spada
Author photo by Zack Griset
Set in Stix Two

PART
ONE

ONE

THE SUN GLOWED red as it dipped below the horizon. In the distance, metal spires gleamed, stretching to the sky as if hoping to escape Earth's brutal grasp. Dark shapes moved about below. Great pillars of scaffolding rose in the distance, the light of welding torches gleaming amongst them in points like stars.

Quynn smiled darkly at the city stretched out before him. From his vantage point high atop a narrow skyscraper, he could see the fruits of his labors. The seventh city; the final piece. Too long had it been since the city was destroyed. Now, at long last, the time had come. The device was nearly complete.

The Conjunction was at hand.

Quynn turned, surveying the newcomer at his side. The woman was small and slim, with skin as black as night. Her hair was short and she carried herself with aplomb, as if nothing could hurt her.

He very much doubted that was true.

"State your purpose," Quynn said. Surely this woman knew better than to interrupt him now, of all times.

The woman lowered her head in deference. It wasn't much, but the gesture at least showed that she knew her place, if only by a little.

"I am merely a curious engineer," she said, though her eyes belied her tone: an intelligence lurked there, far beyond what he would normally expect for one such as her. "I came to gaze upon what you have wrought."

Quynn watched her as she looked out across the city. "Do you like what you see?"

The woman turned to look at him, her gaze piercing into his very soul. Her finely-pointed ears were delicate and beautiful, her cheekbones high. She was a perfect elven specimen, yet there was something else about her, something almost *too* perfect. They watched each other, the moment growing between them, until she finally dropped her gaze, thick lashes covering her eyes.

"I mean no offense, of course," she said quietly. "I simply wanted to see what all the fuss was about."

"Very well," Quynn said. "And what do you think?"

"You have done well," the woman said. "The Twins will be pleased."

The Twins? This seemed like an odd time to bring *them* up. Quynn narrowed his eyes. "I didn't catch your name," he said, his hand moving to rest at the lip of his pants pocket.

"You may call me Magona," she said. "I thank you for allowing me to see this. I will trouble you no longer."

She slipped away into the darkness.

Quynn watched her with a puzzled expression, not bothering to follow. Perhaps he'd tell Lorelei about this strange woman.

His communicator vibrated, and he tapped it. "Yes?"

"The meeting has begun," a voice said. "We trust you will be here momentarily."

"Yes," Quynn repeated. The Small Council could not be kept waiting. He stepped off the edge of the building and disappeared into the night.

TWO

"COME ON," Elanil said. They had run all night, using leafrunning and fallfoiling when necessary, but trying to do most of the journey on foot to conserve their wood. She couldn't face her people, not after what she'd done.

She'd started that fire.

She'd destroyed their magic.

It hadn't been on purpose, of course. But when had *that* ever mattered? Everything was always Elanil's fault. She was always barreling into things, trying to do what was right. But no matter how hard she tried, nothing ever came out the way she'd meant it to.

So she ran, tears streaming down her face, wondering if she would ever be able to go back home.

At first she led them in a random direction, but after a time she realized it wasn't random at all: they were heading toward the strange metal city with the big hole in the ground.

Fennas Elenathon. The Cothellon device.

Why was she going there? It felt like running from the fire right into the kettle, or however that saying went.

She thought about taking them to Gulthurub, but

discarded the idea immediately. The Remnant would just kill them on sight. Jalnab and Martan weren't there anymore, anyway. They'd been banished by their own people. So Gulthurub was not an option.

No, there was no escaping what she'd done.

So they ran through the forest, heading ever closer to Fennas Elenathon. At least it was somewhere to go.

"Why don't you like berries?" she asked.

They were resting under a redwood, eating nuts and berries she had gathered from the forest. The rain had just let up, water still dripping on them from the wet leaves above.

"They taste weird," Rylan said. "Too sweet."

"How can something be too *sweet*?"

He shrugged. "Where I live, we don't get sweet stuff very much. No berries. The only sweet thing I ever had was Coke."

"What's...Coke?"

"It was a long time ago."

"What was the city like?"

Rylan leaned back against the tree. "I don't know much about topside," he said. "I lived in the Under, under the city. With my Crew."

"*Under* the city? What was that like?"

"Hot, mostly. Stifling and dirty. Smelly. Loads of kids down there, all fighting for scraps of food. You have to get in a Crew or you're done for in the Under. And you have to earn an undername or they don't let you in."

"What's an undername?"

"Just a name. Something they call you when you do something big. Like do a really tough job, or kill someone, or—I don't know—just be really good at something. It's a name you have to earn for yourself."

"Don't you already *have* a name?"

"It's not the same thing."

"So why not give yourself an undername?"

"You can't. It doesn't work that way."

"Okay," Elanil said. He wasn't making much sense. "You said you live with a...Crew? What's that?"

"It's like a gang," Rylan said. "Just a group of kids, living together and looking out for each other. Whole Under's full of them. It's the best way to survive."

"Who's in your Crew?"

"Oh, there's Dill. He's the captain. And Small, Grid, Shot, and Grime. And then there's Con."

"Con?"

"Yeah. She's..." he trailed off, and she could see a wistful look in his eyes.

She was clearly someone special.

She nudged him with her foot. "You okay?"

He snapped out of it, his eyes sad. "She was captured."

"Oh."

"I wanted to go after her, but then..." He paused.

"Then you fell out of the city."

"Yeah."

"Con's your girlfriend?"

"Just my friend. We looked out for each other before I got into Shock Crew. She's a good girl. I hope she's alright."

He fell silent, then. They sat that way for a few minutes, listening to the water dripping from the leaves. It was peaceful, in its way. Comforting.

Then she heard a *snapping* sound, and something black was shoved over her head.

She screamed.

ELANIL WOKE UP. She rubbed her eyes, trying to clear her vision. Her head hurt terribly.

They were in some kind of small room made of cement, cold and dark and unfriendly.

She hated it.

Their room had one door: a row of vertical metal bars. They must be in some kind of jail cell, then—but where?

Rylan was sitting against the wall, fiddling with a piece of darkprime wood. She shivered, suddenly realizing how *cold* it was in there. So she crawled over to him, leaning next to him against the wall, their arms touching. He flinched a little when she sat so close, but he didn't move away.

"Where are we?" she asked.

"Some kind of city," he said. "They knocked us out and took us here. I saw a little bit of it as we came in, but I pretended to be unconscious. I think this is the place you told us about: Fennas Elenathon."

"So it was elves that brought us in."

"Elves with guns."

"They must have lowered the forcefield to let us in. I wonder how they knew we were out there?"

"They're elves," Rylan said. "They probably know *everything*."

He did have a point.

But what now?

They were stuck in here, that was what. And what had her plan been, anyway? Had she really thought the evil Cothellon with the deadly guns would be a better option than her own parents, her own people?

She had been so stupid.

She leaned on Rylan, resting her head on his shoulder. He twitched a little when she did it, but he didn't move away. She felt so tired. All that magic, all that running about—it had all been for nothing, and now she was stuck with a boy she barely knew. They were probably going to die in here, cold and alone.

She shivered. Rylan reached over and rubbed her arm. The gesture felt alien coming from him, but she appreciated it, snuggling closer. He rested his head on hers.

They sat like that for a long time.

After a while, Rylan drew in a deep breath, as if marking the end of an age. "You ready to get out of here?"

Elanil sat up straight. "What? How?"

"Well," he said, "I figure we can get through this door if we both try hard enough."

Oh, with magic. Why hadn't she thought of that? Probably because she'd never done anything like it before. She'd only ever used leafrunning to jump and fly and dance in the air— never for destruction.

Never to set anything on fire.

She shuddered, remembering what had happened at the Primestore building. Another of her many mistakes.

"Do you think we're strong enough?" she asked.

"Only one way to find out."

"Okay. Let's do it."

They rummaged about in their pockets. Luckily, their captors hadn't thought to remove any wood from them. They must not have been expecting mages to come this close to their little outpost. Rylan pulled out two more pieces of dark-prime wood, adding it to the piece he had been playing with. Elanil had some bits of elm left in her pocket. She'd had an entire sheet of it before, but she must have dropped it in their escape.

"We don't have much left," she said. Rylan grunted his agreement.

Just then, footsteps echoed in the hall outside their cell.

Rylan and Elanil quickly hid their wood chips and sat back, pretending to be asleep.

Through barely cracked eyelids, Elanil saw a guard appear in front of their cell. He was big and tall, with a dark black jumpsuit and a nasty-looking gun and a really mean face. He just stood there for a moment, watching them. Then, without a word, he left.

After he'd been gone a few minutes, Elanil opened her eyes. "Patrol?" she asked.

"Yeah," Rylan said. "We'll have to time this right."

"It'll be loud."

"I know. But we have to try."

"Let's get it over with, then."

They stood, joints and muscles creaking from so long on the hard cement floor. Then they approached the door.

It was big, of course, made from thick metal bars and a metal frame and hinges and a lock. The lock was just a keyhole, actually, where a knob would normally be.

"Can you pick the lock?" Elanil asked.

"Probably," Rylan said. "If I had a lock pick set."

"Oh."

They were screwed, then. But wait. "Could we pick it with magic?"

Rylan looked at her, obviously working the problem in his mind. "We'd have to combine our powers."

"Would it work?"

"Worth a shot."

They joined hands. Elanil could feel his heartbeat underneath the rough skin, his fingers strong. She wondered how much of his confidence was real.

"Ready?" she asked. "I'll have to dance again to make this work."

"I know. Do it, then we'll try."

She had an instinct, then. She grabbed Rylan, pulling him into a partner dance. His eyes widened with surprise, but he allowed himself to be led, stumbling over her as she moved. She repeated the figure several times—just a simple waltz. He started to understand the movement, not bumping into her as often, moving instead to her internal beat. She hummed faintly, an old elven tune in three-quarter time.

"Shh," Rylan said, but he kept dancing with her.

They twirled and moved about the cold, dark cell. She pulled him close, still leading the dance, feeling their bodies touch. His breathing intensified, his eyes locked on hers. She smiled at him. She knew she must look a fright after their narrow escape and flight through the woods. Truth be told, he looked terrible too. Still, it just felt *right*, dancing there with him.

The elm in her hand suddenly Invested, all at once. She yelped, surprised, then clapped a hand to her mouth. Rylan stopped, still holding her awkwardly in a half dance position, looking out the door of their cell with alarm.

Had anyone heard them? They waited, but nothing happened. No one came. So she let out a breath—quietly—and stepped away.

"Ready to try?" she asked.

"I think we need to be touching for it to work."

"Oh. Right." She stepped back to him, grabbing his hand. They walked over to the door, bending down together until their heads were level with the keyhole.

"Go," she breathed.

She closed her eyes, feeling herself connect with the primewood in her hand. The connection extended into her body and out through her other hand, encompassing Rylan. She felt something stir inside him, as if his very soul had responded to the touch of her power.

Then she felt the connection to him *truly* take hold.

Her eyes flew open. She could feel power flowing through her, thrilling through her veins. Rylan was part of her, part of her very being, their souls intertwined. Prime magic flowed over and around them, a symbiotic flood, a river of energy.

It felt intense. Amazing. Like nothing she'd ever felt before. Her body tingled, and she felt a warmth between her legs.

Then his thoughts *bent* toward the lock. She could feel it, could almost visualize what he was doing. His mind was moving up and down in thin little lines. She lent her thoughts to the action, granting him her ability, and suddenly the motion broke free, able to move in three dimensional space. It was like rescuing a mouse from a trap it had been forced to stay in its entire life. It was like suddenly seeing color where only black and white had been before. It was like the moon rising in a clear evening sky, full and bright and majestic amongst the stars.

Rylan made quick work of it, taking control of their symbiotic power and wrangling the lock with ease. He split the magic in two, using the halves like he had his lock pick set earlier. It seemed easy, feeling him deftly work the lock, but she knew there was no way she'd have been able to accomplish it.

The lock *snicked* and the door opened.

Rylan let go of her hand, and the whole world crashed down on her. It was like waking up from a dream. Like stepping out of an icy lake. Suddenly he was just *gone* from her mind, and the pain of it hurt like a thousand needles in her brain.

"Ow," she cried, rubbing her temple.

Rylan had a completely different reaction. His face was red, and he looked very, very happy. His breathing was shallow, his eyes fluttering back and forth. He stepped backward, almost losing his balance, his hand flying out to touch the wall, trying to keep from falling over.

She could see his hand shaking.

"You okay?" she asked.

He shook his head, looking down at the floor, trying to regain his breath. "We need to go," he said after a moment, his voice raw.

Whatever had just happened between them had been powerful—and somehow also dangerous. She didn't understand it, but she knew they would need to be careful with it.

Very careful.

Just then, footsteps echoed loudly down the hall outside their cell.

The guard had returned.

THREE

RYLAN REACTED QUICKLY as the guard approached their cell, reaching into his pocket and throwing him up into the ceiling with violent magical speed. The guard's head cracked against the cement and he fell back down, limbs askew. Blood pooled around his head where he had fallen.

He was dead.

Rylan saw a shocked expression on Elanil's face. Maybe she hadn't known he could do anything like that, anything so violent.

He hadn't known it himself.

But now wasn't the time to worry about such things. Now was the time to *leave*.

He grabbed Elanil's hand, pulling her out of the cell. They stepped over the guard and headed down the hallway, moving as quietly as they could.

Rylan checked his pocket: just three chips of wood left. Not nearly enough—he would have to use magic sparingly.

They rounded the corner and found themselves in a long hall. Metal doors dotted the walls on either side—locked, no doubt, and probably not an exit. They tried them all anyway as they passed, just in case.

None of them opened.

And so they wandered, hoping to make their escape before someone caught them and killed them. They only encountered one other guard in the place. This time Elanil dispatched him—not with magic, but with a deftly placed punch to his throat.

Where the hell had she learned to do *that*?

Now they were even, although Elanil's kill hadn't involved as much blood. She was perking up noticeably, acclimating to the adventure. This was a girl he could see himself spending a lot of time with, he realized. Even if she was an elf, and her face was too clean.

They kept trying to find an open door. But all of them were locked, and they didn't want to waste the wood to try their magic trick again. They didn't know if any of these led out.

The last door they came to was the lucky one—it opened, revealing a metal staircase that spiraled up into darkness.

They looked at each other for a moment before proceeding up the stairs.

They emerged outside above ground, in the middle of a city of some kind. It was smaller than Rylan was used to, though—most buildings were only two or three stories tall. They were all made of metal, their edges reflecting the light. It was strange to see so much metal after his time in the forest.

It almost felt like home.

He took a deep breath and led Elanil out from the shadows.

ELANIL NOTICED that Rylan was taking charge now, leading her through the maze of hallways and buildings, always alert for trouble. Maybe his survival instinct was coming out. Maybe it was the cement and metal, a familiar environment for him.

She liked him leading like this.

But where were they going? So far, they'd managed to avoid the guards she knew were patrolling the grounds. But she knew it was only a matter of time before somebody caught them. There had been a lot of guards last time she was here.

Rylan led them on, darting from building to building, keeping out of sight as much as possible. They saw one patrol pass, guns clearly visible on their waists as they marched in unison. Rylan and Elanil shrank back against the wall, hoping it was enough to remain hidden.

It was.

They moved onward, heading closer to the center of the metal city. Fennas Elenathon, Orym had called it. A strange name for a strange place.

"Hey," she whispered. Rylan stopped and looked back at her. "Where are we going?"

He pointed. Through the buildings up ahead, she could see one of the metal prongs sticking up from the big hole in the center of the area. Why was he taking her there? That was probably *not* where they should be going.

"Hey—" she started, but suddenly a patrol was in front of them. They scurried back, flattening themselves against a wall. Elanil held her breath.

"Did you hear something?" one of the guards said. Rylan and Elanil shrank back against the wall, trying to remain unseen.

It didn't work.

"You, there!" the guard shouted, rounding the corner of the building. Two other guards approached as well, guns pulled out and trained on them.

Should they run? Should they attempt more magic?

Elanil suddenly felt cold steel up against her temple.

"Got you," a voice said right into her ear.

ARRA OPENED the door to Trey's room and peeked in. He was asleep, his chest rising and falling as he breathed. It was the middle of the day, but he had gone back to sleep already, his magical exertions having gotten the better of him. Prime Mages clearly had a lot of power, but that power came with a price.

Arra still couldn't quite believe any of it had happened. That storm, the way he'd just *killed* all those Remnant...she hadn't even known it was *possible* using simple leafrunning.

It had been gruesome.

But it had been necessary.

Silanar had let slip what had made it all possible: the Book of Amplification. He had finally brought it out—not for her, to see if maybe she really was a mage. No, he had brought it out after a hundred years the moment Trey, a total stranger, had landed in town.

She wasn't sure if she should feel jealousy or anger. Maybe neither.

Whatever wrong her father had done, Trey's intentions at least seemed honorable.

But there was no choice now, in her mind. She had to know. She had to know if the Book could turn her into a mage.

She padded silently over to Trey's dresser, sliding open the top drawer as quietly as she could. The wood groaned a bit as it moved, and she froze, looking at Trey. He remained asleep. She let out the breath she had been holding and pulled the drawer all the way out.

Nothing.

Where was it? She checked all the dresser drawers, but they held only clothes and essentials. She moved to the table, looking at the various items strewn on top: a comb, a small mirror, a bowl of water, some dried flowers. It wasn't there, either.

There was a chest at the foot of the bed. She crouched down, lifting the lid. Luckily, it wasn't locked. The lid creaked loudly as she opened it, and she froze again. Trey shifted in his sleep, turning on his side before settling back down, his breathing even. Arra finished opening the lid.

There it was: a thick book bound in gilded leather. The words on the cover were written in High Eldrim: The Book of Amplification.

FOUR

"YOUR PROJECT HAS BEEN AN ABJECT FAILURE," Argus said. Quynn twisted in his seat to look at him, ancient wood creaking as he moved.

"Failure is a relative term," Quynn said.

"Your breeding program has produced no viable results in the entirety of its existence. Surely even you cannot disagree that this constitutes failure?"

Quynn bowed his head slightly in acknowledgement. "It has not produced the results we hoped for," he said. "That much is true. Yet I feel I am growing close."

"You *feel?*" said Morgian from the other side of the room, her expression a mask of contempt. "Now is not the time for *feelings.* You should know that better than most."

"And the subject you just detailed doesn't fall into your usual parameters," Argus said. "He's not even part of your breeding program, is he? Where did you pick him up? Perhaps you are losing your touch."

"I assure you, I have not lost my touch," Quynn said. "You will have good news soon." He offered no more information;

these petty imbeciles didn't deserve anything else. The program was his and his alone—his idea, his execution, his genius. He had been progressing steadily for hundreds of years, and he was *close*. He would be damned if anyone stood in his way now.

Besides, the breeding program had been a sham.

Garrik cleared his throat. "Let us move on to other matters," he said. "The Tree Ring Staff. The time has come to use it." He looked at Quynn pointedly.

Quynn's lips compressed into a thin smile. "I will obtain it tonight."

"Very well. I believe that just leaves Fennas Elenathon. Grathgor?"

Grathgor stood to give his report. He was always old-fashioned like that, always standing to attention when called upon. Quynn caught himself sneering, but forced himself to wipe the expression from his face. The organization required all kinds of people, and Grathgor was a good friend. Still, he could not help but belittle him sometimes. In many ways, these people were beneath him. He fingered the dark yew in his pocket.

"The device is nearly complete," Grathgor said. "Builders are finishing the skin on the last few buildings, and the engineers have completed the network. We will be ready for synchronization within the week."

"Very good," a disembodied voice said. The husky female voice echoed loudly in the chamber, emitting from a black device at the center of the table. "This time no one will stand in our way."

Quynn smirked, eyeing the other Councillors in the room. Lorelei was in another one of her moods.

"Council," Lorelei's voice continued, "the time is drawing

near. Please order another increase in Civil Service Selection. We need to be sure we have as many resources as possible. I expect they may grow thin soon."

"There is one more thing," Grathgor said. He sounded unsure how to proceed.

"Continue."

"We had an...incursion...recently."

"Explain yourself."

"It was an Eldrim girl. She somehow managed to enter the receiver site."

"I trust you dealt with her?"

"She escaped," Grathgor said. "My most humble apologies. The guards gave chase, but she was more Talented than we expected."

Quynn frowned. How had an Eldrim even *found* the site, much less infiltrated it?

"You will deal with the situation," Lorelei said, sounding displeased. She was always displeased.

"Yes," Grathgor said, bowing.

"Wait," Quynn said, and everyone in the room looked at him. "Allow me to take care of this matter. I have certain assets in play that will require somewhat...delicate treatment."

The room was silent for a moment, then Lorelei spoke up. "Very well," she said. "But Quynn?"

"Yes?"

"Treat the situation with circumspect. We have not acted directly against the Eldrim in three hundred years. Not without the Remnant doing it for us."

"I will use all of the gentility at my disposal."

Argus barked a laugh from across the room.

"Do what you must," Lorelei said. "We will meet again in three days."

The Councillors filed out of the chamber silently, Quynn still gripping the yew chip in his pocket. There would come a time when it would become necessary.

That time was fast approaching.

FIVE

ELANIL STRUGGLED AGAINST HER BONDS, but it was no good. She was tied up tightly, forced to sit in a metal chair. Her feet were free, at least. For whatever good that did her.

She looked around the room they'd been taken to. It was dark and big and mostly empty, with a high, flat ceiling. Wires crawled around the floor, and metal pipes were everywhere. There were racks and racks of electronic equipment lining the walls, flashing and whirring quietly. The room was illuminated by small electric lamps set into the walls every so often.

Rylan and Elanil had their hands tied behind their backs. They had been seated on little metal chairs, back-to-back, their hands touching each other. Oddly, the guards hadn't actually tied them to the chairs.

Two Cothellon guards were standing a short way away, large guns of some kind angled on their shoulders. A tall elven woman was pacing in front of them, wearing a uniform that made her look like some sort of officer, with badges on her lapel and a white stripe slashed across her heart. She had her hair pulled tightly back, and she carried a little hand gun of her own.

Elanil looked to her left, away from the guards, trying to get a view of what was on the other side of the room. There was something strange there—it looked like a metal dais of some sort, with some kind of swirly light in the center. All the wires in the room were leading to it.

But before she could figure out what it was, the woman slapped her in the face.

Hard.

"Ow!" Elanil yelped, tears springing to her eyes. "Why would you *do* that?"

"If you answer my questions," the woman said, "things will go easier for you." She had an accent Elanil didn't recognize. "Where did you come from?"

"Uh," Elanil said. Should she tell her anything?

"Answer me," the woman said, looking at her with cold malice. Elanil wondered what had gotten this person so angry.

"We came from Sylrantheas," she said, and Rylan grunted behind her.

The woman began pacing again. "How did you find this place?"

"I—" How *had* she found this place? "It was an accident. Honest."

"You are lying."

"I'm telling the truth, I swear!" She was, actually. It *had* been an accident. The first time, anyway.

She could feel Rylan behind her—he was moving subtly, doing something with his hands behind his back. She hoped he wouldn't try anything stupid.

"How did you get out of your cell?" the woman asked.

"Well," Elanil said, "that's kind of a long story."

The woman stopped pacing and just stood there, staring at her icily. "Try me."

Rylan was still moving, just a little bit. Not enough for the woman to notice, apparently. Then he slipped Elanil something, his fingers passing her a piece of primewood.

Yes! But where had he gotten it? He must have grabbed it from her before they were captured. She hadn't even noticed.

The woman was still looking at her menacingly, waiting for an answer.

"It's better if I show you," Elanil said, standing up slowly.

The woman aimed her gun at her. "Stay where you are," she said. "Guards! Tie them to the chair."

"It's just a little dance," Elanil said. "It won't do any harm. Here, let me show you."

She tapped her right foot, setting up a pattern. Then she tapped her left foot, repeating the pattern. The woman's eyes narrowed, and she kept the gun pointed at Elanil.

"It's okay," Elanil said. "I just want to show you this."

Her hands were bound behind her back, but that didn't stop her from doing things with her feet. She broke out into a small tap dance, shuffling about inside a small radius. She didn't want to push gun-lady's patience by moving too far.

Inexplicably, Rylan started humming. It was mostly tuneless—the boy obviously couldn't sing—but it had a beat to it. It matched her dance.

She found herself smiling.

The guards were watching her, their heads bobbing to the beat of Rylan's song. It was a little funny seeing them there like that, big menacing men watching a little girl dance.

"Stop it!" the woman shouted. "Stop it this instant! Sit back down. Guards!"

The guards took a step forward, and Rylan changed the tune.

They both struck in the same instant.

Elanil flung the two guards away as hard as she could, shooting them into the wall with incredible force. She could hear their heads crack against the wall and they slumped down, motionless.

Rylan attacked the big woman, throwing her up to the ceiling. But something went wrong—a field of light shimmered into being around the woman, and she floated back down to the ground. It looked like a ball of energy surrounding her, sparkling and strange. A forcefield. More magic?

"I don't think so," the woman said, brandishing the gun and stepping forward.

Elanil could see Rylan trying again, but nothing happened. The woman stayed put on the ground. And Elanil was out of power—her one chip had been expended.

She couldn't help.

They both stepped backward, away from the woman that was advancing on them.

"Who are you?" the woman asked, her voice low and threatening. The gun glinted as it reflected light from the lamps in the room.

Elanil and Rylan stepped backward and to the side, avoiding the chairs they had been sitting in. The woman with the gun just kept on coming.

"Tell me," she said. "Who sent you? Who are you working for?"

"It was just an accident," Elanil said, continuing to inch backward. What was the plan, here? Would they keep going until they were up against a wall, or until the woman shot them? She looked around. Surely there must be another way out of here, some way to escape. But she had no more primewood.

There was nothing else to do.

"Stop moving or I'll shoot," the woman said. She probably meant it, but Elanil wasn't about to stop moving. Next to her, she could sense Rylan thinking the same thing.

Suddenly there was something under her feet. Wires. She tripped on one of them, losing her balance. She lunged sideways, bumping into Rylan. They both started tipping, stepping rapidly, trying to keep from falling over. The metal dais loomed in front of her and she stepped instinctively up onto it in order to avoid falling. Rylan's momentum carried him along with her, tripping over more wires that led onto the platform.

"Stop!" the woman shouted. A shot rang out but it went wild, zinging off the dais and ricocheting off the wall.

Elanil couldn't see where she was going. She was still trying to regain her footing amidst the jumble of wires and pipes running over the dais. The weird swirly thing filled her vision suddenly, and she looked up, finally able to stand on her feet without falling.

It was an oval, taller than it was wide, made of light. It looked like a moving picture, constantly waving and flickering. The picture depicted metal and glass—tall, sheer surfaces with hard, unending lines. There were people moving about in the picture, their faces wavy and distorted.

What *was* this?

"Turn around!" the woman shouted. "Now!"

"Jump," Rylan whispered.

"What?" Elanil whispered back.

"TURN AROUND!" the woman shouted. She shot at them again, but the bullet missed, hitting a nearby pipe. The pipe broke off, white steam hissing out of it, and the picture started flickering more than before.

This woman was a terrible shot.

"Now!" Rylan shouted.

They jumped into the picture made of light.

ARRA WENT TO THEIR TREE, Fenian's and hers. Their summer tree, the oak tree. The one they'd made love under, their skin glistening from the fog, shivering in the night air, without a care in the world.

In love.

She hadn't thought of Fenian as much these past two days —the humans had intruded too deeply into their world. She felt guilty, for a moment. She promised herself it wasn't because of Fenian's leg. She still loved him. She'd just been busy.

She'd been fighting a war, after all.

Well now she was here, at their tree. Fenian was back in Sylrantheas. He'd survived the fight with the Remnant with nary a scratch, luckily.

Many others in the village had not been so lucky.

Arra tried not to get misty-eyed as she looked at the Book. This was why she was here. She hefted it in her hand, turning it over. It felt dense, unexpectedly heavy. She wondered if there was more than just wood inside it.

Who had made it, anyway? Elves couldn't create magical artifacts anymore—everyone knew that. It was a lost art, one that no one spoke of. She'd known about this one, but could there be others?

What secrets was her father keeping?

He always avoided talking about the time before she was born. As if it were too painful, or too complicated. And now with Orym in their midst, the two men constantly shared glances, unspoken words. There was some kind of history between them, one that Arra was not privy to.

Perhaps it didn't matter.

Well, it was now or never. She had to try the Book. She pulled six pieces of primewood from her bag, one for each Way. She'd taken them from the little primestore in the kitchen, the wood left there by her father.

Her thoughts strayed again. She shuddered as she remembered the Primestore fire. They'd nearly lost *all* their primewood earlier that night. If Trey hadn't been there, if he hadn't been a Prime Mage with this Book, well...

Magic would be *over*.

As it was now their supply was dangerously low. Half the Primestore *had* burnt down, after all. So unless they drastically curtailed their usage, they'd be completely out within a year. That likely meant the School was going to close—or at least all magical training would stop.

She shouldn't have taken the primewood from the kitchen; it was reckless and irresponsible. They might need it in the days to come.

But it didn't matter. She had to know.

SIX

FENIAN FOUND Arra there an hour later, crying underneath the tree. She had tried and tried, hoping the Book would make it possible for her to be a mage. She had exercised her Will, pushing her mind until it hurt, but nothing had happened.

She was cursed to be Mundane for her entire life.

Fenian just held her, not asking her to explain, not forcing her to talk. He was just there, his strong arms surrounding her. She wept into his shoulder underneath their oak tree.

He kissed the top of her hair. "It's going to be okay," he murmured. "You're going to be okay." She sobbed into his shirt. "You're the strongest woman I know," he continued. "Mage or not, Talent or not, you're everything I need. You're perfect just as you are. I wish you could believe in yourself as much as I believe in you."

His words were soothing; her crying subsided into sniffles. She felt the emotion of it wearing out, running through her like a river, out and down and away. Spent. It left her feeling at peace.

She could be happy with herself as she was, without

magic. If Fenian could live with his crippled leg—if *he* could be happy, then so could she.

So could she.

"I love you," Fenian said. She angled her face up and kissed him, tasting her own tears and his lips. She opened her mouth, wanting more, wanting him. His grip intensified, his strength enfolding her. "I love you," he said again between kisses.

She forgot about the Book as she melted into his arms.

AN ICY WAVE washed over Rylan, and he stumbled as he found himself in bright light. The air was noticeably colder, and everything suddenly smelled different.

Why was he here? He blinked, looking around. His mind felt fuzzy, sort of empty. He couldn't remember anything from the past few days. He could see that this was Planner Central, but how had he gotten here?

He looked behind him, stumbling slightly. He was having trouble keeping his balance. There was a contraption back there, a swirling plane of light surrounded by thick metal. He felt panic starting to rise, his breathing accelerating. His mind was totally blank. He couldn't remember *anything*.

What was going on?

A girl was standing next to him, looking at him with concern in her eyes. Who was the girl? Why was she there?

Suddenly everything slammed back into his mind, and he remembered. It was like a sluice gate had opened, sending water through the tunnels of his memory, filling up the holes. Everything came back to him—the burning building, the flight through the woods, the escape through this gate. How could he have forgotten? That gate they'd passed through...

he'd been through ones like that before, five years ago. Was it to blame for his momentary memory loss?

He looked around. Yes. He was back in the city, having somehow been transported here from the surface. Elanil stepped toward him.

"Are you okay?" she asked. "Where are we?"

Rylan looked behind him. The gate that had led them here was flickering badly. He could see through it to the room they had just left, see the woman with the gun bending down, trying to fix something with the pipe she had shot off. There was a fuzzing sound, and the whole thing vanished.

Where before there had been a picture made of light now there was just a metal platform with a scaffolding of pipes, wires, and tubes.

"Hey!" somebody shouted. "Get away from the gate!" Rylan turned to see a man running toward them. He was quickly joined by several others. Before he could even think of running, they were surrounded.

"You're coming with us," one of the men said, grabbing Rylan roughly. Elanil squealed as they grabbed her too, knocking her down hard on one knee.

Out of the fire and into the inferno, as his mother used to say.

RYLAN WAS GETTING tired of jail. At least these elves— Elanil had assured him that they were, in fact, elves—hadn't tied them up. They'd just thrown them into a jail cell while they figured out what to do with them.

Another damn jail cell.

"So what now?" Rylan asked.

Elanil wasn't looking like her usual self. She was hunched

over, sitting cross-legged on the floor. Her pants were torn, and she had skinned her knee when the guards had pushed her. Her hair was dirty and all messed up, and she had streaks of mud on her face.

She was perfect.

Rylan scooted over to her, putting a hand hesitantly on her shoulder. She flinched, staring down at the floor sightlessly.

"Elanil?" he said. "Are you okay?"

She shuddered, drawing in a breath, and finally looked at him, her expression haunted. "Where *are* we?"

Rylan had seen Con like this once. She'd moped about in their living space for days, depressed and unmotivated. He hadn't known what to do. One day she had just snapped out of it and went back to being her normal self. He hoped that would happen with Elanil.

"This is Newfris," he said, in answer to her question. "We must be in Planner Central." That area of the city was normally cut off from public access.

"I have to pee," Elanil said, looking around the room. There was a toilet in one corner. They were both stuck in this cell together, and that included sharing the toilet.

"I won't look," he said, turning away.

"Can you...go into the corner, or something?"

"Sure." He moved a few feet over to the corner of the cell, facing the wall. He heard the sound of her pants being dropped, followed by her peeing. It didn't really phase him— this was common down in the Under. There weren't exactly public restrooms down there. But he could tell it was bothering Elanil immensely. She must have been holding it for a long time.

Finally, she was finished. "You can turn around now," she

said, and he did. She looked somewhat sheepish, not meeting his eyes. "Sorry you had to be here for that."

Rylan shrugged. "Nothing I haven't seen before."

"You saw it?" She started to put her hand to her mouth, but thought better of it.

"No—I mean, it happens all the time in the Under. We don't have bathrooms down there."

"Oh. That's terrible!" She sat down against the wall, shivering. "It's so cold in here. This place—it's all so...so *sterile*."

Sterile? Didn't that mean clean? Rylan looked around the room. It was anything but clean. She must have meant something else. He sat down next to her.

She had drawn her knees up, wrapping her arms around them. She looked pitiful and scared, sitting there with her bloody knee and bedraggled hair. He wanted to do something to comfort her, but he didn't know what. What would a topsider do in this situation? No, screw that—what would an *elf* do?

He reached out for her hand. They'd held hands several times before, but that had been for doing magic. This felt different. She looked at him quizzically, but she allowed it, placing her hand in his without argument. Her hand was cold.

"I really screwed up back there," she said.

"Back where? That dance you did was awesome!"

"No, I mean Sylrantheas. The fire was my fault. We should never have been playing with that bucket."

"No, it was my fault," Rylan said. "I'm the one who passed out and screwed up the magic."

"What happened to you, anyway?" she asked.

Rylan shrugged. "I'm not really sure," he said. "Just, whenever I do magic, I get a kind of...I don't know, a euphoria or something. For a minute, I just feel really good and I forget everything else. That time with the bucket, it was too much to handle. I had to stop."

"I thought it might be something like that," Elanil said, "but it doesn't seem to have been a problem for you lately. With the guards, and that lock? I didn't notice you acting funny."

"It still happens. I'm just getting better at hiding it. Or maybe I'm getting more control as I practice more. I don't know."

Elanil squeezed his hand. "For what it's worth, even though we've been beaten up and tied up and thrown in jail, it's still been kinda fun."

"It kinda has, hasn't it?" he said, squeezing her hand back. This hand-holding thing wasn't half bad.

"Why don't you have your undername yet?" Elanil asked.

Rylan shrugged. "I haven't done anything big enough, I guess."

"And you can't give one to yourself?"

"Nope."

"Then I'm giving one to you. I think you should be called Ryl."

Rylan abruptly pulled his hand away. "You can't do that," he said.

"What?"

"You can't give me my undername."

"Why not?"

"Because you're not an underkid."

"So I'm not good enough?"

"No! If anything, you're *too* good. You didn't grow up in the Under. You didn't scrape by every day just to eat. You didn't get beat up all the time, growing up scared of everything and everyone. You're used to being clean, having bathrooms, having parents. We have none of those things down there. And unless you've lived that life, you don't get to give me a name."

He slouched against the wall, glaring at the floor. Elanil was silent.

"Well," she said after a moment, "it's good to know you feel that way."

Rylan let out a breath. "I'm sorry," he said. "It's just that... I don't know. I've wanted an undername my whole life. When it finally happens, it's gonna be a big deal. You just don't understand."

"I think I do understand," Elanil said, inching toward him and taking his hand again. He almost resisted, but thought better of it. She didn't mean him any harm, after all. She was just trying to be nice. "Can *I* call you Ryl, at least? You can call me Lani, if you want. It's what my best friends call me."

Rylan saw her golden eyes looking at him, and he couldn't say no. "Okay," he said, "fine. You can call me Ryl. But only you."

"Goody," she said, settling back against the wall. Her shivering seemed to have stopped. "So what do we do now?"

"Do you have any primewood left?"

Elanil shook her head. "We used it all up."

Rylan felt around in his pockets. He'd lost the pack of darkprime wood somewhere along the way, and there were no more chips of it in his clothing.

They were stuck there, without magic to get them out.

Rylan thought about where they were. Planner Central was a lot like the rest of the city, except with hordes of guards and weapons and electric fences. He knew there was a large group of buildings in the center, with clusters of smaller buildings around the edges. He hadn't really gotten a good look at the area before—visiting Planner Central wasn't exactly high on the list of underkid activities. Oh, they could get into Planner Central if they wanted to, but they rarely had reason.

They could get in if they wanted to. Of *course*.

"I think I can get us out of here," he said.

THE SOLUTION TURNED out to be a simple one, thank the Twins. Elanil watched as Rylan went over to the toilet and fiddled with it for a bit. It was gross.

"Aha!" he said. "Can you come help me?"

Reluctantly, she got to her feet. Her knee hurt, and she was starving. How long had it been since their flight into the forest? A day? Less? They'd spent half the time locked up or tied up, time compressing and extending until she no longer knew how it flowed. None of this had been a good idea. She really needed to stop being so impulsive.

She went over to the toilet. "What do you want me to do?" she asked. She hoped he wasn't going to make her touch it again. The toilet was disgusting. Sitting on it earlier had been bad enough—*especially* with a boy in the room.

"Here," Rylan said, "push." He braced himself on the floor and pushed with both hands.

Elanil grimaced, wiping her hands on her pants. She would need to take the longest bath ever after this was over. If she ever got back. She joined Rylan on the floor, pushing daintily on the side of the toilet bowl.

Nothing happened.

"You're gonna have to push harder," Rylan said.

"Ew," Elanil replied. But she pushed harder, putting her hands fully on the toilet bowl, trying not to think about how dirty it was.

There was a grinding sound, and the bowl started moving.

They pushed and pushed, gradually revealing a dark hole under the toilet.

"Is that the *sewer*?" Elanil asked.

"Yup," Rylan answered. "We got lucky."

"How is this *lucky*?"

"Most toilets don't move like this. Over the years, under-kids have gotten to some of them, loosening their connection with the floor, cutting the sewer pipe and greatly enlarging the hole. But it's dangerous work, and not many of them are like this. We got lucky."

Elanil turned up her nose. It *smelled* down there in the hole.

"Let me guess," she said, "we have to climb down that hole."

"Yup!" Rylan said, grinning at her.

Elanil felt like crying.

SEVEN

QUYNN STARED at the sign for a long moment. "Walker Books," it read. But nobody bought books anymore. It was a stupid business to have.

He slipped a key from his pocket and unlocked the front door. Then he keyed a code into the security system and it beeped, powering down.

He stood in the dark of the store, gazing at the books. There were so many stories here. So many fantasies. Quynn wondered what the humans would have written if they'd known the truth about things.

The Staff was right where he'd expected it to be. He'd given it to this Simon character, entrusting it to him merely as an object of beauty. Simon—and his son—had no idea what it *really* was.

He stepped into the dark storage room, eyeing the display case. He ran his finger down the edge of the case, feeling for traps or anything else his eyes had missed. He hadn't expected anything to be there, but it was always good to check.

There was a soft *snick* as he opened the case. The glass door swung open silently, and Quynn reached inside.

The Tree Ring Staff was warm to his touch. Unable to help himself, he touched each of the woods in turn, whispering their names.

"Maple. Birch. Poplar. Ash. Oak. Elm."

And the seventh wood. The wood no Eldrim ever spoke of.

"Willow."

He found himself longing for ages gone by, for the distant past when the art of creating magical artifacts had not been lost. For the days when the Prime Trees still towered over everything.

At least they still had the Tree Ring Staff. Not all had been lost.

Quynn wondered what Lorelei's plans were for the Staff. Although it was a nearly limitless source of power, the Staff tired the wielder out too quickly. It was far too dangerous. He remembered all too well the countless mages who had burned themselves out trying to pull too much power.

Soulburned.

It was not a risk worth taking. Not for him.

Quynn's fingers traced the Staff as he thought back to that time. The Prime Trees had died that day, all at once, just keeled over. Dead. Nobody had been expecting that to happen. If the Eldrim had known, the world would be vastly different now.

But they had not known. There just hadn't been enough information. Prime magic was too ancient, too mysterious. No elf alive—and no surviving history—contained the true secrets of the Trees. No one knew where the power actually came from, how it worked behind the scenes. All the elves had to go on was thousands of years of tradition.

Well, it was time to be done with tradition. Time to carve a new way forward. The Cothellon would see to that. And if this Staff could help, so be it.

He left the bookstore, striding confidently along the dark street. The staff warmed his hand as the fog rolled in through City Three.

EIGHT

THE SEWER PIPE was tight and dark, slick with urine and other stuff she didn't want to imagine. Elanil wriggled down it, barely able to breathe.

It took her several minutes to realize they were crawling through her own pee.

They crawled like this for several minutes, Elanil doing her best to avoid throwing up. That was the last thing they needed in the cramped pipe: her vomit. So she wriggled behind Rylan, praying to the Twins that he knew where he was going.

When Rylan finally stopped, she was having trouble breathing. The stench in the tunnel and the confined space were making her anxious, and she could feel panic coming on.

Rylan was doing something up ahead. She heard a click, and a shaft of light appeared ahead of him. It was a little square hatch. Finally, an exit!

They crawled through.

A dank hallway was on the other side, smelling of rot and

fungus and death. Elanil didn't like it one bit, but at least they could stand in here. She would take what she could get.

She followed Rylan down the hall, wondering where they were. She could barely see anything—a few weak shafts of light came in from unseen windows above, but the place was dark other than that. There were doors with metal bars in them, blocking empty rooms of cement.

This was a jail.

It had an abandoned feeling, as if no one had visited here in a while. Was the place still used? She hoped not. Anyone stuck in this jail would likely never see the light of day again. Or another person.

They kept walking, peering into every cell they passed. All were empty of people, filled instead with dust and cobwebs and dirt and maybe a few rats. There were no people in the cells, at least until they got to the end.

Elanil gave a little shriek when she saw it. There was a girl in the very last cell, huddled on the floor. Rylan turned to see what had startled her, the look in his eyes turning to one of horror.

"Con?" he said, his voice cracking.

He fell to his knees.

RYLAN COULDN'T BELIEVE his eyes. Con was still alive! But she looked terrible, like she'd been put through hell and then starved for a week. Her face was a mess of cuts and bruises, and she was so skinny he could see her bones. The cell smelled of feces and urine—they hadn't even given her a toilet! Rylan felt himself growing angry.

"Con," he said. "It's me." She didn't lift her head, didn't

respond. He could see her breathing, but that was it. "Con," he tried again, "we're gonna get you out of there."

She made a mewling sound, barely audible, and Rylan felt anger surging through him even more strongly than before. He grabbed the cell bars, still on his knees, trying in vain to pull them apart. But they didn't budge, of course.

He wasn't that strong.

"The magic!" he cried, feeling about in his pockets, but there was nothing there. He looked at Elanil, saw concern written on her face. "We have to help her. We have to get her out!"

Elanil knelt down beside him, placing her hand gently on his shoulder. "We don't have any primewood," she said. "There's nothing we can do." She looked forlornly at Con. "You poor thing. What have they done to you?"

Rylan was growing frantic. Here she was, his best friend, his only friend. She was right there in front of him. He had to help her! He cast about, looking around the room. Maybe there was another access point, something he could use to rescue her. But no—he could tell within moments that there was nothing. The cell was solid, with nothing but walls and bars surrounding it.

The situation was hopeless.

He felt tears coming to his eyes. He couldn't leave her there, not like this, not this close to death. If he left now, it would be on his conscience forever.

"Ryl," Elanil said, "we have to go."

"No!" Rylan said. He was sobbing now, unable to help himself. Con looked so alone, so damaged. It had been his fault. His fault she was in here at all. His fault she would stay.

"Someone will catch us," Elanil said. "Come on." She pulled at him, trying to get him to come away.

"Nobody has been here in a long time!" Rylan cried. "They're not coming now. We have to try!"

Elanil put her arms around him, hugging him from the side. They knelt there together, watching Con's labored breathing. She didn't seem aware that they were even there, looking at her. She wasn't going to make it much longer. Rylan rocked back and forth, crying bitter tears.

In the end, they left.

There was nothing else they could do.

RYLAN GOT them out of Planner Central and safely into the Under. It wasn't hard—the government idiots didn't police their sewers and ventilation systems as well as they should have.

He knew there was nothing he could do now, but he'd be back. He'd bring an army of underkids with him, and he'd be back. He'd get Con out.

It didn't matter how.

Elanil was breathing hard, struggling to keep up with him. It had been a long time since they'd eaten anything substantial, and he knew she wasn't used to this kind of environment. She kept hitting things on accident, scuffing knees and elbows and wrists as they crawled and climbed through the Under.

He wished she didn't have to be down here with him. She should be out in the trees, instead, dancing.

Rylan scowled to himself and kept moving.

NINE

TREY WAS EATING dinner in a tavern.

Yes, Sylrantheas had a tavern. It was called Meriel's, after the proprietor. Apparently it had originally been called Syndra's, after Meriel's sister. But Syndra now, was dead.

Trey had learned all this from Meriel herself.

The place was entirely made of wood. It wasn't *quite* like home, but it was close enough. He was thinking of The Pig and Whistle as he ate roasted vegetables and potatoes, sipping on a beer. He thought of Lora.

His wife must miss him terribly.

He'd slept another three hours that day. Magic really took it out of you, apparently, at least when you used that much of it. Being a Prime Mage made you very strong, but the power wasn't unlimited. It came with a price.

Trey had the headache to prove it.

The door to the tavern opened suddenly, and Callan stomped in. He saw Trey sitting there and came to join him, swinging into the large booth across from him.

"I've been meaning to ask," Trey said, "what you were doing during the battle yesterday."

Callan gave him a smile. "You know all those swords the Guardians were using?"

"Sure."

"While you were playing around with *magic*, I helped make three of them."

"You—" Trey was speechless for a moment. "I didn't know you could do that."

"Orist taught me. Allain's father. He's a really good blacksmith. Gave me something to do."

But Callan's expression was guarded. Was he mad at Trey for some reason? It sounded like he disapproved of magic.

Before Trey could say anything else, Arra walked in.

She was stunning, as usual, but she looked a little worn around the edges, as if the day didn't quite agree with her. Had she been crying? Maybe she was just tired. He'd lost track of her in all the fighting the night before. How many Remnant had *she* killed?

They all had blood on their hands. Even Callan.

He felt his stomach sour. He'd been so caught up in the moment, in the flurry of emotions after finding out he was a Prime Mage, that he hadn't really stopped to *think*. Why *had* he killed all those people? He didn't know them. He didn't know their lives. Maybe the *elves* were the bad guys, and the Remnant were just misunderstood.

He should have thought about that before he killed them all.

Trey put down the fork, unable to take another bite. What was happening to him? His life had been so simple, before. But now...

Arra was holding the door for someone. Trey watched as Fenian limped in on his crutches, looking for all the world like a perfectly noble, mortally wounded martyr. Trey watched Arra fawning over him and his stomach soured further.

Arra finally caught Trey's stare as she and Fenian made their way over to his table. He thought he saw something buried in her look—was it jealousy? Maybe not. Maybe *he* was the jealous one. Jealous of Fenian.

But no. Why? Why was he having these thoughts at all? His mind was so confused. Magic. Elves. Girls he thought he knew from a life gone by. It didn't make sense.

It didn't. Make. Sense.

He slammed his hand on the table suddenly, and everyone jumped. Instantly his headache increased, setting his teeth on edge. "Goddammit," he muttered. "I just can't win."

"You're awake," Arra said, sitting next to Fenian in the large booth. "Feeling better? That storm you made...it was impressive as hell."

"Thanks, I think," Trey said, putting his hand to his head. It did nothing to help the pain. "I didn't save the wall, though. It still burnt down."

"Most of it," Arra said. "But you did save a lot of lives. Maybe the entire village."

There was no mistaking it now. She *was* jealous about his magic. Trey tried to suppress a sigh, and was more or less successful.

"Never thought I'd see this much action," Callan said. "You elves seemed like such a peaceful lot."

"We are," Arra said. "Were."

"There has always been the threat of an attack," Fenian said, shifting his leg. Trey could see pain lurking behind his eyes, and he was avoiding Trey's gaze. Why? "That's why we have the Guardians. We should have trained them better."

"They did fine," Arra said. "We should have had more Hunters."

"What we *needed*," Fenian said, "was more Prime Mages." He looked at Trey, finally. "At least we had you. Thanks."

Trey dipped his head in acknowledgement. He didn't know how to respond. "Is Silanar right? Will the Remnant stay away this time?"

"Probably," Arra said. "We—well, you—*decimated* them last night. That had to be most of their warriors, if not all. I don't think they kept many in reserve."

"Then Sylrantheas is safe."

"Yes."

"Any word on Rylan?" Callan asked suddenly. "I kinda miss the little guy."

"Still nothing," Fenian said. "The Hunters returned an hour ago. They found tracks leading east, toward Fennas Elenathon, or where we think it must be. But the kids were nowhere to be found."

Everyone knew the name of the device now, the one Elanil had found. Orym had made sure of that. But nobody knew precisely what it *was*, and Orym still hadn't explained.

Trey wondered why nobody thought that was strange. "So what do you think happened?" he asked. "Where did they go?"

"The two of them were running from something," Fenian said. "Together. But the tracks just disappeared. One second they were there, the next they were gone. Nobody could understand it."

"What about leafrunning?" Arra asked. "Could they have gotten up into the trees?"

Fenian shrugged. "Maybe. The Hunters probably sent leafrunners into the trees, though. That's how they track certain kinds of prey. It would have been standard procedure."

"Oh." Arra twiddled her thumbs for a minute. Then a

server came up, and everyone ordered beer. Beers all around, except for Trey. His head was hurting too much for beer.

"Oh, what the hell," he said as the server was leaving. "Give me a beer, too."

Something told him he would need it.

"I'm sure Rylan will be fine," Arra said. "Especially if he's with Lani. She has a knack for surviving *everything*."

That seemed like a strange comment, but Trey let it pass. "Everything sure went to shit on Sunday, didn't it?" That was the day they had fallen from the city.

Callan nodded. "I blame Orym. He knows more than he's telling us."

Trey knew he was right. But it wasn't just Orym's secrets that he was missing. There was a *lot* he still didn't know.

Starting with magic.

"What *is* primewood, exactly?" he asked. "Why can't you get any more?"

"We don't have time for a school lesson right now," Arra said. Was she *mad* at him?

"I can try to answer," Fenian said, and everyone turned to look at him. "All of this was before I was born, of course. I can only describe what I've heard, what I've seen in paintings and photographs.

"The Prime Trees were big. Enormous. Bigger than any tree on the planet. They were beautiful and majestic, towering over the rest of the planet like giant sentinels. And before you ask"—he caught Trey's eye—"humans couldn't see them. They were invisible.

"In fact, the Prime Trees were the source of our illusion. Any elf within proximity of a Tree could—with just a small amount of Will—look like a human. We called it *misting*, a derivative of mistweaving. The Trees are the reason the elves were able to exist on Earth alongside humans without you ever knowing.

"But the Prime Trees were more than that. They were power. The only source of primewood. Simply cut a piece of wood from a Prime Tree, and it grows back almost instantly. And the wood you cut—that's primewood. Material for magic.

"There were Trees of every type—all fourteen species. The elves stayed near the Trees as much as possible, living under them when they could. I've heard my parents speak of a sense of peace, tranquility, that could be found under the Trees. They were...magnificent.

"But I wasn't there during that time. This is only what I've been told."

He stopped, as if that were the end of the explanation.

"That was almost...poetic," Arra said, looking at him with love in her eyes. "I had no idea you could describe things like that."

Fenian blushed. "Thanks. I'm mostly just repeating it from school."

She nestled into his arm, and Trey forced himself to watch.

But he had so many questions. "Where did the Trees come from?" he asked. "Where did they go? Were they destroyed? How? Why? Why didn't they grow back?"

"All very good questions," Fenian said.

"But you don't know the answers."

"Well..." He sat up straighter in his seat, suddenly seeming nervous. "I do know some of them. Not where the Trees *came* from, or why they didn't grow back. But I do know how they were destroyed."

"I'm listening," Trey said.

"Uh," Fenian said, squirming uncomfortably. "I'm not supposed to tell you."

"*What?*"

"The Council ordered everyone to keep it from you. They said you might take it...poorly."

Trey knew he had a murderous expression on his face. He could tell because his headache increased right along with it. "Callan," he said, keeping his eyes on Fenian, "I think these elves owe us an explanation. Don't you agree?"

"I would say so," Callan said.

"All this magic," Trey said. "All this fighting. The Remnant. Newfris. If the virus was a lie, *then why did all the humans die?*"

Fenian shrank back in his seat, his eyes stricken. "I can't tell you," he whispered.

"Then," Trey said, standing, "I'm afraid you're of no further use to me."

He left the tavern in a rush, shaking with anger, head positively *pounding.*

He didn't even notice how much like his father he had sounded just then.

TEN

RYLAN AND ELANIL made their way back to the only place Rylan knew would accept them: Shock Crew. They emerged from the subway tunnel, exhausted and bedraggled, wanting nothing but food and warmth and companionship.

Things they were unlikely to find anywhere in the Under.

The spiky-haired guard girl was there again, wearing a different shirt this time, her tits less obvious in it. She glowered at him, but let them pass. He walked by her without a word.

Shock Crew quarters was the same as it had always been —hot, loud, and raucous. Rylan kept one arm protectively around Elanil as they made their way through the gauntlet, heading toward Dill's tent. She was something nobody ever saw down here: pretty, delicate, and still too clean. Plus there were her ears. But there was nothing for it but to keep moving, hoping he could defend her if someone decided to make the wrong move.

Jeering and catcalls followed them the whole way, and a few pieces of garbage hit them, thrown from somewhere in the rigging above. Nobody did anything dangerous, though.

The Crew didn't know what to make of Rylan, apparently, not now that he'd been promoted to Dill's inner circle. So they largely kept their distance.

They arrived at the tent and faced the guards.

"Ho," Rylan said, exhausted. His voice wasn't commanding or intimidating—just indifferent. The guards didn't matter. He had bigger concerns now. The pair of guards looked at him for a second before silently stepping aside.

Rylan strode forward. "Ho, Dill," he said, announcing his presence. He could hear something rummaging about in the tent, then the flap opened and Dill came out.

He wasn't wearing his usual shirt with the pickle on it. Instead, he was shirtless, perfectly sculpted muscles rippling as he moved. Rylan caught his mouth hanging open, and out of the corner of his eye he could see Elanil with a similar expression. How the hell had Dill managed to become that fit down here in the literal gutters? Where had he managed to find that much *food?*

"Ho yourself," Dill said, smiling. His eyes flicked to Elanil. Rylan expected him to be surprised to see an elf, but Dill's expression didn't alter at all. "Come in," he said. He reached a hand out to shepherd Rylan into the tent. Behind them, the guards had returned to their post.

The tent was as large as he had remembered. The big table in the center was covered with an array of metal pieces that he couldn't identify. All the usual boys were there—Shot and Grid were cleaning some of the metal parts, and Grime was sitting in the corner, his arm in a sling. Rylan was glad to see they had all made it safely out of the firefight, before the room had collapsed.

"Small's out running an errand for me," Dill said, "but otherwise the gang's all here." Dill turned to him, looking him up and down. "We saw what happened to the floor. That must have been an epic fall. How'd you get back up here, anyway?" He didn't ask how Rylan had survived the fall.

"Some kind of gate," Rylan said. "It's a long story."

Dill nodded, arms crossed over his muscular chest. "I bet it is. But first, maybe you should introduce us to your friend."

Rylan looked at Elanil. She seemed confused, her posture indicating fear. He put his hand on her back, hoping the physical contact would comfort her somewhat.

"This is Elanil," he said. "She's an elf."

TREY STOPPED JUST outside the outer door to the Council building. He could hear voices through the door.

"Are guards placed outside the Primestore?" someone was asking.

"Yes," someone else replied. "And Orist is installing two lightning rods on the exterior."

"Do you think we need more than that? Maybe shielding of some kind?"

There was a sigh. "We might. It's all we have left. If anything else were to happen to it..."

"We'd be completely bereft of magic. We should have known this was a possibility. We should have protected the Primestore better. If we lose it..."

"It would be difficult to adapt."

"We've been planning on this for the past decade, haven't we? What is a year in the scheme of things?"

"We aren't ready yet. Not this soon."

"Are we *sure* the other villages won't part with their supply?"

"We're sure. They've all refused."

"That is very unlike elves."

"Times are desperate."

"Let us pray to the Twins that what we have is enough, then. We can't lose that primewood."

"The Twins will guide us."

"What are we doing with that Remnant pair? Jalnab and Martan?"

"My daughter has vouched for them. They've been very helpful with the cleanup, so far—I think they want to make reparations for what their people have done. We should let them stay with us for as long as they need."

"They may just be waiting to murder us at the proper time."

"Elanil did not think so. I believe her."

"Where *is* your daughter?"

"I do not know."

Trey was listening at the door. The elves inside were talking about the Primestore, about the fire he had put out. It had destroyed more than half the building, more than half their primewood. The Remnant had started it, they had said. Trey didn't know who Jalnab and Martan were. He didn't care. He needed answers.

He opened the door.

The Council turned in their seats to look at him, all in unison. Trey felt uncomfortable, but he stifled the feeling, trying to summon back the anger he had felt in the tavern just minutes ago. He needed answers, needed to understand what was going on in the village.

He needed to know why so many humans had died.

"Silanar," he said, finding the man sitting across the room. "Sorry to interrupt."

Silanar nodded gravely. "What is it?"

Trey came in further, shutting the door behind him.

Everyone in the room—the seven Council members, plus Orym—were looking at him closely.

"I need to know what you know," he said.

"About?"

"Whatever happened before. Why the humans died. Why we're stuck in a floating city now. Why the virus was a lie."

"Those are big questions."

"It's important."

Silanar looked around the room. "I don't think you're ready."

Trey wanted to scream. He wanted to hit something. He wanted to *force* Silanar to obey, wanted to summon a storm down on them all, to hit them with lightning from the sky. He wanted to burn every last shred of primewood they had left, to force them, screaming on their knees, to beg him for mercy.

But his head was killing him.

So instead, he simply crossed his arms. "Tell me," he said, his voice deadly calm. "Now."

Silanar sighed. "Very well," he said, "but it's going to take a while. You might want to have a seat." He turned to Orym. "If we're going to rehash all of this," he said, "it would be instructive to hear your side of events, as well. You too, Kharis."

"I wasn't involved," Kharis said. "I was just in a bar the whole time."

"Whatever you can add will be helpful."

The door opened again, and Trey turned to see Arra, Fenian, and Callan filing in.

"Come in, come in," Silanar said. "You might as well all hear this."

He sounded resigned.

RYLAN LOOKED AROUND THE TENT, expecting it to erupt with wild shouts and questions, but everyone was silent. Only the clink of metal could be heard as Shot and Grid continued meticulously cleaning the parts on the table. Grime began whistling softly.

Rylan was confused. He had just introduced Elanil. He'd said she was an *elf*, a being that until just a few days ago had been completely fictional.

But nobody had reacted.

Dill cleared his throat. "Boys," he said, "remember your manners."

Manners? Down here in the Under?

Dill must be out of his mind.

Grime got up first, careful not to jar his arm. "Name's Grime," he said. "Nice to meet you."

"Hi," Elanil said. Her voice sounded shaky.

Shot was next, jumping up and doffing his dirty cap, giving her a bow. "Milady," he said, "Shot, at your service."

Elanil giggled a little bit at that. "Hello."

Grid got up slowly, stepping over to her and looking her up and down. She withered under his gaze. Grid was tall, with tight, curly brown hair and deep brown eyes. He held the moment out, staring her down, frightening her. Rylan started forward, but Grid abruptly stuck his hand out. "Grid," he said. "Welcome to Shock Crew."

Elanil let out a breath, shaking his hand hesitantly. "Thank you," she said, "I think." She turned to Rylan. "This is where you live?"

Rylan nodded. "What's going on here?" he asked Dill. "You're all acting like you already knew about the elves."

"We do know about them," he said. "You did, too.

Remember five years ago? When your mother died? You met the elves, then. You were in their village."

Rylan cast his mind back. In the midst of all the action, in the whirlwind surrounding Phoenix's death, Rylan hadn't even noticed that the people around him hadn't been human. They'd seemed close enough to him.

"I think you're hiding something," he said. "None of you were there five years ago—only Dill and I. So if you all know about them now, it means there's something you're not telling me."

"You're right," Dill said, his eyes veiled.

"We want to know what it is," Rylan said.

"It's kind of a long story."

"You need to tell us."

Dill looked around the tent, surveying the Crew members there. "You boys got the time?"

Everyone nodded, some halfheartedly, some with a keen interest. Grime got up and went over to the big chest, opening it. He pulled from within it a dirty bottle filled with brown liquid, along with a set of tin cups.

"If we gotta listen to this whole thing again," Grime said, bringing the bottle and cups over to the table, "we might as well do it in style."

Dill grinned. "Good thinking, Grime. Now listen up, people. I'm only going to tell this once."

PART
TWO

ELEVEN
SAN FRANCISCO
300 YEARS AGO

JESSICA SURVEYED THE CITY SKYLINE, watching the fog rolling in from the Bay. There was something unnatural about it, as if the fog had developed thoughts, personality. She imagined it floating there malevolently, reaching with grasping tendrils for poor, unsuspecting victims on the ground. She imagined how cold it would be. How empty.

Lately, emptiness was all she felt.

She turned, wiping a tear from her eye as she looked at Jason in the hospital bed. So small. So frail. So much had happened to him so fast. She still knew so little of what was going on.

"Miss Lim?"

A man was standing in the door. A man in a suit and white shirt, carrying a tablet and a clipboard. It seemed redundant to her. She blinked, trying to come back to herself. Why was the room so cold?

"I'm Mrs. Lim," she said. "My husband couldn't make it here today."

"Of course." The man bobbed his head. "I meant no

offense. My name is Doctor Chanchorn. I'm the oncologist assigned to your case."

Jessica stifled a sob.

The doctor bobbed his head again, but his eyes were looking at the television perched in the corner of the room. He flicked them back to her, a thin smile on his face. The air was growing colder. "I have your results, Mrs. Lim. Would you like to sit down? We can do this in my office." His eyes went to the TV again.

"No," Jessica said. "You can say whatever it is right here." She had waited long enough. She had seen enough doctors. She had had enough confusion for a lifetime.

"Mrs. Lim—"

"You can call me Jessica."

"Jessica." Doctor Chanchorn pursed his lips. "I'm afraid your son has melanotic neuroectodermal tumor of infancy. It's a rare form of cancer that we almost never see in children his age. The tumor is in his jaw. It would have been curable with a subtotal maxillectomy, but the tumor is well advanced." He paused for a moment. "I'm afraid there is nothing we can do."

Jessica barely heard the words, barely understood them. She felt the floor sinking beneath her. All the tests. All the waiting. All the fear. Her heart had felt for weeks like it was on the verge of breaking, and it would only take the drop of a pin to make the final cut. She felt her world grow gray like the fog over San Francisco.

"I'm sorry to be so straightforward," the doctor was saying. "We can discuss all this in much more detail. I know this must be a terrible time for you. We can certainly try the surgery, but the odds of getting the entire tumor are not—"

He was looking at the damn TV again.

Jessica turned to follow his gaze. What *was* that on the

screen? She batted at a tear, then fumbled for the remote to turn the volume up.

"—have reported lower pressures than originally expected," the reporter was saying. "Current models"—the reporter shifted his papers—"current models have the storm making landfall...this can't be right." He looked offscreen, his eyes frantic. He seemed to listen for a moment, then returned his gaze to the camera. "Viewers, Typhoon Velma has just been upgraded to Category Five, with barometric pressures projected to break the previous world record set in 1979. The National Weather Service is issuing an immediate mandatory evacuation warning for the entire Bay Area, including the city of San Francisco. Affected areas should be scrolling at the bottom of the screen now. I urge you: get to safety. Do not wait. This storm is like nothing we have ever seen before."

Jessica glanced out the window again. The fog was darker now, almost black. That wasn't right. Was it really alive? Was it there to kill her son before the cancer could take him away? She looked at Doctor Chanchorn, seeing fear written on his face.

Was this the day they were all about to die?

ORYM LEANED into the steering wheel of his Mazda CX-9, wondering why in the hell the sky was so black. He hadn't checked in with Meteorology in quite some time, but surely the sky shouldn't look like *that*. A car whizzed by him in the left lane and he flinched, surprised. He shook his head. He didn't have time for this.

The radio on the dash was fuzzing, playing nothing but static. Radio. Outdated technology. Still, it had its purposes. He could skip the radio, call his team, get an instant briefing.

But a perverse part of him wanted to do things the old fashioned way, the way everyone else in this Twins-forsaken city did it.

He wanted to get the weather from the radio.

He turned the dial as he drove, hearing the clicks and buzzes as the antenna picked up the terrestrial noise in the air all around him. Then it landed on a station, and Orym settled in to listen with grim satisfaction.

"An evacuation has been ordered for the coastal region of Northern California," the voice said in its gravelly tone. "Tolls have been suspended on all bridges in the Bay Area, and the Golden Gate Bridge has been closed, as Marin County is especially at risk. Everyone is urged to take a go bag and head east as quickly as possible. Typhoon Velma is still strengthening as it approaches, and it is projected to make landfall in less than four hours. Again: this is a lethal storm, currently reading as the strongest storm ever to hit the Pacific coast since we've been keeping records. Do not wait. You must leave now. May God have mercy on our souls."

Orym clicked the radio off, grimacing. Humans and their gods.

They had no idea what *real* gods were capable of.

"Mission," he said into thin air, and the device in his ear clicked.

"Mission here," a voice said.

"Sylvis," Orym said, "can you tell me what's going on with the weather?"

"Where are you?" Sylvis said.

"I'm in FiDi." The cars ahead of him weren't moving. "*Stuck* in FiDi, apparently. Bridge traffic is fucked even worse than usual for 1 PM."

"You'll never get out of there before Velma hits. I'll get a gatesender for you."

"No," Orym said, his mouth twisting. "The last thing we need is a light show here. What are you going to do, take my entire car?"

"We can do that."

"It's too risky. How long have we kept this a secret?"

"Gatesending?"

"*Elves.*"

Sylvis was silent for a moment. "Twenty thousand years, give or take a few millennia."

"We're not giving up on it now. The Ascension is in two weeks."

"Fine," Sylvis said, "but that storm is going to kill you. At least let me send some more people down there."

"Keep them misted, and we'll be fine."

"I'll do better than that. I'll send Quynn for a quelling."

"Is that what we've become?" Orym asked. The car ahead of him lurched forward a foot, then stopped. "We haven't even Ascended, and already we're wiping minds?"

"If it comes to that," Sylvis said. "You know the Ascension is more important than this storm. *You* are more important."

"I'm not even a mage."

"Just try to get across the bridge. Alive. I'll send some people to help. Discreetly."

"Thanks. Oh, and Sylvis?"

"Yes?"

"Don't tell Lorelei where I am."

KHARIS TOOK a big pull of his beer, relishing the taste. It was a Fieldwork IPA, smooth and juicy and not at all like the ale they made back in Sylrantheas. They didn't have beer nearly this good in the village.

Or any TVs.

That was why he was here, in a bar on 1st Street with the locals, or at least the people who commuted into the city to work here. He should have been back home, hunting or teaching archery. He should have been doing what his mother wanted him to do: find a wife, have a kid, whatever it took to further the family line. But he'd wanted a day to himself. A relaxing day. A day with a beer and a burger and not another care in the world.

It was too bad the city was so damn foggy.

Lhoris was sitting next to him. His brother was bigger, broader-chested, favoring their father's side. He could pull a seven foot longbow a hundred times an hour without even breaking a sweat.

"This beer sucks," Lhoris said.

Kharis almost spit all over the bar. "I thought you liked IPAs." He wiped his mouth.

"I do, but this one is *weird*. Way too much funk."

"It's better than that swill Syndra serves."

"Shut your mouth," Lhoris said. "Syndra's beer is *not* swill. Kindly refer to it by its proper name: beer-flavored water."

Kharis snorted. "Beer-flavored is perhaps too strong a term."

"Fine. Water-flavored water. Or maybe I was drinking water. I don't know. Point is, this beer is weird."

"So you've said."

The bartender distracted him just then, waving a remote so he could turn up the volume on one of the TVs.

"...barometric pressures projected to break the previous world record set in 1979," the reporter was saying. Kharis perked up. "The National Weather Service is issuing an immediate mandatory evacuation warning for the entire Bay Area, including the city of San Francisco."

The reporter kept going, but his voice was drowned out by the sudden onslaught of noise in the bar. Everyone was shouting frantically at each other, standing up and fleeing the room. None of them bothered to pay their checks.

Kharis looked at his brother. "Should we leave?"

Lhoris actually had fear in his eyes. "Yes," he said, "unless you suddenly know how to fly."

Kharis sighed, taking another drink of beer. So much for a relaxing day.

KEYA LOWERED THE CHART, scanning the streets below. Her patient was recovering from a particularly nasty dose of chemo, but it wasn't anything to be overly concerned about. What was happening outside was far more interesting.

The streets were completely filled with cars.

"What in the Twins—" she started, but Rosemary burst into the room.

"We have to go," she said. "We're evacuating the building."

"What? Why?" The sky had an ominous, black look to it. But the weather in San Francisco was never very good.

"Haven't you been paying attention? The storm was just upgraded. They've issued a mandatory evacuation notice for the entire Bay Area."

"Shit." She couldn't say "Twins." Not here.

"We have to go."

"I have patients to see!"

"You'll see them, Keya. Once we get out of here. Come with me now. We need to help move patients."

"Do you *see* the roads?" Keya pointed out the window. The American Cancer Society was fifteen floors up, but the clogged streets were easily visible from way up there. So was the fog rolling in across the Bay. "We're never getting out of here."

"We're airlifting the most critical cases. Ambulances will handle the rest. We've rehearsed this. Come on."

"Fuck." Keya looked at her patient lying in the bed. He had slept through the entire exchange. Maybe his recovery would be worse than she thought. "What about him?"

"We'll get him," Rosemary said. "Come on."

Keya took one last look around the room, wondering if this was the last time she'd see it this way.

TWELVE

"THEY'RE CALLING it the World Storm," Grathgor said.

Quynn snorted. "That's the stupidest thing I've ever heard. This thing might take out half the West Coast, but that doesn't make it a 'World Storm.'"

He was pacing around his office, waiting for word from Lorelei. Could they begin the Ascension early? How would they do that with all the humans milling about so chaotically? Would the Ascension even work with a storm underway?

He desperately needed some bourbon.

Grathgor just shrugged. "Not my idea," he said. "And anyway, this storm is far bigger than the human news is predicting. They have no idea what's about to hit them."

"The Eldrim aren't *causing* this, are they?"

Grathgor looked confused. "What—you think they're using stormwardens?"

Quynn frowned. "I guess you're right. They haven't had that much power in millennia. No, it's not magic. But I can't help but wonder if it's something else. Something they discovered."

"We have all their scientists."

"Good point." He sighed. "Maybe Silanar was right. Maybe this planet *is* fucked."

"Lorelei seems to think so."

"Is that the purpose of all of this?"

Grathgor shrugged. "That's above my pay grade."

"You and me both. So what now?"

"Now we wait and thank the Twins we're nowhere near San Francisco."

They turned to the screens that filled the east wall, watching as the human news portrayed the end of the world.

LORELEI STARED at the wall of screens in Mission Control, tapping the toe of her red heel against the cement floor. New San Francisco was three hours northeast of the Bay in the Central Valley, luckily, or they would have had a real problem on their hands. Still, the storm was likely to carry significant force by the time it reached them.

She hoped the shields would hold.

"Where is he?" she snapped.

Sylvis looked up from her screen. "Aelwynn just messaged to say he was running late."

"Kindly inform the Fallfoiler Captain that people do not *run late* for a meeting with me," Lorelei said, conscious of her clipped tone. The man had always been far too arrogant for his own good.

"Right away, sir," Sylvis said.

Aelwynn burst into the room just then. The man was thin —too thin, even for an elf—and he walked with a kind of tottering motion, almost as if he were about to fall over at any given moment. His mouth was perpetually crooked, his hair long and stringy.

Lorelei had never liked the man.

But he was their strongest fallfoiler. Without him and the magic he represented, the Ascension would never happen. And so it was that Lorelei swallowed, took a deep breath, and prepared to be as nice as she possibly could.

"Don't be late again," she said, her voice cold. "You *can* be replaced."

That was about as much as she could manage.

Aelwynn pursed his lips, which didn't help. "Apologies, my lady. It won't happen again. I was speaking with the City Director of New Tokyo, and I—"

"You were breaking the lines of command?"

"I—well—no? City Directors can speak with each other directly, can we not?"

Lorelei smiled, and Aelwynn grew visibly more afraid. "What did Alais have to say?"

"She thinks New Tokyo might be the point of entry for an Eldrim incursion, if there is to be one. Apparently the shield was left down for an hour a few nights ago."

Lorelei felt anger seething through her. "What? And she didn't bring this information to me?"

"She wanted to, my lady, but. Well."

"She was afraid."

Aelwynn dipped his head in acknowledgement. "It's probably nothing. The perimeter was well-guarded."

"A mistweaver could have infiltrated with no effort whatsoever. All he would have to do is make himself look like one of us."

Aelwynn cocked his head. "Do you think they have any mistweavers left with that amount of power?"

Lorelei sighed. The man had a point. "Tell Alais to order a full sweep of the city, top *and* bottom. If New Tokyo was infiltrated by an Eldrim spy, they'll likely hole up in the city framework below."

"I'll tell her."

So much for maintaining lines of command. "I brought you here for another reason," Lorelei said. "The fallfoilers. If we need to Ascend early, *can* we?"

Aelwynn's fingers twitched, as if he were imagining magic flowing through them. "At our current numbers and training, we could get five of the cities aloft now. The other two would be...iffy."

"Iffy?"

"We could bring them up. My concern would be whether we could *keep* them that way."

The timing was far too tight. "And recruitment?"

"Would go a lot faster if we could use mindmasters."

"We were saving that for *after* the Ascension."

"I know. But finding darkprime mages isn't exactly a common occurrence. And you know the Cothellon numbers are limited. If we could leverage humans..."

"Fine."

"Really?"

"I'll send Quynn to you. He'll be able to help."

"Thank you. If we can get just a few more fallfoilers on board, I'll feel a lot more confident in us starting this whole thing."

"Make it happen," Lorelei said, eyeing the screens ahead of her. The storm was continuing to move rapidly toward the coast. "We may need to move our timetable up."

"The storm is bad," Sylvis said. "We knew this would happen."

"We did," Lorelei said. "That is why we're leaving."

THALANIL WONDERED if any storm shelters existed in San Francisco. Certainly they did in the midwest, but they didn't get storms so strong out here. He was wishing he had one now. He needed a secure place to escape.

Thalanil was working from home.

"Mission," he said into his headset, and his Controller picked up.

"Thalanil," Gilvas said. "Why aren't you here?"

"The gates are down," Thalanil said. "It's a three hour drive! You know I can't make it with the evacuation ordered."

"You should have done what the rest of us did, Thalanil. Take up residence here."

"You know I can't do that. And you know why."

"I don't particularly care. Anyway: what did you want?"

"I'm ready to push another build."

"What—*now*? This is hardly the time, Thalanil. We're in crisis mode around here."

"I found a bug in the main timer. We won't be able to start the Ascension until I push this out."

"We're not scheduled to start anything for two weeks. It can wait."

Thalanil sighed. Gilvas was always a pain in the ass. "Will you let me talk to Orym?"

"Twins, no," Gilvas said. "You aren't talking to your skip level without a damn good reason. And anyway, Orym isn't here."

"Where is he?"

"That's above my pay grade."

"Fine. It'll have to wait until after the storm, then."

"Good. Now fuck off."

"Nice talking to you, as always," Thalanil said, smiling as he disconnected.

Speaking with Cothellon High Command was always such a pleasure.

"WE KNEW THIS WOULD HAPPEN," Bellas said. "It's why the Twins put us here."

Silanar stared at the man. The religious rhetoric was a bit much, even for him. Bellas was the Organization Mentor, not usually given to flights of fancy. Still, Silanar had to admit that the elves were there on Earth for *some* kind of purpose.

This seemed as good a reason as any.

A little radio blared on his kitchen table, issuing more warnings and instructions. He tuned it out. It had been going on like that for hours.

"Do we have conclusive evidence that this storm is the result of human-influenced climate change?" Silanar asked.

"No one has that kind of proof."

"I bet the Cothellon do."

"Touché. That'll happen when all your scientists defect. Do you think they'll move their plans up?"

"We have no idea what their plans *are*."

"Let's hope Dunedar can learn something. He got in okay?"

"He infiltrated New Tokyo last night."

"Good."

"Silanar, we need to leave. This storm is going to hit us harder than it will the humans. We haven't fortified Sylrantheas for this."

"Sylrantheas will survive," Silanar said. "And we have many elves in the city. I think we should stay in case we need to help."

"You want to head *toward* the storm?"

"You know Marin County will be hit worse than San Francisco. If anything, moving that toward the city would be an improvement."

"We should evacuate east."

"Kharis is in the city. And Lhoris, and Keya, and dozens more. We can't just abandon them."

"They will have to fend for themselves. Undoubtedly they are already evacuating the city as we speak."

"They may not make it out. We can help."

"We can't use magic there. You know this better than anyone."

Silanar sighed. Bellas had a point.

He listened to the radio, wondering what his next move should be.

JOHN SET HIS PHONE DOWN, frowning. "We weren't prepared for this."

"How could we be?" Warren asked.

"We knew this day was coming."

"We didn't know a *storm* was coming."

"I bet the elves did."

Warren sighed. "What do you want to do?"

"This will move their time table up. Gondor isn't ready."

"You insist on calling it that."

John gave the man a level stare. "I can call it whatever I damn well please, and you know it."

Warren nodded.

"And you know *why*."

Warren nodded again.

"Then let's sound the alarm. Bring everyone in. If we're to

survive this thing—if the human race is to live on—we can't screw up now. Tell the People the time has come."

"Let's hope the elves don't detect us."

"They haven't noticed us for this long."

"John," Warren said, "this storm alone will kill millions."

"And if the storm doesn't kill us," John said, "the elves sure as hell will. Sound the alarm. Let's get everyone underground."

THIRTEEN

KEYA STEPPED OUTSIDE STEVENSON PLACE, the twenty-three-story tower that housed the American Cancer Society, among other things. She winced as the wind took her suddenly, whipping around her, hair flying everywhere. She spit it from her mouth as she tried to get it under control.

It was warmer outside than she'd expected. It felt muggy, like the one time she'd been on spring break in Florida, against her father's wishes. It had taken her *months* to live that trip down.

Sometimes Sylrantheas was *way* too conservative.

"How many are out?" she asked. Patients were still streaming from the building, being loaded into ambulances and vans and anything else the Society could rig up.

"Hang on," Rosemary said. She had her AirPods in, listening to a local news station. "Shit. The storm is making landfall sooner than they thought."

"How soon?"

"I—"

A gust of wind blasted through the streets, knocking Keya to her knees. She felt pain lance through her, and she winced.

If only...but no. She had to maintain her secret, no matter what the cost.

She looked up to see Rosemary sprawled on the cement, wind blowing her hair everywhere, face unmoving.

Blood was pooling on the ground beneath the woman's head.

"Wait—" Keya said. "No. So fast?"

She struggled to get to her feet, and failed. The wind was *incredibly* strong now. Rosemary still wasn't moving. She'd obviously hit her head on the pavement. She'd suffer from a concussion, maybe, but surely she couldn't be *dead*.

The storm hadn't even arrived.

Keya crawled on her hands and knees, the wind pushing her from behind. It felt like two men had their hands on her, thrusting her forward with irresistible intent. It felt like gravity had changed, and *forward* was the new *down*.

Then the rain started, and she was instantly soaked.

"Rosemary?" she said as she finally made it to her friend. "Are you okay?"

Nothing.

"*Rosemary?*"

Not a sound. Not a movement.

No breathing.

So Keya did what she'd been trained to do. What she'd done hundreds of times. She did the thing she didn't *have* to do to save her friend, but it was the one thing that would keep her identity a secret.

She administered CPR.

SILANAR STEPPED out of his car on Fremont and Howard, careful not to touch the door too much as he did. He hated cars. There was something about them that drove him crazy. Maybe they reminded him of the many elves who'd gone wrong.

They'd made great time into the city, taking the 580 in from Muir Woods since the Golden Gate Bridge was closed. All the traffic was flowing outbound—thousands of cars at a complete standstill—so it was easy for them to go the wrong way. He'd caught plenty of looks from other drivers, wondering why he was driving to his death.

He'd often wondered the very same thing.

The wind was staggering as he exited the vehicle, barely able to keep his feet beneath him. The rain started moments later, but luckily he'd thought to bring his rain gear. He was prepared, unlike so many others. Perhaps he could help. Perhaps that was what his life was for.

Perhaps he wouldn't die when all of this was said and done.

"Do we know where any of our people are?" he asked, shouting to make his voice heard over the wind and rain.

Bellas was clearly miserable. "Kharis texted me. He's at a bar in the East Cut with Lhoris. Keya is at work, and her clinic is being evacuated. I've got at least a dozen others, but they're all over the map. Why did we stop here?"

"There's someone I need to see."

ORYM SLAMMED ON THE BRAKES, narrowly avoiding hitting the car in front of him. He was in the wrong place—he'd taken the wrong fucking turn a few blocks back. Now he was way too close to Embarcadero nowhere near the bridge on-ramp. "That'll be the last time I trust a Twins-damned GPS," he said to no one in particular.

The wind was blowing against the car *hard* now, rain sheeting down like crazy. The storm was supposed to be four hours out, wasn't it? Orym really needed an update from Meteorology.

"Quynn coming in now," Sylvis said in his ear.

A blast of light illuminated the vehicle, and suddenly Orym could sense a new presence sitting in his back seat. He twisted to see a man sitting there. An elf, of medium height with medium brown hair worn long. His expression was gaunt, as if he'd lived a long life full of torment. Which, Orym knew, was most likely true.

Quynn had always given him the creeps.

"Mission," Orym said, ignoring his new passenger, "I thought we agreed not to use gates."

"This was a precision gatesending!" Sylvis said. "I guarantee nobody noticed."

"It was pretty cool, actually," Quynn said from the behind him. "I've never seen them send a seated person before."

A tapping sound on Orym's window startled him. He jerked, turning to look at what it was. When he saw it, he felt a chill roll through him. This was bad. This was very bad. Possibly the only person who could stop it all, who could end the Ascension, who could out Orym for who he really was, was there. The one person who Orym feared more than anyone else was standing beside his car in the pouring, gale-force rain.

Silanar.

CPR WASN'T WORKING.

Keya felt for a pulse, and there was none. Rosemary wasn't breathing. Blood continued to pool from her head, spreading its thick redness on the cement. Rain pummeled everything, drops mingling with the blood. The wind was insane now, and Keya could barely keep herself upright on her knees.

Rosemary was dead.

But not quite gone. Patients had around four minutes before brain death, and it had only been two. If Keya could revive her—if she could get her heart pumping again, get her lungs moving—Rosemary might yet live. But CPR wasn't working. And Keya was running out of time.

She looked around, seeing people frantic in the streets, soaked and stumbling. Nobody was looking at her. Nobody cared about her and her dead friend. They only cared about themselves, about the storm, about escape from death and catastrophe. So Keya fingered the thing she had in her pocket, weighing her decision.

Should she break the rules?

Should she save her friend?

Yes.

She pulled the thing out of her pocket. The thing she wasn't supposed to have. The thing she wasn't supposed to use. The thing that could, in her skilled hands, bring Rosemary back to life. She pulled it out and looked at it, wondering if she was making the right decision.

It was a piece of wood.

Birch, from a Prime Tree, cut months ago from a Tree in Peru and shipped discreetly through the elven network to California. There weren't many Prime Birch trees in the world, but luckily they regenerated any time they were cut. Prime Trees were impossible to kill, after all.

The wood was warm between her fingertips, despite the chill from the gusting wind. Keya could feel the latent power flowing through it, ready to be brought forward by her Will.

All she needed was a skilled action—a restorative ability—an attempt to heal.

She administered one more chest compression to Rosemary's prone form.

Instantly power blazed through the primewood in her hand, her Talent bringing it to life. She harnessed the energy, touching Rosemary, channeling the magic into her friend's body. She could trace the blood vessels with her mind, feel the muscles and synapses and nerves. She found the heart and palpated it quickly, bringing it to life with the kind of control CPR could never have. She also repaired the wound on the back of the woman's head, and did what she could to ease the brain compression that would result in a concussion. In moments, it was done.

Rosemary gasped a breath, arching her back, her eyes staring upward into the rain.

And the prime birch fizzled into dust, dust that immediately became soaked. Keya wiped it on her pants, tears in her eyes.

"What—what happened?" Rosemary asked.

"You fell," Keya said, raising her voice to be heard over the wind. "You passed out for a few seconds."

"I—" Rosemary felt the back of her head, as if remembering the wound that had just been there. "I feel fine. Holy shit, I'm *soaked*!"

"Come on," Keya said. "Let's get to my car. Maybe we can still get out of this godforsaken city before the storm hits."

They tottered and tumbled their way in the direction of her little Ford Focus, arm in soaking arm. Keya hoped no one had seen what she'd done just then on the sidewalk. The magic she had used. The power she had wielded. For if any human saw the true abilities of an eleven soulsoother, she knew their way of life might come to a crashing end.

FOURTEEN

JESSICA FELT the building vibrate around her, heard whistling from all the windows as the wind blew ever more fiercely outside. Rain lanced the outside walls. Thunder rumbled. She sat beside her dying son on the hard hospital bed while the TV blared its incessant warnings.

"Bay Bridge inbound lanes have been reversed," the reporter was saying. "No one is being allowed into the city from Oakland. Traffic is still backed up throughout the city. Please note that 280 and 101 are also viable routes, however residents are encouraged to cut east at their earliest convenience. The storm is scheduled to make landfall within the hour, and it continues to strengthen. If you aren't already on the road, please find a strong building. Designated storm shelter locations are scrolling along the screen now."

Jessica sighed, looking at Jason. Her son looked so peaceful, lying there. She almost couldn't tell how much pain he was in. How much more pain would he undergo? If they survived the storm, what kind of life would he live? Would he recover? Would he have some shred of normalcy? Or would he be doomed forever to live as a stranger to the world, as a strange boy with a reconstructed face, as an outsider that never quite belonged?

Jessica felt a spear of anxiety overtake her as she realized there were no good solutions. Only bad ones. Only the ones modern medicine could provide.

She wished that there were some other option, some other way to heal her son.

And as lightning flashed in the dark gray San Francisco sky, she wondered just how strong this building actually was.

KHARIS STAGGERED out of 83 Proof, more than a little drunk, and suddenly noticed that he was completely wet. "What..." he trailed off.

"Twins," Lhoris cursed. "The storm's already here!"

People were streaming down the street, running into each other, jumping into cars and shouting. The neighborhood had erupted into total chaos. Kharis stumbled to the right, heading toward what he hoped was Mission. "Our car is this way, isn't it?"

"There's no way we'll get out in time!" Lhoris shouted. The wind was incredible, strong and loud. It was almost impossible to hear. Lightning cracked in the distance.

"We have to find shelter!" Kharis shouted. "But where?"

"Maybe we should help these humans!"

"What? How? Bladedancing is *war* magic, Lhoris. It won't help us survive any more than it would help them!" He fingered the knife at his belt, knowing that it couldn't stop a storm.

"Let's just find somewhere to wait this out. If we can be of help, let's do it."

"Agreed."

A FLASH of light erupted behind Orym in his SUV, and he flinched. "Aelwynn arriving," Sylvis said in his ear, too late.

"Goddammit," Orym said. "Tell Lorelei to stop using her gatesenders! At this rate you'll burn them out."

"You know that's not how it works."

"You're drawing too much attention."

Silanar was still staring at him through the window.

"Who is that?" Quynn asked from the backseat.

"An old friend," Orym said. "Someone I'd really rather not see right now."

Silanar just frowned at him from outside, sopping wet. He seemed impervious to the wind, his back straight, expression neutral. Everyone else around them on the street was running around frantically, barely able to stand up in the gale-force wind.

"He doesn't seem to like you very much," Quynn said. "Would you like me to—"

"No," Orym said. "Definitely not."

"Your call."

"Quynn," Aelwynn said, his voice reedy, "Lorelei has authorized you to help me generate more...volunteers."

"Fallfoilers?"

"Yes."

"Not now," Orym said. "Can't you see we have a situation here?"

"The only situation I see is the one where you refused my offer of assistance," Quynn said.

The cars in front of Orym opened up, finally, and he stepped on the gas pedal, speeding to the right down Howard.

He could see Silanar's eyes in the rear view mirror, watching him.

"WHO WAS THAT?" Bellas asked. "Someone you know?" Silanar watched as Orym's car turned onto Howard, moving six car lengths before getting once again mired in bridge traffic. Silanar could easily walk up to him, continue staring him down.

But he decided to let him go. Now wasn't the time for reunions.

"Just an old friend," he said.

"The way you were looking at him," Bellas said, "he looked more like an old enemy."

"That would also be considered correct."

"How long since you saw him last?"

"A hundred and fifty years, give or take a decade or two."

"Twins." Bellas whistled, the sound barely audible with the wind and rain raging around them. "How did you know he would be here?"

"I didn't. Orym was the *last* person I was expecting to see. Actually, Kharis texted me. He and Lhoris should be arriving…"

A white Prius slammed into the back of a red Mustang that had stopped too quickly for the light. The Prius' hood crumpled instantly, the front end completely destroyed. The crash was barely audible over the wind.

Kharis jumped out of the driver's side, screaming.

"Now," Silanar finished.

"Twins," Bellas breathed. "How much did they have to drink, exactly?"

THE WHOLE BUILDING was shaking in the wind, and Jessica was growing increasingly afraid. Was no one coming for them? Were they supposed to leave? What in the hell was going on?

Was her husband okay?

No one had come for her in thirty minutes. She'd heard sounds in the hall, what sounded like people running and speaking hurriedly. Shouldn't there be some kind of system for this?

She looked out the window again. Visibility was down to almost nothing—the rain was far too thick. The walls of Stevenson Place were almost shivering from it, quivering as the harsh wind pummelled them. She put her hand on the window, feeling the glass shake.

She didn't think it would hold.

"We need to go," Jessica said to herself. "We need to get lower, at least."

But what if the building flooded?

She was suddenly paralyzed, unsure what to do.

"Typhoon Velma has just made landfall," the TV reporter said, his voice barely loud enough to carry over the storm outside. "Seek shelter *now*. Winds are currently tracking in excess of 200 miles per hour and rising. Stay away from windows and upper floors. Do not shelter in basements. Rain is predicted—"

The TV cut off suddenly, turning to snow.

Jessica almost started crying.

But she steeled herself instead. She would not fall victim to this storm. She would not fall prey to circumstance. She would take matters into her own hands. She—and Jason— would survive.

She went over to the bed, reaching down to pick up her son.

KEYA COULDN'T STAND. She could barely even crawl. The wind was *intense*, far stronger than anything she'd ever felt before.

The storm must be well and truly here.

"We can't be out here on the street!" she shouted. Lightning illuminated the dark street. Her mouth filled with water the second she opened it. She had to squint against the wind, barely able to see. It felt like her skin was peeling off her face.

"What?" Rosemary shouted.

"We can't be out here!"

"Where should we—" The rest was lost to the storm. A tree crashed down next to them, landing on a nearby car with a sickening *crunch*.

"Back inside!" Rosemary screamed, looking at the hospital.

Keya nodded. It was the only chance they had.

Just then a line of windows on the top two floors burst apart, shards of glass showering onto the street below. Keya winced, shielding her face with her hands. Pieces of it plinked against her, not breaking the skin. She hoped nobody had been on those two floors. They were about to go back *in* that building?

"Come on!" Rosemary shouted. "It's safer than being out here!"

Keya had to admit she had a point.

"ARE YOU OKAY?" Silanar asked.

Kharis stumbled toward him, looking shaken. "That Twins-damned Fieldwork IPA packs a punch," he said. "And also, these fucking San Francisco drivers have no idea what they're doing."

"When did you drive last?"

"I—" Kharis paused, listing to the side. "I'm more handy with a bow. Or a blade."

"We know," Silanar said. "I'm just happy you're okay."

Lhoris appeared. "I knew that Prius was doomed the moment he bought it," he said.

"A poor attempt to solve the problem at hand," Silanar said.

"What—*climate* talk now?" Kharis said. "In case you didn't notice, the world is coming to an end!" The storm was truly upon them now, driving them almost to their knees.

"I hardly think the world is going to end," Silanar said, raising his voice so he could be heard. "Although I do not doubt this storm was caused by climate change, that is not the topic at hand. Right now we care about extracting the elves present in the city, and keeping everyone as safe as we can."

"So valiant," Kharis said, balancing a little bit sideways. "Always a man of the people. As long as it's *your* people."

Silanar frowned. "You've been drinking."

"And you've always been like this. We grew up together, remember, Silanar? We've had this argument before. Just because we live in the forest—just because our magic lets us hide in plain sight—doesn't make these humans less... *human*."

"You want to help them."

"You're Twins-damned right I want to help them!"

Silanar's phone buzzed. It was Keya. She was a few blocks

away, trying to find shelter and failing. Everyone else had reported in, saying that they'd found safety from the storm. But Keya, the young soulsoother, might actually be in trouble.

"We need to get to the American Cancer Society," Silanar said. "It's..." He looked at his phone, which was streaming with water. "Two blocks away."

"Twins," Kharis cursed, looking around him at the stand-still cars. Everyone was abandoning their vehicles, running for any nearby building. "I don't know if we can get there. Not now, not with this storm raging. I can barely stand! San Francisco blocks are way too long."

Silanar knew that he was right. The only transportation they had was by car, and San Francisco had terrible traffic at the best of times.

"Saved by a woman," someone said, her voice carrying easily over the storm.

Melenora appeared, arcing down smoothly from somewhere overhead, despite the wind. Dust trailed behind her, instantly turning into damp wood as the rain hit it.

"Keya is still at work," she said as she alighted lightly on the street, wet brown hair streaming behind her. Standing upright seemed effortless for her, somehow. Silanar felt his heart swell.

His wife looked *gorgeous*.

"I can get to her faster than you," Melenora said. "You should get to safety."

"Can you leafrun through this storm?" Silanar asked. "And can you do it without being seen? We can't reveal ourselves to the humans."

"Only one way to find out!" Melenora said, flashing him a smile. She drew a figure in the air with her hand; then she was up and away, cheering as she went.

"Come on!" Lhoris shouted. "Let's get indoors!"

Silanar nodded, watching the stormy sky where Melenora had disappeared.

"Quite a wife you have," Kharis said. "It's too bad the rest of us can't fly."

"It's only two blocks," Silanar said. "Let's head to Stevenson Street, even if it kills us."

Kharis nodded, fear filling his eyes.

FIFTEEN

MELENORA CRESTED ABOVE THE WIND, flying through the sky with ease. Her magic could take her far—farther than any other leafrunners in Sylrantheas, at least—but the skyscrapers in San Francisco were awfully distant from each other. Still, she had enough to go on.

She alighted on the top of a building—she didn't know which—feeling the storm raging around her. It took every bit of her balance to stay upright in the face of it.

She needed to keep flying.

She pulled a piece of prime elm from her primewood pouch, feeling its warmth against the storm. Her magic required a skilled action to power up the wood. So she drew figures in the air, envisioning works of art in her mind. It was enough: another piece of prime elm came to life in her hand, power flooding through it. She burnt the wood with her mind, feeling leafrunning magic flowing through her, and leapt.

She sailed off the building in a tall arc, dust from her hand instantly obliterated by the wind and rain. The clinic Keya worked at was only one more block away, but the storm was raging against Melenora with everything it had. This would take every bit of power she could muster.

There it was. She could see it! She burned another piece of elm, shooting down Stevenson toward the building. She could see some broken windows in the top two floors, which would make a good entry point. She let her leafrunning wane just slightly, altering her arc to head for those windows. It was a small target, but she was very skilled. She could make it.

She was just approaching them when a blast of lightning hit her. She saw brilliant light and felt a searing pain, then the building crashed toward her and everything went dark.

JASON WAS EIGHT YEARS OLD. Far too old for the type of cancer he had, but apparently the world didn't care about that. He was eight years old, which made him far too heavy for Jessica to carry.

Still, she managed it.

She had to.

The building was moving as the storm hit, the walls and floors flexing with the wind. She could hear the rain pummeling the shell of it, even from her position deep inside a stairwell.

She was headed down.

On the one hand, a flood might devastate the bottom floors. But on the other, the high winds and low pressure could create a hazard on the higher floors. She knew the building would be earthquake proof, or at least as near as California law could make it. But typhoon proof?

That wasn't a thing.

So she headed down, trying to save her son.

KEYA STUMBLED through the staff door on the west side of Stevenson Place, dripping, her hair completely out of control. The storm was howling outside, pushing against the hospital with audible force.

Rosemary came in behind her and they slammed the door shut, water pooling on the floor beneath them. "This is crazy," Rosemary said. "I've been here my entire life, and I've never seen a storm like this."

"I hope the patients all got out okay," Keya said.

"I wonder if that might not have been worse for them. They couldn't have gotten far, after all. There are only three ways off this island."

"If only we could fly," Keya said. "Let's go upstairs, see if anyone is left."

The building groaned just then, the walls sounding as if they were about to break. "Shit," Rosemary said. "I'm not sure if this thing will hold."

"Should we leave?"

"I don't know."

"Let's stay. These walls will hold better than our skin will against that storm." Plus she knew she could heal almost anything that might come up, if it came down to it. Rosemary, however, could never know.

"Fine," she said. "Let's go further up."

QUYNN HATED how bumpy the streets of San Francisco always were. Couldn't they afford some Twins-damned maintenance on them? It wasn't that hard—humans were just lazy. Orym's SUV handled it nicely, at least, but all the starting and stopping was getting to Quynn's stomach. He wished he'd thought to bring that bourbon with him before he'd been gatesent.

"Where *are* we?" Quynn asked. "This isn't the way to the bridge."

Orym looked at his GPS. "Something called Stevenson Street."

"That isn't right at all. We need to be further south."

"We need to find more fallfoilers," Aelwynn added.

"We need to get the fuck out of this storm," Orym said.

"Your language has certainly gotten worse since I first met you," Quynn said. "Perhaps we can handle both items at once."

"What do you mean?"

The storm was going full blast outside, rocking the car in its intensity. Quynn wasn't even sure if the windows would hold—they were creaking somewhat alarmingly.

"We're nowhere near the bridge, and let's face it: we can't get there in time. So let's get into a nearby building. There must be thousands of humans all over the place."

"Can you really detect Talent using your ability?" Aelwynn asked.

Quynn regarded the man. He had a smug air about him, as if he thought he was the best magician in the world. Which, if what Lorelei said was true, he very well might be. The best fallfoiler, anyway.

Quynn was the best mindmaster.

"I can," he said. "Well, most of the time. The process is a bit invasive, though. It's almost up to the level of a full quelling."

"This is the perfect time to do it. Everyone is anxious with the storm. They'll *welcome* a quelling now."

"I agree."

"I've always hated mindmaster magic," Orym said from the front seat.

"You've always hated *all* magic," Quynn said.

Orym was silent for a moment, the storm raging all around. "You're not wrong," he said quietly. "You're not wrong at all." He shifted, unbuckling his seatbelt. "Let's go."

And just like that, he opened his door and jumped out into the swirling rain.

SIXTEEN

KHARIS STAGGERED AGAINST THE WIND, rain slicing into his face like slivers of cold glass. He wondered, as he pushed inch by inch down the rain-slick sidewalk, if a stormwarden could approach anywhere near this kind of strength. Not any that he'd met, certainly. Maybe nobody alive. Perhaps the Prime Mages of old could have managed it. Perhaps there was one behind this now.

But no. He held his hands in front of his face as he moved, struggling to keep the rain from slicing into his skin, dimly aware of Lhoris, Silanar, and Bellas behind him. No, there was no Prime Mage making this storm. There hadn't been any Prime Mages in almost five thousand years.

This storm was of mankind's making.

They made it to Stevenson, a narrow road that looked more like an alleyway than a street. The buildings of SoMa towered over it, creating even more shadows in the already dark storm. He could see the remnants of a homeless camp at the other end of the block, tattered bits of tent canvas and clothes. There were no people to be seen.

"There!" Silanar shouted in his ear, pointing.

The American Cancer Society. It was a tall building, gray like all the others, imposing as it reached into the San Francisco skyline. Kharis wondered how Keya could work there day in and day out, commuting from Sylrantheas in the Muir Woods. The contrast was stark, to Kharis. He couldn't imagine working inside a building made of concrete and steel. His life was out in the woods, in the trees, beneath the leaves.

Plus the occasional bar.

He wondered if there would be any bars left after all of this.

They arrived at the doors, the storm a whirl of insanity all around. Kharis could barely breathe. He could barely think. Was the building *quivering*, or was that his imagination? It didn't seem solid enough to withstand the storm.

"Let's get inside!" Silanar shouted.

KEYA NOTICED two things as she emerged from the stairwell, sweating despite the chill of the building's air. How many floors had she just gone up? She'd lost count as she'd ascended, trying to avoid any flooding that might occur. She didn't want to go *too* high—the storm would be stronger up there. She didn't know how well the building would withstand it.

The first thing she noticed was all the shattered windows.

The second thing was Melenora's body lying prone on the floor.

"Melenora!" she shouted, her words flying away into the wind that roiled through the building.

"Who *is* that?" Rosemary asked from just behind her.

"A—a friend," Keya said. Melenora's ears were still the

normal kind—the human kind, not pointed. But of course they'd be; their proximity to a Prime Tree ensured their misting would continue, even in death.

She hoped Melenora wasn't dead.

"How did she get up here?" Rosemary asked. "I thought all the patients were evacuated from this floor."

"I don't know," Keya said. Although she did have an idea.

She approached Melenora, struggling against the wind, kneeling as she arrived. The woman looked bad: her skin seemed burnt in places, as if she'd been electrocuted. She was breathing, but shallowly. Keya felt for a pulse, found it weakly. The woman was in bad shape.

"What should we do?" Rosemary asked. "The electricity is out. The staff all left. We can't treat her here."

Lightning struck outside, with thunder almost instantly behind. The building shook with it, vibrating Keya's gritted teeth.

No, they couldn't treat her here. Lightning shock was not something Keya even knew *how* to treat. This was a cancer treatment center, not a hospital. But it was *Melenora*. Her friend, a Mentor, one of the best people in Sylrantheas.

Keya couldn't just leave her to die.

ORYM WISHED they'd thought to bring a forcefinder with them, to shield them from the storm. But there weren't enough of them, and what they had were needed to keep the cities hidden from prying eyes. So Orym pushed forward in the storm, listening to the radio in his ear.

"Wind speed and barometric pressure are having an unprecedented effect on buildings and infrastructure," the announcer was saying. The station was still inexplicably operating, even with all the radio towers in the area down for the count. Orym was glad he'd thought to bring his battery-powered radio with him—a hopelessly outdated piece of technology, but proving useful now.

"Casualties are already estimated in the thousands," the radio continued, "and we're seeing buildings themselves fall to the wind alone. The storm surge has not yet hit the coast, but it is expected to arrive as far inland as Mission Bay. If you are anywhere within a mile of the water, move away *now*."

"Twins," Orym cursed. They were too close to the Bay. "Will this building hold?"

They were standing in front of Stevenson Place, an imposing building made of mostly cement. It seemed heavy enough to withstand the forces of water and wind. Were the walls quivering? No—it must have been his imagination.

"I'm not an engineer," Quynn said. "That's *your* job. But it would seem to be safer indoors."

"Can you check for Talent?" Aelwynn asked, struggling to make himself heard.

"Very well," Quynn said. He raised a fist, closing his eyes. Orym knew what he held inside that hand: darkprime poplar, sinister and shimmering. Orym shivered, not entirely from the wind.

After a moment, Quynn opened his eyes. "I sense over a hundred souls still in that building," he said, "and a good twenty of them have Talent."

"*What?*" Humans were Talented at best one in two hundred thousand. Not like elves, which were closer to one in three. Twenty of them in one place was unprecedented.

Quynn merely shrugged. "Maybe Talent causes cancer?"

It seemed as good an explanation as any. "Let's go inside."

SEVENTEEN

JESSICA STEPPED out onto the ninth floor, still carrying her son, arriving into instant chaos.

There were people *everywhere*, milling about the floor seemingly at random. It seemed to be a mixture of patients and doctors, nurses and technicians. How were all these people still here? Why had all the other floors been empty?

"We'll be safest here," she overheard a nearby man say to a woman in a wheelchair. "We're near the middle of the building, where the wind won't hit us and the storm surge shouldn't reach. We'll be okay until they can send a rescue party."

"Are you sure?" the woman asked. "I didn't—" The rest was lost in a clap of thunder.

Jessica flinched, finding herself frozen. Should she stay here with all these people? Had the man been right? Was this the safest place for them?

A new group of men entered the room just then, striding confidently forward from the stair well at the other end of the floor. They had an imperious air about them, as if they saw themselves as better than anyone else. Jessica instantly got a pit in her stomach as she saw them arrive.

There was something distinctly *different* about them.

Another clap of thunder sounded, and the wind outside picked up even harder. The building was truly shaking now, the floor vibrating beneath her feet. Jessica glanced again at the newcomers, conscious of the weight in her arms. They didn't seem friendly. They didn't seem right. So Jessica did the only thing she knew how to do. The thing she'd done all her life, when her mother was having one of her fits.

She looked for a decent place to hide.

"ROSEMARY," Keya said, "can you check the rest of the floor, see if anyone else is here?"

"What about her? Who *is* that?"

"I told you. She's a friend."

"But how did she get here?"

"Rosemary." She stared at the woman, willing her to listen. She couldn't let her see what she was about to do.

"Fine," Rosemary said. "Stay with her." She left, quickly disappearing into another room.

Keya wasted no time. She reached into her pocket, pulling out another piece of prime birch. She had brought several of them with her, luckily. You never knew when you might need an emergency healing.

Even if doing so was *strictly* forbidden.

She needed a skilled act to invoke her soulsoothing Talent. She cast about, trying to decide what to do. There was a piece of glass protruding from Melenora's skin, just above the knee. She must have hit it as she fell. Had she been leafrunning? Why was she even here?

It didn't matter. Keya had a job to do.

She pulled the glass from the woman's skin, wincing as blood immediately welled. Then she pressed her hand on the wound, giving it enough pressure to staunch the flow. It was a skilled medical act, albeit a very basic one.

It was enough.

The primewood in Keya's hand flared to life, blazing with energy as she held it. She used it immediately, channeling soulsoothing magic into Melenora's prone form. It took mere seconds to repair the damage done by the lightning and the fall. Keya had always been a skilled soulsoother—perhaps the best in Sylrantheas—and this was almost like child's play. With practiced precision she knit up the rent areas of the woman's skin. She repaired the burnt-out capillaries and veins. She fixed the over-extended muscles, and did what she could for the brain. It was easy. It was brief.

Melenora was alive.

But just then a massive gust of wind hit the building. It sounded like what she imagined a trainwreck would sound like: huge and loud and rumbling. The building *shook*, the floor moving beneath her knees. Everything vibrated loudly, walls creaking, things crashing off of desks. Shards of glass shifted on the floor.

Then the wind hit yet again, and she heard an immense *ripping* sound, screeching in her ears.

The floor began to tilt.

EIGHTEEN

QUYNN BRACED himself as a sudden blast of wind hit the building. Had the floor just *moved*? It couldn't be. Surely the humans were capable of making structures that withstood a little *wind*.

He reached out with his mind, channeling power through the darkprime poplar in his fist. Darkprime magic was so much easier—it didn't require a skilled action. All you had to do was Will the magic to happen.

So he did.

A faint purple haze filled the air around him as his mind-master magic permeated the area. He could do so many things with it, if he chose to. He could sense Talent. He could detect the presence of men and women.

He could control their minds.

He could make them forget. He could make them remember. He could make them submit to his Will, doing things they never thought they would do. His was the greatest power in the universe, and the other Cothellon were endlessly jealous of him as a result.

They really should learn to be more respectful.

He cast out with his magic at the humans in the building, his power ignoring walls and halls and floors and windows. He could feel them all, sense their suffering, know their fear. And with the flick of his fingers, he could bring them to their knees. He could force them to submit. He could bring them into the Cothellon fold.

Aelwynn was staring at him, smiling wickedly, knowing what Quynn was about to do. Quynn smiled back, grateful to finally be appreciated. He raised his fist further, preparing to lash these minds to him.

But the storm hit again, stronger this time, and he felt the floor beneath him buckle.

THE BROOM CLOSET Jessica was in was tilting.

She scrambled, opening the door so she could grab the jam. Jason slid a little as the room kept moving, his back against the wall. She knelt, scooping him up, muscles straining as she held him yet again. She had to get out of here.

Something was very, very wrong.

Everyone was screaming as she reentered the ninth floor, struggling to keep herself upright. They ran past her, stumbling as the building continued to shift. She heard a groaning sound, a creaking, then a *tearing*, the sound of ripping metal. The building vibrated, the wind outside howling even louder than before.

Then the windows all broke at once, crashing inward in a cascade of shattered glass. Jessica felt the world shift beneath her, the orientation of her senses suddenly changing. What was *up* was *right*. What was *down* was *left*. She slid, unable to keep her footing, watching tables and chairs and teacups and several computers sliding and crashing and rolling from one side of the building to the other. She felt Jason slipping from her arms. She felt her feet buckling. She felt the world shift, and a sea of purple rose up around her in the air.

SILANAR BRACED himself as he felt the infrastructure shift underneath him. They were in the stairwell, somewhere near the ninth floor, unless he'd missed his guess. Pieces of concrete broke off from the stairs above him, hurtling down with deadly speed. He flinched, fear rolling through him.

This should have been the safest place in the building.

"Let's get out of here!" he shouted as the floor turned sideways, and the four of them burst out into a sea of tilted chaos.

NINETEEN

CONCRETE CRUMBLED OVERHEAD. The room was sideways, people screaming and sliding into each other. It was chaos. It was a nightmare. And as he watched it all, stumbling, Orym wished for the millionth time that he'd been a mage.

Everything went into slow motion.

"We are seeing winds in excess of 300 miles per hour," the radio crackled in his ear.

Orym felt his balance shift inexorably, his center of gravity changing.

"The storm surge is visible now, to the few cameras we still have working."

He tried to correct for it, tried to shift his body sideways, but the room was moving far too fast.

"It looks like a tsunami," the radio said. "It looks like..."

He was dimly aware of people falling. Someone hit their head on a desk as it slid across the floor, blood spatter filling the air.

"...the end of the world."

He felt a quelling as Quynn's magic overtook him,

flooding through his brain like a strong, fresh breeze. He felt contentment, ease. He felt at peace.

A woman fell, glass shards slicing her open instantly.

A child with no hair flailed, a piece of concrete breaking loose and hitting him, pinning him to the tilting floor.

An IV cart sailed through the air, clear tubing fluttering like ribbons in the wind, wheels turning as it rotated end over end.

"It's here. The water is here. Oh, god, the—"

The sound cut off as an ocean full of saltwater blasted inward from the destroyed windows. Orym just had time to take a hasty breath before he was inundated.

TWENTY

EVERYTHING STOPPED.

The building shifted back a little, righting itself by inches.

The water wasn't as high as he had thought.

Orym blinked, suddenly able to breathe, looking around to see what was going on.

Everything had stopped.

Aelwynn was standing there, hands aloft, a look of fierce concentration on his saltwater-spattered face.

"You—" Orym mouthed, but the word came out garbled.

The man was holding up the entire building.

Fallfoilers. Gravity magic.

Aelwynn truly was as powerful as his reputation.

"Take them," Aelwynn said, gritting his teeth. Orym could almost hear a low *thrumming* sound, the mage's power rippling through the building. "Take the Talented out of here while you still can."

Orym looked around, dripping, confused for a minute as the water continued to run out of the building. All around him the storm was still raging, rain slicing through the broken windows. The radio in his ear had gone dead, the last casualty to the horrible storm.

The Talented. That was why they were there. If they could save them—if they could somehow get them free before this castle made of steel and stone collapsed—the Cothellon could Ascend. They could rise again, conquering the world the way they'd always planned.

It all depended on Aelwynn.

It all depended on magic.

Magic that was way too hard to find.

Aelwynn gritted his teeth, and Orym leapt into action.

KHARIS LOOKED AROUND, wondering what in the Twins' name was going on. The building had clearly been falling, but suddenly everything had stopped.

"Magic," Silanar breathed.

"What—"

"That one." Silanar pointed at a man across the room from them. He was spindly, with a sharp chin, a fierce expression on his face. His hands were in the air. "Dark magic," Silanar said. "Cothellon magic."

"But that's…"

"A myth? A legend?" Silanar frowned. "Clearly we were wrong."

"We have to get out of here. We have to help these people!"

"Agreed," Silanar said. "I see my old friend is somehow here. This will not be an auspicious day. Let us leave now."

"We need to take these people with us."

Silanar glanced at him. "Fine. But we may only have

minutes. I do not know how long this strange magic can last, but by the look on that fellow's face—"

The room shifted by an inch.

"Twins," Lhoris cursed from behind him. "We'll never get down nine floors before this thing collapses."

"We have to try," Kharis said. "We can't just leave these people here."

TWENTY-ONE

QUYNN STRETCHED OUTWARD with his mind, conscious of
Aelwynn grunting next to him. The man wasn't going to be
able to hold the building up for long. Quynn had to hurry. So
he gave his fist a *twist*, and the Talented people in the
building—all of them, even the ones not on the ninth floor—
instantly became slaves to him.

Except for one.

There was a woman, almost out of sight across the floor,
looking at him with suspicion in her eyes. She was carrying a
young boy, and her face bespoke anger, fear.

She was *resisting* him.

But that was impossible.

He tried again, reaching out with his mind, and felt her
begin to slip. She was *strong*, stronger than he'd ever felt. He
flexed his magic harder—he could take her, if he put enough
Will into it. But just then the building moved another inch,
and his concentration faltered.

"Leave it!" Aelwynn shouted. "Take who we have!"

"How?"

"Through the windows! *Quickly*!"

Quynn suddenly realized the madman's plan. "Fine," he said, gritting his teeth and flexing his mindmaster magic.

All the Talented people in the building immediately rushed toward the windows, scrambling up the rain-slick tilted floor. They obeyed his magical commands, moving with fervent precision as quickly as they could. And when they reached the windows, when they made it to the shattered edges of the building, they followed Quynn's command.

They jumped.

All except for that one woman. The one with the child. The one who had somehow managed to resist. But Quynn had no time for that. The storm was raging, and the building was about to fall.

They had what they had come here for.

"Now!" Aelwynn shouted, and the three Cothellon elves headed for the windows, too.

JESSICA FELT something intruding in her brain. Something in the air. Something purple. Something almost...*alien*. She fought back instinctively, bringing all her faculties to bear. She pushed it away with her mind, rejecting it wholeheartedly. It retreated, but not before she caught a glare from a man across the room.

What in the hell was going on?

The man next to him shouted something, and the next thing she knew a dozen people were climbing up the angled floor to the broken windows. In seconds, they had reached the edge of the building.

She stifled a scream as they all jumped.

She knew that if she hadn't resisted, she would have done it too.

KEYA FROWNED. The building had been falling, then suddenly it had stopped. Was something holding it up? Was the building stronger than it seemed?

She sensed a *thrumming* sound, a low vibration, and she remembered the stories she'd been told.

"Darkprime magic," Melenora breathed. "It—it's *real*!"

"It might be saving our life right now," Keya said. "Can you walk?"

"Of course I can walk. When have your healing powers ever not been perfect?"

Keya felt herself blushing. "When I was fourteen, maybe. Come on—let's get out of here while we still can. Rosemary?" Where had that woman gone? "Rosemary?"

She stood, staggering as she tried to navigate the tilted floor. Was that—no, it couldn't be.

Blood.

Rosemary was crumpled against the far wall, neck askew, blood pooling beneath her body. She must have fallen when the building tilted.

The woman was definitely dead this time.

"Twins," Melenora breathed. "Friend of yours?"

Keya felt tears coming to her eyes. "She was my best friend," she said, mustering her resolve. "Come on. We may only have minutes left to live."

They shambled to the stairwell, trying to ignore the corpse across the room.

ORYM REACHED the window of the ninth floor, the wind whipping through his hair and clothes, rippling his skin. He peered through the broken window, looking at the swirling storm outside. The twenty or so Talented humans were there, floating in mid-air, the victim of more of Aelwynn's magic. It seemed alien to him, suddenly. It seemed insane to trust his life to a man like that. It should have been Orym. *He* should have been the mage.

But fate sometimes was a cruel mistress.

He jumped out the window, just as the building began to once more fall.

TWENTY-TWO

JESSICA LURCHED as the building jerked suddenly, resuming its tilting movement. She heard a grinding sound, stone on stone, then snaps and creaks and groans. More glass shattered. Cracks rippled through the cement ceiling, steel rebar poking through. The whole floor shuddered, dropping several inches all at once, and Jessica felt the breath leave her lungs. She watched as a strange, spindly man jumped out the broken window.

Then the building was truly falling, and Jessica knew it was the end.

TWENTY-THREE

THE STAIRWELL WAS CRUMBLING.

Keya fell through the nearest door, sprawling as the building continued to tilt. The world was chaos around her: humans pinned to walls, desks and chairs and electronics and medical equipment flying everywhere. A huge rent had opened in the floor, a hole to the room below. The ceiling was breaking into pieces, lights flickering and flaring. The storm raged in through the broken windows, and Keya felt a sickening feeling in her stomach as the world continued rotating beneath her.

This was it.

This was the end of all she knew.

"I'm not afraid of falling," she whispered to herself, knowing that it wasn't true.

TWENTY-FOUR

KHARIS HAD WANTED to *help* people. He had wanted to be of use. Instead he found himself slipping, sliding toward the far wall as Stevenson Place tilted sideways, moving inexorably to the side, falling in the storm.

A desk whizzed by him and he grabbed it, hoping it would shield him from other falling debris. The building was *concrete*. If it collapsed, they would all be dead. Kharis felt fear rushing through him. This might be the end.

There was a sudden *crash*, the motion of the floor stopping abruptly. But the momentum of the building continued, concrete crumbling into pieces. Had they hit the building next door? Could they possibly survive?

His thoughts were swallowed up by an immense cloud of dust, of concrete shrapnel, of twisted steel, of pain.

His ears filled with the sound of cascading rock as the world went black.

TWENTY-FIVE

ORYM FLOATED in the middle of the storm. Wind and rain and lightning and smoke whirled around him, his body held in the grip of Aelwynn's magic. He and all their prisoners hovered there, watching as the skyscraper they had just been in continued to fall.

The structure was at a severe angle, tilting to the west, pieces of it crumbling as it lost its purchase on the ground. The top third of the building disconnected from the rest as it fell, a jagged rip tearing through the cement at around the fifteenth floor. The two pieces of the skyscraper kept moving ponderously, but Orym knew there wasn't much room left.

Seconds later, it hit the building next to it with a sickening *crunch*. That destabilized the entire structure, and Orym couldn't help but watch as the floors began to collapse. The supports failed, each floor falling into each other one by one in a shower of concrete dust and glass. Orym shielded his face with his hands as he watched the building crumble, as Aelwynn moved them higher in the air in order to avoid the blast. A shockwave of debris shot out from the building as thousands of tons of stone piled into itself, destroying everything in its wake. The cloud of dust and glass and stone spread out with astonishing speed, instantly obliterating everything on the block. Orym and the others soared higher and higher, the storm continually buffeting them, as Stevenson Place collapsed.

When the dust cleared, Orym wiped at rain-stricken eyes.

The skyscraper was nothing but a pile of rubble.

It, and everyone in it, had been completely destroyed.

"Let us down!" Quynn shouted over the storm. "We'll find another place to shelter!"

Aelwynn nodded, lowering them slowly toward the ground. Orym waited, trying to ignore the storm against his skin, wondering just how many souls had died that day.

It was high time the Cothellon left this horrible place behind.

TWENTY-SIX

JOHN WAS SITTING at his desk in Gondor Headquarters, watching the destruction unfolding overhead. San Francisco had been woefully unprepared for destruction of this magnitude. Buildings were collapsing as the sea swept in, weakening anything that had been built on the already unstable landfill portions of the city. The lateral forces of the record-breaking winds had been clearly unanticipated by the city's engineers: they'd expected the San Andreas fault to erupt.

They had not expected a storm.

"How many will die in this?" Warren asked, his voice quiet.

"Fewer than the elves will kill," John said. "Fewer than we humans will destroy ourselves."

"You've always been a pessimist."

John looked at the man. "I've been alive a long time, Warren," he said. "I've seen things no one else has ever seen." He shuddered, remembering.

Two Trees beneath a violet sky.

A voice.

Their *voices.*

Malevolent intent.

"Twins," he whispered. "If only they knew how apt a curse that was." He shivered again, drawing himself up. "We will survive this, Warren. Even if it means we have to stay down here forever, *we will survive.*"

"The chosen few."

John glanced at him sharply. "You know we have no choice."

"I know."

"It's what the elves themselves are doing."

"I'm aware."

"I'm trying to save the *human race*, Warren."

The man laid a hand on his shoulder. "You're doing a good job. No one could handle this better than you."

John sighed, watching the storm destroy San Francisco. "I only wish we could have done more."

LORELEI PACED the length of Mission Control, red heels clicking on the tile floor. Every screen was full of death and dying, the storm inundating San Francisco and the surrounding areas. It was destruction on an unprecedented scale, and Lorelei couldn't help but shudder. She clenched her fists, dim memories returning to her like a dream.

She lost herself for a moment.

"Come with us," Tarathiel said. Lorelei blinked, in the throes of memory. Who was this strange man?

Selenia stepped up to Tarathiel, putting her hand on his shoulder. "I thank you for your invitation," she said, "but it is not for me. No, you will go, and you will do great things." She raised her voice, making it audible to all. "The Sending is not in vain, no matter what the Senate voted. It is vital. It is important. You are doing the Twins' work. Thank you for your service."

Everyone murmured their assent. Then Selenia walked toward Lorelei, touching her on the waist and bending to speak in her ear.

"Remember the coordinates," she said. "If something were to happen to you, if you were to lose all memory—" Her voice became a buzzing sound, the rest of her words lost.

Lorelei looked at her, staring into her eyes. There was something distinctly *familiar* about this woman. "I intend to," she said, "no thanks to you."

Selenia moved even closer. "I would have killed you," she said, "if you hadn't gone."

"I know."

Lorelei shivered, snapping back to reality. The memories had been coming more frequently of late. Were they memories? Or were they some sort of fever dream? She wasn't a magician. She wasn't some kind of saint.

She was just the one in charge.

Still, she couldn't ignore the directive that had been burned into her brain. She couldn't prevent the world from dying, but she believed that she could save some part of it.

She gritted her teeth, hoping the Ascension would succeed.

PART
THREE

TWENTY-SEVEN

QUYNN and the others were huddled inside an unused warehouse near Pier 30, waiting out the storm. It already seemed to be waning, strangely. Perhaps the destruction would not be as bad as everyone had thought. Perhaps the end of the world was not yet there.

He curled his lips, remembering that woman, the one who had resisted him. *Resisted*! There was only one possible explanation for it. She must be a *very* strong mage. Still, he'd always been able to overpower mages before. What was different about her? Why was she so special?

Aelwynn interrupted his thoughts. "That's odd."

"What is?" Quynn asked.

"The prisoners we took. The new Talented. We didn't get them all. You counted twenty of them in the building, right?"

"We only got nineteen," Quynn snapped. "That damn woman somehow resisted me."

"Actually," Aelwynn said, his finger waving as he counted the humans again, "we only got eighteen. Somehow we missed *two*."

THE EARTH SHOOK. The world was gray. The air was filled with ear-splitting sounds: crashing, rumbling, cracking, splintering. Crushing forces surrounded Jessica, overwhelming her senses. It sounded like an entire mountain had fallen all around her. It smelled like cement dust and wood. She couldn't breathe. She couldn't see.

But Jessica was *alive*.

The dust cleared slightly, revealing something she'd never expected to see. She blinked, then sneezed, then blinked again. Had she gone insane? Had she hit her head? Was she dead, and this the afterlife? It couldn't be. It was too *strange*. She blinked again, looking at the world all around her.

A blaze of silver light shone everywhere, lining every surface she could see.

It was scintillating, shining, pulsing as she watched. Was it some new kind of technology? She squinted, trying hard to see. It looked like the entire ninth floor of the building was being held up by whatever it was—but only barely. The level had collapsed, leaving only a few feet of room to move. The ceiling had crumpled, huge cement pieces protruding from it everywhere. The floor, too, had been destroyed. But the strange silver substance lined it as well, keeping its integrity intact. For now. But what was *causing* this? What in the hell could possibly be going on?

She heard a whimper below her, and she realized Jason had awakened in her arms, clutching the door frame to the stairwell. It was made of wood, strangely, and the wood seemed to shimmer slightly as she watched. He was holding it with feverish intent, his eyes sharp, focused on the scene around him. It almost seemed...but no. It couldn't be.

Was *Jason* holding up the entire floor?

"I...can't..." Jason said. His voice sounded strained.

"Are *you* doing this?" Jessica asked.

"I...I think so. Yes. I can't keep it up for long."

"But—" She had so many questions.

"Mom," Jason said. "I think it's magic. But you have to get everyone out. *Now.* We don't have much time."

"Shit."

"Mom, set me down. I have to touch this door frame to make it work."

"But how did you—"

"*Just do it!*"

Jessica had no idea what was going on. But she did as her young son bid, setting him gently on the floor, taking care not to disrupt his contact with the strange wood around the door.

Ahead of her, she saw people begin to stir.

KHARIS WAS ALIVE.

Even though the entire world had crumbled in on him, he had somehow survived.

He got to his feet shakily, hunching over because the fractured ceiling was so low. The ceiling and floor and all the walls were surrounded by a silver light, pulsing and shimmering before his eyes. It was magic, he knew. Magic he had only heard dark rumors about.

It was Cothellon magic.

Dark elves. Enemy elves, the word meant in the Eldrim language. They didn't want anyone to know they existed.

There must be one of them here now.

He thought he saw it, then, for a moment. A boy, slumped

in the stairwell door, his hands white-knuckled where they gripped the frame. It *couldn't* be. Was the doorframe made of *primewood*? But no—not the kind he was used to. This was a different kind of magical wood. The kind he had only heard talked about in secrecy.

Darkprime.

But why was it here? And how? And how had this young boy somehow managed to harness it?

These were questions for another time. Clearly the boy was focusing, his energy draining, his face white with effort. Clearly they didn't have long before this mysterious force dissipated.

Then the building would collapse on them all.

"Quickly!" he shouted, seeing humans and elves alike stirring themselves on the floor. "We have to get out of here!"

There was a window still open, though it was mostly crushed. Only a foot and a half remained—just enough to crawl through.

"This way!" he shouted. He hoped it wasn't too far a drop to the ground below.

SILANAR SHOOK his head to clear it, coughing from the dust in the air. What had happened? Was that a *forcefield* around them? How in the Twins' holy name had a forcefinder managed to show up *here*? They were rare. The Cothellon should have had them all.

And he shouldn't even know that they existed.

Still, he would take the Twins' gifts as they came. This was his chance to survive, to make his way back home. Across the way, Kharis was doing his best to help several humans make their way to the exposed window. But something caught Silanar's eye on the other end of the room. A flash of color, a familiar garment, a strand of hair. He staggered closer, gasping as he recognized her.

It was Melenora, his wife.

She'd been crushed beneath a pile of cement.

TWENTY-EIGHT

SILANAR WASTED NO TIME. He dipped a hand into the hidden pocket in his pants, pulling out a piece of prime oak. The wood was warm in his hand, as all prime oak and cedar would be, responding to his Talent.

Silanar was going to save his wife.

But first he needed a skilled action to activate the wood. "Everyone!" he shouted to the room. "We will make it through this! We will get out of here alive!" He did his best to believe what he was saying, his voice growing softer as he approached his wife. She was still unmoving beneath a huge shard of cement. "I'm going to save you, darling."

Power instantly flooded through the primewood in his hand. Silanar was the Inspiration Mentor, after all. Inspiring people was his job. Whether he succeeded or not was another matter entirely.

Apparently the primewood didn't care.

He felt his body strengthen, his muscles growing stronger than before. His senses improved: sight became sharper, hearing clearer. He could smell everything in the room: human sweat and fear, overlayed by a thick layer of cement dust, burnt electric wiring, and smoke. He could see the pulse still beating in his prone wife's neck.

Melenora was still alive.

This was strengthshaping magic. It had been years since Silanar had used it. He felt it return like an old friend, like a second body he could slip into. The power of it was addicting. He could do *anything* with this magic! But he was the Council Leader. He couldn't abuse his position. He needed to maintain decorum.

But not now.

He bent, hands finding the edges of the thick column of cement that had partially destroyed his wife. She was breathing, he could see, but only barely. She was clinging to life, and he would do what he could. He gripped the cement, newly strengthened muscles bulging as he lifted. And slowly, ponderously, the great block of cement angled up by degrees. Kharis was beside him suddenly, and Keya, and the two of them were pulling Melenora out from underneath the cement as he held it up, arms shaking.

Then it was done, and he let the cement piece fall. Silver light still shimmered along the ceiling and floor, illuminating their progress. Melenora was still out cold.

Her legs had been completely destroyed.

KEYA HAD no idea what was going on. Only that some kind of strange energy surrounded them, prying apart the ninth floor like the jaws of a serpent. Soon it would crush them. Soon whatever mysterious power this was would dissipate. Then Keya's adventure would be over.

Perhaps she could accomplish one more thing before she died.

She reached out to Melenora, tears filling her eyes, prime birch in her hand. She felt for a pulse and found it; the woman was barely still alive. It qualified as a skilled action—Keya could feel magic pulsing into the primewood. She wasted no time, sending it flooding into Melenora's body. It rippled into the woman's form, a feeling of intense warmth spreading out from Keya's fingers.

Her legs were the worst. Soulsoothing magic had its limits, and reconstruction of limbs was one of them. But they weren't as bad as they looked: both had suffered from compound fractures, but the muscles and most of the veins were still intact. Everything was fine at a cellular level, and the nerves were good.

This was something Keya could fix.

JESSICA CREPT ACROSS THE FLOOR, conscious of Jason lying there against the strange, shimmering doorframe. She didn't want to get too far away from him, but something strange was happening up ahead. A man had just lifted a cement block—*by himself*—and now he and two others were crouched over a woman. Jessica squinted, moving forward, trying to see through the dust that filled the air.

The woman's legs had been crushed.

Jessica put a hand to her mouth, unable to help herself. It was *horrible*. It was gruesome. At least the illness that had overtaken her son was invisible. At least his limbs were still intact. But this woman—this woman would not survive. Or if she did, she would never walk again.

But suddenly her legs straightened. The bones inside them moved noticeably, pieces of them gathering beneath the skin. She saw them jerk, then straighten further, then suddenly the woman was sitting bolt upright, back arched, taking a deep breath and staggering to her feet unsteadily.

The woman had been healed.

Jessica's brow furrowed. What was going on? First this shimmering light from her son, keeping them alive. Then this man had become impossibly strong. Now this woman, healed of an injury she could never recover from. How could all this be? Were these gods, walking among them? Were they aliens? Were they magical beings from a fairy tale?

Or was Jessica dead, and this was her personal form of hell?

One of the magical beings looked at her. A woman, the one who had done the healing. They locked eyes from across the room, and Jessica almost took another step forward.

"Keya," the strong man said, "we need to get out of here while that boy's magic holds. Let's move as many people as we can."

They leapt into action, shuffling about the shortened floor, assisting anyone they could. One by one they slipped out the open window, the weird light somehow allowing them through. Jessica watched them for a minute, but then she realized something.

She, too, needed to escape. She and Jason needed to leave.

The only question was *how*.

Somehow that wood was powering his magic. If he stopped touching it, Jessica reasoned that the power would stop. They would be crushed.

She had no idea what to do.

Then Jason looked at her, with eyes more knowing than she had ever seen before. He looked at her, and he gritted his teeth, and he pulled at the doorframe with all his might.

A chunk of it came free in his hand.

"Now, Mom," he said. "Help me." He stumbled to his feet.

She rushed to him, hunching so as not to hit the ceiling, letting him lean on her. They made their way over to the window, joining the others on their slow and shambling exodus.

The building creaked overhead, shifting suddenly, the ceiling dropping an inch. Several people screamed, and Jessica was almost among them.

"*Quickly!*" Jason screamed. "The power is slipping!" Bits of shimmering dust were flying away from the wood in his hand.

Jessica nodded, picking up the pace. The window was just ahead of them, the storm still whirling outside. But it was the lesser threat. It might still kill them, but a million tons of concrete and steel *definitely* would. Jason and his mysterious power were the only things between them and sure destruction.

They were the last to leave. She helped him through the window first, then took one last look behind her before she jumped. This concrete land would not be her tomb. This building would not be where her son succumbed.

Jason would *not* die. Not from this, and not from cancer.

Now she knew a way to heal the impossible.

They stood on the rubble-strewn street, wind and rain filling the air, sparkling light streaming from Jason's wood as he looked upward at the angled, destroyed building.

"I did my best," he said, as the last of the wood drifted away into the wind.

And the ninth floor collapsed in a jumble of rock and steel, barely audible over the storm.

Jason slumped in her arms, unconscious. But Jessica smiled.

She finally had a way to set him free.

TWENTY-NINE

ORYM SAT at his desk in Newfris, watching the bank of monitors on the far wall. He reached for a remote, turning the volume up on one of the screens. It was showing pictures of the aftermath of the storm. Brutal pictures, images that Orym had never thought to see.

San Francisco had nearly been destroyed.

"Typhoon Velma was an unprecedented weather event for the Bay Area," the reporter was saying. "At least in recorded history, we have never known a storm to be that strong. But luckily—blessedly—the fury was short-lived. Velma quickly moved inland, losing strength with great rapidity. Damage was mostly focused in the city of San Francisco itself.

"And what damage it was."

The video was from a helicopter, flying far above the city. At least half of it was in ruins. Nearly every building near the water was gone, turned into watery rubble. Coit Tower still stood, miraculously, as did the Golden Gate Bridge. Orym could see that the Presidio was largely intact, assuming the forest there could recover from the great flooding that still ravaged it.

But many neighorhoods were just *gone*.

The Marina. Fisherman's Wharf. Most of the Financial District. South Beach. Some of North Beach and Telegraph Hill. The Transamerica Tower was broken, leaning haphazardly to one side. Salesforce Tower, the Millennial Towers, everything on Rincon Hill—all of it was gone. The helicopter rotated, the camera turning its attention to the western portion of the city, and Orym couldn't help but gasp.

The storm surge had hit the Sunset especially hard. There had been nothing to stop it, nothing to stand in the way of its destructive energy. As he watched the camera pan slowly across the city, Orym could see that everything west of 19th Avenue had been flattened.

The storm had destroyed it all.

How many lives had been lost? How much of the city could have been saved? Could *anything* have been done?

Were humans really to blame for all of this?

Orym couldn't help but remember the old teachings, the old services held in Twins Cathedral in the village of his youth. Even then, over a hundred years ago—even then, the High Priest had spoken of the hubris of man. Of how the elves had been put on Earth to save them from themselves. He'd thought it a load of horseshit at the time.

Now, he wasn't so sure.

"Boss," a voice said, and Orym jerked upright in his chair. Luthar, his chief research assistant, was standing in the office doorway, looking uncomfortable.

"Yes, Luthar? You look like you've been visited by the Twins."

The man's eyes flicked to the monitors, then back to Orym. "I—uh. I've got some unexpected results."

"Yes?" Luthar was just standing there. "Well? Spit it out, man!"

"I—I think you should really see this for yourself."

Orym stood, straightening his slacks, motioning for Luthar to lead the way.

He wondered just how much more trouble might yet be in store.

"WE'LL HAVE the gates open in the next few hours," Gilvas said. "You can come in then. Lorelei has ordered round-the-clock shifts for everyone."

"Has the timetable moved up?" Thalanil asked. The mission timer was still blank, which was good. The software wasn't ready to activate that function, yet.

"Not that I know of," Gilvas said. He sounded much more cordial now that the storm had passed. "But High Command seems agitated. It's probably Lorelei's fault."

It was unlike his commander to speak ill of the Cundu, even in oblique terms. Thalanil was glad he wasn't in Mission Command at the moment—the tension was probably palpable. "Gilvas," he said, "remember that bug I found?"

"Yes."

"It's worse than I thought. The system is too interconnected—an architecture I argued against, but Orym was adamant we proceed as planned."

"What are you saying?"

"It's that damn timer."

"It's a user interface element, Thalanil. Are you such a terrible programmer that you couldn't even properly separate the UI from the business logic?"

Thalanil almost hung up right then. But he couldn't. Too much was at stake.

He gritted his teeth. "It's a subtle issue. The test harness uses dependency injection to feed mission time into the UI element."

"You're telling me there's a bug in the *test* that causes a failure in production code? I should fire you on the spot."

"This isn't even my fucking code, you idiot," Thalanil said. "I'm just the one who *found* it."

There was silence for a moment. Then: "Go on."

"I'm still tracing it through. I need a few more hours. But Gilvas, just tell Mission not to activate the master timer. Okay? Something bad might happen to the entire system."

"Just get back to work," Gilvas said. "And report in as soon as the gates are up."

"Aye, sir," Thalanil said.

He was growing rather tired of this entire Cothellon operation.

THIRTY

JESSICA'S HOUSE had not been destroyed, at least.

That was good.

She and Jason made it there, sopping wet, wind-blown and not a little bit unnerved, to find Alan waiting for them.

Jessica's husband was tall and well-built for a software guy. His eyes were soft and sad, his eyebrows angled in that way that she so loved. It bespoke concern, interest. It might have been too much.

"Hi," she said.

Alan reached for her, and she accepted. His arms felt like soft steel wrapped around her waist.

"You made it," he said. "You're alive. I was so worried."

Jessica felt herself settling into his arms, her body shuddering. "We barely made it," she said into his shoulder. "The building collapsed around us."

"How did you make it out?" He pulled her closer. She was conscious of his smell, of his breath against her cheek.

"It was..." She thought about it for a moment. What could she say? "It was almost like divine intervention."

"Jesus was looking out for you."

She grimaced, but tried to keep the thought from showing on her face. "Yes."

He pulled her even tighter. "I was praying for you. He is not ready to give up on you yet."

Because she hadn't converted, he meant. Her tongue tasted sour. "I think it was something...else."

He pulled away, concern written on his face. "What do you mean?"

She couldn't tell him. "Never mind. Maybe I was imagining things. Anyway, our son is dying—the oncologist confirmed it. He *also* confirmed that"—she let out a sob—"the cancer can't be cured."

Alan paused for a moment. Then: "We will pray for a miracle," he said. "All things through Christ who strengthens—"

"Shut *up!*" Jessica shouted, pulling away. "Your *god* is *not* going to save our son."

But *her* god might.

"I—I'm sorry," Alan said, obviously shaken. "I didn't mean to—"

"I'm just frightened, Alan. I just don't know what to do. All this religious talk isn't helping."

But she returned to his arms anyway, her mind spinning on the things she'd seen. She couldn't reveal them to him. Not yet. Maybe not ever. His faith was too strong.

When had they disconnected?

"I met a friend," she said after a moment. "Someone who might be able to help our son." Jason was asleep in his bed as they spoke, no hint of sparkling force fields floating around him. She still had no idea where he had gotten that power.

"Good," Alan said. "God works in mysterious ways."

She pulled back, looking at him. At his eyes, those hazel pinprick eyes that bespoke...something. Humor? Intelligence? These days she wasn't sure. He cared for her, of course. He cared for their son. But he was never *there*. He was never—

He kissed her, suddenly, and all her thoughts scattered.

The kiss lasted a lifetime. A second. An eon. A moment. She was a girl, there in his arms. She was a woman. She was the mother of a cancer-stricken child, of a *magic-using boy*.

She held the secrets of the world.

She pulled back, eyes dim, blood hot. "Were you here the whole time?"

Alan nodded. "They sent us all home when the storm was a few miles out. I tried to call you, but—"

Jessica pulled her phone out, saw the twelve missed calls from him. And the three from Rosemary. When had she—

Jessica burst into tears.

Alan gathered her up again, and she nestled into his shoulder. It was comfortable, being there. Even if he didn't know everything that was going on.

"Rosemary is dead," she said, her voice muffled.

"No," Alan said. "I'm sorry. How?"

"I guess she fell," Jessica said. "Everything was a blur."

Everything was a *sparkling* blur. But she couldn't tell Alan that.

"I'm just glad you made it out okay."

"I just want our *son* to be okay."

"He will be, honey. He will be."

Oh ye of so much faith.

"Come on, Jessica," Alan continued. "Jason's okay. Let's go lie down."

She looked around their miserable little apartment, with the sun shining in on the engineered hard wood floor. It wasn't *that* bad. They lived in the most expensive city in the country. They had a son. They were happy.

It wasn't *that* bad.

Still, she couldn't help but feel a pang of anxiety as she thought of him. Of her son, dying. Of her husband, looking at her as if through glass. Alan lived his life in a computer. Sometimes she wished she could live there, too.

All she really wanted was her son to survive.

"HEY," Alan said, his white software arms surrounding her as they lay in bed.

She snuggled up to him. "Hey."

"We made it through. Do you know how lucky we are?" His bulge ground against her in their bed.

She looked out the window. There wasn't much to see out there. Just the Mission, which had been spared. It was one of the only neighborhoods that had survived.

Just a few streets away from the end of the world.

"We're lucky," she admitted. He didn't know the half of it. "But sometimes I wonder."

He rubbed against her. "Wonder what?"

She turned, facing him. His eyes were wide against the window's glow. "Death," she said, and he pulled back. "Magic."

But she'd said too much.

"Magic?" he breathed, software eyes narrowing.

She pulled his arms tighter, and he welcomed it. "Just a feeling. There is magic in this world, Alan. There are things we do not understand."

"I've always believed that," Alan said. "You know how much I believe."

"Perhaps," Jessica said. "Or perhaps gods are not gods. They are simply men with superior technology."

"Do not blaspheme," Alan said. "I know you don't believe, but—"

"Shh," she said, kissing him, pressing herself against his body. He was what she needed. He was what she had. There was a kind of magic in his hands, in his lips, in his form. There was a kind of healing in his touch, in his gaze, in his tongue.

Perhaps his was the only kind of magic they all needed.

Or perhaps *magic* was the magic they all needed.

As she felt him thrusting inside her, as she threw her head back in pleasure, as she pushed and pushed and pressed and cried, she knew that it wouldn't be enough.

She needed magic to fix her son.

She needed Keya.

THIRTY-ONE

THE SUN WAS SHINING as Keya strolled through the main thoroughfare in Sylrantheas. *Enda Taurë* wound through the center of the village, brushing up against the huge redwoods that made up the bulk of Muir Woods. Humans didn't come here—not even the hikers or the incessant cyclists that loved to traverse Marin—thanks to a clever network of diversionary paths that steered everyone away.

She stepped lightly over the bridge that ran over *Celeth Ezel*, the stream that was so named because of the way it reflected all the leaves from overhead. The humans didn't call it that, of course, but Keya far preferred the ancient Eldrim language. It was music in her ears, like the stream babbling as it flowed.

Here in Sylrantheas, it was almost as if the typhoon had never happened.

The trees would be here long after mankind had died.

"Keya!" Chasianna called from somewhere off to her left. The woman was swinging down from the roof of her shop in Builder Plaza, dusting off her hands as she landed on the ground. Keya could see that the plaza had sustained more damage than she'd first noticed: pieces of the stonework had ripped free, leaving rough edges that were crumbling as she watched. A whole section of the plaza had been destroyed, but the elves had already cleared the rubble —so Keya hadn't noticed. Even here, in the sanctuary of Sylrantheas—even in the elves' domain—even here the storm had made its presence known. Keya shuddered to remember.

"You okay?" she asked as Chasianna came walking up to her.

The Architecture Mentor nodded. "The village sustained some damage, but nothing we can't recover from. The redwood trees shielded us from the worst of it, thankfully.

"None of them fell?"

"A few did, of course. And we are sorrowed by their loss."

Keya nodded. "San Francisco was all but destroyed."

"I heard," Chasianna said. "Syndra had TVs installed at the tavern today. We've all been watching the news."

Sylrantheas was actually joining the new millennium. "It was...horrible," Keya said. "So many died."

"*You* almost died, from the sound of it."

Keya nodded. "There was some kind of strange magic in play. That's the only way we survived. I think I saw a boy...but it couldn't be."

"A boy was using magic?"

"Darkprime magic, as far as I could tell. I've never seen it before, of course..."

"None of us have."

"Kharis keeps his mouth shut about what he knows. Do you think Orym told him anything?"

Chasianna shrugged. "Perhaps we'll never know."

Keya regarded the woman. She was nearer to the same age as Orym and Kharis—in their mid-three hundreds. They had all grown up together, at least until Orym had suddenly disappeared.

Keya was only seventy-five. She wasn't in the same generation. She had always wondered what had happened way back then—what this enigmatic Orym had been like. By all accounts, he had been happy here in Sylrantheas. He had been a valuable member of the village.

Nobody knew exactly why he'd left.

123 YEARS AGO

A SHADOWY FIGURE APPROACHED. Orym was standing in the rain on the cobblestones of Acorn Street in Boston. He was wearing a long, woolen overcoat over a sack suit, a top hat on his head. The stifling clothes were welcome on this cold evening, though he hated how they itched. He held an umbrella over his head, watching a man walk toward him. The rain ran in little rivulets over the stones, rushing between the cracks and making the footing perilous.

"Jones?" the man asked as he arrived.

Jones. Yes, that was the alias Orym had been using. He eyed the man, distrusting his large mustache and cane. Orym had never liked to follow the ever-changing human fashions, but he'd been forced to. He fingered his own beard with a slight grimace.

"Yes," he said. "Why am I here?"

"My name is Smith," the man said. A likely story. "Will you come with me?"

Orym hesitated, looking up and down the otherwise empty street. Had he been followed? He thought not, but one could never be too careful.

More importantly: could he trust this stranger? The message had been cryptic—he'd been told to stand on this corner at this exact time, holding an umbrella. Whether the writer of the message had known that it would be raining was unclear.

He who hesitates is lost. A friend of his had coined that phrase, years ago. A man going by the name of Addison. Not his real name, of course, but Orym would do his part to keep up appearances. Well, hesitation would certainly cost him in this matter.

He resolved to go along with the stranger.

"By your leave," he said, bowing slightly. The stranger nodded, turning and leading him down the street. Tiala would have enjoyed this night, Orym knew. She had always loved the rain.

He brushed away what wasn't a tear and continued moving.

They skirted the town, heading out toward the river. Smith eventually led him into a suspicious alley, down a flight of stairs, and through an unmarked door.

Another door immediately awaited them beyond the first. Smith waited while Orym folded his umbrella, shaking off the excess water. A small candle on a shelf was the only light in this antechamber. Satisfied that he was ready to proceed, Smith knocked on the second door, tapping an intricate figure that Orym memorized. After a moment, a little window in the door slid open and a face appeared.

"Where do gods and men go to die?" the man on the other side of the door asked.

"Underneath a violet sky," Smith responded. It sounded like an oblique reference to the Twins' realm—a fable for children. Orym filed the exchange away for future use.

The door opened and they went through into a hallway

beyond. The man at the door nodded sagely to Smith, then glared at Orym as they passed. Orym nodded at him anyway. The hallway led to another set of doors, with another guard and another passphrase. This continued several times, until Orym was growing tired of it. He knew these people valued secrecy above all else, but this was getting a bit ridiculous.

Eventually they reached their destination.

Orym found himself in what looked to be an old saloon, dark wood lining the floor and walls. Deep booths were set along one wall, with tall dividers between them and curtains for privacy. A thick, wooden bar took up another portion of the room, the bar top gleaming. Oil lamps were placed sporadically, their light flickering on the surrounding wood. The place smelled of stale smoke and old beer.

Orym would have preferred a little bourbon.

Smith led him to one of the booths. The curtain was open, and Orym could see another man sitting there. The man gestured for him to sit, and he did so. Smith left without another word.

"Good evening," the man across from Orym said. He was young looking, with long, brown hair and striking blue eyes. He was handsome, well-built but not overly muscled, with a perfectly groomed handlebar mustache and no beard.

"Good evening," Orym responded.

"Will you take whiskey?" the man asked.

"I will." Things were already improving.

"Very good." The man snapped his fingers and a barman appeared, bringing with him a bottle and two glasses and leaving them on the table. The man poured them each three fingers of whiskey and set the bottle back on the table.

"Now then," the man said, "for introductions. My name is Quynn."

"Jones," Orym said. "Pleased to make your acquaintance."

"Come now," Quynn said, "your real name, if you please."

Orym pursed his lips. "What assurances do I have?"

Quynn picked up his glass and took a sip, grimacing slightly. "My men are combing the streets as we speak," he said, "determining if you were followed. Or if you brought others here on purpose." He twirled the glass on the table. "If you have proven yourself true, I will give you this assurance." He pulled a photograph from his jacket pocket, passing it to Orym.

He felt his blood run cold as he looked at it. It was a picture of his son. "What is the meaning of this?"

"Your son," Quynn said, "will remain safe, as long as you follow protocol. If you don't, well..."

"This is an interesting way to convince me to join."

"We're not here to convince you, *Jones*," Quynn said. "You came to us, remember. Now you'll play by our rules."

Orym picked up his glass of whiskey, thinking it through. Quynn was right—he *had* come to them. He had learned of their shadowy organization through the friend of a friend of a friend—and even then, the person had been reluctant to talk of it. They'd spoken in hushed tones, confirming what Orym had learned over years of studying them from afar.

They called themselves "enemy elves"—*Cothellon*, in the native elven language. They existed to propel the elves forward into a new era, using magic *and* technology to accomplish great things. Orym had heard they'd been doing great things with electricity and light, and he wanted to join. As a scientist by trade, Orym felt that this Cothellon group offered him his best chance to further his interests. He no longer wanted to be held back by the elven superstitions against technology. He wanted to advance.

He'd learned all this from secondary sources. No one wanted to talk about the Cothellon, but he'd managed to coerce a few of them. It had taken him years to get them to agree to a meeting.

He'd better not screw it up now.

"My name is Orym," Orym said.

"Just what is it you imagine you're here for, Orym?" Quynn asked.

"I want to join your organization," Orym said.

"We already have many members," Quynn said. "What do you think you will add?"

"Science," Orym replied. "Discoveries. Research. Breakthroughs. I'm a trained scientist, much to the chagrin of my parents. I've reached the limit of what the Eldrim will allow. I want to do more."

It was why Tiala had left him, in the end.

Quynn took a drink, musing. After a long moment, he replied. "We can offer you that," he said, "and more. But it will be hard work, harder than you've ever done before in your life."

"I'm ready."

"You think you are," Quynn said, "but this will test you in ways you never imagined."

PRESENT DAY

KEYA SHRUGGED. "Orym doesn't matter, anymore. I'm just glad Sylrantheas made it through the storm intact."

Chasianna nodded, looking around them. The wooden buildings that made up most of the village seemed largely fine, with only minor damage where roofs had blown off or a few windows had broken. Elven craftsmanship was as good as ever, it appeared, despite what seemed to be outdated building materials and an old-fashioned style.

"We're in pretty good shape," Chasianna said. "It won't be too difficult to repair all this. Not like San Francisco. Do you think they'll ever recover?"

"Do you think they'll even be offered the chance?"

Chasianna frowned. "So you've heard what Silanar is planning."

"It's not just him. It's *all* the Eldrim leadership. But Chasianna—do you think it's the right thing to do?"

"Humans are responsible for a great number of atrocities, not least of which is the destruction of this planet."

"But does that give us the right to wipe them out? Who made us the executioner?"

"As Myriani would say: *magic* gave us that right."

Keya sighed. "Great power."

"Great responsibility."

"But it can't be true."

"What if it is? What if this is our *destiny*?"

Keya felt her fists balling. "I don't know if I can accept that. I don't know if I can go along with it."

"You might not have a choice. This is out of our hands, Keya. This is a matter for the High Council."

Keya sighed again. She was so impotent, so powerless. Surely there must be *something* she could do. Something to affect the outcome. Yes, Typhoon Velma had been terrible. Yes, a lot of people had died. But how did that justify the intentional destruction of billions of human beings?

And were elves *really* that different to begin with? They were contemplating genocide. Didn't that, in the end, actually make them *worse*?

"Keya," a voice said, and Keya jumped, startled. She

turned to see Silanar standing there, a stern look on his face. "Come with me," he said. "Now."

Keya didn't like the sound of that one bit.

THIRTY-TWO

"YOUR MOTHER WOULD BE VERY disappointed in you," Silanar said, looking down at Keya with his most disapproving look. He knew it was; he had practiced it for centuries. He could see from the expression on her face that it was working.

They were standing in Town Hall, the Council arrayed in a circle of chairs around them. He could hear them shifting in their chairs uncomfortably, as if unused to witnessing such a scolding.

Silanar let the moment drag out.

Then he let his expression soften. "How was that? Convincing?"

Keya let out a breath. "What in the Twins' names are you doing?"

Silanar couldn't help but laugh. "Sorry. I couldn't resist. I hope to have a child some day, and I wanted to make sure I could discipline her well."

"Her?"

Silanar looked away, up into the rafters of the room. "Sometimes I dream of her," he said. He could see her, hair flying behind her as she flew through the air, the very image of her mother. "I hope it happens soon."

They'd been trying for decades. But elves were notoriously infertile—most families only had one child, and many had none. They made up for it with longevity, though. Silanar himself was almost four hundred, and he likely had a good six hundred years left on this planet.

If the humans didn't fuck it up first.

"I'm sorry for frightening you," he said to Keya. Maybe he needed to rethink his methods. "Actually, I asked you here for an entirely different reason."

All around them, the Council stood. Melenora in particular caught his eye as she came to her feet, long, dark hair draped artfully around her neck. His wife was radiant, and he couldn't help but smile.

She stepped forward, lifting her hands, holding up a bronze medallion in the shape of two Trees twisted together. "Keya Sunwillow," she said. "For heroic actions undertaken in the harshest of circumstances, for maintaining a cool head in the face of adversity, and for exceptional skill with Prime magic, we, the Council of the Eldrim in Sylrantheas, are honored to present you with the *Rian Maranwe*."

The Crown of Destiny.

The Eldrim's highest honor.

Keya's face blanched noticeably, her mouth falling open. "But I—"

"You saved my life," Melenora said, her voice rich and beautiful. "Twice. While the world was crumbling around you."

"It's my job," Keya whispered. "It's what I was trained to do."

"When you Chose the Way of the Protector," Silanar said, "there were those of us who saw doubt in your eyes. There were some among us who wondered if you would truly be happy in that Way. But you persevered. You overcame. You flourished." He felt tears coming to his eyes, unbidden. "You brought my wife back to me."

He embraced Melenora then, a gesture unbecoming for one such as himself. But he couldn't help it. He couldn't stop his emotions.

Even the leader of Sylrantheas was sometimes allowed to *feel*.

He watched as Melenora draped the Crown of Destiny around Keya's neck. It wasn't actually a crown, of course— the naming was symbolic. It was a rare honor; fewer than a dozen had been given out in the last five hundred years. The elves were peaceful, normally. There weren't many opportunities for outright heroism.

"Shall we continue?" Bellas asked, and Silanar realized he'd gotten sidetracked again. He needed to stop that. He needed to be more present in the moment.

"Of course," he said. "Keya, thank you again for coming. Our Council Meeting is beginning now. You are of course welcome to observe." All elves were always welcome, by custom.

"Thank you," Keya said. "I think I will." She went to one of the chairs ringing the outside of the room. Silanar took his own seat in the Council circle, smiling at his wife next to him.

"Humanity is in the process of destroying this planet," Daylor began. "If we don't do something about it—and I mean *now*—we might all lose our homes and our lives. This menace must be *stopped*." His voice was shaking. As the Regulation Mentor, Daylor was in charge of law. It was unlike him to be passionate about anything.

"Does this storm really *prove* anything?" Kharis asked.

The Bombardment Mentor looked no worse for the wear, having survived the building's collapse alongside Silanar.

Silanar regarded him. "Shouldn't you know that more than anyone else?"

Kharis looked confused. "Orym doesn't talk to me anymore," he said. "Why does everyone persist in this? I'm not a scientist. I truly want to understand the connection between this storm and human-caused climate change."

"It's been *studied already*," Nuvian hissed. "Many, *many* times." The Movement Mentor was nearly shaking in his chair. "Why are we willfully ignoring the evidence that has already been gathered?"

Silanar steepled his fingers. "The ritual is not to be taken lightly. Sundering magic is the most powerful ability we have. And it has never been used before. We must be *sure*."

"What will it take?" Bellas asked. "How many more must die? How far must the planet go?"

"There's something else," Melenora said. She may have been the Artisan Mentor, but she was also the village's best leafrunner. That made her the master of spies. "The Cothellon have gone dark."

"What, *all* of them?" Silanar asked.

Melenora nodded. "All of them. But not before they were seen heading inland. We already know there is some kind of site of theirs in the Central Valley, and activity in that region appears to be heating up."

"Twins," Daylor breathed.

"But that's not all. My network reports that Cothellon are disappearing all over the world. Most were seen heading to the coasts, toward where we suspect additional Cothellon construction activity. The ones in New York and Paris just disappeared underground. We don't know what's going on with that."

"Those cities have significant below-ground infrastructure," Bellas said. "It would be a great way for them to hide. Who knows where they went from there."

"Regardless," Melenora continued, "all signs point to an acceleration of the Cothellon plan. No, we still don't know what the plan *is*. It never seemed like they were in a hurry, before. But after this storm, everything changed."

Silanar stroked his chin. "I wonder why."

"Perhaps they caught wind of *our* plan."

"We don't even *have* a plan!"

Melenora cocked her eyebrow at him.

"There were Cothellon in that building," Kharis said suddenly. "Right there with us."

Silanar looked at him in alarm. "*What?*"

"You could tell by their expressions. And by the purple cloud in the room."

"I didn't..."

"You didn't notice?" Kharis almost looked angry. "You're supposed to be the best of us, Silanar."

"I—" He'd been distracted. By the storm, by the building. By his wife.

Kharis smiled, his expression changing instantly. "Just kidding, old friend. Twins, you look like you've seen a ghost."

"What kind of a—"

"I figured if you could do that to poor Keya, I could do it to you. But seriously, Silanar, a few of the men in that room *did* look suspicious. Didn't you think it strange when all those humans ran for the windows and jumped?"

It *had* been strange. But it had all happened so fast. "I assumed they were trying to escape," he said. "It wasn't a bad plan, all things considered. They were more likely to survive that fall than the collapse of the building."

"But did you see any of them? When we got out?"

"I—"

"You were too focused on other things."

Silanar bowed his head.

"It was chaos," Melenora said. "There were bodies every-where. Who could keep track of who was who?"

"I thought I saw him, for a moment," Kharis said.

"Who?" Silanar asked.

Kharis was silent for a moment. "Orym."

"Twins. Really?"

"I can't be sure."

Silanar let out a low whistle. "I saw him too, just minutes before, on the street. After all these years, what are the odds he would find us in San Francisco?"

"What are the odds he would be in that specific building?" Kharis said. "There must have been a reason."

"The Cothellon are moving," Melenora said. "And we need to do something about it."

"Do what?" Silanar asked.

"The Sundering," Bellas said. "We must call a World Council. The time for deliberation is over."

"A World Council will do nothing *but* deliberate."

"Debate is required before we can activate the magic. All elves must be in agreement."

Silanar bowed his head. "Let us put it to a vote."

THE WORLD COUNCIL WAS HAPPENING. The Council had decided. Once invoked, the other Eldrim establishments throughout the world were required to arrive within a fort-night. Silanar couldn't remember the last World Council— had it been fifty years ago? They weren't very common.

"Sil," Melenora said, using a finger to move his face over to hers. "You have to get out of your head."

He couldn't help but smile at her. "You know me, Nora. I'm *always* in my head."

She snorted. "There is nothing you can do tonight. Please. Lay with me."

He caught her blushing even in the dim moonlight. "How forward of you."

"Twins, Silanar. Sometimes I *need* to be forward with you."

He settled into their bed, chuckling. This was what he got for marrying an artist. "I ordered the Council to start stockpiling primewood cuttings."

Melenora let out a loud sigh, pulling him closer. "You'll never let work go, will you? Okay, I'll bite. Why the stockpile?"

"Just a feeling. If this planet is going to shit, should we take anything for granted?"

"You think the Prime Trees might not be here forever."

He snuggled closer, nuzzling her neck. "It's just a feeling."

She wriggled next to him. "Now you're getting the idea." But she pulled away, turning to him in the dark. "I'm worried, Sil. Dunedar hasn't reported back in quite some time."

"Dunedar was one of yours?" He was their only spy that had managed to infiltrate whatever it was the Cothellon had been building.

Melenora nodded. "It was probably a long shot. He's probably dead, or captured. But we've been trying for *centuries*. And he was the *only* one who managed to make it in. I guess..." She turned away. "I guess I just had high hopes."

"Hey," Silanar said, wrapping his arms around her, kissing her cheek from behind. "We're up against a formidable foe that we do not understand. At all. Just getting one person into…whatever it is…was a monumental achievement. Don't beat yourself up that he hasn't reported in. Maybe he's just been busy."

She turned to him, eyes glimmering in the dark. "I feel like everything is crashing down around us."

"We're going to make it through," he said, gathering her closer. "The Twins will watch over us."

She kissed him, hand stroking his cheek. He responded in kind, gripping her waist, surprised at his own sudden urgency.

If the world was coming to an end, the Twins only knew how much longer they might have left.

THIRTY-THREE

DUNEDAR CHECKED BEHIND HIM. New Tokyo was a busy place, even before they'd loaded it up with humans, but he'd managed to find an alley with no one in it. No one that he could see, anyway. He looked up, scanning the rooftops and fire escapes. None of the black-clothed men were there, fists raised to the sky. He wasn't sure what they were for, exactly, but he'd seen them all over the place.

Maybe they were practicing for something.

He returned his gaze to the ground. Surely there was a— yes, *there* it was. He hoped. He took a few steps forward, approaching a metal hatch that had been worked into the cement. It was a pair of doors set into the ground, and all he had to do was figure out how to open them. That was how he would succeed with his plan. That was how he would defeat the horrible Cothellon.

This was the door that opened into the Under.

THE NEXT DAY, Jessica found herself pacing around the house. Alan had gone to work, leaving her alone with Jason.

Jason, who was dying.

But Jessica knew now that a power existed that could heal him. That could reach beyond the bounds of human technology, that could put to right the cells within his body.

It was magic.

Jessica just needed to find it.

All she had was a name. Keya. Not a normal name, at least as far as she knew. Not a normal name for not a normal person. Could she track her down, somehow?

She flopped down on the couch, opening her MacBook. *If* Keya was the woman's real name, maybe she could find her on the Internet. So she opened her browser and googled it.

There were more than ten million results.

Sighing, Jessica scanned them. The first was from Urban Dictionary, something about the girl who everyone wants to date. Weird, and probably true about this girl, but not the answer Jessica needed. There was a food company, a gymnastics studio in New York, a few Instagram profiles. Toward the bottom of the page she saw a LinkedIn profile for someone named Keya Sunwillow who worked at the American Cancer Society, along with a picture.

It was her.

The whole thing had taken less than a minute.

Excited, Jessica googled the woman's full name. A site called mylife.com had her, and for a cool $79 she could access the woman's entire background check, including home address.

She didn't waste any time.

"That's weird," she said when she saw it. It listed an address in Marin: 27799 Muir Forest Avenue. But Muir Forest Avenue didn't exist. Muir Forest wasn't even a real place—the forest was called Muir *Woods*, and nothing in the area had house numbers as high as 27799.

The address was obviously fake.

But what if it wasn't? Or what if it was *close*? Perhaps Keya really did live near the Muir Woods. Wouldn't that be the best place for people with magic? Jessica had been out to the redwood forest before. She'd seen the majesty of the trees. It was a beautiful area, the perfect place for a group of strange, magical people.

Jessica just needed to find them.

THERE WAS a startling amount of outbound traffic on the Golden Gate Bridge. Jessica clung to the steering wheel of her Land Rover, grateful that she'd remembered to use the restroom before leaving the house. She'd been stuck in bridge traffic for a long time.

She'd left Jason at home with the babysitter. She felt bad about that, but what else could she do? She was trying to *save* him, after all. This was her best—possibly her only—shot. She would do whatever it took to make him better. She would sacrifice anything.

The Golden Gate Bridge was still intact after the storm. Traffic finally started moving again, and she looked up at the orange metal pillars that made up the iconic structure. She'd lived in the Bay for her whole life, but somehow the sight of the bridge never got old. She was lucky to be here. For her, one of the world's most recognizable landmarks was just a part of her commute.

Her cell phone rang as she exited the bridge, speeding up the 101. She ignored it, her mind spinning with questions, trees surrounding her on every side.

She would find this Keya, even if she had to hike for days in the Marin County wilderness.

THALANIL SAW ORYM walking briskly down the hall. Engineering Floor 2 was full of people, heads buried in computers or cups of coffee, eyes bleary. Lorelei had called everyone in simultaneously and set them to working double shifts, putting the finishing touches on the Ascension. But the software that powered the immense machine the elves had built was not simple. It was labyrinthian, with millions upon millions of lines of code. The build system alone was a relic from the 1980s, which itself was well after construction on the machine had begun. It was impossible to keep the Cothellon digital infrastructure up to date with the pace of modern technology—it was just too old.

That was why all these stupid bugs kept creeping in.

"Orym," he shouted before he could stop himself, rushing down the hall to catch the man. Orym was Gilvas' boss—his skip level—and the head of the Cothellon Science Division. In truth, the man was closer to a god. He had *discovered* dark-prime magic. He had invented the machine they had built. By all rights, Thalanil should never be able to approach someone of his stature. But Thalanil had something no one else in the entire Cothellon group had.

He and Orym were from the same village.

"Thalanil," Orym said, turning as he puffed up to him. "We haven't spoken in a while. Apologies, but I'm—"

"Fennas Elenathon has a bug," Thalanil said.

Orym gave him a thin smile. "We log hundreds of bugs a *day* in our tracker. Why are you coming to me with this?"

"It's a bug in the original system, the stuff written in the early eighties," Thalanil said.

"What—the *assembly* layer?"

Thalanil nodded. "One of the IRQs. There's an extremely old expansion board in Gate Control that was never updated to the Plug and Play standard. Just yesterday I discovered a cascade effect. When the mission timer is started, a rare corner case can fire every second, with a quarter percent likelihood or so. The bug ripples through the entire hardware architecture, taking the Mission Control UI layer out completely, until rebooted."

"We didn't discover this in testing?" Orym asked. "Twins."

"It's actually our testing that's to *blame* for the problem," Thalanil said. "Some idiot leaked a test into production code."

"That should be impossible."

"*If* he were following protocol, yes. But this guy—I traced it in source control, his name is Malgath—was clearly not qualified to do this work. At all."

"So *what* happens?" Orym asked.

"When the bug is triggered—which has a chance to occur every second—the entirety of the Mission Control user interface layer will crash. We'll have to reboot it, which takes—"

"—ten minutes. Jesus."

Thalanil was surprised at the unexpected human curse. "Yes."

"Do you have a fix?"

"I do, but Gilvas won't let me push a build."

"I'll speak to him." He looked at his watch. "But shit—what are our build times up to these days?"

Orym was clearly a bit out of touch with the Engineering department, but it was to be expected. "Fourteen hours, including integrated tests."

Orym whistled. "Damn. No wonder Gilvas balked. Okay,

I'll get Release Management to start on it right away. You submitted the fix?"

"Of course. And I flagged it Urgent."

"Good." Orym put a hand on Thalanil's arm. "Thank you for bringing this to my attention directly. If Mission Control had failed, I'm not sure what Lorelei would have done."

Thalanil couldn't help but blush. "My pleasure, sir. And, uh…"

"Spit it out. I have to get going."

"We should grab a drink sometime."

Orym looked at him askance for a moment. Then his expression dissolved into a smile. "We should," he said. "We can remember the good old days back in Sylrantheas. Do you miss her?"

Thalanil felt emotion surging. He hadn't expected Orym to bring that up. "Of course, sir. I miss her every single day."

"Really tragic what happened." Then he seemed to realize that he had touched a nerve. "Twins. I'm sorry, Thalanil. I didn't mean to bring that up. We all loved Aelyn-thi. Truly."

"None more than me."

Orym arched an eyebrow at that. "Anyway, yes. When all of this is over, let's grab that drink." He clapped Thalanil on the back. "I'll see you later."

And he left, leaving Thalanil wallowing in memory. He stood there for a moment before rousing himself.

He had work to do.

KEYA STRODE BETWEEN THE REDWOODS, her brow furrowed in concern. The Council Meeting had been more alarming than she'd expected. She'd had no idea the elves were so close to executing the Sundering ritual. It was the seventh power. The magic of willow and cypress.

The magic written in her name.

Keya Sunwillow, daughter of Aelynthi and Tanyl Sunwillow. Her mother was dead now. Her father was a bitter husk. And she was left to carry the family line, to represent the Sunwillows amongst the elves.

But she couldn't condone genocide.

There must be a way around it. There had to be a way to fix the problem without wiping out humanity. Yes, humans were the responsible ones. Yes, it was all their fault. But were elves really any better? Sure, they lived in villages in forests more often than not. Sure, elves eschewed most modern technology in favor of a more esoteric approach. Yes, elves worked *with* the Earth, doing their best to do as the indigenous humans had done. Only using what they needed. Never overhunting. Never exploiting resources. Always looking out for the greater good.

She sighed, stomping her foot as she passed a particularly beautiful tree. Twins dammit. Maybe elves *were* better.

But the Sundering couldn't be the answer.

If elves really lived in harmony like she believed, *surely* they could find a way to live in harmony with humans. Surely there was a way to keep the planet alive without exterminating its dominant species. There *must* be a way.

There must be something she could do.

Things at the American Cancer Society had been weird. Where had that magic come from? She had seen a woman, there. Dark-haired, with haunted blue eyes. She had been carrying a small boy, at least at first. Had *she* been causing all that darkprime magic? Or had it been the boy? Everything about it had been strange.

The Cothellon were the source of all darkprime magic.

The Cothellon had a plan. But nobody knew what it *was*. Nobody even knew if it was a *bad* plan. Could it really be worse than what the Eldrim intended? The Cothellon wouldn't wipe out the entire human race.

Would they?

Or *would* they?

Keya realized, then, that humans weren't the worst thing that had happened to the planet Earth.

That honor, as hard as it was to admit, had to fall to elves.

THIRTY-FOUR

LORELEI TAPPED her foot on the ground, waiting for the Small Council meeting to begin. Where in the fuck was Quynn? He was never late to these meetings.

When the man finally shambled in, he looked disheveled. "My apologies," Quynn said to everyone arrayed around the smooth, black table. "I just received a very interesting email."

"Is there a problem?" Lorelei asked.

Quynn looked at her, and for a brief moment his gaze was haunted.

Then he snapped back.

"No, my lady," he said. "Everything is proceeding according to plan."

Lorelei knew that he was lying. But she also knew that whatever was actually wrong, it would make no difference. He would have it under control. He'd been doing it for centuries.

"Let us begin, then," she said to the room. "Argus. Report."

The pudgy man sat up in his chair, cheeks red.

"Forcefinder Corps is fully staffed," he said. "And trained. I don't anticipate any problems."

"Good. We don't want the cities becoming visible before we're ready. Or at any time, really. Have you perfected the one-way shield?"

"Yes, my lady," Argus said. "Air and toxins are allowed out of the cities, but nothing is allowed in. Transmuters are of course responsible for the rest."

"Of course," Lorelei said. "Morgian, that's your cue."

Morgian nodded. "We're good. Air is easy. Food is a lot harder, but we're good there, too. Fuel is the hardest, but the stockpiles we have are good for at least a few dozen years. We can keep the cities going."

"What if it goes longer than that?"

Everyone looked at each other in alarm.

"What?" Droth said. "Why would that happen?" The spymaster looked distinctly unnerved.

"Just a feeling," Lorelei said. "I want us to be prepared for every eventuality."

Morgian nodded. "We will be fine," she said. "The cities are largely self-sustaining in terms of energy. What little fuel we require, the transmuters will certainly have time to produce. If it comes to that." She looked at Lorelei meaningfully. "Let's hope that doesn't happen."

"Let us hope," Lorelei said. "Aelwynn, over to you."

Aelwynn sat upright in his chair. The man's angular face still rubbed her the wrong way, but she couldn't pick who was and who wasn't the best mage in any particular type. The universe—or perhaps the Twins—had that control.

She was stuck with him, whether she liked him or not.

"We rescued eighteen Talented humans from the American Cancer Society," Aelwynn said.

Down the table from her, Lorelei caught Quynn smirking.

Perhaps he disagreed with the term "rescue." She gave him a pointed look and his expression went blank. Ever the dutiful servant.

"Of those," Aelwynn continued, "eight of them are fall-foilers. It's the most common type of darkmage, so this is to be expected."

"And will that be enough?" Lorelei asked.

"It will. Training is in progress as we speak, and it should be done by this evening. With the additional eight mages added to our existing teams, I feel confident we can keep ourselves aloft indefinitely."

"Excellent," Lorelei said. "Good work, teams." She sat back in her chair, surveying the room. I think we're ready."

Everyone grew noticeably more alert at that.

"We weren't scheduled for another month," Quynn said.

"I think the Eldrim are planning something."

"By *something*," Quynn said, "you mean the Primal Ritual. Don't you."

Lorelei nodded.

"Twins," Morgian cursed.

"They'd really go through with it?" Argus asked.

"They just called a World Council," Droth said. "My spies on the ground state that the subject matter is indeed the Sundering Ritual."

Quynn let out a low whistle. "They have more balls than I gave them credit for."

Lorelei gave him a glare. "In any case," she said, "if Sundering magic is let loose upon this world, we will not be able to populate the cities. Our Ascension will fail."

"Can't we activate the Device without the people?" Argoth asked.

"We can," Lorelei said, "but what if it goes wrong? Or what if we need to delay the activation? The Ascension was designed to be self-sustaining in perpetuity, in case Fennas Elenathon fails to live up to expectations. It is critical that we maintain *all* the failsafes we have spent so many hundreds of years designing. We *must* populate the Device before we use it."

Quynn was nodding in agreement. "Then we need to move now. The Eldrim might wipe out the entire planet before we get the chance."

"Set a new mission timer," Lorelei ordered. "The Ascension begins in T-minus seven days."

EVENTUALLY, Keya went home.

It wasn't that she'd been avoiding it, exactly. She had to go there eventually. It was just how her father had been acting lately. Tanyl seemed very depressed.

"Hi, Father," she said as she entered. The home they shared was a beautiful little cottage on the western edge of town, constructed of wood and filled with the little eccentricities that still reminded her of her mother. There was the statue of a kraken on the entry table. The lamp in the shape of a mermaid. The picture of a UFO.

Aelynthi had always been a student of fantasy.

"Dearest," Tanyl said from the living room. "I was so worried about you!"

She entered the living room and beheld him there in his favorite rocking chair, eyes glazed over like they always were. He'd started losing his vision ten years ago, and now he was far beyond any doctor's help. The cells had degenerated—Keya had checked. It wasn't something her magic could heal.

There were limitations to soulsoothing.

Now her father was blind.

"I missed you," she said, kissing him on the cheek. "Was the storm bad?"

"It was fine, dearest. I had Chasianna to look after me. But where were you? I was worried sick."

"I'm sorry, Father. I tried to contact you, but cell phones were out. I was at work when the storm hit. I, uh…" She didn't know how to continue.

Tanyl laid a hand on hers. "All that matters is that you're fine now. I couldn't—" He shuddered. "I couldn't lose another family member."

He was referring to her mother, Aelynthi. She had died in an accident shortly after childbirth. An accident that shouldn't have happened, that the elves had worked hard to ensure could *never* happen again.

She had fallen off the bell tower of the church.

Keya had been deathly afraid of heights ever since she'd heard the story.

"I miss her," she whispered, a tear trickling down her face. "And I don't even remember her."

"I miss her too," Tanyl said. "Do you want dinner? Chasianna left us a casserole."

"I think I need to walk again," she said, putting a hand on her father's cheek. "I'm sorry. I just need fresh air."

"I understand. Twins guide you." He made the sign of the Twins, two fingers crossed.

"Twins protect you," she responded.

She hoped they would. Something in her felt that their protection would be necessary in the days and weeks to come.

JESSICA'S LAND Rover bumped and rumbled as she drove it along the fire service road through the forests in Marin. She was operating on a hunch: Keya's address had been listed in Muir Forest, which was not the normal way of describing those redwoods. But perhaps Muir Forest was a reference to the larger forest, not the public section frequented by thousands of tourists a year. California had a lot of redwoods, after all.

And so it was that Jessica found herself turning on her four wheel drive, grateful that her husband had convinced her that it was worth it to splurge on such an expensive offroad vehicle when they lived in the heart of San Francisco. She winced as she hit another bump, the tires easily handling the soil and leaves and loose branches beneath them. She saw birds flitting their way overhead, winging through the sky. She imagined what this forest must be like without this crude human vehicle. Peaceful, probably. Full of beautiful scents and sounds. She imagined raccoons, squirrels, maybe even a wildcat making its way. She imagined falling asleep here, lulled by nature in all its glory.

Then the Land Rover hit another bump, and she was shocked from her reverie.

A redwood was *right* in front of her.

She slammed on the brakes, sliding to a stop in a cascade of dirt and leaves. Then she sat there, breath coming quickly, wondering what was to become of her. Why was she out here, seeking the impossible? Why was she trying so hard to save her son?

It was what any mother would have done.

But there was nothing here. Nothing but trees. Nothing but the last vestige of the Earth, untouched by humanity.

It was *beautiful.*

But it was not what she was looking for. Where was Keya? Where were these strange magic users? How could she possibly find them?

She thought she saw something, then. Something small. Something subtle.

A green ribbon tied to a tree.

She stopped the car, stepping out and taking in her surroundings. It was a forest, peaceful and quiet. Beautiful. So different from the city she was used to. Were people actually *living* out here?

She stepped forward, around the tree in front of her, and beheld it.

There was a village in front of her. A village of wooden houses, of thatched roofs, of dirt streets and a bridge across a stream and a tall cathedral in the distance. She saw a garden on one side, with a cluster of huge trees in it, each one different from the next. People were walking through the village, slowly and peacefully, seemingly at ease in their surroundings. People who looked just like her, except for—

Except for their pointed ears.

What?

THIRTY-FIVE

ORYM FOLLOWED Luthar into his office. It was rather richly appointed, with floor-to-ceiling windows granting a view of the beautiful orchards of the Central Valley. Like Orym's office, one wall was completely full of screens. They showed various views of the research labs, of Mission Control, and many dashboards showing the progress of the various teams that made up the massive Ascension project.

Orym noted one screen in particular.

Mission timer.

Where before it had been blank now it showed a countdown of just under seven days. Shit. *Just* after Thalanil had informed him of that bug.

"Did Lorelei move the Ascension up?" Orym asked.

Luthar nodded. "You really should check your email more frequently. The Small Council just finished meeting. The Ascension is happening in a week."

"Twins," Orym cursed. "I hope we're ready."

"We have bigger problems, boss," Luthar said. "Here."

He handed Orym a single piece of paper.

And Orym read it, feeling the world crashing down around him.

Luthar waited with baited breath. "Well?"

Orym didn't respond. Instead he walked to one side of the room where Luthar had a bar setup. He poured himself a double bourbon and downed it in one gulp. Grimacing, he poured himself another and turned to the other man. "How sure of this are you?"

"Extremely sure," Luthar said. "We checked it ten times. We didn't want to bring this to you without being completely certain."

"Shit," Orym said.

"My thoughts exactly, sir."

"But this is all a simulation, correct?"

"It is, sir, but we've been able to gather more data now that the device is in Stage One. The physical properties were impossible to *fully* pin down until we had it operational. That's why the simulations didn't show this outcome until now."

Orym drank the second bourbon and poured a third. "So let me get this straight," he said. "If we let the Device go to Stage Three—if we turn the gate on—the entire *planet* will be destroyed."

Luthar was silent for a moment. "Yes, sir." His voice was strained.

"And everything and everyone will die."

"That's what the simulation says, sir."

"And...none of us will get where we're going."

"No, sir. We'll all be obliterated."

"But Lorelei just ordered the Ascension."

"It will kill us all."

"Then we have no choice. We have to abort."

"It looks that way, sir."

"Shit," Orym said again.

It was all he could think of to say.

QUYNN WAS KEEPING Orym waiting outside his office far longer than normal. Orym tapped his feet impatiently. The world was about to end, and he had to wait in line to deliver the news?

Finally the door to Quynn's office opened, and his executive assistant stepped through. "He'll see you now," she said.

Without a word, Orym got up and went into the office.

"Greetings, old friend," Quynn said as he entered. "Have a seat."

Quynn's office was spartan, a simple metal desk and a wall of books forming the only real decorations. He gestured toward one of the chairs in front of his desk, and Orym took a seat.

"What was so important you had to see me in person?" Quynn said. Never one for small talk.

"I'll get right to the point," Orym said.

"Please do."

"We have to abort this entire project. New data shows that the entire planet is in jeopardy."

"Explain yourself."

"Our simulations show that activating the Device will destroy the planet," Orym said. "And all life on it."

"You've been running the simulations for decades," Quynn said. "Why this sudden discovery now?"

"Like I said before we started all of this," Orym said, "we needed to build the device before we knew if it worked."

"But we haven't turned it on yet."

"The small-scale tests we *have* run have proven to be

enormously helpful in refining our models. And now it's clear: the outcome will be catastrophic."

"How sure of this are you?"

"Nothing is one-hundred percent, but my calculations are always correct. I'm sure."

"So sure, you're willing to abort the entire mission on the cusp of the Eldrim's plan?"

"Just so."

"You know that's not an option," Quynn said. "If we abort, and the Eldrim go ahead, we'll never be able to execute the gate. This is our only chance."

"I know sir, but it's a fool's errand. We will destroy ourselves if we try."

"You said it's not one-hundred percent."

"It isn't."

"Then we have no choice but to go ahead."

"But sir—"

"Do you know what the Eldrim will do to us if they find out about our mission?" Quynn asked, sitting forward in his chair. "Do you have any idea what is at stake? They'll destroy us all *and* wipe out humanity—and not necessarily in that order."

"Then what do we do, sir?"

"We stick to the plan. It's our only choice. Luthar took the liberty of emailing me about this an hour ago. I've already reviewed the data and made my decision."

"Then why did we even *have* this conversation?"

"I wanted to hear it from your mouth. You were no more convincing than he was."

Orym ground his teeth. He *had* to get Quynn to take this seriously. Somehow. "If I take this to the Council directly—" he started.

Quynn stood. "If you do that, I'll have you executed myself." His voice was cold.

Orym froze. This was not a side of Quynn he'd seen before. Always he'd thought he'd noticed a darkness in the man, but it had never come forth. Not like this.

He took a deep breath, standing.

"Very well." He bowed stiffly. "Good day."

He left the office. If he couldn't take this to the Cothellon Council, he would have to find another way.

He couldn't let the planet be destroyed. If the Cothellon wouldn't listen to him, he needed to find someone who would.

He picked up his phone, searching for a contact long forgotten.

THIRTY-SIX

THE WAREHOUSE at the end of Sylrantheas had been emptied of its contents—mostly agricultural equipment and some seeds and grain—and had been repurposed as some new kind of storage facility for primewood. For primewood! Why would anyone need to *store* primewood?

Kharis walked by the large building, watching workers bringing huge palettes of tiny primewood chips, stacked in various types and stored from floor to ceiling in the newly-empty warehouse. It seemed overkill to him, but everything had changed after the storm.

Elves and humans had both gone a little bit crazy.

But Kharis wasn't concerned with primewood now. He wasn't thinking about the storm. He wasn't worried about the craziness of elves, or the ever-erratic behavior of humans.

Today, Kharis was going to church.

He approached the wooden cathedral, admiring the ornate stained glass windows that graced the front face. The building was at least seven stories tall, and the bell tower that rose above it must go up another three. The whole thing was worked from massive planks of wood, carefully cut and engineered by Orist and Chasianna and their teams. It was a new church, having been built in the last hundred years. Their new High Priest had insisted it was necessary.

Kharis stepped inside.

The room was lined with wooden church pews, wide and oaken and filled with elves. Kharis found a seat three rows back and settled in. Services were normally held on Sundays, mirroring a few human religions, but today was a Thursday. This was a special service, having been called in the wake of Typhoon Velma.

Kharis waited while the remaining elves filed in, gazing up at the high, vaulted ceiling. A wooden walkway ringed the room, at least forty feet above the floor. Several wooden beams crossed through the air at that height, lamps and banners hanging from them. Various doors led off of the walkway, leading to maintenance halls, adjunct viewing chambers, offices of the clergy. The building was a vast, vertical complex, the simplicity of the sanctuary belying its true size.

Kharis returned his gaze to the floor, admiring the huge carving of the Twins that ordained the back of the room. They were there in all their glory, one in black and one in gold, twisting together to a height of at least thirty feet. It had taken Sculptors over a year to complete the masterpiece.

That had been before Kharis' time. The elves had always worshipped the Twins, at least as far as he knew.

He just wasn't entirely sure *why.*

He was shocked when Silanar himself sat next to him, along with Melenora. The Council Leader normally sat in the front row, as was expected of him. Kharis shifted in his seat uncomfortably, straightening his posture. He cleared his throat.

"I've had enough of being the center of attention," Silanar said. The man's face looked haggard. "Didn't expect to find you here."

Kharis smiled. "I'm not usually much for religion. But with everything that's going on…"

"Do you believe in the Twins, Kharis?"

"I—" The question took him off guard. How should he even answer? The Eldrim gods were capricious at best, responsible for transporting the elves here so many millennia ago. They were the source of all magic, supposedly.

Assuming they actually existed.

"I have no idea," Kharis said. "I've never put much stock in mysticism."

"But you're a mage."

"Magic is mysterious. Who is to say why it works, or how?"

"And yet you're here."

"I wish to honor the traditions of our people."

Silanar turned to face the stage. "Good enough for me."

The audience grew quieter just then, and Kharis straightened his shirt as the High Priest entered. Myriani was regal to the point of arrogance, dressed in a flowing green gown with a plunging neck. The dress was embroidered in an intricate pattern of two trees, one in black and one in gold. Her long, golden hair descended across one shoulder in waves, and her eyes bespoke deep knowledge.

"Twins," Silanar cursed under his breath. "My mother looks as young today as the day I was born."

He was right. Kharis had seen the pictures. Whatever beauty regimen she used, it was damn effective.

Maybe it was some kind of otherworldly magic.

"Greetings, elves," Myriani said, and the room became completely silent. Her cat—a plain brown tabby—circled her legs as she talked. For some reason the cat was always present at these services. "We are here," she continued, "to give thanks and praise to Velion and Nelenor, those Two Trees forever perched above our eyes. We are here to grant obeisance to them, to know their Will, to channel our strength from their immense Well of Talent." She paused, lifting her hands in front of her in a gesture of entreaty. "We are also here to mourn the deaths of so many during this past storm, and to ask that the Twins grant their souls swift passing. Let us pray."

The audience bowed their heads. Kharis did as well, but he kept his eyes on the High Priest. There was something strange about Myriani. Something slippery. Her ageless form was beguiling, but he sensed some deeper truth.

Myriani spoke:

"Fourteen Trees in a barren land

"Fourteen Souls where the weary stand

"Fourteen Gifts from the wise one's hand

"And two great woes for the Fall of man."

It sounded like a poem, one that Kharis had never heard before. What in the Twins names was going on?

"O great Twins," she continued, her voice taking on a sonorous intonation, "Great Velion and the tree that bears his soul; Great Nelenor and the vessel that holds her; to the Spirits that guide us, that direct us, that tell us right from wrong. To the Great Souls upon the Purple Hill; to the heavens; to the Trees; and to the world they created."

Most of this was new, or a significant departure from her usual script. What was going on? Had Myriani lost it? What in the hell was this reference to the Purple Hill? Kharis felt confused. He'd heard something like that from a children's story long ago.

"We look to you now," she continued, "in this time of great need. Please speak to us, O Twins. Please give us guidance. Please show us your Will, and in so doing grant us peace, that we may continue furthering your great Work upon this planet. In your great names, Amen."

"Amen," the crowd echoed, and Kharis couldn't help but frown.

"As I'm sure my son has told you all," Myriani said, glancing briefly at Silanar, "this planet is at the brink of sure disaster."

Murmurs arose amongst the elves, but Kharis knew they shouldn't have been surprised. The Council had been beating this drum for months.

"Typhoon Velma was but the symptom of the wound," Myriani continued. "If humankind is allowed to continue on their reckless path, this planet is surely doomed. And so it is written in the ancient texts:

"And thus shall mankind be stripped of their knowledge and dominion; for the Twins saw all that man hath wrought, and deemed it unworthy of Their image. For the future and the betterment of Elvenkind, and for the perpetuation of the Twins' Realm, to which elvenkind must surely go, the Twins hath established a Ritual upon which to defend against this rash incursion."

Myriani stopped, gray eyes scanning the room, giving Kharis time to think. He had read those words before—in its original High Eldrim language, no less. It had taken him two days just to decipher that single passage. Elven scholars had long wondered what exactly the Twins' Realm was, and whether it indicated some sort of afterlife. The whole of elven religion depended on it, actually, but there had never been a satisfactory answer.

But everyone knew what the Ritual was.

"To Sunder Souls," Myriani said. "To end a race. But not to *end*, precisely. The Ritual describes a portion surviving. A new beginning. For we shall not destroy this planet and all who live on it. We are not the humans. No, we shall allow a remnant to survive. To survive and grow anew, underneath our watchful eye."

Kharis' lip curled with disdain. The arrogance of these preachings—of the ancient texts—was astonishing. Who had given elves the right to rule over humans? The Twins, supposedly. *If* they existed. And magic—which definitely *did* exist. But did the presence of magic mean they could kill billions of people? Did it mean they *should*? Why *were* the elves here? What in the Twins' damned names was the fucking *point* of all of this?

Kharis realized he was breathing heavily, and Myriani was looking at him.

"Some of us are called," she said. "Some of us are chosen."

Kharis sighed quietly, resigning himself to the rhetoric that would continue for the next hour. He and Orym had used to make endless fun of these services when their parents weren't around. Orym had had a disdain for the church that matched his own. If only Orym hadn't disappeared so many years ago. Maybe then they'd be snickering together in this church, watching Myriani posture and pontificate. Maybe they'd be able to figure out the hidden meaning behind all those ancient words.

Maybe they'd be able to prove that the Twins were a total load of horseshit.

Or maybe they'd realize that the elves were right. That humans were a disease. Maybe they'd—

His cell phone started buzzing in his pocket.

He checked his Apple Watch, his mouth falling open in

surprise. Myriani continued droning on as he looked at it, not daring to hit the button to confirm. The caller was someone he hadn't heard from in over a hundred years. It was pure luck he had even had the contact saved.

The person on the phone was Orym.

THIRTY-SEVEN

DILLON WIPED his hands on his overalls, conscious of the streak of grease they left. Not that his clothes had been particularly clean to begin with. He inspected the timing belt, checked that the battery connections looked good, and ran his dirty fingers through his hair.

"Fire it up!" he said.

The man they all called Oil grunted from the driver's seat of the '73 Camaro. He turned the key in the ignition, and Dillon watched and listened as the engine sputtered once before turning over. It started, and Oil gunned it for a few seconds before letting the RPMs drop. Dillon made a cutting motion with his hand, and the engine settled to a halt.

"Sounds pretty good, boss," Oil said, awkwardly making his way out of the car. His belly protruded significantly beyond the waistband of his dirt-covered jeans, his forehead slicked with sweat. "You always knew how to touch these old parts right."

Dillon winked at the man. "It's all in the wrist, Oil. I still don't know why you made me do this one, though. You're way better than I am."

Oil looked uncomfortable at the compliment. "You know me and Camaros, boss. Never liked me much." He swayed when he talked, his eyes never leaving the floor.

Dillon walked over to him, clapping him firmly on the back. "You're the best mechanic we have, Oil. Which reminds me: how's your Mustang coming?"

Oil let out a snort. "Fords always liked me better than Chevies," he said. "But this damn Mustang is another beast entirely. Can't wrangle her, boss. Just can't."

"You ran out of money again."

Oil looked up at him sheepishly. "Ain't many parts out there for a '65 Shelby."

"That's a nicer car than I will ever set my eyes on," Dillon said. "You'll make it work, somehow."

Oil blinked. "One day. Maybe. What about you?"

"What *about* me?"

Oil shifted his feet back and forth, as if nervous. "I just—I mean—"

"I'm fine, Oil. I'm making ends meet."

"I know. It's just—"

"Dublin is a great place to raise a family."

"You have a girlfriend I don't know about?"

Dillon couldn't help but blush. "No. I just—"

"You like to think ahead."

"Just so." He was conscious of his father's tone just then. Sometimes he sounded uncomfortably like the man.

It had been a long time since he had called.

"You got a place?" Oil asked.

Dillon narrowed his eyes at him. "Why?"

"No reason. I just—if you need some place to stay, you know I'm good for it, boss."

Dillon almost told him, then. He almost admitted just how shitty his life was. That he was sleeping underneath the

580 overpass. That he barely got enough to eat from day to day. That this business of his might end up being the death of him.

But he couldn't put that on poor Oil. The man had enough problems of his own.

"I'm good," he said. "But thanks. I'll keep it in mind. You got beer in the back?"

Oil cracked a smile, finally meeting his eyes. "You know me, boss. I *always* got cold beer."

THE STELLAS WERE as cold as Oil had promised. They took them to the sidewalk in front of the shop, watching the cars drive by. Dublin was a small town. A quiet town. A sleepy little suburb that was just far enough from San Francisco to feel like its own little world.

Dillon wondered if he should have run further.

"You ever want to move away?" he asked.

Oil finished a big swig of beer, looking at him quizzically. "You mean like to Livermore? Nah, man. I like it here."

"I mean like out of California," Dillon said. "Or even out of the States altogether."

"Why? You running away from something?"

Memories of his mother.

Dillon shrugged. "No reason. Just getting antsy, I guess. There are cars everywhere, right? I can always get a job."

Oil gave a great guffaw. "Not if the environmentalists have their way. I heard they're trying to outlaw *planes*! Cars won't be far behind. You know we can't work on Teslas."

Dillon sighed. "It's a whole new world. One I'm not sure I want to be around to see."

Oil shifted forward in his chair. "You're not—"

"No," Dillon said. "I'm not trying to sound morbid or anything. Just...I dunno. Sometimes I wonder if there's more out there."

"More, like...girls, or something?"

Dillon eyed the man. "More. Beyond this reality. Things we can't see. Things we don't yet know."

"You're starting to creep me out."

Dillon put his hand in his right pocket, feeling the thing he always kept there. His father had given it to him in case of emergencies. His mouth twisted at the thought. His father.

The man who'd driven his mother away.

"Hey," Oil said. "You okay, man?"

Dillon snapped back to focus, taking a long drink of beer. He was about to respond when his cell phone started buzzing, nearly causing him to drop the beer in surprise.

He pulled it out, and this time he *did* drop the beer.

It was his father calling.

After all this time, Orym had finally decided to contact his son.

DILLON MET his father in a little cafe in Danville called Sideboard. It was eclectic, a business built into a house, with a back deck and hippie decorations that were filled with messages of love and peace. The coffee was good, at least, as was the freshly baked English muffin he scarfed down.

It had been a long time since he'd had food this good.

"You look...dirty," Orym said. Dillon's father was dressed in an immaculate gray suit, with a blue dress shirt and no tie. He was clean shaven, his blue eyes peering down his nose with what might have been disdain.

Orym always looked at people that way.

"Thanks," Dillon said. "You always know just what to say to people."

Orym put his massive coffee cup down on the wooden barrel which served as a table. "I'm sorry I haven't been in touch much lately."

"Dad," Dillon said, keeping his voice as quiet as he could, "you haven't called in *fifty years*."

"Since your mother died."

"She didn't *die*, Dad. You and I both know that. She ran away from you. Fifty years ago was when you finally stopped writing her."

"She ran away from *us*."

"No, Dad. It was *you*. You and all your new friends."

"She was gone before all that. And anyway, I've made important discoveries. I'm doing good work."

"Was it worth it, Dad? Was *science* worth your marriage?"

Orym slammed his fist down on the table suddenly, startling Dillon. "I loved that woman more than life itself," he said, his voice shaking. "I loved her more than you will *ever* know. If I had known what she would do...if I had known..." He broke down, tears coming to his eyes.

"Would you have changed, Dad? Would you *really* have done anything differently? You're the most driven person I know. Science. Discoveries. Power. This is all you care about, all you've *ever* cared about."

Orym wiped a tear from his eye. "I care about you."

"Really? Then why the decades of silence?"

"I—" He picked up his cup. "You remind me too much of Tiala. Every time I look at you, I see her."

"Shouldn't that be a good thing?"

"It's—it's too painful, Dillon. I'm sorry. I'm trying. I was never cut out to be a father."

"No," Dillon said. "You were not."

They were silent for a time, the sounds of the cafe filling the air around them.

"But I'm here now," Orym said after a few minutes. "There's a reason I contacted you after all this time."

"And that is...?'"

"The world is about to come to an end."

"*What*?"

"I think I can save you from it, but I need you not to be an elf."

THIRTY-EIGHT

ORYM TOUCHED the earring in his left ear, assuming it was working. He didn't have a mirror handy, and he didn't want to check his phone. The Earring of Mist was a powerful artifact, the only one known to still exist.

Quynn didn't know he'd stolen it.

He nodded at a passerby, one of the elves living in Sylrantheas. He didn't recognize her, but she recognized the image his earring showed her. She gave him a deferential nod, smiling and moving on.

It was working.

He strode down the street, scanning ahead just to make sure he didn't meet his doppelganger. The odds of that weren't high—he'd made sure to visit when the man wasn't likely to be out in the streets.

He took in a deep breath of Muir Woods air. It was strange, being back in Sylrantheas after all this time. The place felt smaller, the trees taller. He'd lived his life for over a hundred years amongst buildings made of metal and glass. To be here, to be in his home town…

He *hated* it.

It wasn't him. He'd moved on. But he had a job to do. He had a message to deliver. And he had some precautions to take, in case things went as badly to shit as he suspected they well might.

The church loomed large in front of him as night began to gather in the village. It was quite clearly a church, with the stained glass windows depicting the Twins, with the bell tower rising far into the trees. But it was clearly newer construction than the surrounding buildings. It hadn't been there when Orym was last here.

It seemed as good a place as any to hide what he was holding.

There was a small door on the side of the building, unlocked like most doors were in the village. Orym couldn't help but give a snide smile as he slipped inside the building. The Eldrim were too trusting for their own good.

Or maybe they didn't care. The church was a public place of worship, after all. Perhaps they didn't mind him sneaking around.

There was nobody inside the church. Everyone was likely eating dinner at home or at the tavern. It only took him minutes to find a good hiding place, in an old offering box on the upper walkway. Elves didn't actually use money, of course —the box would have been used for offerings to the Twins. Flowers, pieces of art, written prayers. This box was being stored upstairs, dusty and disused. Orym placed his package inside it, taking a mental note of where it was in case he needed to return.

He took one last look at the brown paper wrapping before he closed the lid. Darkprime wood lay inside of it, wood of every different kind. It was illegal, by Cothellon law, to have taken any of the material. But he was the scientist who had *discovered* the stuff.

Surely he could be the exception.

If the world was about to end, he wanted to make sure that magic survived.

SYNDRA'S WAS ALMOST how Orym had remembered it. The tavern was made of beautifully paneled wood, with booths around the edges and a long, wooden bar forming a straight line down one end. The floors were clean enough, and the whole place smelled like whiskey and old beer. But there was something there that Orym hadn't been expecting.

Televisions.

There was one on either end of the bar, showing footage of the typhoon's devastation. Orym watched them while he waited in his booth, wondering if perhaps Mother Nature might be more vindictive than any elf.

"Greetings, sir," Syndra said, coming up to him with a dishrag draped over her shoulder. "Surprised to see you in here at this hour."

Orym cleared his throat. The earring wouldn't mask his voice, only his appearance. "Felt the need to be out, Syndra. I'll take a beer."

Syndra cocked an eyebrow at him, and he realized he'd made a mistake. The man he was impersonating probably drank wine. Or worse—water. He always had been a little soft.

"You got it," Syndra said, skirt swishing as she turned away.

She brought the beer back without a word, and Orym

winced as he took a sip. The beer in Sylrantheas had never been any good. He found himself growing nervous, anticipation mounting for what was to come. Was he making the right decision? After all this time, could he really do what he had come here to do?

He almost got up right then. He almost walked out, never to be heard from again. But the man he had come here to see showed up just then, stamping his feet and shouting for a beer.

Kharis had arrived.

"Silanar," he said, approaching Orym's booth. "This is a bit unusual. You asked to see me?"

Orym nodded, motioning for him to sit. "I have something very important to tell you."

"Whatever it is, couldn't it have waited until after dinner?"

Syndra brought a beer out for Kharis just then, and Orym couldn't help but notice the way he looked at her when she set it down. "Just the way you like it," Syndra said. "Warm and half full of piss." She leaned forward, flicking a hair out from behind his ear before sauntering off.

The whole thing had been a little strange.

"That vixen," Kharis said, taking a pull of his beer. "I swear she has it in for me." He was still watching her. "And anyway, she was wrong. This beer is *entirely* full of piss." He set the mug down on the table. "What's going on?"

"First," Orym said, "there's something I need to show you."

He waited until Syndra turned the other way, then pulled the Earring of Mist out of his ear.

Kharis just about fainted from the shock. "*Orym*? But—how—why—what's going on? How are you doing that?"

Orym put the earring back in, Willing Silanar's form to settle over him once again. "It's an artifact," he said. "One of a kind. Grants a permanent misting to anyone who wears it."

"A *mistweaver* artifact?" Kharis gave a low whistle. "I had no idea such a thing existed. We don't have any mistweavers left."

"I figured as much. Anyway now you know. It should be obvious to you that I couldn't show my real face here."

"Right. The real Silanar would probably crucify you." Kharis grimaced. "But that still doesn't answer the question of why you're here. What's so important that you'd risk your life to visit me *here*, in your old hometown? Orym—it's been over a hundred years."

"First," Orym said, "I want to apologize. For everything. For disappearing like that. For never contacting you. I've done a lot of wrong, Kharis. And the things I've done might lead to a whole lot worse. So I need to come clean."

"Kharis, I'm a member of the Cothellon."

Kharis took another pull of beer, eyeing him. "And?"

"You knew."

"Of *course* I knew. Twins, Orym, how many times did we speak of them as children? I knew you had it in you to find them. I knew you'd even make it in. I just didn't know you'd disappear from the fucking *planet* once you did."

"I'm sorry."

"So you've said."

"You and I both know Sylrantheas never felt like home to me."

"You were always after something more. Something... *beyond*. I think being a Mundane really got to you."

Orym couldn't help but glare at the man. "You mages have a way of lording it over us Mundanes." But on the inside, he was smiling. He knew something Kharis didn't.

"I never meant it that way," Kharis said. "I'm sorry."

"Is is of no consequence," Orym said. He sighed. "Sometimes I feel like even this *planet* isn't my home. Nevertheless: what matters now is what I'm about to tell you. But first, old friend, we need to go back. After I joined the Cothellon, I made a startling discovery."

THIRTY-NINE
83 YEARS AGO

"YOU DID *WHAT?*" Orym asked.

"He was a volunteer," Sylvis said, shrinking under his glare. She looked stricken.

"That was *not* part of the testing protocol," Orym said. "Not one bit."

"I know," Sylvis said. "It was Luthar's idea. I tried to stop him, but—"

"Never mind," Orym said. "What's done is done. Do you have results to report?"

Sylvis nodded, handing him a sheet of paper, which he scanned briefly.

"If this is correct..."

"It is."

"Incredible." Orym strode briskly into the research room, Sylvis following close behind. "Team," he said, addressing the room. Everyone turned in their chairs to look at him. "We've just had a major breakthrough."

"WE'VE IDENTIFIED SIX CATEGORIES," Luthar was saying. Orym struggled to pay attention. It had been a very long night. They'd been experimenting with the new discovery for months. It was exhausting work, but exciting at the same time. A whole new frontier.

"Six?" Orym asked. It mirrored the Woodways perfectly. How interesting. "There must be a seventh," he said. "A Primal Way. It would only make sense."

"I know," Luthar said, "and we're trying. We'll have it soon, if there is one."

"Very good."

"Sir?" Luthar looked nervous.

"What is it?"

Luthar picked up a metal case that had been lying next to him on the floor. He placed the case on Orym's desk and opened it.

"We brought this for you."

Inside the case were six pieces of what looked to be wood, except darker and strangely shiny. The pieces looked subtly different from each other, yet substantially the same. An odd light seemed to glisten over them, giving them the appearance of something alien, something alive.

They almost looked like wooden metal.

"Darkprime wood," Orym said, reaching in to pick up a piece. It felt cold to his hand.

"Sir," Luthar said, "you are a Mundane, correct?"

Orym looked at the man severely. "That is correct."

"So you've never been able to perform any magic."

"No. And I'll thank you to never bring that up again."

"Yes, sir," Luthar said. "It's just that...well, some of us wanted you to try this."

"You think a Mundane might be able to exercise darkprime magic?"

Luthar nodded. "We don't have enough data yet to prove it, sir," he said. "But we thought you should try. There's no harm in it."

"None that we know of, yet."

"Yes, sir. Of course. It's far too early to be sure."

"Still..." Orym turned the piece of wood over. "I'm not even sure what to do."

"Uh," Luthar said, "as I understand it—I'm no mage, mind you—you're supposed to Will it to do something."

"No Investment is required?"

"No, sir, not that we've seen. It's rather remarkable."

"Alright," Orym said. "Do you know what this wood is supposed to be able to do? I can't very well Will it to do something at random."

"That's what *we've* been doing, sir," Luthar said, "there's no other way to discover what it's for. But of course, you're right, *you* shouldn't have to do that. This one—um," he bent over, looking closely at the piece in Orym's hand. "This one is ash. It makes a kind of energy field, directed in an area. It can be made to be bidirectional, not allowing matter to pass through from either side, or unidirectional, allowing passage from one side but not the other. The unidirectional mode requires less wood. It may have other modes, but we haven't found them yet."

"You discovered all of that in the past few months?"

"Yes, sir. We've been working hard on it, sir."

"Okay," Orym said, "let's give this a shot." He mentally Willed the piece of wood to produce an energy field. Nothing happened. Was he doing it right? He didn't even know what an energy field looked like. "It isn't working," he said, placing the wood back in the case.

"Try the others," Luthar said.

Orym picked out a different wood chip. This new piece

felt warm to the touch. Interesting. Did that signify something important? Perhaps this was one power he could actually access? That would be quite the coup, after being a Mundane his entire life.

"Pine, sir," Luthar said, answering his unspoken question. "Acts on gravity. You can lift things with your mind."

Very useful, that. Orym held the wood in his hand and Willed it to work.

Luthar suddenly lifted a foot into the air. The man yelped. "Ah, v-very good, sir," he said.

Incredible. He was doing it! Orym could feel the magic coursing through him, a feeling he'd dreamed of his entire life. For all his existence he'd been treated like an inferior, a lesser member of his own race. Sure, elves didn't say it to his face, but he could see their looks, feel their pitying glances when he turned away. They despised him for his lack of power.

This changed everything.

He lifted Luthar higher, glorying in the magic. He felt his mood lift, a smile coming to his face.

"Good job, sir!" Luthar said. As if he needed the encouragement.

Yes, with this kind of power he could finally *take* the respect he deserved. He felt himself growing giddy, overexcited. Luthar continued to rise, his head brushing against the ceiling.

"Sir," Luthar said from his perch at the top of the tall room, "Be careful, sir. Not too much."

Orym's heart raced. His face felt flushed. His hand clenched around the wood uncontrollably. Luthar crouched down as he continued to rise, trying to avoid being crunched into the ceiling.

"Put me down, sir!" Luthar cried, his voice alarmed.

Suddenly the wood gave out. Orym's hand closed around dust, and just like that, the magic was gone.

Luthar fell.

Orym felt dizzy, but he couldn't let his best research assistant get hurt. He stepped forward, holding his arms out to catch Luthar. The man slammed into his arms, carrying them both to the floor in a mess of crumpled limbs.

Neither was hurt. Orym got up awkwardly, leaning hard against a nearby desk. "What's going on?" he asked. "I feel... lightheaded. Like I've been drugged."

"Yes," Luthar said, getting to his feet, "we've noticed that as well. It seems to be a side effect of using the magic. We'll keep working on it."

Orym took several deep breaths, steadying himself. He was a mage. He was a *mage!* And it had all been made possible through this one, miraculous, monumental discovery. Now the Cothellon had their own magic. Now they could change the world.

They would be a force to be reckoned with.

FORTY
PRESENT DAY

JESSICA SNUCK around the outskirts of the strange village, doing her best to stay out of sight. It wasn't large—she figured there must be fewer than a thousand people living there, all told. They all had pointed ears, she noticed, except for when they left. As they exited the village, their ears smoothly transitioned into normal-looking ears.

It was the strangest thing Jessica had ever seen.

More magic at work. But who were these people? Were they even human? Why were they out here, way out in the woods? How long had they been here? And what did they *want*?

Questions and more questions. But that was not the reason Jessica was here. She had a son to save. She had a specific person she needed to find.

She worried about her son at home. Her babysitter was good, but Jason had *cancer*. Who knew what might happen unexpectedly? She really needed to get back. But she couldn't return empty handed.

She had to find this Keya.

She skirted the village, flitting quietly between the trees, admiring the workmanship of the buildings she could see. Nearly everything was made of wood, giving the place an almost ancient appearance. There were no cars. No lawnmowers. No lawns, actually—the redwood forest was allowed to coexist with the village, everything having been built around and between the trees. She saw no machines of any kind, except the occasional cellphone. She smelled woodburning stoves, fragrant food cooking. It must have been an incongruous kind of existence, she thought, to live without so much technology, yet to have it within such easy reach. Whoever these people were, they seemed to cling to their way of life with a tenacity that was unheard of in modern society.

Maybe she had stumbled upon a band of Amish.

She stopped short suddenly. She'd seen a flash of blonde hair that looked familiar. Could it be? Had she finally found her?

The hair turned, the person underneath it moving in her direction.

It was her.

Shit.

Jessica scrambled for some place to hide. She was next to a lovely tree—she didn't know the species—that reminded her of a tree her grandparents had had in their backyard many years ago. She'd used to climb that tree when she was young, reveling in her ability to survey everything beneath her.

Maybe that was exactly what she should do.

She reached up to the nearest branch, feeling the roughness of the bark beneath her fingertips, memories of childhood flooding back to her. Then she swung herself up with unexpected ease, scrabbling from branch to branch until she was perched high above the village.

The girl—Keya—was getting nearer.

Jessica settled in to watch.

KEYA STROLLED THROUGH SYLRANTHEAS AIMLESSLY. She wasn't hungry. Something was bothering her. So she walked around at random, and soon found herself near Silanar and Melenora's house. Theirs was a beautiful building near the edge of town, larger than many of the other homes. Which was funny, considering they still had no kids.

She should really get back home, eat dinner with her father. But something was bothering her. Something she couldn't put a finger on. She could hear voices percolating through the forest, coming from the open dining room window in Silanar and Melenora's house. She should move. She should leave the area. But something told Keya that there might be something that she needed to hear.

She moved closer to the house, staying as silent as she could.

"But have you actually *read* it?" Melenora was speaking.

"Of course I have." It was Silanar. "Keya's father was the one who found it, on one of his expeditions to China. He gave it to me for safekeeping."

"Why didn't you tell me about it? I'm your *wife*, Sil."

"I—I'm sorry, Nora. I wasn't trying to keep things from you. It's just...this power. It's too much. It could *destroy the world*."

"Could one person do that?"

"Well, no. It requires fourteen mages, one for every type of Prime Tree."

"Including willow and cypress?"

"Yes."

"Do we even *have* any mages Aligned with that woodpair?"

"Not in Sylrantheas."

"So it's not nearly as dangerous as you say it is."

"In the wrong hands, it could be."

"Are your hands the right ones?"

"I'm just trying to do what's right, Melenora."

Keya could hear the strain in his tone.

"What else does the Book of Souls contain? Twins, Silanar, how many more artifacts exist that we don't know about?"

"Doubtless many exist," Silanar said, "but that doesn't mean I know about them. And the Book of Souls contains many things, but only the one Ritual of Sundering. There are whole sections devoted to primewood magic, how it works. Some kind of advanced modes that I haven't deciphered yet. The rest of the Book is devoted to what seems to be religious teachings, the kind of stuff Myriani says in church. There are words that I don't recognize, too. Perhaps an archaic form of Eldrim. Something about souls."

"Is the Ritual complex?"

"Too much for me to remember. We need to keep the Book safe. If we lose it, not only does that mean that somebody else could perform the Ritual..."

"It also means *we* can't perform it."

"Exactly."

"I wonder where it came from. Who wrote it."

"Those answers are lost to time," Silanar said. "Anyway, enough about the Book. I'll clean things up. Thanks again for cooking."

Keya heard the sound of a kiss, then dishes rattling. She moved on as night continued to fall, pondering the things she had just heard.

There was a previously-unknown artifact called the Book of Souls. This was how Silanar knew how to enact the Sundering. It sounded like the Book was the source of most of the Eldrim teachings. And what were those advanced magic modes he had mentioned? It seemed far too important a thing to dismiss offhand.

And how could her *father* have been the one who had found it? He'd never gone on any expedition to China. He wasn't the expedition type.

Something about all this wasn't adding up.

But then Keya realized something else. Something bigger.

The Book of Souls was the only thing that would allow the Sundering to happen at all.

If it were lost—if it were destroyed—no one would need to die. The Sundering wouldn't happen. The elves wouldn't commit genocide.

If Keya were to somehow eliminate the Book of Souls, she could save the elven race from making the biggest mistake in their entire history.

Unexpected movement caught her eye up ahead. Was there someone loitering in a tree? That on its own wasn't very unusual—elves loved climbing trees, especially the children. But this was no child. And this was no elf.

This was a human.

And not just *any* human. Keya recognized her from the storm.

FORTY-ONE

THE BRANCH JESSICA was standing on was remarkably large. The trees grew strong here in the Muir Woods, reminding her of her childhood. Sometimes she missed it. Sometimes she longed to escape the city and all its endless distractions. Sometimes she—

Wait. Where had Keya gone?

"Boo," a voice said suddenly from behind her, and Jessica nearly fell out of the tree.

She turned, taking care to keep her grip intact on the over-head branch, heart beating wildly in her chest.

Keya was standing next to her.

"Hi," the woman said. "Don't I know you? You were at the American Cancer Society. Your son was a patient there."

"I—" This woman had her at a disadvantage. "Yes." Might as well be honest. "My name is Jessica."

Keya made a strange sign at her, two fingers crossed. "Greetings, Jessica," she said. "I am Keya. And *you*, somehow, have found your way to Sylrantheas, something few humans ever do. Tell me, Jessica: why are you here?"

"I—" Once again, she was at a loss for words. "I want to save my son."

"Your son. Who has cancer."

"How did you know that?"

"Why else would you be at the American Cancer Society? I work there, Jessica." She reached out and laid a hand on Jessica's arm. "You don't need to be afraid. Not unless I report you."

Jessica's heart beat faster. "Please don't do that."

Keya's grip on her arm tightened. "Then tell me why you're here."

"I saw you," Jessica said. "In the Society. You *healed* that woman. You stitched up broken bone—instantly!" She leaned in closer, her voice dropping to a conspiratorial tone. "I think it was *magic*."

Keya started laughing, the sound unexpectedly loud in the growing night. She pulled away. "You got *that* right, sister," she said. Then her eyes narrowed. "But I'm not the only mage here."

Jessica put a finger on her heart, questioning.

"No," Keya said. "Not you. Your *son*."

"How did you—"

"He's a forcefinder. Isn't he."

"I—"

"He's the reason we all survived that terrible collapse."

"I don't—"

"Are you an elf?" Keya moved forward suddenly, startling her. She flicked Jessica's long, dark hair back from her ears, eyes widening as she saw them. "You're not. Or...a mist-weaver, perhaps?"

Jessica just shook her head. "I don't even know what that means."

"Twins," Keya said, making the word sound like a curse,

like taking the Lord's name in vain. Something her husband *hated* her to do. "You really *are* a human. But that means... that means humans can be mages?" She looked around. "No one will believe me if I tell them."

Jessica surged forward, both hands clasping around the woman's neck. "Don't you *dare*."

Keya had a look of shock in her eyes. Jessica just stood there, pressing her fingers into her neck, willing the life out of her.

Then she stepped back, suddenly realizing what she was doing. She was not a murderer. She was not an animal. "I'm sorry. I didn't mean to surprise you."

"That's not why I'm surprised," Keya said. "Look." She pointed down.

And Jessica realized she was balancing easily on her feet, two dozen feet up from the ground.

FORTY-TWO

"ARE you *sure* you're not an elf?" Keya asked. "You certainly stand a tree like one."

They were sitting on the branch, dangling their feet into thin air like a pair of schoolchildren.

Jessica had certainly never expected *this*.

"What?" she asked. "Elves? Like in *The Lord of the Rings*?"

Keya let out a tinkling laugh. "You actually know what that is? I thought no one read fantasy anymore."

Jessica frowned. "I didn't *read* it. I saw the movies."

"Oh." Keya looked into the distance as the sun continued to set. "Yes, we're elves. But Tolkien didn't invent us—he met some of us and told the tale. Much like you're doing now."

"So you'll let me live?"

Keya regarded her. "Perhaps. Yes. Your son *is* a mage, after all. And you made it this far. I think we should compare notes. You can tell me what you know of your son, and I will tell you what I can of us. Elves. The Eldrim. Sylrantheas."

"Magic?"

Keya smiled. "Even magic."

"Then let's get started. How long have you...*elves*...been here?"

"Our teachings tell us twenty thousand years, give or take."

"Give or take?"

"Much like humans, our records are inexact."

"But twenty thousand years...that's before modern humans even *existed*."

"That's still the subject of some scientific debate, but I'll concede the point."

"Where did you come from?"

"No idea."

"Where did *magic* come from?"

"No idea," Keya said, "except the Trees."

Jessica could hear the capital letter on that word. "Trees?"

"Prime Trees. You can't see them, since you're a human. You can even walk right through them as a human, which is pretty cool. They're *huge*, like dozens of times bigger than the biggest trees humans know about."

"And?"

"And you can't kill them. They do not die."

"That's...interesting. But what about magic?"

"The Prime Trees give us magic," Keya said. "There's power in the wood itself."

"So anyone with this...wood...can do magic?"

Keya laughed. "Not in the slightest. First, you have to be Talented. About one in three elves are. Then you need to find out your Alignment, which is which woodpair you are Talented in."

"Woodpair?"

"Just how it sounds. A pair of Trees, one coniferous and one deciduous. You can use either type of wood for your magic."

"Odd."

"I didn't invent it," Keya said. "Just repeating the facts."

"So we have Talent and Alignment and wood. Is that all?"

"One more thing: Investment. The mage must *do* something, some kind of skilled action that is related to their specific Talent. Like for me, I have to perform an action of healing. It can be as simple as taking a pulse, or as complex as performing open heart surgery."

"Why would you perform surgery when you can use magic?"

Keya gave her a glare. "Elves aren't allowed to use magic in front of humans."

"Oh? Why?"

"Why do you think? We've gone in secret this *entire* time."

"Not *entirely* secret."

"You think people believe *The Lord of the Rings*?"

"I bet some do. The internet is full of wack jobs."

"Conceded. Still, none of them have proof. Because we don't use magic where we can be discovered."

"Until that storm."

Keya looked down at her hands. "It was a mistake. But Melenora would have died." She looked back up at Keya. "And anyway, I was *hardly* the most egregious mage in that room."

Jessica felt herself blushing, but she wasn't sure why. "I have no idea how he did it," she said. "I don't even know if he can do it again."

"Where did he get the wood?"

"The door frame, I think. He seemed to know that it would power his magic."

Keya pulled at her shoulder-length hair. "That is exceedingly strange. Why would a Cothellon plant darkprime wood in the American Cancer Society? And why a *door frame*, of all places?"

"Cothellon? You lost me again, I'm afraid."

"Sorry. Cothellon is a word in the Eldrim tongue. It means *enemy elf*. They splintered off from us, oh, a thousand years ago? Maybe more. They're the science and technology faction, as it were. Also a bunch of dicks."

"You know them personally?"

Keya gave a great guffaw. "Oh, no, I do not. *No one* knows the Cothellon. They're not supposed to exist. That entire class of magic isn't supposed to exist."

"You called it...darkprime?"

"Yeah. It's a whole set of alternate powers, driven from a type of wood we can't create. We have no idea how it works, actually. How any of it works. I'm not even sure we know what all the powers *are*."

"Jesus," Jessica said. "And my *son* is one of them? But he's not a...whatever you said. Cothellon."

"True, you're not an elf," Keya said. "I can tell by your ears. See, elves lose their natural misting when they enter Sylrantheas. Outside of here, the nearest Prime Tree takes over automatically, granting us a human illusion. But here—and in all the other Eldrim strongholds throughout the planet—the Trees consider it a safe zone. We're allowed to look like our natural, beautiful selves." She narrowed her eyes. "Of course, there's always cosmetic surgery."

Jessica clapped a hand to her ear. "I haven't had anything done."

"The funny thing is, I believe you." Keya sighed. "There's something going on here, something beyond my knowledge. Maybe humans *can* be mages. Maybe you and your family are just particularly strong. Or maybe your son's father is actually an elf."

That stopped Jessica cold. "No."

Keya smiled. "Relax. I'm kidding. Elves only *very* rarely interbreed with humans, and the resulting child is almost never a mage. I'm sure that's not the case."

Jessica was starting to feel impatient. "I need to help him. That's why I'm here. You're a healer, right?"

"A soulsoother. Yes."

"Then you can help him! You can save my son."

"I, uh, hmm." Keya was looking at the ground. "There's a reason I was working at the American Cancer Society, Jessica."

"Of *course*! You use magic to heal the patients."

Keya's look was sad. "I studied for *years* to be there," she said. "I took on a ton of student debt. Do you think I would have done that if I could have used magic to wish all that cancer away?"

"You would just have to do it in secret. When no one was looking. Don't you want to *help* people?"

Jessica thought she saw tears growing in Keya's eyes. "If *course* I do. That's why I was there! But Jessica, it's not because of the prohibition on magic."

"Then what?"

"It's because," Keya said, "soulsoothing has limitations. I can't bring people back from the dead. I can't regrow lost limbs or missing organs. And I can't, despite my best attempts, cure cancer. It just can't be done."

They were silent for a minute.

Jessica felt tears threatening to break loose. "But I thought...I wanted...I came all this way. There's *nothing* you can do?"

"I'm sorry. I truly am."

"Then I'm lost." The tears came, then, and Jessica couldn't hold them back. She shook with the force of them, with emotions long kept silent. Her son would die. Her baby, the love of her life, would not survive. And even though she'd discovered a miracle—a magic found in movies and in books —even *that* wasn't enough.

There was no fix for her life. There was no fix for her son's. He would die, and everything Jessica had done would be for naught.

"I can ease his pain, at least," Keya said, reaching out and placing a hand on Jessica's back. The gesture was meant to be comforting, she was sure, but instead it felt threatening.

She jerked away. "Maybe you should just *kill* him instead." A sob jerked her body.

"Jessica. Dear. You don't mean that."

"Don't patronize me, *elf*. You must be half my age."

Keya gave a sad smile. "I'm seventy-five."

"I—Jesus. Shit. How long do you people live, anyway?"

"About a thousand years, give or take."

"Fucking elves. A thousand years, and you can't even heal my son."

"It's not my fault, Jessica. I'd do *anything* to help your son. It's literally my job. I made it my life's work."

Jessica realized then that she was being foolish. This woman only wanted to help. She wiped her eyes, turning to her. To the elf. To the girl who looked all of twenty, but was actually somehow forty years older than her. "I'm sorry," she said. "It's just—"

"I know. I don't have any children, but I work with them every day. I can only imagine what you must be feeling right now."

"Thank you." They were silent for a time. "Keya?" Jessica asked after a minute. "What should I do now?"

Keya thought for a moment, then reached into her pocket,

pulling out a piece of wood. "I'd like to try something," she said. "Hold this."

Jessica frowned at it.

"It won't bite," Keya said. "I promise. Just put it in your hand."

Jessica did so, immediately jerking her hand back in surprise. "The wood. Is it supposed to be warm?"

Keya was staring at her with great interest. "Are you quite sure it's warm?"

"*Very* warm," Jessica said. "And I almost feel something... pulsing...inside." She handed the wood back. "This is weird."

"Jessica," Keya said, "what did I say when first we met? Humans can't be mages. Darkprime mages, maybe, but *certainly* not lightprime mages. To my knowledge, it's never been done."

"So?"

"So, dear Jessica of San Francisco, *you* are just like me. You're a soulsoother. A healer. You, my new human friend, are a *mage*."

FORTY-THREE

JOHN SET ASIDE the document he'd been working on, taking off his glasses and rubbing the bridge of his nose. It was a dictionary, of sorts. A lexicon. Languages had always been his forte, but this one was proving to be a bit of a nightmare. He needed it to be ugly, and he *hated* ugly languages.

"There's someone here to see you," Warren said, opening the office door a crack.

John cocked an eyebrow, eyeing the clock. "At this time? How did they even know I was here?"

"No idea, sir. I haven't seen her in Gondor before."

John frowned. This was most unusual. Was their security that bad? Unexpected visitors did not bode well, not if they were going to survive what was coming. "Send her in."

Warren nodded, closing the door. It opened a minute later, revealing a short woman in a tight, purple dress. Her garment revealed ample ebony skin, and John couldn't help but raise an eyebrow. The woman had flashing black eyes and pursed lips, her expression one of someone who had seen a lot of things. Her eyes were much older than her face.

"Who in the hell are you?" he asked.

The woman gave him a thin smile. "Not the greatest way to greet a guest, wouldn't you say, John?" she said. Her voice was thick, the words rolling off her tongue with languor.

There was something intensely creepy about her.

"You're only a guest in Gondor if I know who you are," John said, his finger sliding under the desk to where the alarm trigger was hidden. "This place is strictly invite-only." There was a spider on his desk, he noted somewhat incongruently.

The woman's smile widened. "My apologies, John. It was my not wish to offend. I have many, many names, but you may call me Magona."

"Magona. A strange name. What do you want?"

Magona's grin bore teeth, giving her an almost feral appearance. "I want to make sure the human race survives."

John crossed his arms. "And what will it cost me?"

Magona's grin got wider still.

DUNEDAR SLIPPED through the maintenance hatch and found himself in another world. He pulled a flashlight from his massively heavy bag and shone it around, taking stock. He'd heard of this place from some of the Cothellon up above. He just hadn't known quite what to expect.

This was the Under.

Each of the cities had been built with a place like this, he had learned. They were cities unto themselves, stretching below the streets deeper than anyone was sure. All the necessary infrastructure to keep the city running was down here: electrical plants, water purification, sewers, plumbing, storage. The subway system wasn't running yet, but it, too, was here. But there was more, he had heard. *Far* more, and nobody was quite sure what it was for. He'd heard whispers of strange, dark forests, of rooms filled to the ceiling with dark-prime wood. And there were vast unmapped areas, parts of the Under that had no purpose at all.

All of this and more he had learned, but he had never thought to behold *this*.

It was a tiny cement tunnel, leading into darkness.

He shouldered his bag, grunting with the weight of it, and set out into the unknown.

QUYNN STOOD in front of the display case in his sumptuous apartment, taking a moment to admire the contents. The Tree Ring Staff was still his most beautiful possession—*and* the most powerful. Six feet tall, it was made up of six different kinds of woods that were separated by small bands of a seventh, darker-colored wood. It might be the most powerful artifact ever created.

And somehow it had fallen into Quynn's possession.

He opened the case with a soft *snick*, taking the Staff in his hands. The wood was smooth, carefully sanded and lacquered, cold in his hands except in one specific spot: the band of poplar that was near the middle. The wood provided an endless source of mindmaster magic, with no need to replenish it as was used. With this Staff, and with Silanar's enigmatic Book of Amplification, he could control an entire city on his own.

Too bad the Book of Amplification had been lost.

No one knew how old the Tree Ring Staff was, exactly. Some thought it had arrived with the elves, twenty thousand years ago. Some thought it had been created during the era of the Prime Mages, which Quynn thought was the most likely story. The Prime Mages had been all-powerful, the only mages that could access all seven powers simultaneously. They were supposed to live forever.

But five thousand years ago, the last of them had disappeared.

And the art of creating artifacts had disappeared with them. Despite the best efforts of Artisans, Builders, and others, no one could figure out how the various elven artifacts worked. Quynn fingered the Earring of Mist, which he always kept in his—wait.

The earring was gone.

What in the Twins' names was going on?

"Quynn," a sultry voice said from a dark corner of his room. "Quit playing with that thing and come to bed. I have a different staff in mind I'd like to play with."

A slow smile creeping over his face, Quynn replaced the Tree Ring Staff in its case and went to bed.

After all, it wouldn't do to keep Lorelei waiting.

WHEN DILLON HEARD what his father had had to say, he knew he had to do something about it. He had to warn people —at least those he was close to in this life. He had no home. He had no possessions. All he had was a handful of friends, scattered throughout the Bay, friends he might just be able to save.

So Dillon picked up the phone.

"Oil," he said when the man picked up. "Can you get to the shop? There's something I need to tell you."

"Sure thing, boss," Oil said. "Everything okay?"

"I'll tell you when you get here. I have a few other calls to make. Oh, and Oil? Gather up the rest of the boys, will you? We might need everyone we can get."

"Sure. See you soon."

Dillon hung up, tapping on a second contact on his phone.

"This is Alan," the person at the other end said.

"Alan," Dillon said. "This is Dillon. Is now a good time?"

"Sure," Alan said. His voice sounded strained. "I just got home. My wife apparently left our son here with the babysitter unexpectedly, and drove off into the woods. She left a note, at least. I have no idea what's going on."

"The woods? Like Marin?"

"Exactly. What's going on, Dillon? I haven't heard from you in a while."

"Uh," Dillon said, suddenly unsure how to proceed. "Something very big and very bad is about to happen."

"Something bigger than the typhoon?"

"*Much* bigger."

"Dang. Is this about those...people...you warned me about?"

"Elves, Alan. You can say elves. And yes. It is."

"I was never quite sure if I believed—"

"Alan." Dillon cut him off. "Look. I know you believe in God, and creation, and everything. But elves are *real*. And they are very, very dangerous. So, bud, you gotta listen to me. Here's what you need to do..."

THALANIL SENT AN IM TO PHAROM, the VP of Release Management. "How's it looking?"

"Just got it," came the reply. "It's in code review."

"We have to hurry this up," Thalanil wrote back. "The bug is far worse than I thought."

"What now? A ten minute reboot isn't the end of the world."

"Because we're dealing with such old hardware, when the bug triggers it will modulate the voltage on the bus."

"That's...unusual."

"Yes. And this particular component is capable of spiking voltage to +24V."

"Why in the Twins' damned names would it be capable of *that*? That's double the ISA high pin."

"I wasn't around back then. I have no idea why they built that stuff the way they did."

"It'll fry the bus."

"Yep."

"Thalanil, that's a *hardware* replacement on a decades-old system. The downtime on that...shit, I'm not sure we even *have* replacement hardware!"

"An electrical event of that level could have ripple effects," Thalanil said. "I've got one of the hardware engineers looking into it."

"Twins," Pharom wrote. "We'll get this into QA immediately."

"*QA*?" Thalanil wanted to shout at the man, but he wasn't even on the same floor. "We have to push this *now*!"

"Thalanil," Pharom replied, "if we push a build without integrated testing and QA, we run the risk of shutting down far more than the UI of the bridge."

Thalanil ground his teeth. Like it or not, he knew the man was right.

MELENORA WAS PUTTING the dishes away after dinner, her mind on other things. The Sundering. The Book of Souls. The elves' role in all of this. Was now really the time? Was there *ever* a time for this kind of action? She didn't doubt her husband's resolve.

She just doubted his morality.

A plate slipped out of her hand, ceramic shattering on the hardwood floor. The plate had been over a thousand years old, handed down through three generations of her family. It had been painted with a depiction of a Prime Elm Tree, the Tree of her line. The Artisan Tree. The leafrunning Tree.

Now it was in pieces on the floor.

She bent to clean it up, tears coming unexpectedly to her eyes. It wasn't the plate. She had a dozen more of them, and it was about time for redecorating anyway. No, her tears were coming from another place.

Her husband was about to commit the elven race to the worst possible outcome.

Her husband was about to kill billions of people.

And even though he might be right—even though the planet itself was being destroyed by those very people—she just couldn't countenance it. It just didn't sit right.

There had to be another solution.

Silanar came bustling into the kitchen, a stack of papers in his hands. He stopped when he saw her on her knees, shards of broken ceramic around her on the floor. "Everything okay?" he asked.

She looked up at him, revealing her tears.

"Twins," he said. "What happened? Are you hurt?"

"We have to stop this," she said. "It isn't right."

"Have to stop what? Honey, what's wrong?"

"The Sundering. You know you can't go through with it."

She saw his expression harden slightly. "It's what's best

for the planet. You *know* this. You've seen the studies. It's our *job*, Nora. It's why we were put here on Earth to begin with."

"Because of that stupid *Book*?"

"Because of the teachings, yes."

"Myriani twists their words."

"Why would you say that?"

"Your mother was always a wiley one. You haven't seen her when you leave the room. She gets this look on her face, Sil." Melanora felt a shiver roll through her. The woman was sometimes *seriously* creepy.

Silanar's expression was carefully guarded. "I know it isn't easy," he said, "but I appreciate all you do to treat my mother civilly. She is not an evil person. She just—"

"She just doesn't like me."

"Well..."

"It doesn't matter. Silanar, *please* think this through. I mean *really* think it through. We can't just casually destroy the human race."

Silanar turned away. "I need to deliver these executive orders to the Council. You can leave that broken plate for later—I'll get it."

And he left, leaving Melenora crying on the floor.

SILANAR STEPPED into the Council chamber, the orders rustling in his hand. The message he'd received a few minutes before had been cryptic at best, from an unknown source. But if it were true...

"You look like you've seen a ghost," Bellas said.

"You look pissed," Daylor said.

It was just the three of them in the room—ever the three

of them, the Mentors who carried out the law and execution of it in Sylrantheas.

"Melenora is questioning me," Silanar said. "And worse—she's questioning my *mother*."

"Myriani?" Bellas said. "But she's the High Priest, for Twins' sake. Why would she question *her*?"

"An intuition, probably. Sure, my mother did not give me the easiest upbringing. She disappeared a lot, off on her quests around the world. And I'll admit it—sometimes she can be a little creepy. But that's no reason to attack her."

"It's a trying time for us all," Daylor said. "We must band together and find the right and proper solution to the problem at hand."

"I couldn't agree more," Silanar said. "But I, too, have an intuition. How are the primestores coming?"

"We've already reached twenty percent capacity in all three buildings," Daylor said. "And we're ramping up efforts significantly. We can have them filled within a few days, I would think. Maybe inside twenty four hours."

"Add more people to it," Silanar said. "We need to get those buildings filled *now*."

"Do you know something we don't?"

"Just a hunch," Silanar said. He thought he'd caught a glimpse of Orym in the tavern on his way over here. That did not bode well. But he hadn't wanted to spook the man, so he'd moved on. And besides: Kharis had been with him. Silanar would speak to Kharis later, find out what was going on.

"We'll get it done," Daylor said. "I hope you're wrong about all this."

"So do I," Silanar said. "But that's not all. I'm also ordering the immediate transfer of fourteen mages to various Prime Trees throughout the world. From their local villages, if possible—I want them in place inside the day. I have the orders here."

Bellas accepted the papers. "We'll communicate with the Eldrim network. But Silanar, the World Council hasn't even assembled yet, much less put this to a vote. Why move the mages now?"

"About that," Silanar said. "We also need to get the World Council going. *Now*. This is a Code One emergency." It was an article that had never been exercised before, to Silanar's knowledge.

"You'll have to give us a reason," Bellas said.

"It's the Cothellon," Silanar said. "I believe they intend to end the world before we can."

FORTY-FOUR

"YOU'RE A MAGE," Keya repeated, and Jessica could hear the awe in her voice. Humans weren't mages, or so she'd said.

"How could that be possible?" Jessica asked.

"We must be wrong," Keya said. "It's not as if we elves have really experimented with humans, or anything. And it's not like humans have access to primewood. What if there have been mages all this time, and no one knew?"

"Do you have any human friends?"

Keya looked down at the ground a dozen feet below them, a sad look in her eyes. "I have many. One of them died in the storm." She looked up at Jessica. "Shit. Maybe more of them did. I haven't heard from everyone yet."

Jessica laid a hand on her new friend's arm. Could she call her a friend? Yes. She felt she could. Keya was kind, in a way she hadn't quite expected from what seemed to be an alien race of magic users. "I'm sorry," she said. "Were you two close?"

"Rosemary was my best friend," she said. "I saved her once, the day of the storm. She died when I wasn't even looking."

"Shit."

"It's harder for a soulsoother. You'll learn that, I suppose. I still can't believe you are one too."

"Are we sure about that?"

Keya pursed her lips. "There's only one way to find out. Come on."

And she jumped off the branch.

Jessica put a hand to her mouth in surprise. But Keya landed spryly on the ground, the impact apparently not giving her much pain. "How did you—"

"I'm not afraid of falling," Keya said, looking up at her and smiling. "All elves learn to do that. Or maybe we are born with it. We grow up climbing trees, after all. Our magic is *based* on them. Come on! But, uh, maybe don't jump."

"I agree," Jessica said. Seventy-five, and the girl still seemed younger than she was. Maybe humans matured at a different rate than elves. "I'm gonna climb down. Just—"

"I'll wait."

It took her several minutes to make it, the bark rough beneath her fingers. When she finally reached the ground, Keya stood next to her excitedly. "You still have that prime-wood, right?" she asked.

Jessica pulled it from the pocket she had stored it in. "Yes." It was still warm in her hand, a strange sort of life pulsing through it. The whole thing was *weird*.

"Good," Keya said. "Now, soulsoothers belong to a larger Talent—those who are aligned with birch and spruce. We call this the Way of the Protector, and it encompasses three disciplines."

It had been a long time since Jessica had been in class. She wasn't sure if she was ready for one now.

"You know Restoration, the art of healing. There is also Preservation, which is focused on maintenance and prevention. And finally, there is Cultivation: gardening, the growth of living things. All three disciplines use the same magical Talent, the same woodpair, the same rules."

"Why are you telling me this?"

"Because we need to test your magic, Jessica. And no one here needs healing."

"Oh."

Keya walked a few yards into the forest, stopping in front of a fern that looked like it was wilting. "Here. This plant needs our help."

"Okay," Jessica said. "What do I do?"

"First, you must perform a skilled action. See that dead frond? Why don't you pluck it from the plant. Pruning can be a skilled action."

"Alright." Jessica did as she was bid, bending to the plant and ripping the dead frond off. Instantly she felt the prime birch in her hand flare to life, growing noticeably warmer. The sensation was almost as if the wood had become awake, just then, one eye opening to the world.

For a moment, she thought there was a *person* there.

But the moment quickly vanished, and Jessica found herself standing over a dying fern. "Now what?" she asked.

"Now hold your primewood, and Will the plant to make a full and complete recovery. Envision it in your mind. *Feel* the plant. You can do this."

How did one Will something to happen? What would that even feel like? Jessica didn't know. She just knew she had to try.

She bent and touched the plant, probing with her mind. She could almost feel its energy, the hurt that was inside it. The plant was dying, and somehow she could see exactly *why*.

The wood was pulsing in her hand. And so she used it, opening her mind to it. She created a kind of gateway, a bridge, a channel between the primewood in her hand and the fern on the ground. And as she did so, she felt power flowing forth.

Magic, warm and powerful, surged through her into the plant. And she felt it growing, then. Repairing. The cells of the plant multiplied, growing as she touched it, its overall health improving as she channeled power into it. She could feel the magic flooding through her, a torrent of energy moving from the primewood to the fern. And the fern grew, growing noticeably greener, twisting a little as its fronds reached upward to the sky. Then it was done, and a perfect, healthy fern was sitting there beneath Jessica's fingers.

She felt a new world opening in front of her, then. New horizons, new possibilities. She *was* a mage. She could *heal*. She just needed more of this magic wood, and there was no limit to what she could do.

She tasted bitterness on her tongue. Except their *were* limits. No resurrection. No regrowth.

And no curing of cancer.

She was a healer, but she could not heal her son.

"Well done," Keya said, touching her lightly on the arm. "How did that feel?"

Jessica let out a breath. "Amazing," she said. "And yet..."

"You're thinking of your son."

Jessica nodded.

"Maybe..."

"What?" Jessica turned to her.

"Well, you're the first human mage in, like, *ever*," Keya said. "What if the limits don't apply to you?"

Jessica felt adrenaline coursing through her. "I have to get home. Now. Do you have any more of this wood?"

"I'm coming with you," Keya said. "And I'll give you all the primewood you will ever need."

JASON WAS STILL SLEEPING when they arrived at Jessica's house. The babysitter was gone, and Alan was home, doing something on his computer. Jessica didn't want to bother him —or explain any of this to him—so they snuck directly into Jason's room.

"My husband is religious," she said to Keya. "He won't believe any of this stuff is real."

"In my experience," Keya said, "religious people are often *more* likely to believe in magic. They were raised to expect the impossible."

"Hmm," Jessica said. "Well I don't want to interrupt his work. To be honest, you're probably right. Even *I* am having trouble believing that all of this is real."

"You've done it now," Keya said. "You've lived it. You know it must be real."

Jessica nodded. "Shall we try?"

"We shall. This is all on you. I've tried to cure many cancer patients over the years. For me, it never works."

"Let's hope I'm somehow different, then."

"Let's hope. Here: more primewood."

"Thank you." Jessica accepted a handful of wood pieces, each of them feeling warm in her hand. "Should I—"

"Use them all," Keya said. "Give it as much power as you can."

"Okay." Jessica felt a little thrill roll through her. "How do I begin?"

"You need a skilled action," Keya said. "Healing, in this case. Do you know how to check a pulse? It's often the easiest."

Jessica nodded, putting her fingers on Jason's neck. The boy was sleeping peacefully, no evidence of the disease upon his face. He was a beautiful boy, her Korean heritage mixing with her husband's European. He would be a hit with the ladies, she knew.

If he only had the chance to get there.

She focused on his pulse, looking at her watch to count the beats. It only took a few seconds for the action to work, power flaring up in all the primewood in her hand. "Wow," she couldn't help but say. There was a *lot* of magic there. She could feel it, pulsing in time with her own heart. With this magic, she could do miracles. With this magic, she felt like she could bring back the dead.

It was time to see what she could really do.

She kept her fingers on her son, Willing the magic to flash forth.

A torrent of it hit the boy at once, flooding from the primewood into him. There was a canker sore in his mouth—gone. She felt a weakened muscle in his heart—fixed. His lung capacity improved, blood flowing freely in his brain. She fixed two bruises, a minor sprain in his ankle, and she eased the allergies that were affecting his sinuses. These were all the work of but a moment, the magic easily fixing everything he had.

But then she reached his jaw.

That was where the tumor was. She could feel it there, in her mind's eye, the magic pulsing and shimmering around it. It was evil, a foreign mass of pain and death, standing out like a black blot upon the brightness of his soul.

She struck at it, then. She used her magic to rail against it, to destroy it with everything she had. She pushed all her power into it, all her ability, all the primewood in her hand.

But it did not budge. It did not move. It just stayed there, almost glaring at her, as if it were daring her to try again.

The cancer would not move.

She gasped, the magic leaving her all at once. Sweat broke out on her brow, tears reaching her eyes. "It didn't work," she said. "The magic almost felt too...blunt. Like there wasn't enough control. I was able to heal *everything* else...but not that. I need to get deeper, somehow. The magic needs to... *change*."

Keya's eyes were wide. "You felt all that?"

"I did. Didn't you, when you tried to cure cancer?"

"It was like a black box to me," Keya said. "I couldn't sense it, I couldn't affect it. The magic just avoided it entirely, as if it didn't want to be involved."

"It wants to," Jessica said. "I can feel it. It just doesn't know *how*. It's almost like it needs something new. Some other way to use it."

"The advanced modes," Keya breathed.

"What?"

"The Book of Souls. I just heard about it tonight. It's something Silanar has. He's the Council Leader, basically the guy in charge of Sylrantheas. If we can find that book, I heard him say that we can learn more advanced ways to use this magic."

"Can we cure cancer with it?"

"I don't know," Keya said. "But it's definitely worth a try."

FORTY-FIVE

"I THOUGHT you were up to something," a male voice said, and Jessica nearly fell over in surprise.

Alan was standing in the bedroom doorway.

"Hi, sweetie," Jessica said. "I didn't want to bother you."

"What's going on?" Alan asked. "Who's your friend?"

"This is Keya," Jessica said. "I met her at the Cancer Society."

Alan was staring at Keya very intently. "This is about Jason?"

"Well, we *are* in his room."

His eyes narrowed. "Are you...praying for him, or something?"

Jessica couldn't stop herself from laughing. "No, sweetie. We're...uh..." She stopped. Should she tell him? Ah, to hell with it. "We're doing *magic*."

Now it was Alan's turn to laugh. "What? You can't be serious."

Jessica gave him her most serious expression. "I am. Keya is...an elf." Keya took in a sharp breath at that. "I'm sorry,

Keya, but Alan is my husband. I have to tell him." Keya nodded.

"Elves?" Alan asked. "Like in Tolkein?"

"Tolkein didn't invent us," Keya said. "He just met some of us and lived to tell the tale. And yes—we're magic users. Well, some of us, anyway. And so is your wife."

Alan turned to Jessica, shock evident on his face. "Is this true?"

"Think of it like a miracle," Jessica said. "Like prayer. I can heal things—people, plants—using magic."

But Alan's face was growing darker, the lines on his forehead creasing. "Is the devil in you?" he asked. "Demon, show thyself!"

"This isn't *The Exorcist*," Jessica said. "Honey, maybe you should just go back to work. We've got this handled."

"Don't patronize me," Alan said. "Just because you don't believe, doesn't mean something evil isn't going on here."

Jessica opened her mouth, a retort at the ready, but then she realized that he might, in fact, be right.

The elves might be just as evil as Alan thought.

She looked at Keya, who was looking at the floor. "That Book," Jessica said. "Do you know where it is?"

"I'm afraid not," Keya said. "But I can try to snoop around, figure it out. I have no idea where he might have hidden it."

"Fine," Jessica said, turning back to her husband. "Sweetie, we need to go. I have my phone on if you need me. Take care of Jason, okay?"

"I don't like this," Alan said. "Whatever you've gotten yourself into, I don't like it one bit."

Jessica gave him a quick kiss on the cheek. "I can look out for myself," she said. "Thank you for your concern."

KEYA WAS SITTING in the front seat of Jessica's Land Rover, watching the city pass her by. So much of San Francisco had been damaged by the typhoon—it almost didn't look like the same city as before. She felt sadness overtake her as she rumbled in the car. If the Sundering came to pass, this city would never get the chance to recover.

"There's something I need to tell you," she said.

Jessica glanced at her. "There's more?"

"I'm afraid so."

As it turned out, explaining the Sundering was just as painful as Keya thought it would be.

"You're kidding," Jessica said when she was done.

"I truly, *truly* wish I was."

The car slowed as they entered the Golden Gate Bridge. "Well then, what's the point of all of this?" Jessica asked. "I'm trying to heal my son, but why? Shit. My husband was right. You elves really *are* evil."

Keya wished she had a retort. She wished she could refute that claim, could protest in any way. But she couldn't. She knew that it was true.

If demons were real, she knew that they would look like elves.

"I intent to stop them," Keya said.

"What? How?"

"I'm not sure yet. First, we need to find the Book of Souls."

THEY PULLED into Sylrantheas in the dead of night, the village completely silent around them. She could still see lights on inside Syndra's, of course. The tavern was the only place in the village that was open around the clock. The Land

Rover crunched over leaves and twigs as it rolled to a stop, and the two women got out of the vehicle.

"Nice car," Keya said.

"My husband's idea," Jessica said. "We're still making payments."

"Isn't everyone. So what's our game plan?"

"We need to find that Book."

"Agreed," Keya said. "And I can't just ask Silanar directly, for obvious reasons. It could be in his house, I suppose. But he's the leader of Sylrantheas. It could be *anywhere*."

"Should we search the village, then?"

"Sylrantheas is bigger than you think. It could take us months, and that's assuming we somehow avoid getting caught."

"We have to try. We need those advanced magic modes."

Keya looked at her new friend. The woman was so intense, so focused on saving her son. And she couldn't blame her—she'd felt that way every second at the Cancer Society. But the Book of Souls wasn't just the source of advanced magic.

It would also be the reason the world ended.

"We'll find it," Keya said. "We can't let this world be destroyed."

"We can't let my son die."

"We'll stop all of this. Somehow."

"Somehow."

Keya only hoped that it was true.

"I'M GOING TO ASK AROUND," Keya said. "Stay here for now."

"Fine," Jessica said. "I need to call my husband, anyway." She was pretty sure he would be fuming at home. She watched as Keya slipped away into the night, waiting until the girl had disappeared. Then she pulled out her phone.

"Jess," Alan said. "Are you okay? Where are you?"

"I'm fine, sweetie," Jessica said. "I'm up here in the Muir Woods with Keya. We think we have a way to save Jason."

"More of this...magic?"

"Yes. There's some kind of advanced mode, apparently."

"I don't know what you're mixed up in, Jessica, but it doesn't feel right to me. Promise me that you'll be careful."

"I promise."

"Dillon called me today."

"What?" Jessica was struggling to remember who that was. "An old friend of yours, right?"

"Yeah. He, uh..." She heard a loud sigh. "Dammit, Jessica, this isn't the first time I've heard about elves."

"But that *is* the first time I've heard you swear, sweetie. What's going on?"

"Dillon told me about the elves years ago, in college. I never really took his word for it, you know? Figured it was some kind of hippie thing. But he kept at it, all this time. He insisted that *he* was one of them. He told me about their magic, Jessica."

"And you kept this from me?"

"I didn't think you'd believe it, sweetie. Heck, *I* didn't believe it! I'm still not sure I do. But he called me today, claiming that something terrible was about to happen."

Jessica felt her blood run cold. "The Sundering."

"That's what he called it."

"Then it must be real. Keya just told me about it a few minutes ago. Could the elves really wipe out the human race?"

"Is there anything we can do to stop them?"

"I just want to save our son."

"So do I, Jessica, but doesn't the survival of the *human race* preclude the safety of our son?"

"I don't know," Jessica said. "I honestly do not know."

"Keep me updated," Alan said. "I want to know what's going on. I feel like we're in over our heads with this."

"I will, sweetie. Try to get some sleep—it's getting late."

"Good luck. I'll take care of our son."

ALAN HUNG UP THE PHONE, glancing at one of his monitors. His wife still didn't suspect, which was good. But it was becoming harder to keep his secrets. It was getting harder to remember which lie he'd told to whom.

He looked at his screen, at the text that was displayed prominently in the middle.

The mission countdown had begun.

PART
FOUR

FORTY-SIX

"SO YOU DISCOVERED YOU WERE A MAGE," Kharis said, taking a sip of his beer.

"Not just a mage," Orym said. "A *dark* mage."

"That makes you sound so evil."

"You don't already think I'm evil?"

Kharis just eyed him, sipping his beer.

"I didn't know it was possible," Orym said. "To be a Mundane my whole life, but still be able to access darkprime magic. It doesn't make sense."

"There's a lot we don't know about magic. Where does it come from?"

"The Twins, supposedly."

"Is that where darkprime magic comes from, too?"

Orym just shrugged. "Who knows. I gave up on the idea of the Twins long ago. If they're real, they're not here."

"Will you tell me how darkprime magic works?" Kharis asked. "Where do you get the wood?"

Orym pursed his lips, considering the request. If the Eldrim found out the exact method the Cothellon were using... "No," he said. "I can't divulge that at this time."

He didn't want Kharis to think less of him than he already did.

Kharis snorted. "Fine. Some contrition, this is. Why are you here, anyway?"

"I'm trying to *tell* you," Orym said. "Will you let me continue?"

"Fine. Be my guest."

Kharis crossed his arms as Orym returned to his tale.

83 YEARS AGO

ORYM CHUCKLED at something the engineer had said, making his way back into his office. He was surprised to see Quynn sitting there waiting for him. It was unlike his superior to visit unannounced.

"How are things going?" Quynn asked as he came in. "Any luck with the Primal Way?"

"I was just preparing a report to send you," Orym replied, setting his things down and taking a seat. "As it happens, we discovered it this week. I don't know why it took so long—the dark wood types exactly mirror that of the light Woodways. It should have been easy."

"Perhaps the lack of volunteers for your...method...has become a bottleneck," Quynn said.

"Yes. That's it in a nutshell. If only...but no, this has already gone far beyond what we originally intended."

"Tell me what you found."

"Our engineers—"

"Mages, you mean."

"You might say it's a little bit of both. Anyway, our engineers were able to make it work after much trial and error.

We didn't know what we were looking for, you see. We had to try everything."

"Spare me the details, Orym."

"Yes, sir. Well, in short, it makes a portal."

"What does that mean?"

"A portal. A gate. A doorway, if you will, to another place. The magic creates a field where matter can be transported instantly from one place to another. We're calling the mages gatesenders, for lack of a better term."

"You have someone Aligned with the Primal?"

"Two of them, in fact. It was a very lucky thing."

"Keep them safe," Quynn said. "Gatesending might be our ticket out of here. I'll bring it to the Council. In the meantime, if we lose those mages...we would need to find a Prime Mage to activate the magic. And you know that's not going to happen."

"Yes, sir. We'll keep them secure."

"Good man."

"There's just one problem, sir," Orym said.

"Yes?"

"Well, gatesending seems to only work over short distances and for small objects."

"You didn't think to mention this sooner?"

"I'm mentioning it now, sir."

"And is there any way to fix this shortcoming?"

"I don't know yet, sir. We're working on it."

"Well, keep working on it. This is your new top priority."

"Yes, sir."

Quynn left, no doubt off to another important meeting. Orym sat in his office, staring at nothing in particular. He stayed that way for several minutes, then roused himself. He had work to do.

PRESENT DAY

DILLON WAS STARTING to freak out a bit. Orym wasn't answering his calls. Dillon didn't have enough details about the Cothellon plan, their so-called Ascension. And he *needed* details if he was going to survive, if he was going to save his friends.

He needed details if he was going to be able to stop them.

And then there was the surgery Orym had suggested. Ear tip removal, cosmetic surgery that only select Eldrim surgeons could perform. It was rare, and it required that he remove his misting from the Prime Trees. He would look like an elf, until the surgery was done, so the whole thing had to be performed by Eldrim.

Dillon wasn't sure if he was ready for such a permanent change.

"Boss?" Oil said, lumbering into the shop's little kitchen. "You ready to address the crew?"

Dillon blew out a breath, then took a swig of the beer he was holding. "Let's do it, Oil. This'll be an awfully big surprise."

QUYNN TOWELED off his hair and put his uniform back on. Lorelei had been insatiable, as always. They'd gone at least four times in a row—he'd lost count. It was just lust for her, he knew. There was some kind of primal instinct that few men could really satisfy. But there was also something missing. Something in him. Something that she wanted, but couldn't ever find. He had no idea what it was.

He shrugged at his reflection in the mirror. Maybe she would come around. Maybe she would eventually see him like he saw her. Perfect. Regal. Strong. Sublime.

Or maybe not. Maybe she would always look just past him into the pillows, just off to the left to his picture of the Trees. Maybe she would only use him for her pleasure, and nothing real would ever come from any of it.

At least she was a damn good lay.

"The Eldrim are moving," Lorelei said from the bed. She was still naked, breasts dangling tantalizingly as she tapped the glass of her tablet. "Silanar invoked a Code One."

"Twins," Quynn swore. "When was the last time they had one of those?"

Lorelei twirled her hair, a thing she only did when she was in his bed. "I think it was during the Great War. I can't remember. They certainly don't use it often." She looked up at him, red lips glistening. She had reapplied her lipstick. "I think they're going to run the ritual. Soon."

"The Sundering? I still have trouble believing they'll actually go through with that."

Lorelei put the tablet down, standing, and Quynn had to remind himself to keep from drooling. She had the kind of body that models would have dreamed of, but he had never seen her enter a gym in her life. Nor did she look any older than when he'd first met her, at least a hundred years ago.

Some people had all the luck.

"They'll make a pretense of debate," she said, bending to slip on her red negligee. "But Silanar has his mind made up. I know him."

"You've never met the man."

Lorelei clucked her tongue. "That doesn't mean I don't know him, Quynn. My intelligence runs *deep*."

"If you're right, we need to move our countdown."

"Yes," Lorelei said. "We need to start the Ascension tomorrow, if we can. I'll convene the Small Council to make sure. But first: come back to bed."

"I *just* showered and got dressed." But he felt himself stirring as she slid the strap of her negligee off one shoulder. He heaved a sigh, unzipping his pants. "Fine, but let's make it quick. I actually do have work to do."

"Yes you do," Lorelei said, dropping the garment and stalking toward him.

Yes he did indeed.

FORTY-SEVEN

IT TOOK Dunedar two hours to find a suitable place for the contraption. He'd been there for eight hours since, eating nothing but the canned food he'd brought with him, slowly but surely assembling the device. It was *very* complicated—and very finnicky—and one wrong move could easily kill him. That was why he had been chosen for this role.

He was the best bomb maker the Eldrim had.

They'd uncovered an architectural diagram of New Tokyo a few weeks earlier, poring over it to determine the best place to trigger a single, large explosion. Disabling the city would be difficult, especially since they had no idea how it was supposed to work.

Eventually, they'd discovered it.

Magic.

The bomb didn't need to destroy the city. It didn't need to punch a hole in it, or vaporize the streets, or eliminate any critical infrastructure. It only needed to blow up a single room, one small chamber where at least a dozen people would be standing at all times.

That was where Dunedar was now, in the Under just below Fallfoiler Troop.

He would destroy their mages, and the city would fall.

The Ascension would fail.

It was all up to him.

AELWYNN WISHED he could be in Mission Control. The center of the entire device, Mission Control was where all the *important* people were. Sure, Aelwynn was important. It wasn't just *anybody* that could be City Director of New San Francisco. True, not just *anyone* could also be Fallfoiler Captain. Still, the titles rang hollow to him somehow.

Aelwynn wanted more.

"Quynn!" he called as he spotted the man walking briskly across the city square. It was unusual to spot him outside of Planner Central. Planner Central. The name seemed odd, but Aelwynn needed to get used to the terms the populace would use. "Wait up!"

Quynn's face looked distinctly annoyed as he paused, turning to face Aelwynn. "What do you want?"

"Do you think it will work?"

"Do I think *what* will work?"

"The Ascension."

Quynn turned away. "I don't have time for this."

"I'm serious, Quynn. How many years have we been planning this? How many elves are involved? How many pieces are there in it?"

"A lot," Quynn said. "To all those questions. And yes, I think it will work. I have Orym reporting directly to me, remember. I see all his reports." Was there something dark behind his eyes? Quynn almost had a haunted expression for a moment, but it went away as quickly as it had appeared.

"Good," Aelwynn said. "And, uh…"

"Spit it out. I have places to be."

"Do you think any of this is *necessary*?"

He watched as the blood drained from Quynn's face.

"Careful what you say," the man said. "The Cundu will not stand for treason."

"But *why* is she the Cundu? Why is she in charge? What in the Twins' names is her grand plan *for*?"

Quynn raised a fist, suddenly, and Aelwynn was aware of a purple cloud enveloping him. Then he felt nothing. Nothing but bliss, but peace, happiness that he was in the position he was in. He was City Director! He was Fallfoiler Captain! He was the man in charge!

He would see Lorelei's plans through to the fullest. That was his life's wish.

"Thank you, sir," he said to Quynn. "Always a pleasure to talk to you. Sorry for taking up your time."

Quynn narrowed his eyes at him. "Always my pleasure, Aelwynn. As you were."

And Aelwynn turned and strode away, heart swelling with pride.

LORELEI ALLOWED a faint smile to touch her lips as she entered her private office, red heels clicking on the hardwood floor. She had never met any man with the stamina Quynn had. It was almost like his soul was somehow concentrated on sex, erotic energy pulsing through his veins. He had his bad boy charms, too, even if he was a bit incompetent at times. There was something mysterious about him—almost ancient—as if he wasn't quite connected to the world at large. She found him fascinating.

It also helped that he was well hung.

She brushed an errant hair away from her face and sat at her desk, biometrics automatically unlocking her computer and turning on the displays across the far wall. The mission timer looked odd, for a second—had it just glitched? Maybe she was imagining it.

"Your operation is falling apart," a voice said, and Lorelei had to stop herself from shrieking.

There was a woman in the room, sitting on the couch that was placed along one wall. Had she been there when Lorelei had walked in? She could have sworn the room had been empty.

With another jolt of surprise, she realized the woman was carrying a small dog.

"Who are you," Lorelei asked, "and how did you get into my office unannounced?"

The woman stood smoothly, still carrying the dog. Lorelei had no idea what breed it was; she didn't much care for the yappy things. She focused on the woman as she stood: curvy, with jet black skin and a revealing dress. A shock of curly black hair surrounded her head, and there was something wrong with her eyes. She couldn't quite describe what.

"Greetings," the woman said. "My name is Magona. I am City Inspector for New Cairo. I had an appointment."

The woman was clearly lying. Why would a City Inspector be here, half way across the world, in the wrong city?

Lorelei narrowed her eyes. "Very good," she said. "Now tell me the truth."

Magona took a step forward, and suddenly she was across

the room and leaning over Lorelei's face. Had she gotten *taller*? And how had she crossed the room that quickly?

"Remember what I told you," she said, her voice low. "The Sending *must* be completed. You still have the coordinates?"

Lorelei felt fear ripple through her. She swallowed, her throat suddenly dry. Memories, murky and dim, struggled to surface. She *knew* this woman, knew her from an impossibly long time ago. But how...where...

"Do. You. Have. The. Coordinates," Magona repeated, dead eyes flashing.

Lorelei finally opened her mouth. "Y-Yes," she croaked. "Everything is proceeding according to the plan."

Magona retreated, finally, smiling. "Glad to hear it. I hope you won't mind, however, if I set up a few...*backup* plans."

Lorelei furrowed her brow. "How would you..." She trailed off, unable to finish the question.

"The Prime Trees," Magona said. "Do you know how they *truly* work?" She leaned forward again, her voice turning to a whisper. "And do you know what happens when one *dies*?"

Lorelei's hand was shaking. "Impossible," she whispered. "Prime Trees can't die."

Magona laughed, then, rich and long. Behind her, the mission timer glitched again. And Lorelei felt the world closing in around her, the darkness of her past finally catching up. She couldn't master this. She couldn't accomplish her plans. She would fail to keep her promise. She would fail everyone.

And trillions of people—thousands of planets— would die.

But she didn't remember *why*. She couldn't think of *how*. The directive that drove her was merely a shadow across her mind, a sliver of an ancient calling that she could not remember or ignore. All she knew was that the device *must* succeed. Fennas Elenathon must do what it had been built to do.

"Cundu?" a voice said, and Lorelei blinked and realized that her executive assistant was standing in the office door. "Did you need anything before I go on break?"

Flustered, Lorelei turned to the mysterious woman.

But Magona—and her dog—were gone.

FORTY-EIGHT

THALANIL HAD BEEN STARING at his monitor for a very long time.

He was at his desk in New San Francisco. The gates were back up, making it easy to come and go between his office in San Francisco and the one in the new city. And while Thalanil had thought he would be more productive at his work office, things had only turned from bad to worse.

The bug he had been tracking was even more powerful than he had thought.

He picked up the phone, waiting until Pharom picked up.

"Thalanil," Pharom said. "You couldn't use Slack for this?"

"I was working with someone from Hardware," Thalanil said, "and we realized we were wrong."

"Wrong about what?"

"This isn't a bug."

The phone was silent for a moment.

"It was put here intentionally," Thalanil continued. "Someone is trying to sabotage the device."

"It can't be."

"It is. And that's not all. The bug isn't just in software—it requires modified hardware in order to make it work. We have old images on file of all the motherboards installed in Gate Control—where the issue lies—and we were able to spot the problem. Whoever this was didn't just modify the software in an extremely hard to detect way. They also managed to tweak one of our old 8088 motherboards with an attack: when the issue triggers, we believe the system will experience mass outages, especially to Mage Comms."

"Mage Comms..." Pharom mused. "That's an interesting system to hit. Why there?"

"Think about it," Thalanil said. "New San Francisco is the only city of the seven that has decentralized fallfoiler mages. It was a security measure, but keeping the city aloft that way requires constant coordination in order to maintain the proper attitude in the air. Without that, the city could start to tilt—or even fall. We believe that once the situation deteriorates, any relatively inexperienced mages could panic, resulting in a total loss of control."

"Let me get this straight," Pharom said. "You're telling me that a *software* bug in a *test harness* interacts with hardware from the 1970s and could result in the *total loss* of City Three?"

"And all hands," Thalanil said. "It's a worst-case, but it could easily happen. We believe that was the intent of the saboteur. Luckily, it's an easy fix."

"Well, shit," Pharom said. "Why didn't you lead with that?"

"Well, maybe not *that* easy. The bug could hit any second, you realize. It's triggered by every tick of the mission timer. Do you have *any* idea how hard it is to find a replacement motherboard from the original IBM PC now?"

"I...guess you have a point."

"But I know where I can get one."

"Goddammit. Are you *trying* to give me a heart attack?"

"I hid it in Sylrantheas."

The line went silent for a second.

"Why in the *fuck* would you have done something like that?"

"It was a long time ago, obviously," Thalanil said. "I was a Cothellon, back then, but certain...elements...of Sylrantheas were still friendly to me."

"Silanar."

"Definitely not him. He'll kill me the next time he sees me."

"Then who?"

"As it turns out," Thalanil said, "my contact is Myriani."

"You need to get it," Pharom said. "And you need to do it now. Does anyone upwards in the chain of command know any of this?"

"Not yet."

"Maybe we can fix it without them finding out. I'll reach out to one of my contacts in Gatesending, see if I can get you down there instantly."

"Sounds good."

The phone clicked off, and Thalanil took a breath before dialing the next number.

"Dillon?" he said when the call connected. "Something just came up. I need you to look after my son for me. Jason can't be unsupervised for long."

JOHN STOOD on one of the high catwalks overlooking Gondor. The city stretched out into the catacombs, strung with glittering lights. Vehicles zipped everywhere along the silver ribbons of the Monorail Transport System, ferrying the humans who had managed to complete their migration here. They needed to pick up the pace.

The end of the world was near.

"I need an update on the infiltration," he said to Warren. "Last I heard, we had a hiccup in City Three."

"Resolved," Warren said. "We're better than the Eldrim at getting in, thankfully." John watched as he inspected his tablet. "I can report that the negative spaces are installed as expected," Warren said, "and we will maintain access. There is a limited window open right now where we can install additional assets."

"By *assets* you mean *people*, yes?"

Warren smiled. "Sorry. That's what you get when you hire out of the intelligence industry. Yes: I mean people. We can get more people aboard, but only if we do it now."

"Draft a list and send it to me within the hour," John said. "I have a sneaky feeling that things might not go as planned." He looked down at Gondor, almost bustling, and sighed. "We may be down here a lot longer than we think."

"Very good, sir," Warren said. "I'll have that list to you right away. And sir?"

John looked at him. "Yes?"

"What you're doing here is good."

"I hope so, Warren," John said. "I truly hope we've thought of everything."

FORTY-NINE

KEYA WAS ALONE IN SYLRANTHEAS.

It was past midnight, and everything was dark except the church and the tavern: the only two places that stayed open around the clock. Why did the village have to go to sleep so early? Keya gritted her teeth. She needed to find the Book of Souls.

But she couldn't just wake everyone up at this hour. Nor could she wait. She needed to find it, and destroy it, and prevent this Sundering magic from occurring.

If only she could figure out where the hell it was.

"You look lost," a voice said.

Keya was proud of herself for not flinching.

Instead she turned calmly, beholding Myriani in the pale moonlight. The woman was stately, statuesque, and other adjectives that Keya didn't feel like figuring out. She'd never *quite* liked the woman, even though she was probably one of the nicest people in Sylrantheas. There was something *off* about her. Keya couldn't quite put her finger on it.

A bat flew by her in the dark, and this time she did flinch.

"You're right," she said, recovering. "I'm lost and confused. Why are you out this late?"

Myriani gave her a small smile. "Sometimes the Twins speak to me. Who can tell when? One must answer the call."

Keya felt her lip curling. The pretentiousness...the arrogance...the—

Myriani burst out laughing.

"I had a beer," she said when she was finished.

Keya looked at her sideways.

"What?" Myriani said. "Am I not allowed to have a beer? Twins know I deserve one with everything that's been going on. This village is in an uproar, even though it doesn't look like it. Twins damn the dignity of elves."

That entire outburst was nowhere *near* what Keya had been expecting. "Are you okay?" she asked.

Myriani swayed a bit. "I'll admit, it's been a while since I've had anything to drink. And the swill that Syndra serves is all bite."

"I'm not a big beer drinker, myself."

"Don't go to Syndra's for that. Go to San Francisco. Or what's left of it." She swayed again. "You okay, sweetie?"

Myriani was clearly drunk.

"I'm fine, Myriani," Keya said. "I'm just—" She didn't know how to put this. "Have you heard of the Book of Souls?"

Myriani went completely still. "Who told you of that, child?"

Keya decided to tell the truth. "I overheard Silanar talking about it. Apparently that's where the Sundering Ritual is described."

"Correct," Myriani said. "The Book of Souls is believed to be the oldest surviving text in the Eldrim language. It was discovered in China, many decades ago, near where the elves are believed to have first arrived on Earth."

"We...*arrived*?"

Myriani looked at her sideways. "No one knows. But some Eldrim archaeologists believe that yes, we arrived here from somewhere else, some eight thousand years before humanity made itself known on this planet. We arrived here with a purpose. With a mission."

"The Sundering."

Myriani's drunkenness had seemingly faded. "Yes."

"I can't actually believe that we are here to eradicate the human species," Keya said. "Are we really even that different? Our *ears* are really the only change."

Myriani clucked her tongue. "You know better than that, girl. Elves are more petite than humans, with higher metabolisms. Yet our bodies carry more strength, thanks to our superior muscular anatomy. We live ten times longer than them. Our eyes are better. Our ears are better. Twins, we can *taste* better than them. We're evolved for more, Keya...and I haven't even gotten to the magic."

"Humans can do magic, too."

Too late, she slapped a hand over her mouth.

She shouldn't have let that slip.

Myriani's eyes narrowed. "That may be," she said, "but by in large the elven race has far more mages per capita than humans do."

"Wait. You *knew* that humans could be mages?"

"It only stands to reason. The Twins hold all in their regard. Not only elves. Not only humans! There are others in their vast purview. Others who may partake in their share of power."

"That is...not at all anything I'd expect to hear in church."

Myriani laughed. "Church is all formula, child. Formula and pretense. Seriously, though, I feel the effects of this beer fading. We should get another."

Keya nodded slowly. "Uh...sure. That would be great." This was already the longest she'd ever spoken to Myriani at a stretch.

Perhaps the Twins had a plan after all.

"TO US!" Keya shouted, raising her glass. Myriani raised hers in return, slamming it into Keya's with a resounding *clink*. Beer sloshed everywhere, and the two women laughed as they took a drink. Keya felt it burn as it went down, but the sensation was welcome.

This was already her third.

Myriani's cat threaded its way along the floor of the tavern, ever curious. It was always at church services, too. Keya had never particularly liked the thing. She glanced at the table on the far end of the room. Kharis and Silanar were there, speaking in hushed tones and occasionally gesticulating. She hadn't expected to see them up at this hour. She took another sip of beer.

"Easy, ladies," Syndra said, swishing up to them in her short skirt. Her breasts were practically bursting out of her top, and Keya couldn't help but smirk at her. "You two should really eat some food."

"You have any?" Keya asked.

"As it happens, I have a whole roast pig out back."

Keya looked into her drink. "Wait...really?"

"No," Syndra said. "Twins. What do you think this is, some kind of ancient fantasy village? I can heat you up a slice of pizza, I think. Or I can turn my fryer back on and do some jalapeno poppers. Either way, you girls should really slow down. I don't think you're cut out for this shit."

"No one knows the Will of the Twins," Myriani said,

taking another swig of beer. Some of it dribbled down her chin. "Do not question the ways of the cosmos!"

"Whatever," Syndra said. "Just don't set the place on fire."

She left, ass cheeks visible beneath her skirt, and Keya couldn't help but wonder why she still didn't have a boyfriend. "I need to find it," she said.

"Find what?"

"The Book of Souls."

"Why?"

"Because—" Keya cut herself short, suddenly scared of what she was about to say. She wanted to *destroy* the Book, but Myriani was the head of the Twins' religion here in Sylrantheas. Surely the Book was considered a sacred object, not to be disturbed. "Because I want to study it," she said. "When I overheard Silanar speaking, he mentioned a particularly difficult translation. I guess it took him a week to figure it out."

"You're a student of Ancient Eldrim?"

"Aren't we all? I mean, we have to learn it just to get around." All their place names and many other proper nouns were still in the language. Keya probably knew a hundred words just off the top of her head.

"I mean more," Myriani said. "I didn't take you for a student of the ancients."

"I'm not," Keya said. "I mean—I wasn't. But lately I've been curious. How did all this come to be? Why are we here? What magic was it that caused all this?"

"I am gladdened by these thoughts," Myriani said, her head swaying. "I always welcome students of history. I myself have long pondered the events that led us here. Perhaps the Book of Souls has some of the information which you seek."

"You know where it is?"

Myriani's eyes were glazed as she took another drink.

"Oh, I've always known," she said. "It's been in the church for a very long time. High up, in the bell tower."

She put the beer down suddenly, hand clapped over her mouth.

"I shouldn't have told you that. Damn this alcohol. Silanar will kill me."

"I just want a glance at it," Keya said. "Silanar won't even know."

Myriani regarded her for a time, but her eyes weren't quite looking at her. "Very well," she said. "I'll turn a blind eye to you tonight, but please be gone by morning." She spread her hands across the table in a gesture of welcome. "The church is open to you, daughter of Sylrantheas."

FIFTY

DILLON ARRIVED at Alan's house, the electronic doorbell letting him in when he arrived. He entered the house to find Jason awake.

The boy had thrown up all over the floor.

"Are you okay?" Dillon asked, rushing over to him. Jason's face looked pale, his breathing ragged.

"Feel...sick," Jason said. His brow was covered in sweat.

"Let me get you some water," Dillon said. "And a bucket. I'll clean this up."

He helped Jason back into bed, bringing him what things he could. The boy didn't look good. Clearly his illness was getting worse.

Dillon wondered how much longer he would last.

A few minutes later, his phone rang. It was Alan. "Dillon," Alan said. "Is everything okay?"

"Jason is getting sicker," Dillon said. "He needs a doctor."

"Rats," Alan said. "I was afraid of that. Listen, I'm tied up with an emergency at work. We need to find his mother."

"Where is she?"

"Somewhere in Marin, I guess. Wait—I think I can find

her. I had her turn on Find My iPhone last week. Hang on." Dillon waited on the line. When Alan returned, his voice sounded shaken. "She's, uh…deep in the Muir Woods, off any known roads or trails. I'll send you her coordinates. I, uh… don't know why she would be out there."

Something was clearly bothering the man. "Do you know why she left?"

"She was searching for some kind of miracle cure for Jason."

"A miracle cure…like magic?"

"You mean elves."

"Just so."

"That's what she said," Alan said. "I didn't want to believe her, but you've been telling me the same thing."

"She found Sylrantheas," Dillon whispered.

"What did you just say?"

Dillon cleared his throat. "Nothing. Never mind. Just send me her coordinates, and I'll take Jason there. Or should I take him to an ER?"

"An ER can't save him," Alan said. "The oncologist said his cancer was incurable."

Dillon gave a low whistle. "The magic of elves might be his only hope."

"Let's hope so." Alan didn't sound so sure. "Let me know how it progresses."

He clicked off, and Dillon went to find Jason in his room. "You okay, bud?" he asked. "We need to get you dressed. We're going on a little trip."

"Right now?" Jason asked. "It's so late. I'm tired."

"I know, bud. But listen—we might have found something that can make you feel better."

"Something like what I did to that building?"

Dillon narrowed his eyes. What was the boy talking

about? "I'm not sure. Maybe. Let's get your shoes and coat. We need to take a drive."

JESSICA WAS BEGINNING to grow impatient. Impatient and sleepy; she could barely keep her eyes open. She checked her watch. It was nearly 3 AM. What was taking Keya so damn long?

Half an hour later, the girl finally appeared.

"Sorry," Keya said, stumbling a little. Was she *drunk*? Maybe so, but that wasn't the strangest thing about the situation.

"Keya," Jessica said. "Why are you wearing a *sword*?"

Keya glanced down at her waist, where a sword and scabbard were swinging. "Oh," she said, blinking. "I forgot to take this thing off. Myriani bet me I couldn't take the tips off three candles without toppling them. Bindfolded. After three beers."

"I don't even know where to start with that. You know how to use a sword?"

"Of course," Keya said, giving a little curtsy. "All elves learn to use them. Swords, bows and arrows, knives, hand-to-hand fighting, everything."

"Why?"

Keya shrugged. "Beats me. We don't graduate until we're fifty years old—maybe they just want to make sure we get a complete training."

Jessica eyed the sword. "Just try not to poke me with that thing."

"Of course not."

"So what happened? Did you figure out where the Book is?"

"As it just so happens, I did. Myriani found me. She told me that Silanar hid the book somewhere in the church. In the bell tower, to be precise."

"She wasn't more specific than that?"

"No. But she did grant us access to the church for the rest of the night. She wants us gone by morning."

"Didn't you say the church was open to everyone?"

"It is, but people aren't supposed to wander around the offices and stuff. Myriani as good as said we could."

"Okay then," Jessica said. "What are we waiting for?"

"Right this way," Keya said, and she skipped off into the forest, sword swinging.

FIFTY-ONE

THE CHURCH WAS AN IMPOSING STRUCTURE, far taller than Jessica had expected it to be. It towered over the village, rising what had to be ten full stories above the ground. The bell tower was beautiful, tall and slender, a spire reaching toward the sky. Yet the place was dwarfed by the immense redwood trees that surrounded it. Even here, Mother Nature reigned supreme.

The elves probably liked it that way.

"Let's go," Keya whispered, leading the way. They stepped between two creaking wooden doors, Jessica marveling at the thickness and the craftsmanship. She hadn't seen this much wood in one place in a long time—humans favored steel and concrete construction, at least in the city. And it smelled of wood, too, the fragrance of good oak or pine or whatever it was.

The sanctuary beyond was breathtaking.

It resembled a Catholic church. The main room was at least four stories tall and lined with wooden pews. The area overhead was crisscrossed with narrow beams of wood, from which hung various electric lights and banners and other decorations. The far end of the room was filled with a statue of sorts, made of wood, depicting two trees twisted together. It reminded her of the traditional altar in a Catholic church, only this one was depicting trees. The lights overhead were soft and almost amber, filling the room with warmth.

Everything was *beautiful*.

"Come on," Keya said, leading the way to the right. No one was in the church at this hour. Their visit would be undisturbed.

Keya took them to a door, and through it to a stairway. This led to a narrow corridor and three more flights of stairs, until finally they were stopped by another tiny door.

Which was locked.

"Twins," Keya cursed. "This is the way to the bell tower. Myriani said we could get in."

"Did she?" Jessica asked. "Or did she say we could get into the *church*."

Keya frowned. "I guess the latter," she said. "Wait a minute. What kind of Twins-damned lock *is* this, anyway?"

She pointed at a rather large device that was affixed to the door, near the handle. It was rectangular, filled with buttons.

On each button was a tree.

"Prime Trees," Keya breathed. "The Fourteen. What in the hell *is* this?"

"It's a combination lock," Jessica said. "Duh."

Keya gave her a quick glare. "Okay. But what is the combination?"

"This is your village," Jessica said. "It's your way of life. What do you think it could be?"

"The combinations are endless. How am I supposed to know?"

"Isn't there any kind of order to this stuff? Don't those trees represent magic to you?"

"I—well—yes. The Fourteen are where all magic lies. They are divided into pairs."

"Okay. That gives us a start."

"But that would be too easy."

"Who said it had to be hard?"

"If the woodpairs are together, that still leaves us with seven different pairs. What order might they be in?"

"I don't know," Jessica said. "Isn't there anything you can think of that designates an order?"

QUYNN PACED IN HIS ROOM, finally empty now that Lorelei had left. The Tree Ring Staff was secure in its case, gleaming beneath the lights. It held immeasurable power, and yet somehow Quynn still felt powerless.

Maybe because he wasn't the one in charge.

But he couldn't begrudge Lorelei the position. She was strong. Capable. She was kind of a bitch, when it came right down to it, but he was okay with that. He liked her.

She had given him the Tree Ring Staff.

He approached it, opening the case and touching the gleaming wood. Ash. Maple. Birch. Poplar. Elm. Oak. With Willow in between. The seven deciduous woods, each representing a different power.

Unfortunately, Quynn could only access one of them.

"THERE *WAS* SOMETHING," Keya said. Jessica was tapping her foot impatiently. Her son was dying, and here they were, stuck behind some kind of fantasy puzzle. "We were taught about it in school. An ancient artifact called the Tree Ring Staff, lost to us for centuries."

"Get to the point," Jessica said.

"No need to get snippy with me," Keya said.

"Sorry. What about this Staff?"

"It has all seven woods, in a specific order. I wonder if that could be it..."

"Do you remember the order?"

"Sure," Keya said. "There's even a nursery rhyme about it:

> *"Ash to bring the coldest storm*
> *Maple for the eyes forlorn*
> *Birch for when the soul is shorn*
> *And Willow in between*
> *Poplar in the archer's phase*
> *Elm that fills the air with praise*
> *Oak to bring the arm true grace*
> *For when the foe is seen"*

"That's a hell of a rhyme," Jessica said. "Let's try it."

Keya set to it excitedly, tapping the Trees in succession.

"You can recognize them from their picture alone?" Jessica asked.

"Of course. All elves can."

"Crazy. You guys must learn so much. Fifty years of school? That's insane."

"Well, we don't start until we're three."

"*Three*? Humans don't start until age five."

Keya shrugged. "I guess we have a lot to learn." She kept clicking Trees. "I'm doing each woodpair in order, starting with deciduous and then doing the coniferous Tree. I'm leaving Willow for last, because...well..." She looked askance as Jessica.

"What?"

"Willow is the Primal Way. This is the wood that powers the Sundering."

"I...see." She didn't see. But she needed to get to this Book, no matter what it took. She wasn't going to ask unnecessary questions.

"Here we go!" Keya said, clicking the last button into place.

There was a loud *snap*, and a grinding sound, and suddenly the door sprung open.

"We're in!" Keya said, sword bouncing as she did a little dance.

"Let's go," Jessica said, sweeping by her.

Into the strangest room she'd ever seen.

FIFTY-TWO

"SO, WHAT'S IT FOR?" Kharis asked. Myriani and Keya had come and gone, and now Kharis and Orym were once again alone in Syndra's tavern. Kharis yawned—it was getting incredibly late.

"What's *what* for?" Orym said.

"The Cothellon. The discoveries. What is it that you do for them, anyway?"

"I'm the Scientist General," Orym said. "It's less of a lofty title than you might think. I'm like three levels down in the reporting chain."

"Three levels down from the top is pretty good," Kharis observed. "But what do you *do*?"

"You're right about the atrocities," Orym said. "Not only am I plotting them, my team *invented* them."

"So it *is* true," Kharis breathed.

"What is?"

"That your...people...are plotting something."

"Oh, yes," Orym said. "Something worse—far worse—than you can probably even imagine."

"I can imagine a lot."

"Not this. That's why I had to come to you. I am going to turn myself in to the Eldrim World Council, tomorrow morning. But I wanted you to be the first to know."

"Why now? Why turn yourself in after all this time? How long has it been, anyway?"

"I was inducted in 1897."

Kharis gave a low whistle. "We had just Chosen," he said. "We were just kids."

Orym nodded silently. "They're going to destroy the entire planet," he said.

"So are we."

"Not like that. Not limited to humans. I mean *the entire planet*. Destroyed. Boom."

"Explain," Kharis said. This was sounding quite far fetched, even for Orym.

"It's a device," Orym said. "A massive device in the sky, made up of seven replica cities. We built them all—it took hundreds of years—and we loaded them up with the technology we needed. Once we've completed the Ascension, Fennas Elenathon will be ready to turn on."

Kharis' head was whirling. "This is crazy. Seven *cities*? Why in the Twins' name would you do that? What is it all *for*?"

"It's the same thing the Eldrim are trying to solve," Orym said. "How to fix the planet. With humans on the edge of destroying the whole damn thing, the Cothellon are seeking a solution. A much different one. We're not trying to *fix* the planet—we're trying to *escape* it."

Kharis was silent for a moment, absently taking a sip of beer. "Escape," he said. "Like in a spaceship?"

"We tried that. We tried very hard. Our space program was at the forefront of the world, although no government ever knew that. But, like those governments, we just couldn't get the technology off the ground. So to speak."

Kharis didn't crack a smile. "You can't get to outer space."

"Well, we can, but it takes too long. We can't break light speed, or even get close to it. And terraforming is completely out of the question—it's impossible. So to identify a livable planet, and to actually get there...let's just say Cothellon leadership is in too much of a hurry."

"But that's the only way off the planet. How else can you escape?"

Just then, Syndra sidled up. "We need something stronger than beer for this," Orym said. "I'll take a whiskey. Bourbon, if you have it."

"I'll have the same," Kharis said. He didn't even have the presence of mind to flirt.

Syndra left, giving him an odd look, but Kharis ignored her. How had it come to this? One way or another, the elves were going to do a lot of damage to Earth. After living in harmony with the planet for so long, the elves were about to become its mortal enemy—either to the people living on it, or to its very existence. The elves would be killers, plain and simple.

It was not what they had come here to do.

"The device," Orym said, "creates a gate. A kind of portal, that transports matter from one place to another. The device is capable of creating a gate large enough for the whole planet."

Kharis whistled again. "You can't get to another solar system using a spaceship, so you *move the planet* there instead. Wow."

Orym nodded.

"But that raises all kinds of questions," Kharis said. "Like, how can you just insert a new planet into an existing solar system? How can you ensure this...gate...will put Earth at the correct distance from the new star? You could roast or freeze everything instantly. And for that matter, what about kinetic energy? Wouldn't the rotational velocity of the planet interfere with the transference? It could cause massive tectonic disturbance on an unprecedented level! What about the magnetic field? The atmosphere? The ozone layer? What about other planets in the system? None of this can *possibly* work."

Orym smiled. "Maybe you should have been a scientist and not a Hunter."

Kharis took a deep breath. "You've thought this through, haven't you."

"You don't get to be Scientist General without thinking it through."

"But then—"

Syndra arrived, bringing their bourbons. The men paused for a moment, taking a drink. Kharis wanted to say something to Syndra, but he couldn't figure out what.

Eventually she left.

"But then," Kharis continued, grimacing from his first taste of whiskey, "why do you say the planet will be destroyed? Why are you outing yourself now?"

"Simple," Orym said. "I discovered a fatal flaw in our simulations. A miscalculation. An error. You see, the device taps into the Earth's core to utilize its immense amount of energy. That's the only way to create a gate big enough. But the mistake...the core will not be stable. Adjusted simulations show it will implode catastrophically into a black hole. It will annihilate the planet before anyone can get off."

"Fuck," Kharis said.

"My thoughts exactly."

FIFTY-THREE
25 YEARS AGO

THE VOICE CRACKLED on the other end of the secure line. "Report," it said. Orym smiled to himself—Quynn had never been much for small talk.

"We think we have something," Orym said into the mouthpiece. Why the Cothellon insisted on using outdated military-grade technology for communication was beyond him. They'd had cellular technology a decade before the general public—why not at least use that instead of dedicated lines?

"By all means," Quynn said on the other end, "please elaborate." The sarcasm in his tone was obvious even over their shitty connection.

"First thing," Orym said, "is we were able to stabilize the gate for much longer than before."

"How long is that?"

"Indefinitely, as far as we can tell. The gate has been up for a year, and it's still stable. As long as the fusion reactor can maintain its power output—which is a very, very long time—the gate should remain stable."

"But it's still too small for much use beyond transporting a few humans at a time."

"Correct, although having a stable gate of that size is still very useful. But you're right—the power ceiling affecting gate size and distance has been an insurmountable problem. Until today."

"You enjoy this, don't you?" Quynn asked.

"Enjoy what?"

"Drawing this out. Increasing the drama."

"Yes, sir. Sorry, sir." He'd been working on this technology for almost sixty years—he deserved *some* amount of drama. But Quynn had never been much for that kind of thing. "We have an idea—a theory, really," he continued. "The problem with the theory is it can't be tested in prototype form. The technology doesn't scale linearly—we have to build the whole thing to find out if it works."

"And what is this theory of yours?"

"In order to move past the power boundary, we need to tap into another source of energy. Something we can't just generate on our own."

"The sun?"

"We thought of that, but it's much too far away. We need something closer to home."

"What, then?"

"The planet's core." Orym let that dangle for a minute before continuing. "We believe we can build a device on the surface of the planet, acting as a director of energy. We would bore a hole nearly to the core, and when the moment is right, breach the core and funnel the energy to our device."

"To the gate device?"

"Just so. The math here is a little tricky, obviously. The device would need to be a precise distance from the core in order for this to work."

"You've run simulations, I assume?"

"Yes, of course, sir. The simulations are ongoing, but we believe we've nailed down the parameters. We've reached the point where we need to actually build the thing in order to know more. But sir, there's one problem."

"There's always one problem, isn't there?"

"Yes, sir."

"Well, spit it out, man!"

"Remember just now how I said the device would need to be a precise distance from the core?"

"Of course I remember, Orym, I'm not an idiot."

"Sorry, sir. Well, that distance ends up being about 3000 feet above sea level."

There was a slight pause on the other end. "So just build it on a mountain."

"We could, sir, but the additional effort of boring that far through the ground would be uneconomical. We need to choose an area where the surface is weak and low. Ideally between two tectonic plates."

"How about the middle of the ocean? You'll get much closer to the planet that way."

"We also thought of that, sir, but it presents us with a whole new set of problems. How to get the energy through the water, for example, without vaporizing it all. And we'd still need the device to be around 3000 feet above sea level."

"We're not trying to *destroy* the planet, goddammit."

"I know, sir."

"At least not until we've escaped it properly."

"Yes, sir."

"So where are you suggesting we do all of this?"

"We have researched several sites across the globe, and we've selected a place near San Francisco."

"The San Andreas Fault," Quynn mused. "I see."

"But that leaves the problem of the device's elevation."

"You're proposing—what—some kind of sky machine?"

"Closer to a sky city," Orym said. "We've calculated the numbers, and in order to make a gate big enough for the entire planet, the device would need to be very, very big. Monstrously big."

Quynn was silent, so Orym continued.

"We propose building the device in seven pieces. Put the pieces over seven population centers all over the planet. Cloak them with forcefinders, levitate them with fallfoilers. When the time is right, combine the pieces and turn it on."

"That's a goddamn *lot* of mages," Quynn said. "Just where in the hell do you think we can get that many?"

"We've been testing human subjects, sir," Orym said.

"Oh." The line went silent for a long time. Then: "I see. Continue."

"I propose we build the cities as analogues to the cities they are hovering over. They will need to be extremely big, big enough to house and feed a large population of humans."

"If we go this route—and that's a very big *if*—why not just outright enslave the humans? Chain them up?"

"The mages will be enslaved," Orym said. This was the part of the plan that made him the most squeamish—he steeled himself to continue. "But in order to fabricate the Darkprime Trees, we need the humans to be in peak physical condition, or as near to it as possible. Frankly, it's easier to make them think they're living in a city, happy with their way of life."

"You're quite the creative thinker, aren't you?" Quynn said.

That was putting it mildly.

"My team has been working on this night and day for years," Orym said. "It's not all me."

Might as well be nice about it.

"Modesty is not becoming on you," Quynn said. "You should know we've been hearing rumblings in the Eldrim leadership recently. Something big is coming. We don't know when, and we don't know what, but it may affect our plans. We will need to hedge our bets as much as possible."

"Understood, sir."

"Just how long will this project take to execute?"

"About twenty-five years, sir."

"*Twenty-five years*? Jesus, man. How could it possibly take that long?"

"I have a report prepared. I'll send it over."

"No," Quynn said, sighing into the radio. "I don't want to read your damn *report*. I'll bring this to the Council."

"Thank you, sir."

"One more question. *Why* would the humans stay in our floating cities? If you don't want to force them, how will you convince them to go up there to begin with?"

"We'll have to give them a very good reason, sir."

FIFTY-FOUR
PRESENT DAY

SILANAR WOKE IN A COLD SWEAT, looking around the dark room blearily. What in the Twins' name had startled him so much?

His cell phone rang.

He jumped, grabbing it before Melenora could wake up. The phone had been ringing repeatedly, he saw. He picked it up.

"Bellas."

"Silanar. Thank the Twins, you're awake. Sir, the World Council is arriving. *Now*."

Silanar blinked, checking the clock. It was 4 AM. "What in the hell…"

"You invoked Code One, sir. So the Council used their supersonic jets to get here."

"Christ," Silanar swore, the human curse feeling awkward on his tongue. "I'd forgotten about that. It's been so long."

"They're arriving here. Now, and for the next few hours. Silanar, we have to put them somewhere. We have to get ready. We have to prepare."

"Okay, okay, I'm getting up."

Things were moving faster than he'd expected.

The World Council was upon them.

ORYM COULD TELL, in that moment, that he'd forever lost his friend. Kharis was sitting silently, sullenly, sipping his bourbon in the near-dark of the tavern.

"We're closing up," Syndra said. "It's 4 AM."

"Sorry, Syndra," Orym said. "We didn't mean to stay this long."

"You're the first customers I've had this late in quite some time," Syndra said. "Not quite sure why I keep the place open as long as I do." She looked around the empty restaurant. "Maybe I'm just lonely."

Kharis roused himself then, Orym saw. He put his bourbon down, looking like he'd seen a ghost. And he stood, turning to Syndra and grabbing her hand. "Syndra," he said. "This world is coming to an end."

If Syndra was surprised, she didn't show it. "And?"

Orym noticed that she didn't pull her hand away.

"I want to spend my last remaining moments with you," Kharis continued. "I really...uh...like you."

Syndra burst out laughing. "You *like* me? Twins, Kharis, you've been ogling me like a school boy for *two years*. I've been wondering when you'd ask me out."

"I. Uh. That is, will you?"

"Will I what, Kharis?"

"Will you go out with me? Please?"

"Begging doesn't look good on you, Kharis." She dropped her hand from his. "But that bow and arrow does. Meet me tomorrow, at the range. And bring your A game, buddy. I want a real competition."

"Um. I'm the archery *teacher*," Kharis said. Orym couldn't help but crack a smile as the scene unfolded. "I'm the bladedancer Mentor."

"Then you'll put up a good fight," Syndra said. "See you at ten."

She turned, skirt swishing away. Then she turned back, eyes flashing, and landed a quick kiss on Kharis' lips.

Seconds later, she was gone.

"Nicely handled," Orym said, taking another sip of the fiery bourbon.

"Uh...thanks," Kharis said. "Twins, she's pretty."

"You should marry her while you have the chance."

Kharis turned to look at the woman, who was wiping something behind the bar. "Maybe I will," he said. "Maybe I fucking *will*."

DUNEDAR PULLED the soldering gun away, taking a step back to admire his handiwork. The device was huge, taking up the entire room. Most of it was made up of fuel tanks he'd smuggled in from various parts of Planner Central. The middle of it was the C-4 he'd brought in, surrounded by various electronics. The whole thing was wired to a cellular trigger with a hardwired failsafe switch. If he had to, he'd trigger the thing himself.

The bomb was done.

And it was *beautiful*.

He hoped it would be enough. He would only have one chance, one shot to take this entire city down. He didn't know what it was for, why the Cothellon had built it. He just knew what his superiors—and his instincts—told him.

Nothing good would come from it.

He heard a sudden scrabbling sound from outside the door and he tensed, reaching for his gun. Yes, he had a gun.

He may be elven, but that didn't mean he only used a sword.

He reached for his sword, too.

The door opened, revealing the face of a Cothellon security guard. "Who are—"

Dunedar stabbed him in the throat.

Sometimes guns were just too noisy.

The guard gurgled, grabbing at his neck, then settled to the ground in a heap of uniform and blood. Dunedar pulled him into the room, closing the door behind them. There was barely enough space for the two elves and the bomb. He hoped no one else had found this place.

That was when the pounding on the door resumed.

LORELEI SAT AT HER DESK, sipping a cup of coffee. It was something like four in the morning, and the exertions with Quynn had tired her out. Still, she had more work to do. Things were beginning to accelerate.

"Grathgor," she said, picking up her phone. "What news?"

"Cundu," Grathgor said on the other end. "Fennas Elenathon is online. We're ready to go whenever you say the word."

"Good," Lorelei said. "The Eldrim activated a Code One, and I can see them arriving in Sylrantheas now. I'll give the Council a few more hours to sleep, but we'll need to invoke a Small Council meeting early this morning."

"Aye, sir," Grathgor said. "The device is ready. Let's hope the others are."

"Let us hope," Lorelei said. "We cannot miss this chance. The Ascension must start today."

The door to her office burst open suddenly, and Droth stepped in. Her spymaster looked tired, dark bags underneath his eyes. Like her, he'd clearly been up all night. "We have a problem," he said. "It's New Tokyo."

Lorelei hung up the phone. "Tell me."

JOHN WATCHED the latest train rolling in from the outside, carrying humans. Only the best of the best had been elected to come here, to survive the destruction of mankind. They had taken great care to select the best of every discipline: scientists, engineers, researchers, construction workers, as well as everyone else that was needed for a functioning city. Sanitation workers. Line cooks. Safety inspectors. Government officials. Teachers. Even athletes. All were represented here, culled from the human race by hand.

It *should* have been random. John should have been fair about it. But he knew the threat they were facing demanded more.

He had a feeling they might need to survive for a very long time.

"John," Warren said, arriving just then. "Thought I'd find you here."

"I wanted to ask you about the Under," John said, turning to the man. Warren was as close a friend as he could have now. As close as he had ever had.

"All ready," Warren said. "And the additional assets you requested are being added as we speak. If this goes as long as you suspect, we'll be able to keep injecting new tech into the negative spaces."

"The elves have no idea we've done this, correct?"

"Not a clue," Warren said. "The Under is largely ignored by the higher-ups. Not unlike how it is in the cities here."

"Powerful people always underestimate the working class," John said. "Ever has it been so. May it be their undoing. In any case, I feel our window drawing to a close. My bug in Lorelei's office says she's announcing the Ascension in a few hours."

"The Eldrim's World Council is arriving, too. I expect they'll make a decision soon."

"Then these last few arrivals will be our last."

"Aye," Warren said. "We'll need to close up Gondor in the morning."

"May whatever gods exist in this world have mercy on our souls," John said. "Lord knows the elves won't."

FIFTY-FIVE

JESSICA FOUND herself in a rotating wooden room. There were eight doors leading in every direction, but the destinations kept changing. She could feel the floor moving beneath her feet, grinding as it slowly spun. The doors were open, leading to passageways that shifted as she watched. Some led to stairs. Others to halls. Still others opened to rooms, murky and dark.

"What in the hell *is* this place?" Jessica asked.

Keya was standing next to her. "No idea," she said. "Perhaps Myriani had it built."

"But why? What is it all *for*?"

"Maybe to confuse would-be thieves."

"Like us. But didn't Myriani say we could have free reign of the church tonight?"

"She didn't say anything about getting us through whatever puzzles might await."

"Why are there puzzles in a *church*?"

"I have no idea. Myriani has always been weird."

"What do we do?"

Just then, the room stopped spinning.

And all the doorways led to stairs.

"That's...odd," Jessica said. "I could have sworn these weren't all stairs before. Which way do we go?"

"Maybe we should split up," Keya said. "I have your cell number. Call if you find something, and I will, too."

"Okay," Jessica said, frowning. She wasn't sure she liked this situation. Here she was in the center of an elven village, in the building that marked the height of their magical power, with puzzles and strange spinning rooms blocking their progress.

No. She didn't like it one bit.

THALANIL STEPPED through the swirling gate. He felt the familiar icy feeling washing over him as he passed the threshold, and for a brief moment he was disoriented. Where was he? What had he been doing? There were trees around him, huge trees, and a church, and—

It all rushed back to him in an instant. The motherboard. The secret stash. The bug that might ruin the Ascension before it could even begin.

The gate had nearly stolen his memories away.

This was always the case with gatesending—momentary disorientation, confusion, loss of memory. But it always came back. His memories always returned.

At least they had so far.

Now he had a mission to complete. He had a civilization to save. He stepped forward, toward the church, hoping Jessica wasn't there.

DILLON DROVE his beater through the Muir Woods, Jason sleeping fitfully in the front seat next to him. The old Honda Civic barely ran anymore, but Dillon couldn't afford anything else.

You'd think a car mechanic would drive a better car.

But Dillon had more important things to worry about. Things like why his father was suddenly back, and what exactly the Ascension was.

More important things like how anyone would survive what was about to come.

As the car bumped and rumbled through the redwood forest, he wondered if bringing Jason here had really been a good idea.

KEYA STEPPED through the first door she could make it through on her left, barely making it before the room started spinning again. The whole thing was insane—what could possibly possess the elves to build something like this? And *how*?

Clearly there was more going on in this church than initially met the eye.

The room she found herself in was a simple cube, made of wood, with no windows, no pictures on the walls, nothing but a single electric light in the ceiling.

She had reached a dead end.

She turned back, but the door had already disappeared behind her.

JESSICA JUMPED through the first door on her left, feeling a breeze as the wooden doorframe swept by her, the room resuming its spin. This place was so *weird*. Why would elves build something like this? Maybe she shouldn't question what she didn't understand.

She found herself standing on a small catwalk high up in the air, overlooking the church sanctuary. The catwalk ran around the sanctuary in a square, ringing the walls. Narrow beams of dark wood jutted out from it at intervals, criss-crossing the room about fifteen feet below the ceiling. Jessica was high—at least forty feet, she estimated—and there were no rails to keep her from falling. She swallowed nervously.

She had to keep going.

But keep going to *where*? She didn't know this church. She had no idea where anything would be hidden. She was out of her element, here. Maybe she shouldn't have suggested splitting up.

She turned, intending to head back to the spinning room, but the doorway had already disappeared.

"Shit," she whispered. Was she trapped up here? Would the door reappear? Everything about this place was strange.

She had no choice.

She took a step to the right, following the catwalk around the room. There was some kind of chest ahead, made of wood. It looked like those old offering chests she'd seen in catholic churches, like in one of those Robin Hood movies. It was probably empty, but it would definitely be a great place to hide a book.

She headed that way.

SILANAR COULDN'T GET BACK to sleep. It was two hours until dawn, and emissaries from Eldrim communities all over the world were arriving in Sylrantheas as he lay in bed. Others were handling it, theoretically. They had decided that he needed to get more sleep in order to handle the delicate negotiations to come.

But Silanar couldn't sleep.

So he got out of bed, careful not to disturb Melenora. She looked so peaceful, lying there, long, brown hair strewn out around her on the pillow. He wouldn't let anything happen to her, no matter what was to come.

He would keep her safe.

He dressed quietly, stepping outside into the brisk forest air. Sylrantheas was deathly quiet in the early morning, everyone still in their beds. Syndra's was lit, but he knew the woman was likely closing things up for the night. The only other source of light came from the west, high up in the forest.

The church's tower was alive with whirling lights.

"What in the Twins'..." Silanar started, before setting out in that direction.

Something very strange was going on.

THERE WAS a sword leaning against the wall, Jessica noticed somewhat incongruously. Why would that be there? This church was a very strange place.

She passed the sword, approaching the wooden coffer, careful not to accidentally step off the edge. It was quite a fall to the sanctuary below. One she didn't think she would survive.

She bent to inspect the coffer. It was a beautiful wooden chest, rendered with ornate leaves and a textured surface much like bark. The elves just *loved* trees, it seemed. They couldn't get enough of them. But what was this coffer for?

There was only one way to find out.

She lifted the lid.

It opened easily, no locks evident. And when she saw what was inside, she couldn't help but quirk an eyebrow in confusion. Perhaps she should have been expecting this. Elves *did* love trees, after all.

The box was completely filled with pieces of wood.

It was weird wood, though. It glinted strangely in the dim light from the overhead lamps, reflecting it as metal would. The stuff looked a lot like that door frame Jason had grabbed.

That was when Jessica realized what this was.

She stuffed handfuls of it in her pockets, acting on impulse, not sure if there would be any use for it. Perhaps she had been brought here for a reason. Perhaps she had been destined to find this thing. She closed the coffer and stood, just as the doorway flashed back into existence.

Jessica's pockets were filled with darkprime wood.

FIFTY-SIX

KEYA CONTEMPLATED CALLING JESSICA. But what could the human woman do? She was more out of place here than Keya was. What in the Twins' names had caused someone to build a place like this? Was it magic? She didn't know of any magic that would make doors *disappear*.

The door suddenly appeared.

Keya darted through it, wasting no time, emerging back into the spinning room. The lights were dazzling in here, different colors moving along with the doors. It was all so extravagant, so unlike Eldrim society.

Maybe Myriani had had something to do with it.

The Book of Souls. It was here, somewhere. Couldn't Myriani have given her a hint? This whole thing was a bit ridiculous. But she didn't have a choice. She didn't have much time. She had to choose a door.

She picked the one in the center, leaping through it before it disappeared.

DILLON'S HONDA crunched to a halt at the outskirts of Sylrantheas. It was the dead of night, and nobody was awake. But was that *light* he saw, shining high up in the trees? That was strange. He wondered what was going on.

"Come on," he said to Jason. "We need to find your mother."

KEYA WAS IN A ROOM. A tiny room, bounded once again by wood. She felt a rumbling beneath her, heard something like an engine far above. What in the hell was going on?

Then another door opened, and she had no choice but to step through.

And almost instantly fell to her death.

"What the fuck—" she whispered, grabbing a wooden beam and gazing at the dizzying fall before her.

She was near the top of the bell tower.

She could see all the way down to the sanctuary from up here, more than a hundred feet below. The bell tower was positioned above the statue of the Twins, sharp branches pointed upward toward the sky. She imagined what a fall from here would be like, shuddering.

She was not afraid of falling.

She remembered this place, in her mind's eye. She remembered it from the stories she'd been told.

This was where her mom had fallen.

This was where her mom had died.

It had been an accident. And now, seeing this place, she could easily see why. One slip, and she would fall, too.

But she was not afraid.

She turned, looking up at the bell ten feet above her. It had not been used in decades, she knew. Now it was more for decoration than anything else. A rope had used to run from it to a room far below, where a bellringer would be positioned. But not these days. The church itself was dwindling. Faith in the Twins was in decline.

Keya wondered if that was good.

There was a coffer, just ahead of her on the floor. A wooden chest, carved in beatiful leaves, with no lock or any obvious means of keeping it closed. Was there money inside? Was there something else?

There was only one way to find out.

She bent, and opened the box.

And beheld the most beautiful sight she had ever seen.

It was a book, bound in dark wood, with gilded letters on the face of it in Ancient Eldrim. "The Book of Souls," it read in the old language.

That had been easy.

THE DOOR APPEARED ONCE AGAIN in front of Jessica, and she leapt through it, back into the spinning room. She tried to ignore it, focusing instead on where she wanted to go next.

One door in particular looked promising.

So she jumped through it, finding herself in a tiny wooden box. The box rumbled and shook, and a few seconds later another door opened.

Keya was standing in front of her.

She was holding a massive Book.

"That was easy," Jessica said, and Keya let out a tinkling laugh.

THALANIL TOOK the stairs two at a time, breath already coming heavy in his chest. He really should work out more, dammit. This programmer life wasn't good for him.

Eventually he reached the Chamber. It was a stupid name for a clever contraption, one that he and Myriani had worked on almost a hundred years ago. Eight doors spun around a central axis, revealing new destinations as they moved. The lights overhead were in different colors: white and yellow and green and purple, and they were spinning, too. The whole thing was a dazzling display of hubris and special effects.

Thalanil bent down and turned it off.

The control surface was hidden cleverly in the floor. He was pretty sure only he and Myriani knew how the whole thing actually worked: it was a neat combination of technology and magic, leveraging an artifact Myriani had found. It was a mistweaver artifact—incredibly rare and powerful— that could provide illusions on command. Add to that some elevators and some lighting, and the whole place functioned as essentially a trap.

If you didn't know what you were doing here, it was very easy to die.

The doors spun to a stop as he turned the Chamber off, settling into stable positions. The mistweaver illusions dissipated, and the room became nothing more than a set of gears and metal frames, built to spin endlessly. It was extravagant, but Myriani had always been a little weird. And it had been a fun project to work on, honing his skills.

Now, he had another mission entirely.

He set off down the doorway to the right, hunting for his stash of ancient electronics.

SILANAR STEPPED INTO THE CHURCH, wondering what in the Twins' names was going on. Had someone installed a lighting system in the bell tower? Or was it some kind of illusion magic at work? His mother had always been a strange one. Perhaps this had been her idea.

There was no one in the sanctuary. He strode into the center, hearing scrabbling noises overhead, hushed voices. Was there someone in the bell tower?

KEYA HELD the Book as Jessica emerged. The door behind her settled into place, no longer moving, the lights no longer flashing. She could clearly see an elevator beyond the door, which explained how they'd gotten up here. Everything about this was incredibly strange.

"Is that it?" Jessica asked.

Keya nodded. "The Book of Souls. It was pretty easy to find."

"If you don't count that ridiculous spinning room." The woman took another step. "What's inside?"

"I haven't looked yet."

"Perhaps we can look together."

They sat beside each other on the platform, legs dangling out over the edge much as they had on the tree branch before. Only this drop was *much* further than the tree had been. This drop would definitely kill them.

"It's all in a weird language," Jessica said, flipping through the pages as Keya held it. "The letters are normal, but the words..."

"It's Ancient Eldrim," Keya said. "I can read it, but very slowly, and only some of it. But wait. What's this?"

Pieces of white paper were folded in between many of the pages. Keya pulled one out, unfolding it. "English. Is this…"

"…a translation?" Jessica finished.

"I think it is."

"That will certainly make things easier."

"It's in Silanar's handwriting," Keya said. "I recognize it from his Orders of Law. He must have written down the translation so he could refer to it later, without damaging the Book."

"Makes sense."

"We're looking for the magic."

"Yes. Does it say anything?"

Keya kept turning pages, referencing the translation when she couldn't immediately identify the headings. "Here it is," she said. "Advanced Primewood Use." They were about half way through the book. She pulled the translation out, reading.

Motion caught her eye, far below. Was that *Silanar*, in the church with them? Twins. He was probably here for the book.

She couldn't let him have it.

She had to save the human race.

FIFTY-SEVEN

THALANIL'S STASH was right where he had left it: in a hidden cubby just off the east catwalk above the sanctuary. The old 8086 motherboard was still intact, dust-free and gleaming.

He hoped that this would work.

He paused for a moment before picking it up. He could just leave it there, after all. He could never return, never fix the issue he had found. And the Ascension would fail. The cities would fall, or at least one of them would. Lorelei's plan would not come to fruition.

The human race would not be subjugated.

Millions would not be displaced.

Elves would not reign supreme.

It was all in his hands.

But it was his job. And this was one *heck* of a bug. If he solved it—if he actually saved the Ascension from demise—he would definitely be promoted. He would never be looked down on again. He would go on to be known as the elf who had fixed the Cothellon's plan. All he had to do was finish what he'd started.

He picked up the motherboard.

Now he needed to get back to the gate, back to Newfris so he could replace the faulty part. But something caught his attention, first. Something overhead.

He thought he heard his wife's voice.

JESSICA STRUGGLED to read the translation over Keya's shoulder. The paper was shaking, making it hard to do. Keya's attention was elsewhere.

Certain additional behaviors can be unlocked via the lower layers. Orientation, vibration frequency, and distance all play a part. In order to access this portion of the power spectrum, the user must be attuned to the proper—

The paper was shaking too much for her to continue.

"We need to get back home," Jessica said. "We need to try this magic on Jason."

This could do it. This could actually save him. She didn't know much about elven magic, and she'd only read the first paragraph, but the methods described in this Book sounded like they could actually work. She'd *felt* the block, when she'd tried to heal him. This would let her get through it. All she had to do was read the rest, and then get back to her son.

Keya closed the Book, her face clouded. "We can't."

"What?" Jessica was confused.

"I can't let you take this."

"Why? Just let me read the rest of it. I can heal him, then."

"No."

Jessica felt anger surging through her veins. "What is *wrong* with you?" she asked. "I thought you wanted to help."

But Keya's eyes were filled with tears. "This Book contains

the Sundering ritual," she said. "It will kill all of mankind. We need to destroy it. We can't let humanity die."

Jessica felt the blood rush out of her all at once. "Oh," she said. "Well, *shit.*"

JASON WAS STAGGERING as Dillon helped him into the sanctuary of the church. He needed to get the boy to his mother. Had Jessica found what she was seeking? Could soul-soothing magic really help her boy? He had thought there were limitations—every Way had them—but he couldn't remember what they were.

He heard voices from above. And just ahead, he saw Silanar.

Shit.

He ran, pulling Jason with him, ducking into a stairwell. He couldn't let the leader of Sylrantheas see him—not after all this time.

He headed up the stairs, hoping Jessica would be able to help.

Jason wasn't looking very good.

"I CAN'T LET you have it," Keya said, standing and trying not to sway. She shouldn't have had those beers. "We have to prevent the Sundering."

"I understand," Jessica said. "I want to stop it, too. But I also need to heal my son. Will you help me?"

Keya felt her expression grow cold. "I'm sorry," she said. "I was lying about the magic. Soulsoothing cannot heal cancer."

"*What?*"

"I've tried, Jessica. I've tried *thousands of times*."

"But you haven't read this Book."

"I just did," Keya said. "I read that section before you even got here. It's meaningless, Jessica. It's all bullshit. It's not going to help."

"At least let me read it," Jessica said. "Maybe you're wrong."

"You *just* discovered soulsoothing," Keya said. "I've been doing this since I was twenty. For fifty-five years, I've healed people. For nearly that long, I've tried to cure cancer. If the words in this Book could suddenly teach me how, *trust me*. I would know. But they won't. They can't. Magic will not save your son."

"Fuck you," Jessica said, lunging for the Book.

Keya had no choice. She had to stop the Sundering. She had to destroy the Book of Souls.

She drew her sword.

FIFTY-EIGHT

DILLON HEARD FOOTSTEPS BEHIND HIM. Had Silanar followed? Had they been seen? There was a little alcove up ahead, dark and hidden. "Come on," he said to Jason. "We need to hide."

Somewhere in the distance, he thought he heard women shouting.

"WHAT ARE YOU *DOING*?" Jessica demanded. "Are you going to kill me with that thing?"

"I'm not going to kill you," Keya said. "But I can't let you have this Book."

"I just need to *read* it, Keya. Don't you want me to help my son?"

"Silanar's here," Keya said. "He's come for the Book. If I let him have it, billions of humans will die. *You'll* die, Jessica, and so will your son."

"He's going to die anyway," Jessica said, taking a step away from the other woman. She couldn't fight a sword with her bare hands. "Won't you at least let me *try*?"

"No," Keya said. "We need to destroy this Book. I'm leaving. Let me pass."

"No."

"Don't make me hurt you." She gestured with the sword. "I know how to use this."

It appeared that she did. Jessica couldn't deny the skill with which she held the weapon, brandishing it as if it were an extension of her arm. She had no doubt that Keya could kill her where she stood.

Assuming she didn't slip and fall, first.

But Jessica didn't want to hurt her new friend. She wasn't violent. She just needed to save her son.

"Let me pass," Keya said, stepping forward, and Jessica had no choice but to squeeze to the side, letting her through.

This was it. This was her opportunity. One small push, and Keya would be dead. The Book would be hers, and all the secrets it contained.

But she couldn't do it. It wasn't right.

So Jessica let the woman pass, following her back into the small, wooden room. They stood together for a moment, waiting as it rumbled around them. Then a door opened, and they emerged into a chamber of metal and gears.

"What in the..." Jessica said.

"The whirling chamber," Keya said. "It was all a *machine*. But why? And how?" She stared at the walls, questions in her eyes.

This was the chance Jessica was waiting for.

She lunged for the Book.

But Keya was too quick. She slashed upward with the sword, narrowly missing Jessica's face, and Jessica had no choice but to swerve to the side to avoid being struck. She stumbled, trying to regain her balance, and something clicked beneath her foot.

The room transformed into wood again, the lights whirling overhead. Eight doors resumed their rotation, their destinations continually changing.

"Twins dammit," Keya said. "Now it will be a lot harder to get out of here." She lunged toward one of the doors, and Jessica had no choice but to follow. She needed to save her son.

She barely made it through the whirling door.

She found herself back on the sanctuary catwalk, where she'd picked up the mysterious pieces of wood. The sword she'd spotted earlier was still here, leaning against the wall near where the door was.

She grabbed it now.

It was much heavier than she'd expected, much harder to hold. But she needed *something*. She couldn't go up against Keya's weapon without one of her own. This would be her best shot.

She had to get that Book.

KEYA WASTED NO TIME. She danced out onto one of the narrow wooden beams, balancing as easily as she had in the tree, unafraid of the immense drop below. There was another door at the far end of the room, she saw.

She headed that way.

And was stopped by a sharp *nick* on her shin. She almost fell right there, almost toppled off the beam to her death. She turned, ignoring the pain, anger beginning to take over.

Jessica was holding a sword.

That infernal woman. "Just let it go!" Keya shouted. "This isn't your place! We aren't your people!"

"It *is* my place," Jessica said, advancing on her, balancing just as easily. The damn woman may as well have been an elf. "Just hand me that translation. It's easy! You can keep the Book, and I can save my son."

"It won't work!" Keya shouted. "I told you, the instructions are meaningless! It's nonsense."

"Let me be the judge of that."

Keya took a step toward her, sword brandished. She didn't want to hurt the woman, but she had to see this through. "How long have you been using magic?" she asked. "How long have you even known it *existed*? Why won't you just *believe* me?"

Jessica's face was dark. "If you had a son," she said, "you'd know."

And she struck with everything she had.

JESSICA DID her best to hit the elven woman with her sword. But Keya had had years of training and experience. Jessica had never even *seen* a sword before.

And so it was that her first attempt went wide, nearly sending her careening off the platform into thin air. Keya's swipe, meanwhile, nearly cut her face completely off.

But Jessica managed to avoid it, barely, managing to stay atop the tiny beam of wood. Whoever had designed this place had been insane. Of course, she was sure they hadn't intended a *sword fight* to occur up here.

"I'm not just looking out for *your* son, here," Keya said, holding her blade aloft. "I'm looking out for *everyone's* sons. And daughters. For the people of this world."

"By all accounts, you were here first," Jessica said. Her arm was already starting to hurt. She lifted the sword, readying another strike. "And by all accounts, the human race is doomed, anyway. Haven't you heard of climate change? Isn't that why this whole thing got started to begin with?"

"Yes, I've *heard* of it," Keya said. "And I choose to believe that there's a better solution. We elves cannot wipe out the entire human race."

"Just give me the fucking translation."

"No."

And Keya struck. She came forward in a flurry of slashes, each one faster than the next. It was all Jessica could do to block them one by one, retreating back across the wooden beam step by perilous step. She could tell that Keya wasn't trying to actually kill her. She knew that if she'd wanted to, she could. She was simply trying to drive her back. But Jessica had no choice. She couldn't defend against this onslaught. She was way out of her depth. So she stepped back and back, and then she was once again amongst the swirling lights.

"Goddammit," she said. "This stupid room, again."

"Catch me if you can," Keya taunted, and leapt into a different door.

Jessica followed.

In her brief times with the elves, she'd seen strange things. She'd seen magic. She'd seen whirling lights and doors. She'd seen impossibly old yet impossibly young people, people who could change their appearance at a whim. She'd seen forcefields. She'd seen swords.

But she'd *never*, in a million years, expected to see *this*.

FIFTY-NINE

THALANIL STUFFED the motherboard carefully into his backpack and headed back through the door. The Chamber was back on, he saw with vague annoyance. Clearly somebody else was up here. Was it really Jessica? He hadn't seen her anywhere. But the church was big, he knew. Labyrinthian. He wasn't even sure if he had seen all the secrets that it held.

But now was not the time for that. It was not the time to see his wife, either. He needed to return to Newfris, to fix the hardware problem that could doom the entire thing.

Now it was time to leave.

Luckily, he had helped design this Chamber.

He took the correct door, barely sliding through as it shifted around the room.

And ended up in the completely wrong place.

"Rats," he said, turning back. But the door was already gone.

Thalanil had ended up in the stupid bell tower.

JESSICA WAS SURROUNDED by strange colors. The sky was purple, oddly, and the ground was black. She saw stars overhead, little pinpricks against the violet heavens. And there were trees along the ground, painted in a violent green that contrasted sharply with the black surroundings.

The entire place was *very* weird.

There was a path that led through the trees, and she could see some kind of hill in the distance. Two trees were on that hill, larger than all the others. Two trees that stood together as if they were lording it over all the others, one black, one gold. They stood stark against the violet sky, and Jessica could feel the power emanating from them. She could feel their purpose.

She shivered. None of this was good.

"You," a voice said, and a tall woman appeared as if from nowhere. Her skin was black, and she was dressed in purple to match the sky, her clothing revealing her curves. Her black eyes flashed in the otherworldly light from the stars and trees, and she took a step forward.

Jessica found herself more scared than she'd ever been before.

"Why are you here?" the woman asked, her voice as dark as her skin. "This place is not for you."

"Who—who are you?" Jessica asked. To her left, Keya was slack-jawed, speechless.

"You were not meant to see this place," the woman said. "It is not your time." She raised a hand, and something silvery and strange passed over both of them.

Jessica shivered, feeling ice wash over her, and then she remembered no more.

THE NOISES SILANAR was hearing were very strange, especially for this time of night. Was somebody using *swords*? Why were they up so high in the building? What was going on up there?

He trudged up the stairs, regretting his lack of sleep, hoping he wasn't heading into tragedy. An alcove to the side caught his attention briefly—was there someone hiding there?—but he decided against investigating it.

He didn't need more trouble than he already had.

THALANIL WAS FEELING around the wall. He knew the door was actually still there, but there were two mechanisms obscuring it from him. First, there was the mechanical side. The door was rigged to shift, moving so people couldn't easily go right back through where it had been. The second part of the illusion was powered by the mistweaver artifact: it made it so he couldn't *see* the door. He wondered once again where Myriani had gotten it, and whether she knew where he could get more. It was probably one of the most powerful artifacts in existence.

He had almost found the door when something flashed behind him. He turned and saw a gate appear, transitioning vertically from top to bottom, revealing Keya Sunwillow and Jessica Lim.

His wife was here.

Rats.

He ducked to the side, hiding behind a pile of ropes that had been hung against the wall. As he did, he noticed through a window that the sun was just beginning to rise.

JESSICA SHOOK HER HEAD, feeling dazed. What had just happened? She couldn't remember anything. She felt as if she'd just been dragged through a river of ice. There was a woman standing next to her. A woman with a sword in one hand, and a large book in the other.

Everything came rushing back to her.

She lunged at Keya, who was still reeling, intending to take the Book from her hand. But something stopped her. Something surprised her.

Her *husband* was standing there in the shadows.

"Alan?" she asked.

"Rats," Alan said. "I guess the jig is up."

SIXTY

DILLON WAITED for several more minutes after Silanar had passed them. He knew Jessica was up there—he could hear her, arguing with someone else. Something about a book? He was confused. Still, he knew what he needed to do.

He needed to bring her her son.

Jason was stumbling, barely able to stand upright. Dillon put the boy's arm around his shoulders, helping him make his way up the stairs.

"EXPLAIN YOURSELF," Jessica said. Her husband was just standing there. And his ears...*shit*. "You're an elf."

Alan fingered the tips of his ears. "I'd forgotten about the safe zones," he said. "I guess Sylrantheas forced me to reveal my true identity."

"You *knew* about this place?"

"I grew up here." More people were arriving, filing out of the door and onto the narrow platform of the bell tower.

Jessica recognized the first one from the American Cancer Society.

"Silanar?" Keya said. "Twins. I didn't know you'd still be up."

"You found the Book, I see."

"I'm sorry. I just—"

"Did you talk to Myriani? She always has something up her sleeve."

"You can't do it, Silanar. You can't do the Sundering."

"I can, and I will, young lady, if that's what the World Council votes to do."

"Not if I destroy the Book."

Silanar took a sudden step forward, his expression fierce. "You wouldn't."

"Quite the party here," a new voice said, and a young man walked into the bell tower.

Holding her son.

"Jason!" Jessica cried. "How are you here? *Why* are you here?"

"Mom," Jason mumbled. "It...hurts."

"Shit."

"I'm Dillon," the young man said. "Your husband's friend. We usually talk on the phone."

He had pointed ears, too.

Jessica turned back to Alan. "Explain," she said. "Now."

But Silanar was already standing next to him. "I should throw you off this tower," he said, seething. "I should end you right now."

Alan sighed. "I tried to tell you, Silanar. How many times did I try? It wasn't my *fault*. I didn't make this happen!"

Keya was staring at him oddly. "Why does Silanar want to kill you? Who *are* you? I thought I knew all the elves around here."

"This man," Silanar said, "is one of the Cothellon."

Jessica felt her blood run cold.

"Oh," Keya said. Then she shrugged. "Kill him, or not. I'm leaving with this Book."

But Jessica had her sword ready. She leveled it at Keya's throat. "Not so fast. Give me the translation first."

Silanar looked at her. "A human," he said. Then he glanced at Jason, and his face blanched. "The boy from Stevenson Place. He's a dark mage! And you..."

"I'm a soulsoother."

"Lies," Silanar hissed. "Humans cannot be lightprime mages."

Jessica shrugged. "I don't care if you believe it. I just know that with the Book she's holding, I can heal my son."

"Wrong," Silanar said. "Soulsoothing has limitations."

"So I've been told. You're both wrong."

Silanar turned to Keya. "Give me the Book."

"No," Jessica said. "Give it to *me*."

"Guys," Dillon said, "surely there's a peaceful resolution to all of this."

"I'll just leave you to it," Alan said, slinking away.

Jessica rounded on him. "Not so fast, mister. You need to explain yourself. You're an *elf*? I married an *elf*?"

Alan sighed. "My real name is Thalanil. I'm three hundred twenty seven years old. And *this*"—he pointed at Jason—"is not my first child." He turned to Keya. "*She* is."

SIXTY-ONE

"*WHAT?*" Keya cried. "But that...that's impossible." Silanar was simply shaking his head. "Wait. You *knew*?"

"I'm sorry to keep it from you," Silanar said. "Yes, I knew. I banished Thalanil myself for what he did."

"Explain," Jessica said, her voice incredibly cold. "Now." Her sword was still touching Keya's throat.

"I was born here," Thalanil said, shifting his backpack on his shoulders. "In Sylrantheas. In Silanar's generation. I was friends with all those guys—Orym, Kharis, Orist, the lot. But like Orym, I was more of a scientist than anything else. I wanted to build technology, but you've seen this place." He gestured around him. "This isn't exactly the height of modern technology."

"Careful," Silanar said.

"Apologies. But you know it's true. That's why Orym left, is it not? So a few years after he joined the Cothellon, he reached out to me. Gave me the chance to join. I took him up on his offer."

"And Silanar banished you?" Keya asked.

"No. All he knew was that I had moved into the city. Same

thing Orym had told him. It took him decades—maybe more —before he had any idea."

"True," Silanar said. "We didn't even know the Cothellon existed, yet."

"Years passed. Decades. And I was happy. But I missed the old life, sometimes. You know? I missed it here, in Sylrantheas. Still do. It's so…quaint. So quiet. So…peaceful."

"You came back."

"Seventy six years ago, that's precisely what I did."

Keya felt an unsettling feeling enter her stomach. "You met my mother. But she was married!"

"Aelynthi was beautiful," Thalanil said. "Perfection. And yes, she was married to your father at the time. Had been for many years. But we met, and dare I say we fell in love. Our affair only lasted for a month, but that was all it took."

"It can't be."

"When I found out she was pregnant, I begged her not to keep the child. But that was a human's way of thinking. Elves are so infertile—so she refused. She wanted the baby. She wanted *you*, Keya."

"She lied to Father?"

"She didn't want to hurt poor Tanyl. He was good to her. She loved him. She would always stay with him, and I knew that. She felt terrible for what she'd done with me. She wasn't a cheater. She wasn't unfaithful."

"And yet she was." Keya tasted bitterness on her tongue, the Book of Souls forgotten in her hand.

"Yes, she was. I loved her, Keya. I loved her like I had loved no one else—not until I met you, Jessica."

"Finish the story," Jessica said, and Keya could see that she was seething. This must be as hard for her as it was for Keya.

"So, yes," Thalanil continued, "Aelynthi lied to Tanyl. She

told him the baby was his, and he believed her. Why would he not? She had always been faithful to him. Adultery is almost unheard of in elven culture. And so he played the ever-devoted father, helping her carry you to term.

"But on the day of her delivery, she became stricken. I was there, you see, hiding in the shadows. Silanar had not yet caught on to things—he would, later that day, when he caught me lurking in the village. But in that moment, I could see her face. I could see the hurt I'd caused. I could see it eating her alive, tearing her up from within.

"I knew that I had ruined her.

"A week after you were born, she came here. To this very spot. To the bell tower of the church, with a clear view of the floor a hundred feet below."

"She fell," Keya said. "It was an accident, and I can clearly see why."

Thalanil reached into his pocket. Were his eyes watering? Looking at her, he pulled a piece of paper out and handed it over. Keya sheathed her sword, taking the paper wordlessly. A tear dripped down Thalanil's face.

This pain is too much to bear. I cannot live with it, and so I must bid you farewell. Goodbye.

— Aelynthi Sunwillow, wife of Tanyl

"No," Keya breathed, breath choking in her throat. "No."

"It was suicide," Silanar said. "I'm the one who discovered her body, saw the note. I'm the one who hid it from you—from everyone. I didn't want you to grow up with this hanging over you."

"He came upon me later that night," Thalanil said, "and wrested the story out of me. He threatened to kill me, then, but he was too kind to follow through. So instead he banished me, never to return. He gave me Aelynthi's suicide note. I've kept it ever since."

"Mother*fucker*!" Keya screamed, lunging forward. But Jessica's sword was still at her throat. The woman was looking at Thalanil fiercely, but she did not yield the sword.

"That. Is not. All," Silanar said, his voice the quiet of the grave.

"No," Thalanil said.

"Tell them," Silanar said. "Tell them all of it."

"You are wrong, Silanar."

"*Tell them!*"

"I will not speak lies! You slandered my name then, and you will not slander it now!"

Silanar turned to Keya, his jaw visibly shaking. "Thalanil is a dark mage," he said. "Thalanil—your father—this woman's husband—is a *mindmaster*."

"Fuck," Dillon whispered.

SIXTY-TWO

"I DON'T KNOW what that word means," Jessica said. All of this was a whirl of information, but most of it didn't affect her directly. Her husband was an elf—that affected her. That could make a difference. But that he'd had a life before he'd met her? That he had a daughter she hadn't known about? These were things she could come to grips with. These were things he had a right to have. He had always been cagey about his past, and she had let him. It hadn't mattered to her.

It shouldn't matter now.

"Mind control magic," Silanar said. "Thalanil can make people do whatever he wants."

"You think..." Keya was shaking, tears rolling down her face. She didn't complete the sentence.

"You *didn't*," Dillon said. "Did you? Old friend?"

Thalanil was crying, too. "I never used mindmaster magic on Aelynthi. I swear it. Everything she did, she did of her own accord."

But Silanar stepped up to him, jaw clenched. "You saw her," he said, "you wanted her, you approached her, and you *took* her. You can't lie to me, dark elf scum." He spat off the edge of the platform, and Jessica watched it fall.

Alan—Thalanil—was sobbing. "I swear I didn't," he whispered. "I would never do such a thing. Even in the Cothellon, such a thing results in capital punishment. They'd kill me."

"And so they shall," Silanar said. "I'll see to that myself."

Just then, Jason collapsed to the floor.

"Twins," Dillon cursed. "You have to *do* something. I don't think he'll last much longer."

"Let me go," Thalanil said to Silanar. "I have to go."

"No," Silanar said, and he grew larger before her eyes.

"What in the—" Jessica started.

"Strengthshaper," Dillon said. "Don't do this here..."

But Silanar was clearly too mad to listen. "You will pay for the crimes you committed!" he shouted. His voice was ten times louder than it had been before, the sound nearly bursting Jessica's ear drums. It echoed around the walls of the bell tower, sending shivering vibrations through the floor. "I may have been too weak to kill you then, but *I am not the same man now!*"

He launched himself at Thalanil, but Jessica knew that Thalanil was quicker than he looked. He dodged, and Silanar slammed into the wall instead.

Or rather, he slammed almost *through* the wall.

Wood clattered down around him, and Jessica could see daylight shining through. Was it already that late? The sun was coming up in the distance.

And Silanar was stuck inside a wall.

"Stop this," Thalanil said, inching toward the door.

But Silanar was somehow *incredibly* strong. He reached around himself, ripping whole chunks from the wall with ease. Then he pulled himself back into the room, face red as he glared at Thalanil. "This ends here," he said, and launched himself at the man again.

He might have been strong, but he was not clever.

Thalanil dodged again.

This time Silanar crashed through several support structures in the interior of the building, sending wooden shrapnel flying. Ropes snapped, the bell overhead swinging perilously. Jessica felt the platform beneath her begin to shift.

"Stop!" she screamed. "You're destroying the entire building!"

"I will *not* stop," Silanar said, his voice a guttural roar.

Jessica dropped her sword, lunging for her son as Silanar rushed at Thalanil again. She heard the sound of shredded wood, creaking nails, ripped fabric, fraying ropes. The bell at the top of the tower began dinging, the sound reverberating throughout the church. Jessica wanted to clap her hands over her ears, but she needed to help her son.

Jason was awake.

"Mom," she thought he said, but she couldn't hear.

"Here," Jessica said, acting on impulse, thrusting chips of darkprime wood into his hand. "Help us, if you can."

The sounds abated for a moment. "Can...barely..." The rest was lost in a cacophony of broken wood.

Jessica coughed. Dust was everywhere. Silanar was on a rampage. He was trying to kill her husband, but there was nothing she could do.

She was focused on her son.

"Quickly," she said, grabbing Jason and helping him to his feet, slipping him a few pieces of the wood she'd grabbed earlier.

She hoped her hunch was right.

The platform buckled underneath them as Silanar

destroyed another section of the wall. Thalanil was over by the door, which was finally stable for the moment.

"I'm sorry, Jessica," he said. "I love you. Save our son."

And then he was gone.

Silanar followed him, roaring.

"That was—" Keya started.

But Jessica saw her opportunity.

She didn't think.

She didn't hesitate.

She didn't shirk from her responsibility.

She took the Book from Keya's hand.

And while the tears were still drying on the woman's face, she pushed her off the platform's edge.

And Keya fell, screaming, just as the entire bell tower began to fall apart.

SIXTY-THREE

EVERYTHING AROUND HER FROZE.

Shimmering light surrounded the remnants of the bell tower, just as they had that fateful day in San Francisco. Jessica looked down to see that her gamble had paid off.

Jason was using his magic once again.

Keya screamed, the sound horrible in Jessica's ears. Her scream was cut off abruptly as she slammed into the sanctuary floor, and Jessica could see the light go out of her eyes.

Keya was dead.

Jessica had killed her.

Perhaps it was poetic. Perhaps Keya had been meant to die here, in the very place where her mother had killed herself.

Or perhaps Jessica had just committed the greatest sin of her entire life.

She shook her head, rousing herself. They needed to get out of here.

"Mom," Jason said, and he slumped over, unconscious.

The magic dissippated all around her.

And all around her, the bell tower began to crumble once again.

SIXTY-FOUR

JESSICA FELT the world topple around her as the bell tower began to fall. Her son—the light of her world—was unconscious. Dying. Maybe dead. His magic was gone, and now she was going to die, too. Now she would die like poor Keya, so many feet below her on the floor.

Jessica's whole world was coming to an end.

But she still had something in her pocket.

Something else besides the darkprime wood she'd given Jason.

Something Keya had given her.

Primewood.

She grabbed it quickly, reaching out to touch her son. She had only read the first paragraph in the Book. She only had the vaguest idea of what to do. But she only had seconds before everything around her would come crashing down.

She had to try.

And so she did.

She touched Jason, feeling for his pulse. Power instantly flared through the prime birch in her hand, the warmth of it suffusing her. And she cast it into him with a thought, feeling it surging into his very soul.

She felt the cancer, then.

She felt the blackness of it, the blight. She saw it as a huge black box, pulsing and ugly, wicked, evil. It was insurmountable. It would be his end. But something in that paragraph she'd read had sparked her ingenuity. Something about it gave her an idea.

Power spectrum.

Frequency.

Attuned to the proper—

Jessica focused her mind, looking closer at the power she held. She could feel it, there, beneath her fingertips, flowing into Jason, being stopped by the blackness of the cancer in his jaw. But there was more to it than just a flow. There was more than just raw *power*.

With her mind, she looked even closer.

There. She could sense them, underneath it all. There were pieces to the magic, little particles, tiny things almost like atoms, making up the power itself. And if she *twisted* them just so...

The cancer blasted away, ripped to shreds by her modified magic. She felt the cells around it heal, re-forming, the body shaping itself back to the way it once had been.

The cancer was gone.

It had been that easy.

Jason woke with a start, gasping, and silver light once more filled the room.

PART
FIVE

SIXTY-FIVE

THE LAND ROVER pulled into their driveway, and Jason followed his mother into the house. He felt perfectly awake, perfectly fine. His body had been completely healed. He was cancer-free, full of energy.

His mother looked like a complete wreck.

They'd made it out of the disaster of the church, just barely. It had taken them the better part of an hour, carefully using his forcefinder magic to ease the collapse. Without his cancer, Jason found it easy to manipulate the strange force-fields he could create.

Now they were home.

And so much had happened.

Keya was dead. Jessica had killed her.

His father was an elf. His father had a daughter.

And Jessica had just *killed* that daughter.

But Jason had been healed.

His mother collapsed on her bed, but Jason wasn't tired. So he went into his room instead, doing something he hadn't felt well enough to do in quite some time.

He took out his set of Legos and started to build.

THALANIL WAS SWEATING as he made his way deep into the Under of City Three. He had escaped Silanar, barely. The Council Leader had not been expecting a gate to be there, shining in the forest next to Sylrantheas.

He hadn't followed, when Thalanil passed through.

Thalanil had heard the sound of the church collapsing as he left.

Now he was back in Newfris, hoping his wife would still be there for him when all of this was done. Just then, she sent him a text.

"Made it home," he read. "The church was destroyed, and Keya fell to her death. Sorry to give you that news—we need to talk when all of this is over. Jason is better."

"What?" he texted back, trying to move through the corridors without running into anything. "Jason is okay?"

But Keya was dead? His brain was frozen. He wasn't able to process what was going on.

"Healed him," Jessica sent back. "What's going on?"

"It's the Cothellon," he wrote. "Their plan is starting now. You need to get into the new city with me. That's the only way to be safe. Here's what you need to do..."

He finished the instructions, locking his phone and putting it back in his pocket. He needed to fix the timer bug, or this entire plan might fail. He also needed his wife and son safe in New San Francisco, where the Sundering couldn't affect them.

He hoped he could accomplish it all.

The Under around him was dark and cold. He had never

been this far down, before. He was lucky the infrastructure was even there. The sabotaged hardware was in one place and one place only, and Thalanil was running out of time.

As he continued running through the cement passages of the Under, he hoped he wouldn't be too late.

SIXTY-SIX

"ORDER! ORDER!" World Council Leader Vargoth pounded his gavel on the table. "I will have order!" The room quietened, men and women shifting in their seats.

Silanar looked around at the other elves sitting at the large round table. At least one delegate from every major country was there, except for Sweden, which had refused to participate. Their absence most likely made the upcoming decision a foregone conclusion.

He helped himself to a muffin and another cup of coffee. It was only 6 AM, but everyone else seemed wide awake. Perhaps he shouldn't have visited the church. Perhaps he shouldn't have used his magic. Now the church was in shambles, and at least one person was dead.

Thalanil had gotten away.

And Silanar could barely keep his eyes open. Everything was going to shit. He was grateful Vargoth had stepped up at the last minute, offering to run the meeting. Silanar couldn't seem to keep a clear head, lately. He wished his wife was there.

Vargoth addressed the room. "Thank you all for

answering this Code One summons to a World Council. May I remind the Councillors that this meeting will be conducted using modified Parliamentary procedure. This is not one of your regular Council meetings. We have but one motion before us today."

"Genocide," someone said.

"It is *not* genocide!" someone else cried. "It's a course correction!"

"You can't call killing billions of humans a *course correction!*"

The room erupted into shouts again. Silanar sat back, trying to stay awake, studying Council Leader Vargoth. The man seemed entirely too calm about what should be a very contentious topic. But calmness was needed, here. That was why Silanar was not in charge.

"Order!" Vargoth shouted, banging his gavel repeatedly. "The representative from Italy has the floor. You may begin, Horith."

"My fellow elves," Horith said, his English carrying a faint Italian accent. "We are here to discuss the Sundering Act. You have all by now read the final report. This planet is about to cross a critical tipping point, beyond which it will be very difficult—if not impossible—to recover. We have monitored the situation for the past two centuries, and we have attempted to affect actual change for the past sixty years. Thus far, our efforts have been fruitless."

Someone raised their hand, and Horith motioned for him to speak. It was Ettrian, the representative from Canada.

"Have we exercised every option available to us?" Ettrian asked. "What is the good of having embeds in nearly every government on Earth if we can't use that influence to fix the problem?"

Silanar raised his hand, and Ettrian yielded the floor. "The

United States is perhaps the best example of the issue," he said. "We've attempted change through regulation for the past several decades, but nothing sticks. The citizens in this country simply do not wish to recognize the problem, much less do anything about it. Everyone passes the problem on to somebody else, or insists it isn't real."

"What about the upcoming elections?" Ettrian asked. "The democratic candidates—surely they understand."

"One President is not enough. We need widespread change across the entire planet, and we need it now. The United States is too slow-moving to make it happen, even if they did have the influence."

"But surely we can regulate it anyway," Ettrian said.

"Worldwide? No. Short of taking over every government wholesale, it's not going to happen. We simply don't have the manpower for that kind of thing. And besides, running the planet as a benevolent dictatorship is not much better than the current plan on the table."

"It is certainly better than killing everyone outright."

Silanar nodded. "Agreed, but that is not what is being suggested. We are only going to cull the population down to manageable levels.

"If a political solution is infeasible," Ettrian asked, "what about a technological one? Surely we can use bioengineering to reverse the situation."

"Firstly," Horith said, "we do not possess the level of technology needed to make that happen. Any scientific minds we once had have long since been subverted by the Cothellon. And even if we could successfully perform bioengineering, the risk to the planet is too great. It's likely we would create an even bigger problem than if we had done nothing."

"And *is* doing nothing an option?" Ettrian asked.

"Regrettably, it is not. If we allow the situation to deteriorate much further, we will be past the point of no return. Even if we immediately arrest all carbon output, resource overconsumption, and overbreeding on a global basis, the planetary ecosystem would barely recover—and we still face at least two degrees of warming. What we are proposing here will do all of what I just said, and do it instantly. There is no other way to make it happen so quickly."

"But surely we have more time to decide."

Ytharra, the delegate from Japan, raised her hand, and Horith yielded to her. "Gentlemen and women," she said, "our eyes and ears in the Cothellon are reporting that their activity has increased markedly. We believe their operation goes into effect very soon—within a week. Possibly sooner."

The room was silent for a moment. Silanar raised his hand. "Do we know yet what they're planning?"

"Unfortunately, no," Ytharra replied. "We have not succeeded at planting any assets at a high enough level. We know there is a great deal of construction involved, much of it taking place out in the oceans, but our embeds are reluctant to speak of it."

"Our worldwide spy program certainly has deteriorated lately," Silanar said.

"With respect," Ytharra said, "the Cothellon group has always been remarkably secretive. They kept their very existence hidden from us for over a thousand years. Getting *anyone* inside their organization has been difficult at best."

Silanar knew that she was right. Still, he felt it was all too perfect, too neat for the Cothellon. They were too good.

They would have to slip up at some point.

"What Ytharra is saying," Horith said, "is that the time for action is now. If we wait any longer, the moment of opportunity may pass us by forever."

"For all we know," Silanar said, "the Cothellon might have the same plan we do."

"We do not think so," Ytharra said, "although it is certainly a possibility. We have not seen any Cothellon near the Prime Trees in many years. We believe they are utilizing a new set of technologies, something they discovered. To what end, we do not know. We have been completely unable to infiltrate their research division."

"It's magic," Silanar said. "Dark magic."

"That remains to be proven."

Deryth raised his hand. The representative from the United Kingdom was tall, towering over the other delegates as he stood. "This is our divine right," he said.

"Not this again," the representative from New Zealand whispered next to Silanar.

"We were put here by the Twins as a safeguard," Deryth continued. "We, the elves, are intended to be the final arbiter of change if this world needs it. We are to keep it pristine until the final Plan is revealed."

Various grumblings could be heard around the round table. Vargoth pounded his gavel once and the room became silent.

Silanar raised his hand. "With respect, Deryth, this World Council should concern themselves with facts, not super-stition."

Deryth bowed to him slightly. "With respect," he said, "our earliest writings speak of this moment. They prepared us for this day. Are the Twins not present in our every day lives? Is it not the Twins' power which we are proposing to use to cull this threat? The gods put us here for a reason. They gave us this power, this ultimate Primal Way, for a reason. And that reason has come upon us now, at this very moment. We are the arbiters of change for generations before, and for generations to come."

He sounded just like Myriani.

Deryth sat, and an uncomfortable silence followed. They'd been debating this for years, exhausting every possible argument—even the religious ones. Nobody had any energy left for another last stand.

"Council members," Vargoth said, "we will take a short recess, after which we will put this issue to a vote."

He banged his gavel on the table.

SIXTY-SEVEN

GATE CONTROL WAS a madhouse when Thalanil arrived. Elves were everywhere, tweaking instruments and watching monitors, shouting at each other as they did. He could hear the hiss of steam, smell the acrid stench of burnt electronics.

Clearly things weren't going well.

He wiped his brow, straightening his back, walking slowly and purposefully through the crowd. If he looked like he belonged, he reasoned, no one would question why he was there. But where was the system he was meant to fix? He'd never been down here before. He had no idea.

Across the room, he caught sight of the mission timer.

It had stopped.

LORELEI WAS STANDING in Mission Control, wondering where in the Twins' names Orym had gone. He was Mission Commander. It was his duty to be here.

The Ascension was beginning.

She looked up at the wall of screens that filled the front of the room. A lot of information was displayed up there, but one thing in particular caught her eye. She frowned.

Something was wrong with the mission timer.

SILANAR FILED BACK into Town Hall with the others and took his seat. He felt dejected. Depressed. He didn't *want* to order the murder of nearly every human on the planet. He wished it wasn't necessary to take such a drastic step.

But it was.

"The matter before us," World Council Leader Vargoth said, "is the activation of the Primal Woodway. We, the Eldrim, are resolving to perform a soulsundering upon ninety-nine one-hundredths of the human population on this planet. Furthermore, the proposal calls for relocation and assistance for the remaining one percent of the human population, along with the outlawing of most technology, in order to prevent a reoccurrence. The details of the proposal are in your docket. Do I hear a second?"

"I second," Silanar said.

The time for hesitation had passed.

The room was silent for a long minute. Only the sound of papers and shuffling feet could be heard. Someone sniffed.

"Let me remind you that this motion requires an eighty percent majority to pass. Please indicate your vote by raising your hand when I call for it. Those voting for?"

Nearly everyone raised their hand.

"Those voting against?"

There was no show of hands this time. "Abstain," said Deryth.

"The ayes have it," Vargoth said, rapping his gavel on the table.

It had been decided, then.

It was to be mass murder on an unprecedented scale.

Silanar hoped the Twins would have mercy on their souls.

Someone was shouting in the hallway outside. "Let me in!" they yelled. It sounded like...but no, it couldn't be.

The door to the Council chamber banged open, and Orym burst through.

"What is the meaning of this?" Vargoth demanded.

"The Cothellon," Orym said, breathing heavily. "They're going to destroy the planet. And it's my fault."

Silanar stood. "What do you mean?"

"It's my device," Orym said. "My invention. I've been working on it for them for decades. And it's going to destroy the planet."

"Guards!" Vargoth shouted. "Arrest this man immediately!"

SYNDRA'S HAD ALREADY REOPENED. The woman hadn't slept, and neither had Kharis. They both could sense that something important was happening. Something monumental.

Perhaps the world was about to end.

The sun was up, and Kharis sat at the bar and watched her work. His mind was whirling. He'd learned so many unexpected things. Orym was a traitor to his race, had lied to him for over a hundred years. Orym was responsible for the planet's impending death. Kharis nursed another whiskey, hoping to dull the pain.

There was nothing wrong with drinking at 6 AM.

The new television was on above the bar, the volume up. Kharis watched it idly, his mind someplace else.

"Reports are spreading of rising action in the Middle East," the reporter was saying. "Insurgents are targeting a place out in the desert, away from all known settlements. Military forces in the region have determined that the action does not appear to be threatening at this time."

Kharis took another drink of bourbon. There was always fighting somewhere—this was nothing new. Humans were such a hotblooded race, ready to shoot first and never ask questions. Such a waste.

"Elsewhere in the world, we bring you to Japan, where we have breaking news. Angela Devereux has the story."

"Good morning, Sean," Angela said, trying to keep her hat on her head and not succeeding very well. "I'm reporting from Tokyo, where as you can see, the wind is very strong. Scientists are reporting seismic disturbances earlier today in the Pacific Ocean, near Tokyo. No cause has been confirmed yet, but officials are issuing tsunami warnings throughout the coast of Japan. Citizens of other countries bordering the Pacific Ocean may be in danger, as well."

First a strange uprising, and now natural disasters. What was the world coming to? Kharis ordered another whiskey, trying to ignore the television. Syndra gave him a smile.

Thank the Twins for simple blessings.

SIXTY-EIGHT

"THERE'S BEEN A CHANGE," Lorelei said. She was standing in the Small Council chamber, wearing another of her smart red suits.

"Yes?" Quynn asked.

"I've ordered City Seven to move. We're bringing it over to the US."

"Why?"

"We've received new information. The Eldrim did indeed infiltrate New Tokyo, and their intent is sabotage. We are moving up the timetable for that city in order to be safe."

"You believe this information?"

"We are taking every threat seriously at this point," Lorelei said. "We picked up a million people from Japan, but the rest of the city will be populated in the United States."

"Very well," Quynn said. Why was she telling him this?

"I need you to do something for me," Lorelei said. "Investigate this threat to City Seven. I want to know if it's safe to proceed."

"Of course," Quynn said, bowing.

"And Quynn?"

"Yes?"

"I want you to do this privately. I don't want the rest of the Council freaking out."

THE GUARDS POUNCED ON ORYM, throwing him to the floor and handcuffing him. He didn't struggle. This was what he had signed up for.

"Wait," he heard a voice say. It was Silanar. The guards helped him up, letting him stand in front of the World Council. Everyone had various looks on their faces, ranging from shock to disgust.

"Why have you turned yourself in, Orym?" Silanar asked. He didn't ask why Orym was a traitor, why he'd done the things he'd done.

Perhaps he'd already known.

"I'm the Scientist General for the Cothellon Research Division," he began. He told the story, keeping it as brief as possible. "I don't want to hurt anyone," he said after he had finished. "When I found out the calculations were flawed, I brought it to my superior officer. He dismissed it out of hand, so I came here." His voice broke, the emotions of the day catching up with him. "I don't want to be responsible for this planet's death."

The room was silent for a moment, then it abruptly broke out into chaos. Everyone shouted at each other, gesticulating wildly and running about the room. Orym stood there, letting it all happen around him. Silanar stayed in his chair, watching him.

Council Leader Vargoth didn't try to control the chaos. He appeared shocked, unable to act. He just sat in his chair, eyes staring blankly ahead.

Silanar got up and made his way over to Orym.

"Why?" he asked. It was difficult to hear him over the noise in the room.

Orym looked at him. "I just wanted to do science," he said. "I didn't want to hurt anyone."

Silanar nodded, looking at him as if weighing his soul. Then he turned to the guards. "Release him," he said.

"Are you sure?" one of them asked.

"Do it. I'll answer to the Council."

The guard did as he was bid, releasing Orym from his handcuffs.

"If you get back to them now," Silanar said, "the Cothellon, I mean—if you get back to them right this minute, will it be soon enough for your...defection...to go undetected?"

Orym nodded. "I've only been gone one night. They won't know."

"Then do it," Silanar said. "See if you can get word to me about what's going on. Try to stop them," he laid a hand on Orym's shoulder, "but don't let on to anyone that you told us about this."

Orym nodded again, not quite understanding. "Why?"

Ytharra was standing near them, listening. She moved closer. "Dunedar," she said, at once making a statement and asking a question.

"Yes," Silanar said. "If he is successful, we may be able to avoid this outcome altogether." He turned back to Orym. "If you can't stop this, stay under cover. Remain a Cothellon. Raise a rebellion if you must, but do it slowly, carefully. You may only get one shot at this."

Orym looked at his friend. Silanar seemed older than his years, as if dealing with these decisions had cost him. How far ahead had Silanar been planning things? Who was

Dunedar? Had Silanar already known that Orym was a Cothellon?

"Orym," Silanar said, looking at him steadily. "Don't get yourself killed."

Orym clasped his old friend's hand.

The Council chamber was still in an uproar when he left, unnoticed by anyone else.

SIXTY-NINE

THE COTHELLON SMALL COUNCIL meeting was dragging on and on. Quynn just wanted it to end, to get this thing over and done with. He was tired of the years of planning, the decades of work it had taken to get this far.

He wanted the Ascension to begin.

But still the meeting continued. They were putting the finishing touches on the Tactical Technology Defeat program, which would simultaneously destroy all orbiting satellites and most communications centers throughout the world. This part of the project was tricky, relying on perfectly-coordinated timing across thousands of individual moving pieces. They had embedded assets across most major government organizations, including NASA and the Department of Defense. It wasn't part of Quynn's responsibility, though, so he mostly tuned it out.

"Let's move to the media portion," Lorelei said. This was the removal of books, documents, computer systems, and other forms of media. The new cities had been pre-populated with a selection of approved media, those things which would best support the fiction they would be creating, mindmastering the population. Everything that didn't fit was to be destroyed. Some of it had even been created from scratch, fabricating a false history in case somebody got it in their head to do some research.

Quynn, of course, had secretly brought thousands of banned books and other things up to City Three, where he intended to make his home after the Ascension. He loved books—there was no way in hell he was going to let them all get destroyed.

"Is everything in place?" Lorelei asked.

Garrik, the man in charge of media removal, nodded. "Yes, ma'am," he said. "We will be ready to trigger everything on your command."

"Very good," Lorelei said. She turned to Morgian. "Transmuter Legion?"

Morgian nodded. "Up and running as we speak. By the time we launch the Cities, we'll have a steady flow of resources."

"Excellent. Forcefinder Corps?" Lorelei addressed this to Argus, who nodded.

"We've been conducting escalated drills for the past seventy days," he said. "We're ready."

"Very good." She turned to Quynn, who snapped to attention. "Mindmasters?"

"Ready, ma'am." This was his favorite part—the part he was truly good at. "The population won't know what hit them."

"We won't be hitting them with anything," Lorelei said.

"Very good, ma'am," Quynn said, smiling inwardly.

"And now for the overall device," Lorelei said, turning to Grathgor. "Where do we stand with Fennas Elenathon? You reported it running, as of a few hours ago."

"One of the engineers reported an anomaly earlier today,"

Grathgor said, "but we believe it is under control. We'll be ready for the Conjunction within seventy-two hours of launch, as planned."

"Good. Droth, please update us on the Eldrim."

"My plant on the World Council tells me that they ratified the Sundering Act just minutes ago," Droth said. "It will likely take them at least a few days to execute those plans, assuming they decide to move forward with it quickly."

Lorelei sighed. "That's what I thought," she said. "The timing on this is too tight. If they pull the trigger on that magic before we're up in the air and populated, all our plans will be destroyed."

Everyone knew that she was right.

"Do we have any way to disrupt the ritual?" she asked.

"Not without putting undue strain on our existing plans," Droth said. "We could divert resources to it and delay the launch. But I fear it would only delay the Sundering Act, and alert the Eldrim to our plans before we're ready."

"Understood," Lorelei said. "If this is the case, we need to get moving now. Grathgor, accelerate City Seven to maximum velocity. Get her over here now, preferably within range of another city. Use City Three, if you can get her that far. I want her near Mission Control in case we need to transport people across for any reason."

Grathgor nodded.

"Droth, where do we stand with the population gates?"

"We're about three hours out from being able to drop them," Droth said. It was to be one of the final steps in the plan, to occur just after the communication blackout—or concurrently, if possible. Once the gates had been dropped throughout the selected population centers, the general public would be alerted to the Ascension. All hell would break loose. The timing was tight.

"I may need you to move that forward," Lorelei said. "Grathgor, how fast can New Tokyo get here?"

"It's been underway for five hours already," he said. "If we accelerate to maximum—which has never been done, I might add—we should be able to have the city on the west coast by around noon."

"Good. Do it. We're going to pull the trigger today. Will the city hold together at maximum speed?"

Grathgor shrugged. "You'd have to ask Orym. He designed it."

"Where *is* Orym, anyway? I expected to see him in Mission Control today."

Nobody knew.

"I hope nothing has happened to him," Lorelei said. "That would be very bad."

Quynn had an inkling what might have happened.

"Let me remind you all," Lorelei said, "that we must ensure our contingency plans are in place at every level. If something goes wrong—and with so many variables involved, it most likely will—we go to our backup plan." She looked around the table at everyone. "Worst case, the cities have been engineered to survive indefinitely. Let's hope it doesn't come to that."

Everyone nodded their agreement.

"Stay on your communicators at all times, folks," she said. "Dismissed."

Quynn got up and left.

The Ascension was finally at hand.

SEVENTY

THE FLOOR SHOOK and there was a sense of sudden acceleration, knocking Dunedar off balance. He grappled with the nearby railing, trying to hang on for dear life. What in the hell had just happened? Was the city speeding up?

The pounding on the door finally stopped. Dunedar waited another ten minutes, until he was satisfied that whoever it was had left. Then he opened the door, heading back out into the Under. He had hidden his communicator in a different room, in case he himself was discovered. But now he needed to warn the others.

The Cothellon plan was accelerating.

ORYM HAD time for just one more stop before he returned to Mission Control. He sped into the hospital parking lot, brakes squealing as he came to an abrupt stop. Moments later, after sharing a look with the embedded elf on duty, he was in room 221.

"I don't have long," Orym said. "Are you sure you want to go through with this?"

"I'm sure, Dad," Dillon said. He was lying there in bed, already prepped for surgery. It was relatively minor, as these things went—just some reshaping of the ears.

"This is permanent, you know," Orym said. "You'll never look like one of us again."

"I know. I want to help, if I can."

"I told the Eldrim Council today. About who—what— I am."

Dillon sat up, his elbows on the bed, a shocked look on his face. "What happened?"

"Silanar let me go. He wants me to remain undercover, to try to stop it from the inside."

"So we'll be working together." Dillon smiled.

"Looks that way." Orym sat on the bed, reaching out to put a hand on Dillon's shoulder. But Dillon grabbed his hand instead, taking it in his own. The gesture was sweet. "Son," Orym said, "whatever happens today, I want you to know that I love you."

"I love you too, Dad." Dillon squeezed his hand.

Orym looked around the room. He had so much more he wanted to say, but time was running short.

"What will you do?" he asked. He didn't want to leave just yet.

"Well, you're at the top," Dillon said, "so I'll get into the bottom. That stuff you told me about the infrastructure beneath the streets—the Under—it sounds like people could live down there. I might check that out, get a group of low-lifes together or something. Maybe take a codename like you." He smiled.

"Dillon," Orym said, "I received word on my way here that

the Ascension timetable has been moved up. They're starting it in just a few hours."

"Will that be enough time for me to get out of surgery?"

"As long they only use local anesthesia, I believe so. I'll speak to the doctor on my way out, get you released immediately. But Dillon—"

"Yes?"

"You have to get yourself into the city. There's going to be a gate dropped on Taylor and California, in front of Grace Cathedral. I don't know where the other gates will be. Get yourself over there, will you?"

"I'll do my best, Dad."

"Stay safe. We'll reconnect in New San Francisco." Orym squeezed his shoulder.

"Good luck, Dad."

Dillon lay back on the bed, and Orym released his hand.

He took one last look at his son before he left.

It would be the last time he ever saw him as an elf.

AELWYNN INSPECTED HIS TROOPS. His fallfoilers had been training for years, and they looked ready. Each of the dark-mages started with simple objectives—raise a ball to the ceiling, that kind of thing—and progressed to harder and more complex tasks. The final phase of fallfoiler training involved working together, a hundred of them at a time, to raise a single, extremely large object.

An entire city.

He strode down the field, walking confidently, the very image of a successful officer. He was proud. He was a City Director. He had a right to be proud. He loved being in charge.

He stopped in front of his officers, watching as they snapped to attention. "Men," he said, "the timetable has been moved up. The Ascension begins shortly."

"Yes, sir!" they said in unison.

Aelwynn swelled with pride.

This was going to be a great day.

"SILANAR," Vargoth said, "we just heard from Dunedar. He says their plans are accelerating."

"Has he offered any additional detail on what exactly those plans are?" Silanar asked.

"No."

"Well, if he's right, we have no choice but to move our plan forward. Send a message to the mages. Give them a time: noon, Pacific time. I hope they can all get to their Trees in time."

"But won't you be able to coordinate them during the ritual?"

"I have a feeling something might end up standing in the way of that. In the absence of communication, they'll know what to do. Give the order."

Vargoth nodded.

Silanar was glad he'd had the foresight to order the mages into position.

SEVENTY-ONE

THE CITY Three mindmasters were gathered together in the common room of their headquarters. Quynn's words would be relayed by video to the other six cities as well.

The meeting was set to start in five minutes. Quynn was sitting at the head of the room with his officers.

"Selwyn," Quynn said, gesturing to his second-in-command, "do you think the virus story will work?"

"It's easy to imprint and maintain," Selwyn said, "since this type of story has been common in popular entertainment amongst the humans. Most of the time we won't even need magic to enforce it. And after a while, once it has become part of common knowledge, our job will be completely done."

Quynn nodded. The logic made sense. He wasn't normally one to second-guess himself, but there was nothing wrong with making sure.

"Not completely done," he said. "There will always be rebellions. Uprisings. Those will require active mindmasters to quell."

"That's why we'll always be there, waiting in the shadows. Ready to correct what needs correcting."

Quynn stroked his bare chin, musing. "We can't very well call ourselves mindmasters. The public should fear us, but they shouldn't know what we truly are. We need a different name."

"What about...Monitors?"

"Yes," Quynn said. "Monitors. I like it."

He stood.

He started to leave, but Selwyn stopped him. "Sir," he said, "what about the other thing?"

Quynn turned. "What other thing?"

"The side effect of the gates. The effect on memory."

"That's a myth," Quynn said. "And even if people do lose their memories, that just makes our job easier."

Selwyn frowned as if he wasn't sure he agreed. Then he nodded. "Very good, sir."

Quynn spun and left the room. It was time to begin the mindmaster's final meeting.

DUNEDAR THOUGHT HE HEARD SOMETHING. He looked behind him, trying to see in the dark. Was someone there? He continued walking, proceeding through the Under, heading back to his bomb.

He had done his job. He had warned the Eldrim.

Now it was time to see this through.

THALANIL MADE his way to the heart of Gate Control, trying to look like he belonged. Everyone ignored him, luckily. But he still had no idea where he was going.

He stepped as lightly as he could along the narrow metal

catwalk, eyeing the drop below. New San Francisco hadn't Ascended yet, so it was still resting on the scaffolding structure that supported its immense weight. Still, a fall from here could easily kill him. Gate Control was open to the world below.

He knew from the architectural diagrams that the computer system in question was somewhere in this area. It would be old, he knew. Very old, compared to the other electronics in this room.

He hoped the motherboard in his backpack would work.

ORYM WALKED INTO MISSION CONTROL, straightening his uniform. "Where do we stand?"

"Systems are coming online as we speak," Sylvis said. "New Tokyo has accelerated to one-hundred percent velocity. They're approaching fast."

That was a surprise. What had happened while Orym was gone?

"How's her infrastructure holding up?" he asked, as if he had expected to hear the news.

"She'll make it," Sylvis said. "Although the transmuter staff will be exhausted by the time they arrive."

Orym nodded. They'd be using a hell of a lot of fuel to move so quickly. The Council must have ordered the acceleration of the Ascension.

He'd returned just in time.

"Stations, report," Orym ordered.

"Forcefinders online, ready for decloaking," Nuovis said. She was sitting at her console, tapping rapidly at the keyboard.

"Fallfoilers are reporting in, sir," Erlan said. "Ready for liftoff."

"Transmuters have been operational for twenty-four hours and holding strong," Estelar said. "Once New Tokyo comes within range, we'll transfer some of our reserve staff from New San Francisco to freshen their ranks."

"Very good," Orym said. "Keep me updated. Incidentally" —he looked around the control room—"what is our mission countdown?"

Erlan looked at him with surprise. "Sir," he said, "it's on-screen." He pointed to the lower-right quadrant of the main screen on the front wall.

"Of course," Orym said, "my apologies. It's been a long day." Some of the staff looked at him strangely. He hoped they weren't suspecting anything.

He looked at the countdown. T-minus seven minutes and counting.

Except...it wasn't counting.

What the hell?

Maybe this would give them more time. He hoped his son would make it before the world ended.

"Something's wrong," Lorelei said from her position two desks down. "That timer has been stuck for several minutes now. Orym, I want you to start things now. Get us up in the air."

"Yes, Cundu," Orym said.

He had no choice but to obey.

There was no stopping the Cothellon now.

THALANIL FELT a lurch as the city shifted, then suddenly it was rising in the air. He fell to his knees on the tiny metal platform, just in front of a large bank of computers, watching as the Earth descended from his view. It dropped precipitously, the city surging upward like a comet in reverse, and Thalanil couldn't help it.

He threw up into thin air.

He watched as the vomit spewed into nothingness, spraying hundreds, thousands of feet toward the world below. The city was still rising, fallfoiler mages commanding it with their great power. He felt dizzy as it flew, motion sickness overtaking him. The entire structure vibrated and shook, but it was otherwise completely silent.

This was it.

After all this time, the Ascension had begun.

SEVENTY-TWO

THEY'D ERECTED a tent for Silanar and the others near the Prime Oak in Mount Tamalpais State Park. The Tree itself was invisible to humans, of course. And it wasn't just invisible: it was also incorporeal for humans.

They could walk right through it.

All it took was an elf to lay a hand on the Tree and Will it to become invisible. From that point on, the Tree would be Aligned with elves and elves alone, visible only to them.

At least that's what the ancient writings said. No new Prime Tree had appeared in centuries.

No one had any idea where they came from.

Silanar had been given a chair to command things from. Not a very nice chair, of course, but it would do. The Eldrim hadn't been prepared to execute their plan quite so soon, after all. He took a seat, the Book of Souls in hand. The human woman had dropped it in her haste to leave.

"Are the mages in place?" Silanar asked.

Bellas put his cell phone down and nodded. "Almost," he said. "We haven't heard from the leafrunner in Spain, yet. Hopefully she'll make it in time."

"What about our two soulsunder mages?"

"They are being guarded by our best Hunters," Bellas said. "They're safe."

Silanar hoped so. They'd had to travel to Oregon and Mississippi to find the nearest Prime Trees representing willow and cypress. The mage network would be stretched very thin. He hoped the magic would work as it had been described in the Book of Souls, even over such long distances. Surely whoever had created this magic hadn't expected to find all fourteen Trees in the same place?

"Let me know when everyone is in position," Silanar said, fingering the Book. Bellas nodded.

It was almost time.

He prayed to the Twins that the elves would be forgiven for the terrible transgressions that were about to occur.

"HAVE you considered that the saboteur may have already left City Seven?" Quynn asked.

"We have officers combing the city as fast as we can," Lorelei said. "But it's a big place. If we can find him, we can find out what he's done. Maybe we can stop it in time."

Quynn nodded, running his fingers absently over the Tree Ring Staff. It was warm to the touch, comforting him in its own way. It was his insurance policy in case anything went wrong.

"Everything is in place," Lorelei said, her voice quiet. She moved up to Quynn and put her hands around his waist. "You ready for this?"

Quynn quirked an eyebrow. "Are you?"

"Win or lose," she said, "this day will definitely go down in history."

"The question is," Quynn said, "whose history?"

THALANIL TRIED to ignore the fact that he was three thousand feet in the air, suspended by nothing but a metal platform, holding on to nothing but a set of old computers.

This was not how he had expected this day to go.

But he'd found the system he needed. He'd identified the box. Now he just needed to open it, replace the motherboard, and hope that taking the system offline didn't crash the entire city.

He wished they hadn't Ascended so soon.

THERE WAS SOMEBODY FOLLOWING DUNEDAR.

He ducked into an empty room, hoping the person hadn't seen him. It was less of a room and more of a hole—a place where two cement walls didn't quite connect properly, leaving a small, triangular room just behind them.

He had his communicator with him now. "To whoever hears this," Dunedar said into it, keeping his voice low, "I think I've been discovered. This city is still in flight, heading to Twins-know-where. I intend to follow through with the plan." He stopped, then thought of one last thing to say. "May the Twins have mercy on my soul."

He placed the communicator on the floor and flicked a switch, hearing a quiet whine from the charging circuits. Dunedar left the room, heading down the Under toward the bomb.

Moments after he'd left, the communicator burst into flames.

SEVENTY-THREE

DILLON'S HEAD FELT WOOZY, and his ears were still bandaged from the surgery, making it hard to hear. His taxi was braving the traffic to Nob Hill, having picked him up from the hospital. The news on the radio was reporting fires in Afghanistan and tsunamis in both the Pacific and Atlantic —caused, no doubt, by the liftoff of the invisible cities. The news stations hadn't caught on to the significance of today's events.

Not yet.

"Almost there," the taxi driver said.

Dillon wondered if it would be in time.

·

AELWYNN WAS PREPARED. He was the strongest of the fallfoilers, the Director of City Three. The man of the hour. He had taken it upon himself to welcome the newcomers to his city.

He straightened his robe, admiring how he looked in the mirror. It was something he'd commissioned a few weeks ago, in order to look the part of City Director. He enjoyed how regal the robe made him look.

"This will be a day to remember," he said to his attendants.

He looked out the window at New Pier 39, where many of the gates were being setup. He was ready to greet his new subjects.

"ALL OF OUR Cothellon assets have just gone dark," Ytharra said, walking up to Silanar where he sat in the command tent. "I fear the worst."

"Do you think we've been discovered?" Silanar asked.

"I do not know. But whatever it is the Cothellon planned, it is clearly happening today. Right now."

"And we still don't know what their plan is."

"We do not." Ytharra looked at the ground. "I regard this as a personal failure."

Silanar stood, putting a hand on her shoulder. "This is not your fault," he said. "You did the best you could. We all did."

"Twins guide us," Ytharra said, making the sign.

"Twins protect us," Silanar returned.

He went back to his seat as Ytharra left. The growing Cothellon threat was troubling, but there was nothing he could do about it. His attention needed to be focused on the soulsundering that was about to take place.

He had read the Book of Souls. He knew how hard the coming ritual would be. For the magic to work, he would need all the skill and energy he could bring to muster.

If only he had gotten more sleep.

"WE HAVE A PROBLEM," Luthar said, running into Mission Control, his assistants trailing behind him. His hair was starting to gray—unusual for an elf.

"Yes?" Orym asked, eyebrow raised. Luthar wasn't supposed to be here. He was supposed to be back in the research office.

"It's the gates," Luthar said. "There isn't enough range to make it to the ground at this altitude."

"How could you possibly have made that mistake?"

"My apologies," Luthar said. "It was a simple error, one that we overlooked. We've had a lot of details to cover." He did look haggard, Orym noticed. Probably no better than he himself looked. They had all been run raw trying to pull this plan off.

"How much lower do we need to be?" he asked.

Luthar fumbled around in his notes. "Um," he said. Then one of his assistants whispered something in his ear. "Five hundred feet should do it," he said.

"Very well," Orym said. "Sylvis, will that be a problem?"

"No, sir," Sylvis said, "I don't believe so. Fallfoilers!"

"Yes, sir!" Erlan said.

"Drop City Three five hundred feet. Now!"

"Yes, sir!" Erlan tapped on his keyboard frantically and said something into his headset.

The city immediately lurched as it fell precipitously. Papers and tablets flew everywhere. Orym fell against a desk.

"Don't kill us all in the process," he said.

"Sorry, sir!" Erlan said, face red. He tapped again on his keyboard, and the city began dropping at a more tolerable rate. A great low sound sprang up suddenly, filling the air, causing vibrations to spread everywhere.

"Shit," Orym said, "does it have to be this loud?"

"Sorry, sir," Erlan said. "I'm not sure, sir. Many of the

darkprime magics have an audible component." He looked embarrassed.

Orym's communicator beeped and he flicked it on.

"Well," Lorelei's humorless voice said, "if the humans didn't know we were here before, they sure as fuck do now. Drop the gates."

SEVENTY-FOUR

EVERYTHING WAS SUDDENLY SO LOUD.

Jason put down the Lego he was holding and looked out the window. People were running down the street, shouting at each other and looking back and forth frantically. A car drove by, tires squealing as it swerved to avoid a man in the middle of the road. Jason turned from the window just as his mother came through the door.

"Jason, honey," Jessica said. "We have to go. Now."

Jason looked up at her. "What's going on?" He had just been healed. He felt *great*. Surely nothing else terrible could happen today.

"We don't have time for that now," his mother replied. She held out her hand and gestured for him to take it. "Let's go. I got a text from your dad. He told me what to do."

Jason looked out the window again. A woman was standing in their front yard with a lawn rake, shaking it at the sky and shrieking something he couldn't understand. A loud crack sounded in the distance.

His mother took his hand and pulled him hastily out of the bedroom. They ran to the front door and opened it.

Jason's father was nowhere to be seen, of course. He was gone.

Because his father was an elf.

Jason looked up at the sky and wondered what was going on.

DUNEDAR SPRINTED THROUGH THE UNDER, ducking under crossbeams and jumping over pipes. He knew this area like the back of his hand, having inspected the maps for months. He checked behind his shoulder as he ran. He could swear someone was still following him.

He only needed to get to the bomb in order to activate it. Simple. Except the distance from here to there was entirely too far. He cursed his stupidity for allowing himself to get distracted so far away from it. Now that his communicator was gone, the timing was entirely up to him.

He hoped he could make it without being discovered.

Suddenly the whole city lurched, and Dunedar fell hard, sprawling on the cement floor. His wrist and knees felt like they'd been skinned badly—they hurt like hell. What had just happened? Was the city about to crash without his help?

When nothing else happened after a few moments, Dunedar got up painfully. He was thankful he hadn't broken anything in the fall. He was close now. He could do this. He just needed to make it a little further.

Suddenly there was a click behind him.

"You're coming with us," a voice said.

Shit.

"ALL CITIES, REPORT," Orym said. Sylvis relayed the order, and in a few moments the various Mission Leaders started reporting in.

"New London is up in the air," the first one said over the satellite connection. "Shields holding."

"New Paris reporting. Launching in T-minus thirty seconds."

"New Sydney reporting in, sir. We are airborne and ready for gate drop."

"New Manhattan is online. We're seeing increased media presence in our vicinity. Waiting for the order to decloak."

"New Moscow reporting. Ready for launch."

"Any word from New Tokyo?" Orym asked.

Sylvis spoke into her headset for a minute. "They're almost here, sir," she said. "There's been some disturbance en route. Something to do with air traffic."

Of course. That was one reason the cities were never supposed to move this quickly. They would inevitably collide with something else.

"How bad is it?" he asked.

"Bad, sir. Local media is reporting on it now. It's been picked up by the AP and should hit national news in minutes."

"Was the city damaged?"

"No, sir. The forcefields held."

"Good," Orym said, "but Lorelei was right. We need to go now. Drop the gates."

Mission Control sprang into action, everyone furiously tapping consoles and speaking into microphones. Orym could feel small vibrations in his feet as the gate infrastructure descended rapidly, coming out from underneath the city. The infrastructure would remain invisible until it breached the forcefields, at which point the gates would look like big metal doors with tubes and wires running off of them. The gates themselves were designed to disconnect from the city once they'd been placed.

If they'd only had more gatesenders, the mages could have just opened the gates manually, using magic. None of this dropping nonsense. But the mages were far too rare, so the gates had been placed ahead of time, ready to drop.

And now was the time.

The first gate dropped. It must have gone down faster than intended, for it made a loud *cracking* sound as it hit the ground.

"What the hell was that?" Orym asked.

"One of the gates, sir," came the reply.

"Is it still operational?"

"I believe so, sir."

"Keep it together, people. We're not off to a good start, here."

"Yes, sir."

LORELEI WAS STARING at the screen in Mission Control. Something was definitely wrong with it. "Why is the timer stuck at seven minutes?" she asked.

Orym glanced at her. "Uh…"

"You know something, don't you."

"Twins. I didn't take it seriously at the time. One of my engineers—Thalanil—he told me yesterday about a possible bug in the timer."

"Thalanil," Lorelei mused. "One of your old village friends." Orym nodded. "How serious is this bug?"

Orym opened his mouth to respond, but Sylvis cut in, instead. "Guys," she said, "we have a problem."

"What's going on?" Orym asked.

"We've lost all mage communications."

"*What*?" Lorelei asked. "That's not good."

"No," Sylvis said. "It's not good at all."

That was when the city started tilting in the air.

SEVENTY-FIVE

THALANIL ALMOST FELL RIGHT off the platform when the city shifted. It tilted off its axis by less than a degree, but it was enough to send everyone almost flying into empty space.

Gate Control was an *incredibly* dangerous place to be.

Everyone was chattering around him. "Mage comms are down," he heard someone say.

"What? How could they be down?"

"Some kind of malfunction. The fallfoilers can't calibrate their magic."

"Twins," the other person said. "This city might not fall, but it sure as hell won't stay upright!"

"Mission is pointing the finger at us," the first person replied. "Some kind of broken hardware."

"What? Where? How in the Twins' names are we supposed to fix something like that?"

Thalanil almost raised his hand, almost acknowledged them. He almost told them that he knew where the issue was, that he had the fix right here in his backpack. But something else distracted him. Something that he hadn't expected to see. Someone that his wife had told him couldn't be here.

Keya was standing on the platform next to him.

And she was very much alive.

THE TV WAS BLARING AGAIN. Kharis stared at it blankly, not really paying attention. A crowd had gathered in Syndra's, bleary-eyed elves drinking coffee and eating bad fried food. The citizens of Sylrantheas had caught wind that something was going on.

A report came on that caught his eye.

"We're just getting word of a series of plane crashes," the news anchor said. "Passenger flights in Iowa and Nebraska have gone down for unknown reasons. I'm being told all lives were lost on both flights." The man cocked his head for a moment, listening to his earpiece. "We take you now, live, to the scene of the crash in Nebraska."

Kharis heard gasps in the tavern as the television cut to a horrendous scene. A Boeing 747 was on the ground, smoke pouring out from it. The entire jet had been crumpled, as if it had run headlong into something at full speed.

"Officials are investigating the crash," the reporter said. "There is no word yet as to what could have caused this devastating nightmare."

Nightmare was certainly the word for it. The plane looked like it had been crushed, as if someone had stepped on a tin can lying on the sidewalk. It was a miracle the thing hadn't exploded.

Kharis sat back in his seat. Something about the situation wasn't right. He picked up his phone and dialed Silanar.

KEYA. She was alive.

She was here.

"How did you…"

She launched herself at Thalanil, sword suddenly in her hands. But the city dropped just then, and both of them went flying to the metal deck.

Thalanil had narrowly avoided being sliced across the cheek. "Jessica said you died!"

"You'd *like* that, wouldn't you!" Keya shouted. "*Father*."

"I—I'm sorry, Keya. I didn't know your mother would do what she did."

"It doesn't matter," Keya said. "It's still your fault."

"How did you get into the city? How are you still alive?"

But she ignored his questions, anger flashing in her eyes. She came at him with everything she had, sword blade reflecting the electronics' light.

THE TAXI CAB was really speeding now. Dillon clung tightly to his seatbelt as the driver weaved wildly through traffic. It was his fault—he had told the driver to go as fast as humanly possible.

Humanly.

That was Dillon's life now, for better or for worse. He picked out a cluster of prime elm from his pocket, fingering the pieces idly. He was still an elf, even if he no longer looked like one. It would always be a part of him.

The car was moving incredibly fast, hurtling down the street at a very unsafe speed. Dillon hoped the driver knew what he was doing. They were close now, almost to the gate at Taylor and California.

A lady with a baby stroller appeared in front of them, as if out of nowhere. The taxi driver swerved violently to avoid them, tires squealing.

The car swung to the left, but its momentum carried onward, down the street. The taxi flew into the air, flipping sideways toward the woman and her baby.

The scene froze, everything moving in slow motion. Dillon made a quick, practiced motion with his hands— enough of a Movement to Invest the elm he was holding. It was the minimum possible motion, something Dillon had been perfecting for years. With the prime elm Invested, Dillon held his hand out, concentrating.

The car flipped over once in the air, then righted itself, sailing smoothly down and to the left of the street, narrowly avoiding the lady with the baby. Dillon breathed a sigh of relief as he focused on setting the car softly down on the street.

Then there was a terrible crash, and something hit Dillon hard in the side of the head.

He blinked, trying to clear his vision. His head was bleeding, and the window next to him had been shattered. He looked in front of him blearily.

The car had crashed straight into a tree. Dillon had been so focused on their lateral motion that he'd failed to look in front of them. He could see the taxi driver in the front seat, out cold, possibly dead.

Dillon put his hand to his head, trying to stop the flow of blood, and struggled to get out of the car.

The handle was stuck. The door wouldn't open.

"STOP!" Thalanil shouted. "You don't mean this! This isn't

you! I'm your *father*, dammit!" The curse felt terrible as it crossed his tongue.

"It's not just you," Keya hissed. "It's your *wife*. She *killed* me, Twins damn you both. She pushed me off the bell tower! I could have fucking *died*, you terrible excuse for an elf. First you kill my mom, then your wife kills me. Well, I've had enough. I've had enough of you *dark elves*. This ends now!"

The city tilted further, nearly throwing them both off the platform. Thalanil heard creaking all around him as the infrastructure was stressed in ways it was never intended to be. Too much angle, and it could all fall apart.

The ground was three thousand feet below.

"I have to fix this!" he shouted. Everyone in Gate Control was screaming. "The city is going to crash if I don't!"

"Fuck you," Keya shouted, and she took another step forward on the tilted platform.

SEVENTY-SIX

ANOTHER CRACK SOUNDED, closer this time, and the ground trembled. Jessica squatted down to look at Jason.

"Everything's going to be fine," she said. "But right now, we need to move fast, so I'm going to pick you up. Okay?"

Jason nodded mutely, glancing again at the sky. It was a clear, hot day, with just a hint of a breeze. The lady with the rake had stopped shrieking and was standing in place, rocking back and forth. Jessica reached down and picked Jason up, groaning.

"You're way too big for this," she said. She hefted Jason into a better position in her arms. "Here we go."

They set out down the street, walking rapidly, taking care to avoid the other people moving about on the sidewalk.

"What the hell..." his mother started, looking behind them at something Jason couldn't see. There was a loud crashing sound, but he couldn't see what had caused it.

"Shit," she said. "This is worse than I thought."

SILANAR'S PHONE WAS RINGING, but he ignored it. "I need an update, please," he said, standing next to the command table.

"Almost everyone is in place," Bellas said. "Except for Kaladar. He has not reported in."

That wasn't good. Silanar needed every mage present and accounted for in order to initiate the ritual. "Call him again."

His phone was still ringing incessantly. Annoyed, he looked at the display. It was Kharis. Silanar picked up the call.

"Now's not a good time, Kharis," he said.

"Are you watching the news?" Kharis asked.

"I'm nowhere near a TV. Why?"

"I think the Cothellon are making their move."

"Any idea what they're doing? Will it affect the ritual?"

"It might," Kharis said. "It's—"

The connection cut out. Silanar tried to call Kharis back, but he had no signal. The cell tower nearby must have gone out. That was strange.

Silanar turned to the command table. "Check your phones," he said. "I think everything just went dark."

This would make it very difficult to conduct the ritual.

QUYNN HAD JUST CONCLUDED his final mindmaster meeting. Everyone was prepped and ready to receive the population. He himself wouldn't be doing the grunt work, of course. He'd just be on hand to ensure things went smoothly.

But now the entire city was tilting in the air.

He stumbled into Mission Control, wondering what in the hell was going on. "TTD program is ready," one of the officers was saying as he entered. The room was bustling, dozens of commanders and technicians sitting in front of rows of consoles, each wearing headsets and fingering thick manuals. A massive row of screens took up the entire front wall, looking like something out of Star Trek. Quynn suppressed a moment of glee. They were really doing this. It was really happening.

"All departments," Orym said, his amplified voice coming out of speakers around the room, "keep yourselves in your chairs, and standby for synchronization. We're working on the fallfoiler problem, but in the meantime we must continue with the mission." Quynn watched him carefully. Was there something different about the man?

Lorelei was standing next to Orym, still wearing that fiery red outfit of hers, listening to her communicator. After a moment, she nodded briskly and said something to Orym.

Orym put his mouth back to the microphone. "TTD program, activation in 5...4...3...2...1...mark!"

Quynn imagined he could hear it, the sound of all communication technology being destroyed around the planet. Then he actually *could* hear it—a series of explosions rippling through the city below them. City Three had moved in the past hour, lifting itself over the original San Francisco.

"Prepare for decloak," Orym said.

"Shields ready," came the response.

"Decloak." A loud whine filled the air, thrumming through the desks and monitors, vibrating the floor under Quynn's feet. The forcefields were coming down. All around the world, the seven great sky cities were becoming visible.

This was it. There was no going back now.

THE TELEVISION WENT OUT, displaying nothing but snow.

Kharis set his drink down carefully on the bar. Everyone

in Syndra's was already on their feet at that point, watching the news with rapt attention. The plane crashes had been just the beginning. Reports had been coming in one after another: hurricane force winds in Utah; rioting in Manhattan; two dozen fishing boats missing off the coast of Australia; the Russian government suddenly declaring martial law; strange cattle stampedes in Texas; animals fleeing from the forests in Northern California for no apparent reason; the sudden disappearance of clouds over London.

And then, just before the video cut off, the strangest report of all. Odd metal doorways were appearing in locations around the Bay Area, funny metal contraptions with wires and tubes that led to nowhere. Eyewitnesses had claimed that the doors came down from the sky, but reporters weren't taking them seriously.

And now the TV had gone dead. The whole world had gone to hell in less than six hours. Kharis felt the pit growing in his stomach. His friend—or the man he'd thought of as his friend—was responsible for all of this.

What would the world look like tomorrow?

A loud, high sound suddenly pierced the air, louder than anything Kharis had ever heard before. The bar erupted into screams, everyone dashing for the exit. Kharis ran with them, caught up in the flow, jostled violently about as he made his way through the door to the tavern and out into the village itself.

When he saw what had made the sound, his jaw dropped.

SEVENTY-SEVEN

THEY BROKE INTO A RUN. Jason clung to his mother, arms around her neck, bouncing up and down as they moved. He looked up into the sky, squinting at the bright sunlight.

Something was wrong with the air overhead.

The ground trembled again, and a piercing sound filled the air. As Jason looked up, the sky disappeared and something huge shimmered into being high above them, blocking the sun.

It looked like a city.

Jason knew San Francisco. He lived there, after all. This looked like that city, but upside down, with huge towers of metal thrusting down from a vast platform. Scaffolds and frameworks hung from the platform in a complex array of metal shapes. The massive structure cast a sudden shadow on the streets below.

The shouting around them increased as everyone frantically ran in the direction Jason and Jessica were headed, their necks craning up to look at the incredible city floating in the sky.

His mother started running faster.

"WHEN WERE you going to tell me about this bug?" Lorelei shouted.

Orym looked stricken, his face all white. "I—I didn't think it was actually going to be a problem."

"You're useless," Lorelei said. "Remind me to fire you when this is over. But first: how are we fixing this? We're about to fucking *crash*."

The city tilted ponderously, moving to a fifteen degree angle. Everything shifted, sliding across the floor: desks, people, chairs. One of the displays disconnected from the wall, falling to the floor in a shower of sparks and glass.

Sylvis looked up from where she was sprawling on the floor. "Cundu," she said. "That engineer. Thalanil. He's down in Gate Control now, trying to fix the problem."

"Well, tell him to fix it *faster*," Lorelei said.

This entire plan was about to be foiled by a goddamn *bug*. Lorelei had known she shouldn't trust computers.

"THALANIL," a voice said in his ear. "Come in."

It was Sylvis in Mission Control. Sylvis, second in command to Orym himself. Thalanil was honored to be hearing directly from her.

But he was far too busy dodging Keya's sword to respond.

"I'll make you pay," his daughter said, slashing at him. But the city moved again, and the swipe went wide.

Thalanil had the computer case open, the new motherboard in his hand. He had to pull the power to this system, finishing the replacement as quickly as he could. But all of this was difficult to do with a sword hovering about his head.

"You sound like a cliche," he said. "Like the villain from some movie. Is that who you really are, Keya? I've been following you, you know. Keeping an eye on you."

Keya's sword dipped. "What?"

Thalanil nodded. "Sure. You're my *daughter*, remember? And even though I couldn't contact you, I wanted to make sure you were okay. I even helped you, from time to time. Remember that job at the American Cancer Society?"

"I got that job myself."

"You did. And I'm very proud of you for it. But Keya, your father wasn't happy about it. I talked some sense into him."

"You...spoke with my father?"

It was actually working. Thalanil nodded, choosing that moment to pull the power to the affected computer system. The motherboard was next: he used his screwdriver to quickly unseat it from the case, the movements practiced from many decades of building PCs.

"I had to," Thalanil said, focusing on the task at hand. "Tanyl might not be your flesh and blood, but he's your father just the same. I wanted to be there for you, but I couldn't. So I did the best—the only—thing I could."

He glanced at Keya, saw the tears in her eyes. But he couldn't focus on that now.

He had a city to save.

SEVENTY-EIGHT

AS HE BOUNCED up and down in Jessica's arms, Jason got brief glances behind them. A taxi cab had crashed into a tree in someone's lawn, smoke from the car spewing up into the air. A guy with blood dripping down his face was stumbling away from the crash, looking toward him with a haunted expression. Wait—was that *Dillon*? He couldn't tell.

He turned his head to look in front of them. A device of some sort had been setup in the middle of the street, and everyone was running toward it. It looked like a door, but with a metal frame and metal joints holding it upright on the ground, pipes and wires running up to it from somewhere else.

The view beyond the door was hard to understand—everything was warping and swirling and shifting as he looked through it. Were those buildings he could see? Little wisps of white light escaped from the edges of the door, curling into the air and disappearing a moment later. It was like nothing he had ever seen before.

The street was growing crowded, with people from all over the neighborhood running toward the door. Some carried children, some had bags and bicycles, and others pulled their dogs with them on strained leashes. One lady looked like she had just gotten out of the shower—she was wearing nothing but a robe, her wet hair flying every which way as she ran.

Jessica pushed forward, pressing her way through the crowd and up to the door. People bumped into Jason, jostling him as they moved. He clung tighter to his mother, grateful that he didn't have to run through the press of people on his own.

Moments later, they were at the strange door. A huge rumble started from somewhere far to their left, and the ground shook harder than it had before. Scared, Jason buried his face in his mother's shirt as she stepped forward and through the door.

He felt something cold wash over him, as if he'd been drenched in icy water. There was a moment of disorientiation, as if he'd forgotten where he was, but it only lasted for a second.

Then he opened his eyes to look around.

They were no longer on their neighborhood street, but in a large square flanked by tall buildings. Metal edges gleamed in the suddenly bright sunlight, their bulk casting heavy shadows on the pavement below. The whole thing seemed angled, somehow, as if the city was floating in the wrong direction. But Jason and his mom stepped forward anyway, fighting the angle, heading toward the edge of the square. Jason held tightly to her neck as they neared the edge. As they approached it, he heard his mother give a small cry. He looked out over the railing to see what had caused her distress.

They were floating in the sky.

There was no other way to describe it. Their feet were on

pavement, and large buildings surrounded them, but the ground—the ground they had just come from—was far below. Jason could see houses and buildings and trees and parks underneath them. People on the ground were running back and forth, looking like that ant nest he had accidentally disturbed the week before.

Why were they here? What was going on? Where was his father? His mind was filled with questions, questions that he wasn't sure he'd get the answers to.

He reached into his pocket, feeling the darkprime wood that was still there.

He hoped he would never have another occasion to use it.

THE CITY TILTED FURTHER, and Lorelei heard screams as everything slid to the back wall of the room. She herself was already there, pinned against the sheetrock and cement.

"We need a fix for this!" she screamed, but nothing was happening. Everything was chaos.

The Ascension was about to fail.

THALANIL DIDN'T BOTHER SCREWING the new motherboard in place. It wasn't necessary, and he didn't have the time.

Keya was still hovering over him with a sword.

He pulled the single ATA daughterboard from the old system, replacing it on the new motherboard. Then he plugged the power supply back in, praying to Jesus that it would work.

"Mission," he said, and his earpiece activated.

"This is Orym," a voice responded. "Thalanil, please tell me you fixed the problem."

"It's fixed," Thalanil said. "But you need to reboot the control plane for it to take effect."

"Twins," Orym cursed. "We'll do it. Thanks."

He clicked off, and Keya gave him another glare. "Tell me why I shouldn't kill you now."

"Because I'm your father," Thalanil said, conscious of his pleading tone. "Because I love you!"

"You don't *love* me," Keya said. "It's because of you my mother died! You could have stayed. You could have taken her out of Sylrantheas, made her one of these...Cothellon. You could have *done* something, Thalanil. You didn't have to leave me be."

"System rebooting," a voice said over the PA system. "Please stand by."

"But look at you!" Thalanil said. "Look at who you've become! You're a nurse. You help cancer patients every day. You're a talented mage, and a loving daughter. You're everything every elf strives to be!"

"But there's something missing," Keya said, sword pointed at his throat. "My *mother*."

"Communications will resume in two minutes," the PA system said, and just then the city tilted even further to the side.

Keya lost her balance. She slipped, teetered, and fell off the edge of the metal platform.

Just like that.

But Thalanil was quick. He was there, grasping for her hand, keeping her from falling to the Earth so far below. It was difficult, but he held here there, swinging.

He really should have worked out more.

"I've got you," he said.

Keya had fear in her eyes. "I just wanted to have a family."

"I know, sweetie," Thalanil said. His grip was growing weaker. "Let me pull you up, and we can talk about it more. Somehow make amends."

"I—I'm sorry," Keya said. "I didn't mean to hurt you. I was just so *angry*. At Jessica, at you. At my mother." She was crying. He felt his heart break.

He tried to pull her up, but he wasn't strong enough. "Can you help me? Grab my hand with your other hand."

But Keya didn't seem to hear. "This isn't what I was meant to do."

"What? Keya, sweetie, I can't pull you up."

The city shifted further, metal groaning all around them.

"System reboot will be complete in ten seconds," the PA system said.

"I wasn't meant to wear a sword," Keya continued. "I wasn't meant to fight like this."

"I'm losing you!" Thalanil shouted. "I can't hold on!"

"Five," the PA system said.

"I was meant to *heal*," Keya said.

"Four."

"That Tuesday I was born must have been the worst day of your life."

"Three."

"I love you, Father. I'm sorry for causing so much trouble."

"Two."

"I'm not afraid of falling."

And Keya released her grip.

Thalanil watched her fall, her shape dwindling until it met the Earth far below.

Keya, his daughter, was truly dead.

"One."

He hadn't been able to save her.

"System reboot complete. Communications have been restored."

"Thanks, old friend," Orym said in his ear, and Thalanil clung to the metal deck as the city quickly righted itself.

He'd saved the city. He'd saved the Ascension. He'd saved the Cothellon plan.

But he'd lost his only daughter along the way.

SEVENTY-NINE

KEYA FELT her stomach drop as she fell, wind whipping through her hair and clothes. She could see the ground, see it rushing up to meet her, see the buildings and the streets of San Francisco far below. She had tried. She had tried to get revenge.

She knew now that it had been the wrong thing to do.

Her father didn't deserve that. Her father only wanted what was best for her. And he wasn't her father, anyway—not the one she knew. Tanyl was her father, the one who mattered.

But nothing mattered now. Now she was about to meet her end. There would be no healing through this one, not like in the church. No amount of primewood could fix a flattened corpse.

No matter who her father was, she hoped they would remember her fondly.

SOMETHING in the distance caught Jason's eye. It was below them—a shape that looked like a person. "Look," he said, pointing. Next to him, his mother gasped.

"Is that *Keya*?" she asked. "But I—"

"You thought you'd killed her," Jason said.

The woman was falling, falling quickly. In a matter of seconds, she would hit the ground. Then she would truly be dead, despite whatever miracle had kept her alive this long.

No one could survive a drop this far.

Acting on impulse, Jason activated the darkprime wood in his hand.

A forcefield appeared around Keya in the air, a shimmering bubble in the sky. His mind tracked her descent as she fell, moving the bubble alongside her. He could *sense* her now, feel her presence inside his magic.

"I felt it when you healed me," he said to Jessica. "I know what you did."

"You...you do?" Jessica sounded confused.

But Jason was focused on Keya. Keya, the woman who hadn't wanted him healed. Keya the elf, whom his mother had tried and failed to kill.

Jason didn't want anyone dying for him.

So he dove into the magic, looking *inside* it for the answers.

There. The particles. He could *feel* them, sense them.

He knew what he had to do.

A BRIGHT CIRCLE of light sprang up around Keya, surrounding her in the air. It touched her briefly as she fell, sending agonizing pain into her body. What was this? What was happening?

She recognized this magic.

It seemed a forcefinder had noticed her fall.

The forcefield touched her again as the ground grew closer. She wasn't slowing. She wasn't stopping. This energy field wasn't going to keep her from dying. But something happened when it touched her, sending shivers down her spine.

She felt something *changing* in her mind.

It was like an unlocking, like a heavy weight lifting from her. She felt new pathways opening, new Talents appearing. Memories returned to her.

Memories that should not have been hers.

She had no time to contemplate these things before the ground hit her, hard, and her last thought was one of—

She opened one eye.

What?

She was on the ground. Safe. Unharmed. She caught a glimpse of the forcefield dissipating around her, leaving nothing but the sun and air upon her skin. She was lying in the middle of Mission Street, and cars were honking at her to move.

None of this was making any sense.

She stood, staggering, as yet more memories assaulted her.

No. It couldn't be.

Impossible.

She needed to speak to her father.

EIGHTY

SILANAR CAUGHT himself gaping and closed his mouth with a snap. He needed to appear calm, in control. He needed to be the authority figure here.

But it was becoming increasingly difficult.

Above him, the Cothellon creation had finally appeared.

It was a replica of San Francisco, hovering above the city like a mirage. It was a nearly perfect copy: the Transamerica Pyramid was there, its triangular shape pointing upward like a giant dagger. Coit Tower was also there, and the Ferry Building. Neither of the iconic bridges were part of this new city, though, which somewhat spoiled the effect.

Still, it was an incredible feat.

Silanar was bewildered. Why in the hell would the Cothellon create a copy of a city? And how was it floating? Questions hurtled through his mind, spinning and tumbling.

"The phones still aren't working," Ytharra said.

"They did this," Silanar said. "It must be part of their plan."

"I fear you may be right."

Silanar shook himself, trying to regain his composure.

The Sundering must be completed, regardless of Cothellon actions. But as he looked out at the strange double skyline of San Francisco, Silanar had just one question.

What was the floating city *for*?

"SIR," Sylvis said, her voice urgent, "New Tokyo still hasn't reported in."

"Goddammit!" Orym exclaimed, earning him several looks. Maybe he'd overacted the part a bit. "Do we have them on satellite?"

"Satellites have all been destroyed as ordered, sir," Sylvis said, her face showing concern. "Are you okay?"

Orym looked up at the Mission Control screens. Secretly, he was hoping that New Tokyo would somehow fail. It would at least delay the plan, possibly by a long time. But he couldn't show that face to the crew members in Mission Control.

He leaned against the nearest desk. "I'm fine, Mission Leader," he said. "Go back to your station."

"Yes, sir."

Orym looked at the screens again. Six of the seven cities had completed their Uprising, and were now floating in their designated locations over major cities.

Now they would populate the cities with humans. It was time for the mindmasters to go to work.

DUNEDAR WAS BEING ESCORTED by two uniformed policemen from the New Tokyo Department of Corrections. They were taking him the wrong way, away from where he needed to be, but at least they hadn't killed him yet. Or hand-cuffed him, for that matter.

They must have been new to the job.

"Can you at least tell me the charges?" Dunedar asked, trying to get a look at the guys behind him. They were taking him through the Under, and it was dark. Hard to see.

"Shut up and move," one of the men said. "Eyes forward."

Well, there was nothing else for it. He would have to do something drastic.

DILLON STUMBLED away from the car, clutching his forehead. He'd had to kick the window out and crawl through it in order to escape the cab. The bandages around his ears were starting to itch, but the pain in his forehead captured most of his attention. He felt dizzy.

Then he looked up, and he felt even worse.

The city was there—City Three, as his father had told him —hovering over San Francisco, at once beautiful and terrible.

This had all been his father's invention. The great work of his life. The great, deadly, horrible work of his life.

Now Dillon would do what he could to help unravel it.

He struggled toward where the gate should be, people streaming by him in droves. Everyone was screaming or crying. The whole city was in an uproar. Dillon walked on, trying not to pass out.

He hoped he would make it in time.

SILANAR'S WATCH was still working, at least. 11:50 AM. It was almost time to start the soulsunder ritual. New San

Francisco was hanging motionless in the sky, intent on whatever dark purpose it had been created for. Silanar closed his eyes for a moment, gathering his thoughts. It was time to focus.

"We need to start," he said, looking around at the other elves under the command tent. "All the mages received my message from earlier, correct?"

Ytharra nodded. "We confirmed with them a few hours ago, before communications dropped. They will start the ritual with or without you, right on time."

"What about Kaladar?"

"He was still trying to get to his Tree when we spoke earlier. He got the message, but things were starting to get a little crazy in Spain at that point. He might not make it."

"What's going on over there?"

"He didn't say, exactly. Some kind of disturbance off the coast of France. Had everyone in the vicinity spooked."

Maybe it was another one of those damn city replicas.

"Well," Silanar said, "it's now or never."

He walked over to the Prime Tree they were camped under. The Tree was absolutely massive—the trunk alone was hundreds of feet in diameter, the wood filling his vision as he approached. He looked up, taking care not to lose his balance. The great Oak Tree's canopy must have easily been five hundred feet up—maybe more. The scale of it was hard to interpret. The trunk twisted slightly as it rose out of the ground, forming a slight corkscrew.

Silanar put his hand gingerly on the trunk. The wood felt warm to him, as all Prime Oak did. He imagined he could feel a heartbeat within it, an intelligence deep inside the enormous tree. He closed his eyes, just for a moment, relishing in it. It wasn't every day that he got to stand next to a Prime Tree.

He let out a deep, contented breath, feeling calmed by the Tree. He felt centered. Ready. He could do this.

He could murder billions of innocent souls.

His vision went black, suddenly, his ears filled with a screaming sound. A face flashed into his mind, all red, mouth gaping, eyes closed.

It was doing the screaming.

The sound got louder, piercing into his skull, vibrating into his very bones. Silanar found himself screaming along with the face inside his head. Then the eyes opened, and he felt pure terror slam into his soul. He fell to the ground, hunched into a ball.

The world went dark around him.

MOMENTS LATER, Jason's father appeared.

"Alan!" Jessica said breathlessly. "Where were you?" She narrowed his eyes. "Or should I call you Thalanil."

"I had to work," Alan said. "And you can call me Alan." His face was flushed, his brow covered in sweat. His eyes seemed dark, as if he'd seen something he regretted. "I guess we have a lot to talk about, but it will have to wait until all of this is over. I'm here now. I'm not going anywhere, and I'm glad you made it safely. Thank God you were in time."

"We saw Keya. She was falling out of the city. Did you have any hand in that?"

Alan's face was white. "She attacked me, claimed it was my fault her mother committed suicide."

"So you pushed her out of the city?"

"I tried to *save* her, actually. I had her in my hand, but she let go." His eyes were wet. "I didn't want her to die."

"Then it was a good thing I was here," Jason said.

His father turned to him. "What?"

"Your son saved her," Jessica said. "Using his magic."

Alan nodded slowly. "Of *course*. I'd always heard about forcefinders being able to cushion falls, but I'd never actually seen it in action. But how did you know what to do?"

"I felt it," Jason said. "It was inside me the whole time."

"Amazing. You must be a very powerful mage." He turned to Jessica. "Something about all this feels off, to me."

"What do you mean?" Jessica asked.

"It was something she said, just before she fell. That she'd been born on a Tuesday."

"What's so strange about that?"

"Well, Keya wasn't born on a Tuesday. I remember it. I was there."

"You were in the delivery room?"

"No, of course not. I was hidden elsewhere in the village, but I remember the day it happened. Aelynthi looked stricken, afterward. And I also remember quite clearly: I had been at church earlier that day. It wasn't a Tuesday, Jessica. It was Sunday."

"Maybe you're misremembering. Or maybe she was wrong."

"Maybe." He looked out at the world below them. "Or maybe we've been lied to this entire time."

EIGHTY-ONE

DUNEDAR FINALLY SPOTTED his chance to escape. They were just about to round a corner in the Under, a corner that he knew very well. There was a pipe up ahead, right at face level. He knew it, but the two policemen holding him evidently did not.

He ducked.

The officers ran headlong into the pipe, as he'd known they would. He used their brief moment of surprise to make his move.

The man on the left was easy to take out. Dunedar punched him swiftly in the crotch, then threw an elbow up into his face.

He spun, aiming a kick at the other guy, feeling his foot connect with the man's shin, hard. The policeman howled, turning to face him, but Dunedar already had his hand in the guy's hair.

He smashed the man's face into the wall. Once, twice, three times, hearing the crunch, seeing blood spatter on cement. That was enough.

The guy was done.

He let him drop.

Both policemen were down, and Dunedar hadn't even worked up a sweat. He wiped his hands on his jeans and continued down the tunnel.

A shot rang out just then, and the pipe next to him broke, cold water spraying into his eyes. He turned, trying to see through the water to where the shot had come from. A man was standing there, dressed all in black, with a gun pointed right at Dunedar's head.

Damn. Back to square one.

The man moved forward slowly, keeping the gun trained on him. He didn't say anything. Was he just going to shoot him, or did he want something?

"Hello?" Dunedar said. The water was still spraying, coating the wall and forming puddles where the cement floor was uneven. The man just kept approaching silently.

That was when the city *stopped*.

Inertial motion threw Dunedar and the strange man violently through the corridor, slamming them against the wall at the far end. Dunedar heard a sickening crunch as he hit, and his arm erupted in pain. Shit—he'd probably broken something. He blinked, trying to clear his head, and saw that the man with the gun was lying on the ground, crumpled up against the wall.

He wasn't breathing.

Dunedar stood up slowly, cradling his useless arm. He took a quick look around to get his bearings, then headed off toward where he needed to be.

He only made it a few feet before stopping. Then he turned around and came back to pick up the fallen man's gun. Better safe than sorry. Armed, he jogged off through the Under, his broken arm throbbing painfully with every movement.

He relished the pain.

He had far more killing to do.

SILANAR OPENED HIS EYES. Ytharra and Bellas were standing over him, concern written on their faces.

"What happened?" Ytharra asked.

"A vision of some kind," Silanar said, getting up. His head still hurt, but he felt the pain rapidly receding. The whole thing had been awfully strange. He'd never heard of anything like it before.

But then again, no one in written history had ever attempted a soulsundering before.

"Are you okay?" Bellas asked. "Can you continue?"

"I'm fine," Silanar said. "Assuming it doesn't happen again." He frowned at the Tree. It didn't look any different, but he could swear there was a malevolence lurking underneath the bark. He approached it warily, laying his hand on the trunk once more.

Nothing happened. The wood was still warm to the touch, but no face appeared, no screams pervaded his mind. Maybe it was safe.

It was time to begin.

He took a deep breath, intoning the words from the Book of Souls. Words that had been there for tens of thousand of years, just waiting to be spoken. He did not know where the Book had come from, who had created a ritual such as this. He only knew that it was necessary. It was required.

It was the only thing that would save this planet.

He completed the words.

Now the preparation was done. Now he needed Will. He

closed his eyes. In his mind, he sought a connection with the Tree.

Most elves never had the opportunity to connect directly with a Prime Tree. He himself had only done it once before, as a sort of test to figure out the process for the soulsunder ritual. The feeling was strong, intoxicating. Much purer than using primewood chips.

Much, *much* more powerful.

If he were strong enough...but no. Trying to use the entire Prime Tree at once would burn him out instantly. Oh, there were mages who had tried it. Luckily, their experiences had been written down for others to learn from. Or rather, outside observers had written it down.

The mages who had tried it themselves were very dead.

There was a reason Woodway mages used small pieces of wood, and not the Tree itself.

But this was the Primal ritual: the Sundering. This required the actual Trees, all fourteen types. He hoped he could control the magic. He hoped the other mages could, too.

He was about to kill billions of humans.

It would be a shame if he died along with them.

It took a moment for his Will to connect. But once it did, awareness flooded into his head like a lightning bolt. His senses sharpened, his vision becoming that of the Tree's: impossibly tall and wide, overshadowing the land around it, visible for miles. The Tree uncoiled in his thoughts, becoming aware.

Becoming *visible*.

Silanar's thoughts expanded, then, zooming out, out, out, until he could see the curve of the planet. Clouds shifted in his vision, wind whipping by his mind. And he could see them. The Trees, thirteen of them, shaking off their millennia of stupor, their eons of concealment. Connecting together with invisible lines of power, surrounding the planet with their might and wonder.

The Tree he was touching rose, getting suddenly taller, twisting slightly as it moved. Its colors grew stronger, more saturated.

And Silanar knew that, for the first time, the whole world could see—*truly see*—the splendor and majesty of the Prime Trees.

EIGHTY-TWO

QUYNN WATCHED THE SCREENS, keeping tabs on the mission progress. He wasn't in charge—that was Lorelei and Orym. He wasn't even City Director—the idiot Aelwynn had been given that position. No, Quynn was stuck as the lowly mindmaster in charge.

He really needed a title.

But Quynn didn't need to be in charge to feel important. He was, after all, the one who was fucking Lorelei.

That had to count for something.

"New Tokyo has arrived!" Sylvis exclaimed, out of breath.

"About time," Quynn muttered.

"Status report?" Orym asked.

"They sustained some damages," Sylvis said, "mostly to the Under. But all systems are reporting as operational at this time."

"Good," Orym said. "Tell them to decloak and finish populating. They're behind schedule."

"Yes, sir."

THE SQUARE WAS FILLING up with people, milling about and talking excitedly with each other. There was a feeling of anticipation in the crowd. Jason was wondering if any of his friends from school would be up there with them, when suddenly his mother let out a gasp.

"What *is* that, Thalanil?" she asked.

Jason looked out over the railing to where his mother was pointing. An enormous tree had appeared in the distance, in the middle of a forest. It was a hundred times bigger than any tree Jason had ever seen, towering far above the rest of the forest. A wide canopy of green topped a massive trunk of gnarled wood, lifting up, up, far above the ground. As he watched, the tree twisted and seemed to grow even larger. Something about it pulsed, as if the very color of the leaves was growing stronger bit by bit.

His father grunted. "That's a Prime Tree. The source of elven magic."

Further away, nearly to the horizon, Jason could see another great tree. It was easily taller than the hills and houses near it, rising what must have been hundreds of feet above the ground.

The air above the second tree shimmered, and another floating city faded into view, high up in the sky a long way away. It looked like a vast island of metal, hovering motionless above the tree. Jason could see skyscrapers rising in great spikes above the city, and long metal stacks jutting down from the bottom, pointing toward the ground below. It was all so strange, so frightening.

DILLON STRUGGLED to make it to the gate. His head was hurting terribly, and he was feeling woozy from loss of blood.

But this, he knew, was his only chance. He needed to get into the city in order to infiltrate it. There would be no other way on board after that.

The others on the street had cleared away, passing through the gate or running in other directions. The neighborhood was now eerily silent.

Dillon was almost there.

DUNEDAR DIDN'T RUN into any other resistance on the way to his destination. He barreled through the little doorway, ducking his head as he entered, keeping the gun out in front of him. The room was dark, and he didn't see anyone inside other than the body he had left there.

Good.

He felt around on the wall until he found his electric torch. He clicked it on, and stark white light suddenly illuminated the space. He waved the torch, letting the light play across the device he had assembled. It had been painstaking work, but it was ready, and it was beautiful. A beautiful mechanism, built for pure destruction.

He ran his finger along a wire, lovingly touching where it connected to the ignitor. It was a shame such beauty must be destroyed, but such was life. Such was death. Such was the lot he had been given.

He knew that what he was doing was right.

He put the gun down carefully on the table, taking one last look at his handiwork. He didn't need the cellular trigger. The city was going to die in any case. All he needed was himself and his conviction.

He flicked the manual switch, and the short countdown began.

In his final moments, Dunedar knelt and prayed to the Twins.

AELWYNN STOOD IN THE DOORWAY, watching the Citizens arrive, his chest swelling with pride. They weren't there for him—they were there for a greater good. And he had been chosen to lead them to glory.

The humans arriving here would be eternally grateful to him for this chance.

He went back into the room, checking his reflection in the mirror. The darkprime misting still held—his ears looked like that of a human. It would not do to frighten the new Citizens on this, the day of all days. Satisfied with his appearance, he walked out into the square to welcome his people.

"COMMANDER," Sylvis said, "we're getting reports of retaliatory strikes being readied by the US military. Recommend pulling out now."

"What is our population level?" Orym asked. He could see Lorelei pursing her lips out of the corner of his eye, but she didn't say anything.

"Nearly full, sir," Sylvis said. "Within ninety percent."

"Very well," Orym said. "Close the gates on City Three, and give me a status update on the other cities."

"Yes, sir."

DILLON FELL, skinning his knees and wrists badly on the asphalt. He was within a few feet of the gate. He was the only one left on the street, the only one remaining to enter the great city above. He forced himself up, ignoring the pain, trying to keep his eyes open. His body felt numb. His muscles wouldn't respond properly.

The gate in front of him flashed suddenly, emitting green wisps of light from its edges instead of white. The vision of the crowded city square beyond the gate clouded for a moment, then became clear again.

Shit. They were closing the gate. He probably only had seconds to get through.

He was so close.

Dillon closed his eyes and jumped through the gate, hoping it wouldn't close while he was partway through, severing his body in half.

He felt an icy chill wash over him, and he opened his eyes.

THE GATE FIZZLED ONCE, then shut down. Aelwynn caught a glimpse of one final, desperate human flying through the gate just before it collapsed. The poor boy had barely made it in time.

Aelwynn strode forward into the square, eyeing everyone in it. They were a disheveled bunch, with mismatched clothes and wild hair. Children were crying. Men were speaking to each other with rough voices. There was an air of great concern throughout the square.

Aelwynn frowned. This wasn't quite what he'd been expecting. It wasn't the proud populace, happy to welcome their new leader. The crying children hurt his ears, and he grimaced. He hated children and all their mewling.

Well, he would have to make the most of a bad situation. It was the lot he'd been given. He took a deep breath.

"Citizens!" he said, giving what he hoped was a magnanimous gesture. "Thank you for coming." He'd prepared a speech for this moment. It wasn't a great speech, since he hadn't been given a speech writer, but it would do. "You have all been chosen for a reason," he said. "This will—"

Suddenly the communicator in his ear buzzed. "There's been an explosion on City Seven," the voice said. It was Orym, Mission Commander for the entire fleet of cities. Aelwynn felt honored to be hearing directly from the man.

"A moment, please," Aelwynn said, addressing the crowd.

He saw smoke in the distance, and New Tokyo started tilting.

"DAMMIT," Orym said as the floor lurched beneath him, "stay focused, people." He looked at the screen as the aftermath of the bomb on City Seven became visible. The city had started tipping already, beginning to fall.

"We don't have much time," Sylvis was saying. "There are a few mages left, but they can't keep the city floating for long."

"Aelwynn is strong," Quynn said, "but can he keep the whole thing up?"

"No," Lorelei said. "Give him the Staff."

Quynn looked at her dubiously. "Are you sure?" he asked. "What if he burns out? Or worse, destroys the Staff?"

"We can't lose that city," Lorelei said. "Go. Now. Get the Staff to him."

All of their planning was about to come to ruin, thanks to

a bomb that had somehow completely escaped their attention.

Quynn ran out of Mission Control, cursing the Eldrim.

EIGHTY-THREE

AELWYNN CONTINUED LISTENING to Orym's voice over the communicator. "We lost nearly all the fallfoilers on active duty," he was saying. "The bomb was positioned in *just* the right place. They're trying to activate new mages now, but the city is already beginning to fall. Aelwynn, you're the strongest fallfoiler we have nearby. We need you to keep the city up until we can get more mages on it. Quynn is bringing you something that will help."

Aelwynn looked over to where City Seven was, a few miles away in the sky. New Tokyo was smoking, listing to one side.

Something had gone horribly wrong.

Aelwynn frowned. There was no way a single mage could keep an entire city aloft, especially from so far away. That was why fifteen of them were supposed to be on duty at any one time. Doing it himself was impossible, unless there was a way to amplify or channel more magic.

Quynn burst through the door just then, carrying with him the Tree Ring Staff.

Of course! Aelwynn recognized the Staff. This was the

artifact he needed. With it, he might be able to keep New Tokyo afloat. He'd long wanted to try it, to see if all the rumors about its power were true.

This was finally his chance.

"Use this," Quynn said in a loud whisper. "But please be careful. We don't want anything to happen to it."

Aelwynn took the staff from Quynn, gripping it around the maple portion, which was warm to the touch. "Will this work for darkprime magic?" he asked.

"Yes," Quynn said. "Now hurry!"

Aelwynn concentrated, holding the staff forward at an angle and raising his other hand, Willing the magic to come forth. He felt it instantly, a torrent of power rushing through him from the Staff. It was like suddenly being thrown into a rushing river. He gasped from the suddenness of it, from the raw energy that now cascaded through him. He almost lost consciousness, then, succumbing to the pure power of the Staff. He swayed, struggling to keep his balance.

"You can do this," he said to himself.

He concentrated harder.

He felt the power take form, his mind shaping it into a line, a beam of energy. He directed that energy out over the crowd of humans, over to the falling city of New Tokyo. As he worked, shaping and forming the magic to do his bidding, he could see lights swirling in the air around him. He'd never seen that before with fallfoiler magic, but he paid it no attention, focusing instead on the city. He felt sweat break out on his brow.

There—he had it! The city was within his grip, magically held in the air by the force of his mind and his immense power. He could feel it, feel the incredible weight of the city being buoyed by the magic. It was incredible, this feeling of power.

It was intoxicating.

He felt his face flush, his breathing growing more rapid. The power continued to surge through him, channeling out of the Staff through the core of his being.

He was doing the impossible.

His heart was pumping almost audibly in his chest now. He could feel it, thumping there as if trying to get out. He felt blood rush in from his extremities, and suddenly his hands and feet were very cold. The lights continued circling around him as his vision began to swim. He heard a roaring sound in his ears, and the weight of the city pressed in all around him. It was so heavy, so ponderous. He couldn't keep it in the air. It was going to crash if he didn't stop it, and all the Cothellon's plans would be ruined.

He couldn't let that happen. Struggling to see through increasingly blurry vision, he dug even deeper into the Staff. He just needed a little bit more power, and he could keep the city afloat. He would be the one who saved the Ascension. He would be a hero! He would be—

Aelwynn felt the energy burn through him, tearing through his body as if a volcano had erupted in his veins. It ripped through him in a flash, and he felt as if his very soul was being torn apart. He opened his mouth to scream, but everything around him had suddenly disappeared.

Aelwynn fell to the ground, dead.

EIGHTY-FOUR

JASON, still held in his mother's grasp, looked out again at the other floating city. As he watched, it tilted slightly, then more, starting to lose altitude. Black smoke billowed out from underneath the city as it slowly fell, tilting ponderously, its tall buildings shining in the bright sunlight.

The crowd had seen it too, and now everyone was watching, their attention riveted on the distant falling city. The metal monolith continued listing to one side and dropping slowly, inexorably to the ground.

It was on a collision course with the massive tree below it.

The floating city fell and fell, and as Jason watched, it hit the tree, snapping branches and flattening leaves. The tree was nearly as tall as the city itself, and Jason stared open-mouthed as the two behemoths collided. Even from such a great distance away, Jason could hear the crunching and squealing as wood and metal ground together in mutual destruction.

The metal city now twisted and broken apart, crashed into the great tree's trunk, splitting it down the middle. The sound was almost deafening as the destruction continued. Explosions rocked the city, and fires broke out along the great tree's branches. A cloud of dust and smoke billowed out from the area, pieces of wood and metal flying rapidly through the air.

It was all happening very far away, but Jason could still feel his father's fear. Jessica held on to Jason and watched as the destroyed city reached the ground, pieces collapsing in a rain of metal and smoke.

His mother was crying.

"That could have been us," she said, looking up at Thalanil through tear-filled eyes.

His father shuddered. "It could have," he said, his jaw tight. "Maybe God is watching out for us."

"Or maybe we're just the lucky ones."

As Jason dared a glance behind him, he thought he saw a ghostly tree somewhere in the sky. "What is that?" he asked.

"What is what?" his mother asked, squinting at the sky.

The tree was already gone.

"ALL HANDS LOST," Sylvis reported, her voice mournful.

"You can't be sure of that," Orym said. He was taking care to keep an even expression. Inwardly, he was relieved that City Seven had been destroyed. The Eldrim must have had someone embedded in that city. For how long? How had they known what to do? Regardless, it had been an incredible feat, sneaking a bomb of that power through Cothellon security, and keeping it hidden for that long.

But he couldn't show those thoughts. Outwardly, Orym tried to look sorrowful—angry, even. He looked over at Lorelei. She was slumped against a desk, mouth slightly open, eyes staring at nothing.

He had never seen her react like that to anything before.

"Nobody could have survived that," Sylvis said. She turned away from him and sat back down at her desk.

The room was silent for a long moment.

"Interesting turn of events," Quynn said quietly in Orym's ear. Orym jumped, startled. He turned to Quynn.

"What do you mean?" he asked.

"How long has it been since you discovered the fatal flaw in the device?"

Orym cleared his throat uncomfortably. "That was yesterday, sir," he said, an icy feeling sinking into his stomach.

Quynn seemed to think about that for a moment, then shrugged. "Well, then, it couldn't have been you." He looked up at Orym, eyes narrowed slightly. "Not enough time."

Then he turned abruptly and strode out of the room, laying a brief hand on Lorelei's arm before exiting.

Orym watched him go.

"Lorelei?" he asked after Quynn was gone. The leader of the Cothellon was still leaning on his desk with a vacant expression. "Lorelei, what should we do?"

His words seemed to rouse her. She straightened, drawing in a deep breath, and turned to look at him. Her eyes were red to match her dress.

"Cloak the device," she said, so quietly that Orym had to strain to hear. "Mission aborted."

Orym swallowed, turning to face where Sylvis was sitting at the front of the room, her back to him. "Mission Leader," he said firmly, "mission is aborted. I repeat, mission is aborted. All remaining cities are ordered to cloak and move off-position two city lengths."

"Aye, sir," Sylvis said from her position at the desk.

"What population did we achieve?" Orym asked.

Sylvis was silent for a moment, tapping on her screen. "Most cities reporting ninety percent or higher," she said.

"City Seven had achieved forty percent population before it was destroyed."

The cities were designed to hold about two to eight million humans each. New Tokyo had been the largest, with capacity for ten million. At forty percent capacity, that meant around four million people had died during the crash. Innocent humans.

Wasted lives.

Except not wasted, for those four million poor souls had actually saved the planet from sure destruction. The Cothellon device could no longer work, as long as that city was gone.

Orym found himself gripping the desk, knuckles white. He forced himself to let go, turning to Lorelei. "What will we do?" he asked.

"We will rebuild," she said. "This is not the end."

JASON LOOKED toward the center of the square. The man with the staff was still on the ground, and it didn't look like he was breathing. Several attendants in dark uniforms were huddled around him, speaking frantically. Jason couldn't hear what they were saying.

He looked at his father, who was still staring resolutely out beyond the rail.

"Can we go home now?" he asked.

His father looked at him, eyes dark. "Son," he said, taking in a deep breath, "this is our home now."

Jessica whimpered next to him.

EIGHTY-FIVE

THE GROUND WAS SHAKING, leaves and small branches falling from the Tree. Silanar held himself flat against the trunk, trying to shelter himself from the majority of the detritus. Through the Tree's expanded vision, he had seen the floating city crash, seen it destroy the Prime Tree it had been hovering near. He had felt it like a shot to the gut, the Prime Trees reeling with pain from it. The network of trees had fragmented, separating into distinct Trees. Silanar had lost his ability to see the whole planet, had been thrown back down into the Oak he was next to. Then the network had been restored, minus the poor Prime Pine that had died.

The Oak that Silanar was touching felt like it was shivering, but Silanar realized it was more of a mental thing. He could still feel the Tree's thoughts, knew its distress. Silanar himself was upset—he could feel his heart beating rapidly, and he struggled to get his breathing under control. The death of a Prime Tree was a terrible thing. It had never happened before, to his knowledge.

And it was his fault.

If he hadn't uncloaked the Trees at that moment, there

was every likelihood that the city would not have destroyed it. Silanar wasn't quite sure how it worked, but the Trees didn't seem to take up physical space when they were cloaked, at least in the human world. Elves could see them, could even touch them, but humans could walk right through them without knowing it.

Silanar believed that the Tree would have been safe if he hadn't begun the ritual. He knew that the death of the Prime Pine would haunt him for the remainder of his days.

He sensed someone near him, and he opened his eyes. His vision was strangely doubled—he could still see through the eyes of the Tree network, but he could also make out the world around him. Ytharra was drawing near.

"Silanar," she said, her face downcast, "I'm so sorry."

"Edyrm is dead, isn't he," Silanar said. Edyrm had been the mage assigned to that Prime Pine.

Ytharra nodded. "Communications are still down," she said, "likely permanently. But yes, he must be dead. No one could have survived that."

Silanar looked up at the sky, where he could still see the floating San Francisco skyline. The Cothellon would pay for this, he vowed. He would make them pay.

The city suddenly shimmered away, disappearing from view.

"We must continue," he said, scowling at the sky. "But there are only twelve Trees now. Where is Kaladar? And how can we replace the Pine that was just destroyed?"

"I do not know," Ytharra said. She followed his gaze to the sky.

"HOW FAST CAN THIS THING GO?" Quynn asked. The fallcar was shooting through the air, forests and rivers and farmlands passing underneath them in a blur. Quynn wished they were flying a bit higher.

"Fast enough," the captain said. He was a very strong fallfoiler, and one of the most skilled fallcar captains Quynn had had the pleasure of meeting. "We'll be there in five minutes."

That must explain why the fallcar was so damn loud. Fallfoiler darkmages were capable of raising and lowering the aircraft with incredible precision and power, but they couldn't move the car laterally. That was where traditional engines came in, lending forward momentum, like a plane. But unlike a plane, the car had no need for aerodynamic lift, so there were no wings, and the vehicle itself could be rather small.

Small, but loud. And apparently *very* fast. Lorelei must have approved one of the emergency transports. He'd never been on one of those before.

They arrived in New Manhattan within minutes, as promised. Quynn thought it was a bit excessive bringing him all the way across the United States just to reign in a few moronic humans, but he didn't mind being of use. He'd been feeling a bit useless in Mission Control.

As soon as he stepped out of the fallcar, Quynn realized the depth of the problem here in City Four. Sound assaulted him, screams and crashes and honking horns. Apparently some idiot had activated the electric cars before the Citizens had been properly subdued. Grathgor had made a mess of things, which was unlike him. Or perhaps these Citizens' minds were particularly unreceptive for some reason.

It happened, sometimes.

He walked down the steps leading from the landing platform, turning his gaze to the edges of the crowd, trying to find the mindmasters. Here and there he saw them, in trim uniforms of dark blue, with stripes of white on their sleeves. There weren't as many of them as he expected, which was strange. Perhaps that explained why the Citizens were revolting.

He reached about halfway down the stairs and stepped out onto a metal dais that overlooked the main town square, where all the Citizens had entered the city. Opening his case of dark yew, he clicked on his communicator.

"Grathgor?" he said.

"Thank the Twins, you made it," Grathgor said.

"Are the riots contained to this area?"

"For the most part, yes," Grathgor said. "Although it's spreading. You got here fast."

"I'll update you soon," Quynn said, clicking off and staring out at the crowd. It was a frenzy, for the most part, with people fighting each other, breaking things, and setting things on fire. Had the mindmasters here not properly softened the people before dropping the gates?

As he scanned the crowd, Quynn thought he saw a pattern emerging. The people's movements seemed to center around a smaller group. It was difficult to see it, but he had a great deal of experience with this sort of thing. Yes, there was definitely an epicenter to the madness. A source. Cutting out the core would help a great deal. But first, he needed to quiet the masses.

He reached into his case and pulled out a handful of dark yew. The familiar wood was warm to the touch, almost pulsing with glee at being released. He could feel the wood's sickly sweet allure, longing to reach its dark tendrils up through him, to grasp his very soul. He held the wood tightly.

It would not control him.

He burned the wood then, closing his eyes as the familiar ecstasy of darkprime magic took hold. His thoughts went sideways, veering into madness, but he reeled them back. He was in control.

He opened his eyes, raising his fist with the wood in it out over the crowd. From his vantage point on the dais, he could see everyone, could visualize their emotion, could empathize with their pain.

He could control them.

Quynn released a massive dulling effect, then, a blanket of emotion-sapping that settled over the crowd like a thick fog. Almost immediately, fights became slower, voices less pronounced. Some people sat down on the ground, no longer certain where they were or what they were doing. Others turned around in circles, their minds no longer working correctly. A woman near Quynn fainted, her mind unable to cope with the intense field he had summoned.

It was perhaps the strongest mindfield he had ever created, but it still wasn't enough.

The leaders, the ones who had started this whole thing, were still resisting. Quynn could see them there, nearly unaffected by the mindfield, still inciting the people around them to madness. How were they doing that?

He set out down the stairs, heading for the troublemakers. He'd deal with them the old fashioned way.

With his fists.

EIGHTY-SIX

"ARE there any other Prime Pines in California?" Silanar asked,

"There is one other," Bellas said. "But it's four hours away. Can we delay the ritual that long?"

Silanar could feel his strength failing already. "No," he said. "If I stop the magic, there is only a ten minute window to start it again. And if we don't complete the ritual now, the Book says it will be a year before we can attempt it again."

"A *year?*" Bellas asked, dumbfounded.

"I didn't make the rules," Silanar said. "The Trees operate by their own set of laws—we just follow them. I have to hold this magic until we have enough Trees, and my energy is failing. I'm not sure how much longer I can last."

Bellas turned to Ytharra. "What are we going to do?"

Just then, Ytharra's phone started ringing.

THERE WERE FIVE OF THEM: big burly humans, ruddy-faced and sweating. They looked at Quynn as he approached, as if daring him to move against them. Their anger was palpable. Quynn wondered what had triggered it, why the mindmasters had failed to subvert their thoughts.

He raised a fist as he neared them, trying again with dark yew. He felt the magic enter his bloodstream, cascading through his body in a riot of energy. He expelled that magic in a puff around him, directing the mindfield at the five humans. He could see it move, a purple haze flowing shapelessly through the air. The humans couldn't see it, of course. Only mages could visualize the magic.

The mindfield enveloped the troublemakers. Quynn twisted the field with his mind, Willing the humans to lose their anger. The effects of mindmaster magic varied depending on the subject—some people were better able to resist the effects. But Quynn was a strong mage, and he had found that he could easily master most people.

Not these humans, apparently. The mindfield didn't seem to have any effect on them, which was strange. Usually only other mages could resist a mindfield this easily. Did these humans have some innate Talent?

Quynn tried again, stronger this time, burning five pieces of dark yew at once. The mindfield strengthened, thick purple smoke wafting around the humans, permeating their bodies. He twisted the field *hard*, using all his Will to make them obey.

"Kill the fucker," one of the men said.

Someone threw a punch at Quynn. He was so surprised that he didn't get out of the way in time, and the punch landed squarely on his jaw. It hurt like hell, and Quynn saw stars for a moment. How was his mindfield not working? He should have used his Talent scan, instead. Probably all of them were mages. But there was no more time for questions —the men had all turned on him.

Now it was time to fight.

Quynn deflected the incoming kicks and punches from the group of men, spinning and dodging to avoid them. Within moments, he had dispatched the first of them, sending him crashing to the ground with a swift kick. Then he whirled, ducking under a punch and striking another of the men hard in the stomach. The man buckled reflexively, and Quynn straightened, chopping down on the man's neck. The man dropped, unconscious. The next man proved harder —they sparred back and forth, neither of them gaining the upper hand. Quynn finally managed to get the man into a choke hold, but not without taking a punch to the kidney from one of the remaining men. Quynn threw his target to the ground, kicking him savagely in the face, blood spattering out from his ruined nose.

Three down, two to go.

The last two men circled Quynn warily. He flicked his communicator on, holding himself in defensive stance—fists ready, not allowing his opponents to get behind him. A space had formed in the crowd, people watching the fight with rapt expressions. His first mindfield still seemed to be holding, at least—the riots had stopped.

"Grathgor," Quynn said into his communicator. "I've got a group of humans who are resisting me. We need to eject them."

"What?" Grathgor said, his voice crackling. "How are they resisting?"

"I don't know," Quynn said, dodging sideways as one of the men tried to land a punch. "They're completely impervious to the magic."

"My men are all busy trying to quell the crowds," Grathgor said, "but I'll see what I can do."

"Don't take all day," Quynn said.

Suddenly, one of the two men moved in, striking Quynn hard across the cheek, then sweeping his legs out from under him. The man was *fast*, and Quynn hadn't had time to react. He fell, rolling on the rough pavement. He felt a kick on the stomach and another on his leg, and he struggled to get up amidst a blur of limbs. The crowd was cheering now, urging his attackers on.

Quynn huddled on the ground as the two men continued beating on him.

EIGHTY-SEVEN

"YES?" Ytharra said, answering her phone.

Silanar was beginning to feel weak—the energy required to keep the Tree network running was eating away at him.

Ytharra listened on the phone for a minute. "Excellent," she said, "good job. The ritual will continue momentarily." She hung up.

"Who was that?" Silanar asked, fatigue creeping into his voice. "And how is your phone working?"

"It was Chasianna," Ytharra said. "She managed to get me through a satellite that wasn't destroyed. She's with Kaladar in Spain."

"Oh," Silanar said.

"She said Kaladar should be arriving at his Tree shortly," Ytharra continued. "Chasianna was calling me from a Prime Pine she found in Spain. *Pinus pinaster*, a breed specific to that region. Will it work?"

"I believe so," Silanar said. His head was getting foggy with the effort of holding the ritual. "Why is she there? How did she know?"

"Chasianna was accompanying Kaladar to his Tree," Ytharra said. "As for how she knew...I have no idea."

Silanar bowed his head. It must have been the Twins looking out for them. "The ritual must continue now," he said, eyes closed.

He heard Ytharra and Bellas retreating, giving him space.

QUYNN WAS SUDDENLY FLOATING in the air.

He opened his eyes, looking around. A dozen or more humans were also floating with him, including the five men who had attacked him, the ones who had incited the riot. Quynn's body was hurting all over from the beating, but he had managed to remain conscious. The men were brutal, and far more skilled than he had expected them to be.

He looked around, trying to determine the source of the magic that now lifted them. Why hadn't the darkmage left him on the ground? Most skilled fallfoilers could selectively target individuals. This one had apparently just grabbed a circle of people indiscriminately.

He had his answer when he found the darkmage. It was a young elf—just a kid, really—standing nearby. The boy was concentrating hard, obviously trying not to drop them. Quynn didn't recognize him, but he was obviously inexperienced. Was this really the best Grathgor could do? The whole situation had been mismanaged from the beginning.

They floated in the air for several minutes, about twenty feet off the ground, twirling idly. Quynn could feel the magic's hold on his body, keeping him weightless but fixed at this altitude. Fallfoilers over the years had tried to figure out how to move objects anywhere other than up and down, but it had proved impossible. The best they could do was lift them.

Many Citizens were staring up at the floating people. Quynn didn't mind being the center of attention, but this was ridiculous. When was the fallfoiler going to let him go? He started to reach for his communicator, but suddenly a droplift flew into the square. The vehicle had an open platform on the back, probably used to transport materials.

As the droplift flew into position under the group of floating people, Quynn began to understand what was happening. Sure enough, the fallfoiler mage lowered them onto the deck of the vehicle, and the droplift sped away.

Quynn and the rest of the dozen humans stood up, struggling to maintain their balance on the flying platform. Air rushed by them, pushing them inexorably toward the back railing. It was a dangerous situation—if any of them fell or were pushed off the droplift, they wouldn't survive the fall. He suddenly felt a bit queasy. He'd never been good with heights.

The droplift sped across the city, making its way between buildings, heading to the Edge. Quynn felt his stomach drop as it flew beyond the city, out into mid-air three thousand feet above the ground.

This wasn't quite the ejection Quynn had envisioned.

The five ones who had attacked him had recovered. They gathered in a group, talking amongst themselves and shooting angry glances at Quynn. Quynn kept away from them, preferring to stand against the railing at the back of the droplift. The handful of other humans on the deck looked confused, most of them hanging on for dear life as the vehicle swooped away from the city and began descending. They were caught up in this now, along with Quynn's original five targets.

The five muscle-bound humans who had instigated the whole thing stayed away from Quynn as they flew on. Perhaps they understood what was coming. Or perhaps they had tired of fighting.

As Quynn looked out at the world below the droplift, his eyes were drawn to the massive silhouette of a Prime Tree in the distance. It was Prime Ash, if he wasn't mistaken. As he watched, he thought he saw the Tree grow larger, its colors strengthening. Was he imagining it, or were wisps of golden light surrounding the Tree, circling around it? The light looked like it was dancing. But it couldn't be—Prime Trees didn't do that. It must be a trick of the distance. The Tree was very far away, after all.

The droplift continued descending, spiraling down to the ground far below.

SILANAR CONCENTRATED on the Tree he was touching, his thoughts joining fully into the network. He felt a surge of power, and he was once again able to expand his vision, zooming rapidly out until he could see the whole network of Trees at once.

The original twelve were there, all of them except the Pine that had been destroyed by the falling city. They were connected together with glowing beams of light that arced from Tree to Tree, spanning countries and oceans and continents in a shining mosaic of lines.

But where were Kaladar and Chasianna? They needed to reach their Trees soon. Silanar felt his hand start to quiver where it touched the Tree. He wouldn't be able to keep this up much longer. He waited, the seconds feeling like days.

Then he felt them: first one, then the other, joining the

network of Trees like lights in a desert. He could feel them, feel their spirits joining the others, spreading their power across the vast world.

He queried the network, using a technique he'd read about in the Book of Souls, asking if the other mages were ready. One by one, they pinged back with "yes," their lights becoming brighter. Silanar felt his energy depleting, but he was almost done.

Just a little bit further.

He began uttering the Words of the Sundering. He'd memorized them that morning, reading them repeatedly from the Book. He'd felt the weight of them then, as he felt it now. This was it. This was the end.

This was the final blow to the humankind of Earth.

As he said the last word of the verse, he felt power spark from his Tree, shooting out along the connections it held, scintillating across the network of Trees like giant fireworks. The power leapt from Tree to Tree until it had touched them all, each one reacting in turn as it received the token of light and power.

Silanar felt the power of the Trees increasing, ratcheting up in verve and intensity, until he thought they were likely to burst. A pitch filled the air, at once too high to hear and too loud to bear. It was life. It was death. It was the sound of a billion souls caught up together, held forever in a single moment.

The soulsundering had begun.

EIGHTY-EIGHT

THE DROPLIFT DEPOSITED Quynn and his prisoners on the ground below New Manhattan. He'd been tasked with bringing a group of especially unruly passengers out of the city.

They hadn't responded to mindmaster magic.

And Quynn had wanted to get out, to take one last look at Earth before his great imprisonment in the sky.

He held one of the new mergeguns, ushering the five angry men off the droplift. The humans seemed at least a little bit frightened now. Magic hadn't worked, but it seemed they understood what a gun was.

"That's it," Quynn said. "You're free. Run along."

They just stood there, staring stupidly at him.

Well, Quynn's job was done. He could hitch a ride back home with this droplift, then take up office in his new city. He started to turn, but something caught his attention.

He stopped, looking around. What had he seen? It had seemed like a golden glimmer, a flash, just for an instant in the corner of his eye. He cast about, trying to determine what it had been. Probably nothing.

Then he saw a distant Prime Tree, an Oak. It was truly large now, towering what must easily be a thousand feet over the ground. Was this just his imagination? Had the Tree always been that large? He didn't think so, but he didn't spend much time around them. Perhaps he just had the scale wrong. Maybe it was an illusion due to how far away it was.

The Tree started glowing.

Quynn frowned. Now *that* definitely wasn't right. He knew for sure that glowing wasn't one of the things Prime Trees did. What was going on?

It must be the Sundering. The Eldrim plan.

He looked up to where he knew New Manhattan was, floating calmly far above him, cloaked in invisibility by forcefinder magic. Lorelei's timing had been perfect. With all the cities populated, the Eldrim were too late to stop the Cothellon's plan. They simply needed to rebuild the fallen city, and they'd be back in business.

Right?

The Tree *flashed* suddenly, becoming brighter than the sun. Quynn squinted, holding a hand to his face, unable to look directly at it. It still held the vague outline of a massive tree, the trunk and crown shape obvious, even though the thing was blindingly bright.

Then the Tree dimmed, and a sound began. It started as a high pitched kind of whistle, almost too high to hear. But then it got louder, permeating everything, and Quynn could hear a lower component, a bass rumble. Soon everything around him, the very land itself, was vibrating to the sound. Quynn felt his head start hurting from it, and he clapped his hands over his ears.

The humans were very agitated. They were shouting at each other, trying to be heard over the noise. The Tree was pulsing, growing brighter and dimmer every second, like a giant, golden, tree-shaped heart. Quynn wasn't sure what to do. Soulsundering wouldn't affect him, right? He thought of the city up above him. Would the forcefields protect it from the Primal magic? Would it even reach that far up?

He didn't know.

The sound grew even louder. The humans were down on their knees now, sobbing, obviously in great pain. Quynn's head was pounding, his heart beating in time with the Tree's pulsing.

That was not a good sign.

He looked around, suddenly frantic. The Tree. The soulsundering.

It was going to kill him.

"IT'S BEGINNING," Lorelei said.

"What is?" Orym asked.

"The Sundering."

Lorelei looked out at the bank of screens along the front wall, and Orym followed her gaze. Some of the cameras were pointed at the nearby Prime Trees, and Orym saw now that they were glowing a strange, golden, pulsing color.

"Will it affect the cities?" Orym asked.

Lorelei shook her head. "I do not know."

"Will it affect *us*?" He meant the elves.

"Not if they're performing the ritual correctly."

"And if not?"

"Then may the Twins protect us," Lorelei whispered.

Orym looked at the pulsing Tree with growing alarm.

SILANAR CONCENTRATED. He could feel his soul intertwined with the Tree somehow, as if his very being were connected to the magic. There was no way he could escape it now, even if he wanted to. From his vantage point high above the planet, he could see all the Trees. They were glowing, pulsing, building up strength for the final magic.

Silanar directed his thoughts into the Tree in front of him, focusing on doing what he could to control the magic. The Book of Souls had been unclear about this part of the process. The magic could be controlled, yes, but it was less of a science, more of an art. His goal was to sunder ninety-nine percent of the humans, leaving the one-percent and all the elves untouched.

He hoped the magic would do his bidding.

EVERYTHING WENT DEATHLY SILENT.

Quynn stood still, staring resolutely at the distant Prime Tree. It was still glowing faintly, but it had stopped pulsing to the beat of his heart. Or had his heart stopped? No, no, he had it all turned around. The humans around him had frozen, too.

All of them were looking at the Tree.

DILLON STOOD at the edge of New San Francisco, peering down at the dizzying ground below. The gate had done some-thing funny to his mind, had made him momentarily forget the moments leading up to his jump through it. Luckily, the moment had passed. His memory seemed fine. So he stood, his gaze focused on the Prime Tree at Mount Tamalpais, clearly visible from his location. The Tree was emanating a brilliant golden glow.

This was it.

The final moment of humanity.

He looked around him at the others gathered there, at the edge of this new world. They were scared, or sad, or excited, or confused. Everywhere he saw loved ones holding each other; old ones destitute and alone; calm ones helping young ones; distraught ones seeking comfort.

Everywhere he looked, he saw humanity.

He felt a tear come to his eyes as he looked once again, and for the last time, at the Earth that was.

WHEN IT FINALLY CAME, it came as a whisper.

A vast river of golden light, like fine strands or grains of sand, swept silently out from the Prime Trees. The wave shimmered across the planet: irrevocable, resolute. Gentle. Primal.

Death.

Quynn found himself shaking as it flew across the land, heading straight towards him. This was his final moment. This was the end. Had he lived the life he wanted to live?

He had no idea.

Then the river of golden sand swept over him and the others, hissing faintly as it passed. And as a group, every single human near Quynn dropped to the ground.

Dead.

He felt the energy pass through him. He could almost imagine it weighing him, testing him, deciding if he were true.

And as it passed, it made its decision.

Quynn lived.

The others died.

In the waning light of day, he almost thought he could see the very souls of those who were dead, carried up and out of their bodies, joining the wave of golden sunder, caught up and taken away into the sky.

Forever.

EIGHTY-NINE

"WE WERE SPARED," Lorelei said.

Mission Control was subdued. Nobody clapped or cheered. Nobody said anything, they simply watched their screens. Silent.

She was right. The cities had been spared the soulsundering—not a single person on them had died. Either the forcefields had kept the magic at bay, or their elevation had.

Orym sat at his desk, feeling alone. "I can't believe they went through with it," he said after a minute.

But then something else caught his attention. Something was happening on-screen. He looked at the camera that showed the Prime Oak on Mount Tamalpais, his eyes widening in shock.

What in the Twins'—

"SILANAR," someone was saying. He heard it dimly, as if from a great distance. The world was a fog, colors all blurred and muted.

He felt exhaustion. He felt accomplishment.

He didn't feel sorrow.

Not yet. In the years to come, he knew it would haunt him, but not yet. Not now.

He had saved the planet.

Him.

"Silanar!"

The shouting was more insistent, but Silanar couldn't bring himself to move. His mind felt like sludge, his body disconnected. He tried to rouse himself, tried to look in the direction of the voice, but everything was a whirl of senseless shapes and color.

"Silanar, get out of there! *Now!*" He felt hands grabbing at him, pulling him roughly away from the Tree. He tottered, unable to walk. He blinked rapidly, trying to clear his vision.

"What—" he started, but the words wouldn't come.

"Something is happening," the voice said. Was that Ytharra? His mind reeled. "We have to get away from the Tree!"

They kept walking, moving faster now. Silanar was getting his coordination back, his vision improving. He tried to swing his head to look behind him, but dizziness struck and he almost fell. Hands held him up, keeping him from falling.

"We have to go faster," someone said. A man. Bellas?

"Silanar, come on," Ytharra said.

Then he heard it. A cracking sound. He looked behind him.

His mouth dropped open, and he started running as quickly as he possibly could.

DILLON WISHED he had some binoculars or a telescope. He wanted a closer look. Something was happening around the Prime Tree, something unexpected. He thought he could see small branches of it falling off. Branches and leaves. The Tree looked like it was wilting, like autumn in fast forward. As he watched, the color of the Tree changed, turning from vibrant green to orange, then gold, then rust.

It finally settled on gray.

Then the trunk cracked at the base, and the whole Tree began to fall.

SILANAR WAS RUNNING AS FAST as he could, trying desperately to escape the destruction behind him. The Tree— the Prime Tree, the source of elven magic—was dying.

Maybe it was already dead.

A loud *crack* shattered the air, and the ground trembled. Silanar glanced behind him. The Tree had turned completely gray, and it was shedding its foliage as if it had a disease. Silanar kept running, trying to get glimpses of the Tree as he moved. His companions were keeping pace with him, and he could see the other elves from the camp ranging out ahead. Some were carrying bags or pieces of the tent, but most had nothing.

They were trying to escape with their lives.

He looked behind him again. A massive, dark crack had appeared near the base of the Tree, great chips of wood shredding out from it as it began to tip. As he ran, he could hear it, falling ponderously, tipping over and over as if in slow motion, gravity pulling it inexorably to the ground.

He checked the angle. It wasn't falling directly on them—

that was the good news. The bad news was that with a canopy as massive as this Tree had, any kind of fall would wreak massive destruction on everything around it. Cursing, Silanar kept running, trying to get as far away as possible.

"DO we have eyes on any other Prime Trees?" Orym asked.

One of the technicians tapped on his screen, pulling up camera feeds from a few of the satellites the Cothellon had left. One by one, Prime Trees came on-screen.

They all appeared to be dead or dying. They had each turned dark gray, the color of ash. Several had started falling over, their trunks cut through near the base. One had split down the middle vertically, its two halves falling away from each other.

"What *is* this?" Orym asked. "What's happening to them?"

"They're dead," Lorelei said.

Orym turned to her. "But why?"

She shrugged. "It must have been the soulsundering. It's never been used before, right?"

"As far as I know."

"Maybe this is what was always supposed to happen. The final safeguard, to prevent misuse of the power. The soulsundering destroys the Trees."

"But surely it's only supposed to destroy the Trees that were part of the ritual! The Fourteen? There are far more than fourteen Trees on Earth." Orym was grasping at straws.

"No," Sylvis said from the front of the room. She motioned toward the screen. "This is a Tree in Ethiopia. It wasn't part of the ritual."

"How do you know?"

"Because I was watching it. It didn't glow like the others did. It couldn't have been part of the soulsundering."

But the Tree in Ethiopia was gray like the others, already lying on its side in several giant pieces, leaves and branches strewn about it on the ground. The area around the Tree had been flattened during the impact.

"This is impossible," Orym said. "If *every* Tree just died…"

"It means lightprime magic now has a limit," Lorelei said. "Whatever primewood anyone stored before this moment, that's all they will ever have."

The room went silent.

"Well," Orym said after a moment, "it's a good thing we have our own source of magic now."

Lorelei nodded.

That was it, then. The Prime Trees were gone. They would never return. People would try, of course, desperately try to discover how to make new Trees. But Orym knew better than anyone living how impossible that task was.

He'd been trying for over a hundred years.

QUYNN STOOD ABOARD THE DROPLIFT, shivering. Not from the temperature, which was quite warm. He was shivering because of what he'd just witnessed.

The deaths of all the humans he was with.

But also something far more important.

The death of the Prime Trees.

He'd never thought it possible, not in a million years. The Prime Trees were eternal, everlasting. They were the source of Eldrim power. They couldn't just *die*.

He held his arms around himself as the droplift took him back to New San Francisco.

It truly was the end of an age.

SILANAR THREW himself to the ground behind a boulder as the Prime Oak finally hit the ground. He could feel the shockwave blasting by, dust and leaves and lethal spikes of wood shooting through the air.

He was spared the brunt of it.

When the ground finally stopped shaking, he peered out from the rock. The air around him was thick with dust. Leaves and twigs fell from the sky, a kind of infernal rain.

And the Tree was dead. Dead and fallen.

Silanar blinked tears out of his eyes. How could this have happened? The Book of Souls said nothing of this. Had he made a mistake? Had he performed the ritual incorrectly?

Or had the souls of seven billion humans risen up together, striking at the very source of magic?

Was this their otherworldly retribution?

He saw Ytharra and Bellas and the others getting up from where they had taken shelter. Many of them were nursing cuts and bruises. A few were limping badly.

What would they do now? Without a renewable source of primewood, their magic was limited. They would run out, and then they would all be Mundane.

It would take time, but the dominion of elves would eventually be over.

Silanar trudged out of the forest, weeping for what was lost.

ON THAT DAY, the Eldrim killed 7,212,627,402 humans, trapping millions more in the great cities in the sky. One percent remained to populate the Earth.

One percent was all humanity had left.

NINETY

"IT IS FINISHED," John said. "It happened just as we had expected."

"So many dead," Warren said. "So many gone." He shook his head sadly. "I still can't believe they went through with it."

"They stopped the Cothellon, at least. New Tokyo was destroyed."

"Along with millions more lives."

"Yes. But you know what our sources said. If Lorelei had activated her machine, this world would have been lost. At least *that* didn't happen."

"The world ended, anyway."

"It did, except for us."

"Except for us."

"Cheers," John said, raising his glass of English ale. "To the ones who remain."

"To the ones who remain," Warren said, clinking his glass.

As they drank, John knew that nothing would ever be the same again.

JESSICA SAT on the bed she'd been given, in the apartment they'd been assigned. It was Thalanil's apartment, in truth.

And it was *nice*.

It was good to be married to the enemy.

But Thalanil wasn't the enemy. At least, she didn't think so.

They still had so much to discuss.

"You lied to me," she said.

Next to her, Thalanil nodded. "When I first laid eyes on you, I knew you were the one. But you were a *human*, Jessica. Elves don't marry humans, and if we do, we can't tell them who we really are."

"You could have told me."

"Would you have believed me? Would you have understood?"

"I—" She honestly wasn't sure.

"But you're right. I should have. I should have *trusted* you, Jessica. Can you ever forgive me?"

"In time," Jessica said. "In time. We've been through so much these past few days. First the storm, then all this magic, then the appearance of elves. It's a lot, Alan. Thalanil. It's been a lot." She looked out their door at Jason, playing with his Legos in the hall. "But at least our son is safe. At least *we* are safe. At least I still have you."

"We saved humanity," Thalanil said. "The Eldrim nearly wiped it out. Perhaps we weren't the bad guys in all of this, after all."

"Perhaps not," Jessica said, snuggling up to him. "I'm just happy to have you."

As she watched their son playing in the hall, she wondered what kind of man he would grow up to be. He was half elf, half human. He was a mage. He would likely live a very long time.

She wondered what kind of world he'd grow up to see.

SILANAR TRUDGED through the streets of Sylrantheas, wondering for the millionth time if he'd done the right thing. It had been him, in the end. He had led them here. He had performed the ritual.

He had destroyed the world.

Now Earth would be free to recover. Now nature could run its course without pesky human involvement. Now the elves would be free to just live their lives, their great purpose accomplished.

But Silanar would always have the death of billions of lives weighing on his soul.

He could feel it there, like a blight. It was a dark spot on his consciousness, a weight around his heart. He was marked for all eternity as the man who had nearly ended an entire species.

But humans weren't extinct. One percent of them still roamed the planet, after all. The Cothellon had destroyed all their technology, though—satellites, radio, TV, the Internet. And Silanar knew that the remaining few would not know how to repair these things. He knew that humanity would be forced to re-learn everything that had come before.

He only hoped they wouldn't make the same mistakes.

But it was out of his hands now. He looked at the rubble of the church, already being set to by carpenters and architects. He saw it as a metaphor for what he'd done.

Silanar the Destroyer.

That was how he would be known.

He trudged off into the sunset, wondering if he would ever be happy again.

KHARIS SAT WITH SYNDRA, underneath a big oak tree on a hill. He loved it here, surrounded by a meadow, overlooking the forest all around. It was peaceful. It was romantic.

It almost helped him forget what the elves had done.

"I had no idea," he said. "I didn't know the terrible things we elves were capable of."

"It wasn't us," Syndra said, squeezing his hand. She was softer, here, outside of her tavern. Softer, but still strong.

He needed that strength.

"Let's get married," he said. "Let's make something out of all of this. You know I've loved you for years."

"And I've loved you," Syndra said. "So let's do it. We can find our happiness. Together." She squeezed his hand.

They sat there for a long while, watching the setting sun.

It was almost enough to make him forget the atrocities of the day before.

QUYNN PLACED the Tree Ring Staff back in its case, giving it one final, loving stroke before he locked it away. It had not been enough, in the end. *Aelwynn* had not been enough. But Quynn should not have been surprised. One man could not lift a city on his own.

In the end, their plan had failed. Fennas Elenathon had been damaged, and it would take a long time to rebuild.

Lorelei had decreed that they would.

Now Quynn needed to look to the future. To *his* future, living here in the city they had made. New San Francisco was a wonder, every bit as impressive as the city they had modeled it after now left to rot on the Earth's surface. There were almost a million people up here. There would be plenty to keep him busy.

But Quynn wanted more. He needed something to *do*. He needed a project of some kind, and he had just the one in mind.

He would discover the next Prime Mage.

LORELEI HAD to remind herself not to rage at everyone around her.

The plan had failed. New Tokyo had been destroyed, and New San Francisco had almost been lost due to a software bug. She wanted to rail and scream, to kill her entire staff. But she could not do that. She had to maintain control.

She was alone in her apartment when Magona appeared.

"I always knew you were a failure," the dark woman said.

"Do I *know* you?" Lorelei said. "What kind of magic are you using?"

"Oh, you know me," Magona said. "You just don't remember. But you will. Oh, you will."

Lorelei felt fear like a spear inside her heart. "What do you *want*?"

Magona leaned closer. "I want you to rebuild," she said. "I want you to fix this device, to do what you set out to do. I'm a patient one, dear Lorelei. I'm more patient than you could *possibly* know. But even I have limits. Get it done."

"As you say," Lorelei said, knowing that she had no other choice. Whoever this woman was, she held power far beyond Lorelei's imagining. "I will do as you say."

"Excellent," Magona said, and she disappeared.

Lorelei sighed, fingering the neckline of her dress, wondering just how long all of this would take.

ORYM SAT AT HIS DESK, grateful that he still had a desk to sit at. He had defected. He had told the Eldrim all about the Cothellon plan. And in the end, it hadn't mattered—Dunedar had managed to stop it all.

At least Orym hadn't been discovered.

"Luthar," he said into his communicator, "there's something I want you to research for me."

"Yes, boss?"

"There's something funny with gatesending magic. Something involving memory."

"I'll get right on it, boss."

Orym needed to bide his time. He needed to lay low. He needed to find a way to defeat the Cothellon from the inside, without being discovered in the process. But he wouldn't do it alone.

Orym had his son.

DILLON CREPT through the sewer tunnel, wondering how in the hell he had ended up here. This wasn't the life he had planned. This wasn't what his father had promised him.

But at least his father was in contact with him now.

He wouldn't have to live under a bridge. Instead, he would live inside the sewer. It wasn't as bad as it sounded. Because this time, it was on *purpose*.

This time Dillon had a plan.

"THE WORLD HAS CHANGED, FATHER," Keya said. She was sitting next to Tanyl in their living room. He wasn't her father —not really. But he had raised her, so she still thought of him that way.

"It has," Tanyl said. "I do not know if I condone the waywardness of elves."

"Neither do I, Father. Neither do I. But..." She had to ask. She'd waited a whole day, but it was eating her up inside.

"Yes, child?"

"I wanted to ask something."

Tanyl shifted in his seat. He couldn't see her, but she was sure he could pick up on her tone. "What did you want to know, Keya?"

"Who is my real father?"

Tanyl sighed. "It is not me."

"You knew? Knew that Aelynthi had slept with Thalanil?"

"I did," Tanyl said. "I knew about it then, as it was happening. And I chose to stay with her, to try to win her back."

"So you know that Thalanil is my father."

"No," Tanyl said.

"What?" But inside, she was not surprised.

Memories had been stirring inside of her.

"I do not know who your true father is, child," Tanyl said. "Silanar and I found you in the forest one day, wandering around. You had no memory of who you were or where you came from. Your features were ageless, but young. We did not know what to do with you.

"So we took you in, and I raised you as my own."

"But...Aelynthi. She was pregnant!"

"Yes, she was," Tanyl said. "With *my* baby—not Thalanil's. We were so happy. But she lost the baby during childbirth. It damn near killed her, emotionally.

"*That* was why she threw herself off the bell tower ledge. Not because of you. Not because of Thalanil. It was because she had failed to have the daughter that she had always wanted to have.

"You arrived two days later."

Keya's head was swimming. So much of this didn't make sense. "So you *lied* to me? All this time?"

"We didn't know who you *were*, Keya," Tanyl said. "You had no memories when you arrived here. So we did the best we could. We integrated you. I raised you as my own. You were the daughter I almost had. You were the soul my wife died in honor of."

"So all this time, Thalanil was beating himself up over *nothing*."

"I regret that, Keya. I wish we could set him straight. But we can't contact him now. He's up there in that infernal city. I longed to reach out to him, but I'm sure you can understand. I'm still angry at him for what he did with my wife."

"I do understand," Keya said, but things weren't fitting into place. She wasn't Thalanil's daughter, *and* she wasn't Tanyl's. So who *was* she? Where had she come from? How had she gotten here?

How *old* was she?

None of this was making sense.

Her strange memories were rising yet again.

She stood from the couch, releasing Tanyl's hand. "I'm sorry," she said. "I'm sorry for all the pain I've caused."

"What are you doing?" he asked.

Keya looked around the room, at the things that no longer felt like hers. "I need to leave," she said. "I need to get away from all of this. From the sins of elves. From the lies of my past. I need to go out into this newly-empty world. To explore. To be on my own.

"I need to find myself, Father."

She leaned down, giving him a kiss on the cheek.

"Thank you for everything you've done. I hope to see you again, in this life or the next."

And so it was that Keya left the village she had thought of as her home, knowing not how long she would remain away.

NINETY-ONE
260 YEARS LATER

KHARIS INSPECTED THE BOWSTRING. It was intact, even if it was fraying around the edges. The bow it was attached to was also old, having been handed down from Kharis' father to himself.

Now, it was being handed down to his own son.

"Welcome to class, Fenian," he said, handing him the bow. The boy was a scant fourteen. It would be a few years before he could even pull the six foot, one inch longbow. "This is the first day of the rest of your life."

He winced at the cliched line, but he knew the boy's mother would have liked it. Syndra had always been a sucker for cliches.

Wiping a tear away, he turned to the rest of the class. "This year will test you in ways you've never experienced before," he said. They were all so young. So impressionable. So unaware of all the tragedies his kind had committed. "Let's begin. Please line up at the shooting line."

He watched as the students—and his son—took their places.

He only wished his wife could have been there to see it.

LORELEI STAMPED HER RED HEEL, the clicking sound echoing in her private office. "How in the *Twins' purple hell* is this taking so long?" she shouted. She sat at her desk, taking a long drink of water.

This day had been too much.

"I told you," Orym said, looking far too regal, "building an *entire city* from scratch is difficult! We could have built the minimal viable apparatus."

"And how long would *that* have taken?"

Orym shifted his weight. "Almost as long. Look—this thing is *complicated*, okay? Fennas Elanathan took over three hundred years to build the first time. Why would you expect it to go quicker now?"

"Because it's *one seventh* of it, Orym," Lorelei said. "You know what? Never mind. Just get it done." She resumed her tapping on the floor.

"Have you seen her, recently?" Orym asked.

Lorelei looked at him sharply. "Who?"

"The dark woman."

"What do you know about that?"

"Nothing, Cundu. Just...I wondered what she'd said."

"She told me that my time was running out, Orym. She told me that my *life* would be forfeit if we didn't get this done."

"It will happen, Cundu. We are making it happen."

"Good."

She pretended not to notice the twitch around his mouth, the way his eyes shifted about the room.

Orym was lying to her.

He had been lying to her for hundreds of years.

"*PULL!*" Dillon shouted, and the kids around him pulled. The car moved an inch, sliding onto the platform with a resounding *clang*. "Good job!" Dillon said, and the kids dropped the ropes, resuming their usual duties. Now they could repair this car. Now they could improve their way of life.

Dillon shivered, despite the Under heat.

"Good job, boss," a voice said, and Dillon turned.

Oil was standing in front of him.

The man had lost a ton of weight, probably owing to the lack of actual food down here in the city slums. "Thanks," Dillon said. "Didn't expect to see you here."

"Things are slow right now," Oil said, his shirt hanging loosely over his flat stomach. "Queen doesn't have much work for us these days."

"Queen," Dillon scoffed. "What a stupid name."

"She's young, I'll grant you," Oil said, "but the girl has a vision. More importantly, she has some *powerful* backers. People even *you* wouldn't want to cross."

"Is that so."

"Just watch yourself, old friend," Oil said, turning away.

"You came here to *warn* me?"

Oil looked back at him, a sad expression on his face. "Not all of us are happy, here." He turned away, walking slowly toward the exit hatch. "Goodbye, old friend. I hope you find your place down here."

QUYNN PUT the book back on the shelf, one finger lingering longingly. He was glad he'd brought the books up here, saved them from the Cothellon's rampant destruction. He loved books. He didn't want to see them die.

"Hey," he shouted to the boy downstairs. He knew the boy could hear him. The apartment wasn't that big. "You done, yet?"

"Almost!" the boy returned.

So weak. So placid. This one was such a terrible specimen. But Quynn knew to look beyond all that. He knew to see *within*.

He knew that this boy might actually turn out to be the Prime Mage he was trying to find.

He wondered how his other projects were doing.

IT WAS on days like this that Jason liked to remember his mom.

Jessica was dead now, of course. She was human, after all. And Jason, well.

Jason was still here.

And alive, thanks to her. And married. And happy.

And a half-elf.

He turned to his wife, the newly-minted Mrs. Karen Lim. He had taken his mother's surname, but his wife was Korean, too. It fit. She didn't mind.

They were happy.

It had been so long.

Life aboard Newfris hadn't been all bad, even if it had been far longer than he had expected. Would they be here for three hundred years? He didn't know. Would he outlive his human wife?

Yes.

But that was the way of things. That was his blessing, and

his curse. His father had counciled him in the way of elves, at least.

It was too bad Thalanil had died.

But now he had other things to focus on. He was two hundred and sixty eight years old, and he was about to have his first child.

A girl.

"Megan," he said. "I like the sound of that."

Karen smiled. "Me too. I wonder if she will be a mage, like you?"

"Undoubtedly," Jason said. "*You* are, after all. The only forcefinder human *not* subjugated by the Cothellon."

"You can thank your father for that."

"I can, and I do. Every day. I love you, Karen."

"And I love you."

"She will be a forcefinder, then."

"Only the Twins know, Jason," Karen said, rubbing her stomach. "Only the Twins know."

Jason wondered if the Twins were real. And if they were, how much they *actually* knew.

Either way, he knew his daughter would be someone very special.

SILANAR TOOK a deep breath of the redwood forest air, desperately trying to calm his nerves. He had no reason to be so uneasy. He had no reason to be so scared.

No reason, other than the murder of billions of living souls.

He shouldn't have done it. He regretted every minute. It had been two hundred and sixty years, and he still hadn't gotten over it.

Silanar had made a terrible mistake.

But the Earth was better for it now. Forests had regrown. Cities were empty. No smoke polluted the sky. Life was better, for the damage he had done. The world would survive.

But so many people had not.

He choked down a sob, trying for the millionth time to keep it together. He had to. He had to for Sylrantheas. He had to for himself. He had to for Melenora. He had to be strong.

He was startled when a face appeared.

"Greetings," the woman said.

Silanar couldn't quite see her. She was shrouded in shadows, her form obscured by branches and leaves. He squinted, trying to make her out. She seemed familiar, somehow. Someone from his distant past. From back when he had ended the world.

"Silanar," she said, taking a step into the light, and Silanar couldn't help but gasp.

It was Keya.

The girl was here, after all this time.

And she looked entirely the same.

"I have returned," she said, and he was dimly aware of something in her arms. "I've brought something for you."

She lifted a piece of gray fabric, unwrapping the bundle she was carrying. And suddenly Silanar's vision shifted, going haywire. He blinked, unsure what had just happened.

A woman was standing next to Keya.

She wasn't carrying anything at all.

"What—"

"This girl came to me in the forest," Keya said. "Like me, she does not remember who she is. Like me, she needs a home. Will you see to her?"

"I—" What was going on? Silanar was lost. Keya was Thalanil's daughter, right? He couldn't understand her words.

"Say it, Silanar," Keya said. "Say you'll help her."

The girl next to her stumbled, long hair matted and dirty. She had a haunted look in her eyes, and her clothes were tattered. She clearly needed help.

And she was clearly an elf.

Like Keya, she was ageless. She could have passed for anywhere from fifteen to fifteen hundred. He didn't know. Yet there was something ancient about her, something mystical and strange. Perhaps the Twins had a plan for him after all.

"Yes," he said. "I'll help her. I'll find her a home, if I have to house her myself. But Keya, have you returned? Will you stay in Sylrantheas after all this time?"

Keya looked past him, to where he knew the village stood amidst the trees. "Yes," she said. "I will stay. But my name is no longer Keya. I have taken a new name, and I bring with me many stories." She turned her gaze back upon him. "Will you accept me amongst your kind?"

It was a strange way of putting things. "Of course," he said. "No matter what your name, you will always have a home here."

"Very well," she said, walking toward him. The other girl followed. "You may call me Kythaela."

"Kythaela," Silanar echoed. "It is a good name."

"Thank you," Kythaela said, passing him and walking onward through the trees. "I hope you have repaired the church. We have many stories yet to tell."

THE
END

TO BE CONTINUED...

THE STORY CONTINUES

Excerpt from THE PRIME TREES, book five of The Metalwood Saga:

Trey sat in his chair in the Town Hall, stunned. The room was silent for a long moment. "That was...quite the story," he said finally. He felt numb at first, but something was growing inside him, suffusing his body.

The Sundering. The Ascension. The things the elves had done. It was almost too much. It was almost far too much to bear.

He stood.

"I would never have believed it," he said, "but I've seen you. I've seen how you work. How you think." He felt his hands start shaking. He walked up to Silanar, finally understanding the feeling that was shooting through his veins.

It was anger.

"You killed them," Trey said. He was standing right in front of Silanar's chair, glaring down at the man. "*You* killed them. Seven billion living human beings. It wasn't a virus at all. It was *elves.*"

Silanar just sat there, looking at him with those elven eyes, expressionless.

Trey leaned down until he was inches away from the man's face. "*How dare you,*" he said, his voice almost a whisper.

Then he spun and left the room.

"Well, that went well," Bellas said. Arra could hear the sarcasm dripping in his tone. She glanced over at Fenian, trying to gauge his reaction. They'd both heard parts of the story before, but never in this much detail. And never from the Cothellon's side.

It was...sobering.

Fenian seemed nonplussed. This business of killing most of the humans didn't seem to bother him much. Well, it bothered Arra. It bothered her a lot. She wondered, not for the first time, just what kind of a man her father was.

"He'll be back," Silanar said, referring to Trey. "I hope. In the meantime, we have a meeting to continue."

"Hold the fuck on," Orym said suddenly.

"That language isn't necessary," Silanar said. "What do you want?"

"You've heard it all now," Orym said, "every detail. You know what the Fennas Elenathon device will do. And I've already told you that they plan to activate it soon. Very soon."

"It's been what—296 years?—since their first failure," Silanar said. "How do you know they'll activate it now?"

"Because I still *work* for them, you idiot," Orym said, his voice dripping with contempt. "How can you not understand, after all this? I've been undercover the whole time. I arranged all of this. Trey, your new Prime Mage, is down here because of me. And this entire planet is going to be destroyed if we don't do something. Right. Fucking. Now."

"And just what do you propose we do?" Daylor said.

"We need to destroy the cities once and for all," Orym said.

"How? They're invisible, and even if they weren't, they're also shielded by those forcefields you described. They can't be destroyed."

"They can be," Orym said. "There's something very few

people know about the forcefields."

"And I suppose you're going to tell us."

"Picture an egg," Orym said, ignoring Daylor. "Picture it standing on end. Got it? Now cut the egg neatly in half." He made a sideways chopping motion with his hand. "Now you have two shells: one on the bottom, and one on the top."

"Very descriptive," Silanar remarked. Orym glared at him.

"The city shields used to be the whole egg—a full circle around the entire city. But over time, forcefinder Talent atrophied in the population. People just aren't as genetically predisposed to it as they are to the other Talents. As a result, we don't have enough darkmages to maintain the full Shield. So only the bottom half is active."

Arra saw her father thinking that over. "But why even keep the Shield up at all?" he asked.

"To keep people like you from getting in."

"Are all the cities like this?"

"Yes," Orym said.

"So all we have to do is get our people three thousand feet in the air—high enough to clear the forcefield—then, what, throw explosives at the city? Shoot it? And we have to do this six times, in locations all over the planet?"

"Seven times," Orym said. "New Tokyo has been rebuilt."

"It's just not feasible," Silanar said.

"That's why I brought you the Prime Mage."

"He's really only half a Prime Mage, and a very weak one at that. How is that supposed to help?"

Arra was looking at the window, watching Trey. He'd left the village, stomping out into the forest with a murderous expression on his face.

"He's not going to be able to do anything if he's not here," she said.

Everyone looked at her.

Arra found Trey in a clearing deep in the forest, nearly a mile away from Sylrantheas. He was sitting on a fallen tree, glowering at the ground. Arra made sure to make noise as she approached so he wouldn't be frightened. He looked up as she neared, his expression dark. She didn't say anything, just walked up and sat beside him on the log.

They were both silent for several minutes. Then Trey drew in a ragged breath. "What kind of person commits genocide?" he asked, still staring at the ground.

She looked at him, at the hunch in his back, at his hair where it met the nape of his neck. She put a hand on his forearm, the touch awkward.

"I'm not going to defend him," she said quietly. "How could I? I think it's unspeakable what he—what they—did."

Trey looked at her then, and she could see tears glistening in his eyes. "What could have become of us?" he asked, his voice quavering. "What could we have accomplished in all this time? We might have *saved* this planet, not killed it." He looked out at the forest.

Arra squeezed his arm. "I know."

She felt something, then, as she touched him. As if in a long-lost life, she had once known him. She withdrew her touch, suddenly confused.

He looked at her again, his blue eyes finding hers. "Everything I've ever known was a lie," he said, "and the truth—the truth is *far* worse."

He reached for her then, needing physical contact, needing comfort. She wrapped one arm around him and held him as he cried.

"So you're an elf?" Rylan asked. The boys in the tent were staring at him, watching his reaction.

"You got it," Dill—Dillon—said.

"How old are you?"

"We don't really keep track in the Under. I guess I'm something like 430, give or a take a few decades."

"Holy shit," Rylan said.

"Well said."

"And you've been down here the whole time? Who else knows?"

Dill looked around the room. "Just these guys, mostly," he said. "Oh, and him."

Someone new stepped into the tent. He was older than most of the boys in the Under—much older. He had shaggy gray hair and walked with a slight hunch, making him seem short. He was wearing a dirty, floppy black jacket made of cloth, and baggy black pants. The strange man walked up to the table and sat, dropping a heavy bag onto it with a loud clanking noise.

"Rylan," Dill said, "meet Smoke. Smoke, Rylan."

The man named Smoke turned to look at him, but he didn't stand. His eyes were gray, glinting like steel. He didn't say anything.

"Smoke here makes mergeguns," Dill said.

"Mergeguns?" Rylan asked.

"Yup. Same as what Shot uses, and the guards that chased you."

"Stupid name."

Dill laughed. "It is pretty stupid now that you mention it."

Rylan eyed the man named Smoke. He seemed like he was hiding something. But then again, it seemed like *everyone* was hiding something around here. He looked over at Elanil. She hadn't reacted much during Dill's story. Maybe she'd heard it before.

Her expression was one of pity.

"I found Con," he said, changing the subject.

Dill quirked an eyebrow. "Oh?"

"She's in an old jail in Planner Central. They aren't feeding her. She looks like she's about to die."

"We don't rescue people from Planner Central anymore," Dill said. "It's too dangerous."

"I thought you wanted to take over the city."

"Sure," Dill said, "but I don't see how saving her will help do that."

"Con can help," Rylan said. "We have to rescue her."

Dill looked at him for a moment as if weighing his options. "If we get her out," he said, "will you help us?"

"I was already going to help you," Rylan said.

"Not much of a negotiator, are you?"

Rylan shrugged.

Dill turned to Elanil. "What about you?"

Elanil looked surprised at being addressed. "I want to go home," she said. That haunted expression was back in her eyes.

"I don't see any way of getting you back there," Dill said. "Unless Dad knows a way. Grime, is the radio working yet?"

Grime shook his head. "Not yet, boss. It works for short-range stuff, but something's wrong with the antenna. We haven't been able to raise Orym on it."

"Get it fixed," Dill said.

"Sure thing, boss."

"In the meantime, there's something I want you to see."

"Not until we get Con," Rylan said. He wasn't going to budge on the subject, not this time. He needed to save her, and time was rapidly running out.

Dill sighed. "Fine. Shot, go find Small. You and him and me will go with Rylan to get Con. Elanil, you coming?"

Elanil looked around the room nervously. She was probably afraid of what would happen if she were left alone with the boys. "I guess," she said.

Dill went over to the big chest and rummaged around. "Here," he said, turning back to Rylan and handing him a handful of dark wood.

"Maple?" Rylan asked.

Dill nodded. "Dark maple," he said. "Heard you were out."

"Thanks."

"I don't suppose you have any prime elm on hand?" Elanil asked.

"Nope," Dill said. "You didn't bring any with you?"

Elanil looked crestfallen. "I used it all getting here."

Dill stroked his chin. "Grime, will the radio reach Greyson?"

"Sure will, boss."

"Get him on the line. See if he can get us some prime elm. Real prime elm, not the dark stuff. I know the Planners still have some. Tell him to use the dead drop just outside Planner Central. And Grime?"

"Yes, boss?"

"Tell him to hurry."

Dill turned to Rylan, sticking out his hand. "We'll get your friend out," he said, "and then we'll fix this city. Deal?"

"Deal," Rylan said, shaking Dill's hand.

He hoped they wouldn't be too late to save Con.

To be continued in THE PRIME TREES...

To purchase, head to **jtf.link/metal5** or scan the QR code below.

ENJOY THE BOOK? HELP SPREAD THE WORD

Reviews are the most powerful tools in my arsenal when it comes to getting attention for my books. Much as I'd like to, I don't have the financial muscle of a New York publisher. I can't take out full page ads in the newspaper or put posters on the subway.

But I do have something much more powerful and effective than that, and it's something that those publishers would kill to get their hands on.

A committed and loyal bunch of readers.

Honest reviews of my books help bring them to the attention of other readers. If you've enjoyed this book, **I'd love it if you could leave a quick review.**

Head to **jtf.link/metalreview4** or scan the QR code.

ABOUT THE AUTHOR

Jeremy is a fantasy and science fiction author, living and writing in the San Francisco Bay Area. Fantasy is his first love —there's something about magic and mayhem that has interested him since he first cracked opened Lord Foul's Bane in the seventh grade. Also archery.

There always seems to be a lot of archery involved.

When not writing, Jeremy is a graphic designer, software developer, game designer, and music composer. He makes a really great Old Fashioned.

Check out his other work and sign up for his newsletter at **www.jeremythomasfuller.com**.

facebook.com/JeremyThomasFuller

instagram.com/jeremythomasfuller

amazon.com/author/jeremythomasfuller

bsky.app/profile/jeremythomasfuller.com

www.ingramcontent.com/pod-product-compliance
Lightning Source LLC
Chambersburg PA
CBHW021153030726
47493CB00029B/1454